ALSO BY JASPER FFORDE

The Thursday Next Series

The Eyre Affair

Lost in a Good Book

The Well of Lost Plots

Something Rotten

~~*The Great Samuel Pepys Fiasco*~~
(No longer available)

The Nursery Crimes Series

The Big Over Easy

The Fourth Bear

The Danverclone seemed to hang
in the air for a moment before a large wave
caught her and she was left behind the
rapidly moving taxi.

“Fforde really unleashes his imagination, and it knows no bounds, especially in reference to specific books, displaying . . . his ‘bibliowit.’ Despite all the allusions, illusions, neologisms, puns, and other literary sleights-of-hand, the reader comes to see that for all its futuristic, alternate-world shenanigans, *Thursday Next: First Among Sequels* is a down-to-earth (well, sort of) cautionary tale about good and evil, as well as a family-centered love story about a good marriage.” —*The Washington Times*

“Warning: Reading one of Jasper Fforde’s Thursday Next novels could, if you are not careful, have the effect of making other novels appear dull, uninspired, pedestrian, and predictable. Outright silliness . . . surrounded by strokes of inspired, demented genius. This is a novel with a deep love for fiction and a respect for how books, more than any other medium, can transform a life.” —*The Tampa Tribune*

“If you’re done with Harry Potter, you’ll need some books to fill the empty space. My suggestion? Anything by Jasper Fforde. He manages to be silly and smart at the same time.” —*Richmond Times-Dispatch*

“Fans of satiric literary humor are in for a treat.” —*Knoxville News*

“The pleasure in reading Fforde is immersing yourself into a satiric, literary world rich in characters, setting and language from your favorite books, made over in a wacky, campy way.” —*The Oregonian* (Portland)

“Reads like a well-edited Harry Potter; *First Among Sequels* is for adults who want sophisticated with their fantasy, but who still possess an appreciation for the intricate world-building of a well-imagined children’s novel. Canonical in-jokes abound. . . . What dedicated reader wouldn’t laugh at the suggestion of a parallel universe in which *Jude the Obscure* is renowned as a comic novel?” —*New Statesman*

“What is most enjoyable about Jasper Fforde’s work is not its silliness—though there is plenty of that. It is admiring the skill that keeps all of those silly balls in the air. *First Among Sequels* does something as highly improbably as the life of its heroine: it continues to surprise and entertain. What makes Fforde’s work such fun is [his] unrestrained combination of wit and lunacy. Underlying that, though, is a love of a good story that rings true. It works magnificently.” —*The Denver Post*

“Recommending Fforde’s novels is a bookseller’s dilemma. You can go on about literature-as-technology in popular culture in the Nextian world. . . . Or you can tackle his Nursery Crime series. But handselling *First Among Sequels* is easy. Just hand [the reader] a copy and tell them to read a couple of pages—and have plenty of earlier titles on hand, because you’ll sell them too!”
—*Publishers Weekly*

“Irrepressibly playful and relentlessly imaginative.”
—Adam Begley, *The New York Observer*

PENGUIN BOOKS

THURSDAY NEXT: FIRST AMONG SEQUELS

Jasper Fforde is the author of four previous Thursday Next novels: *The Eyre Affair*, *Lost in a Good Book*, *The Well of Lost Plots*, and *Something Rotten*. He is also the author of the Nursery Crime Series, featuring Detective Jack Spratt, which includes *The Big Over Easy* and *The Fourth Bear*. All of Jasper Fforde's books are available from Penguin. He lives in Wales.

Visit www.jasperfforde.com and www.thursdaynext.com.

Praise for *Thursday Next: First Among Sequels*

"*Thursday Next* is an invigorating romp for all lovers of literature. In his 2003 novel *The Eyre Affair*, Fforde introduced readers to a futuristic world where books reigned supreme. Now, years later, [Thursday Next is] back, older, wiser, married with children and working for Jurisfiction, the policing agency that works within books. It's not entirely necessary—though perhaps more fun—to read the books in the proper order. Fforde gives enough background in *Thursday Next* to inform readers of all they need to know to find both books hilarious, exhilarating."

—Kim Curtis, The Associated Press

"Jasper Fforde's mind-blowing books consistently defy—nay, mock—easy description. Are they fantasy? Mystery? Espionage? Science fiction? Absurdist humor? Shaggy, gleeful, scrambled combinations of the above? Answer: Yup. *Thursday Next: First Among Sequels* is so jam-packed with goofy jokes and shaggy plot lines that some readers may tire before the end. That would be a shame, since they'd miss the book's exciting conclusion on the dangerous high seas of piratical swashbuckling. Argh! Die-hard Fforde ffanatics can check out [Fforde's] very cool Web sites (all accessible through www.jasperfforde.com)." —*The Seattle Times*

"For the past six years, Jasper Fforde has been . . . churning out one impossibly winning book after the next about Thursday Next. You needn't have spent half your childhood sitting up at night with a flashlight reading these books to enjoy *First Among Sequels*. What captivates here is something that will appeal to any reader—and that's the feeling that there's something at stake in fiction, that characters created in books are every bit as real as the memory of a person. Of all the Thursday books, this one is by far the most busily plotted, but Fforde's greatest gift is on display. He beautifully captures that sense of embattlement which hovers over readers today in a world crowded with other forms of entertainment." —John Freeman, *Newsday*

"[An] incredibly smart novel." —*USA Today*

"[With a] furiously agile imagination . . . Fforde has shaken up genres—fantasy, comedy, crime, sci-fi, parody, literary criticism—and come up with a superb mishmash with lots of affectionate in-jokes for any book lover. There's a good chance the aptly titled *First Among Sequels* is the best of Fforde's novels."

—*The Miami Herald*

THURSDAY NEXT

IN

First Among Sequels

A NOVEL

Jasper Fforde

PENGUIN BOOKS

PENGUIN BOOKS
Published by the Penguin Group
Penguin Group (USA) Inc., 375 Hudson Street, New York, New York 10014, U.S.A.
Penguin Group (Canada), 90 Eglinton Avenue East, Suite 700, Toronto,
Ontario, Canada M4P 2Y3 (a division of Pearson Penguin Canada Inc.)
Penguin Books Ltd, 80 Strand, London WC2R 0RL, England
Penguin Ireland, 25 St Stephen's Green, Dublin 2, Ireland (a division of Penguin Books Ltd)
Penguin Group (Australia), 250 Camberwell Road, Camberwell,
Victoria 3124, Australia (a division of Pearson Australia Group Pty Ltd)
Penguin Books India Pvt Ltd, 11 Community Centre, Panchsheel Park, New Delhi–110 017, India
Penguin Group (NZ), 67 Apollo Drive, Rosedale, North Shore 0632,
New Zealand (a division of Pearson New Zealand Ltd)
Penguin Books (South Africa) (Pty) Ltd, 24 Sturdee Avenue, Rosebank, Johannesburg 2196, South Africa

Penguin Books Ltd, Registered Offices: 80 Strand, London WC2R 0RL, England

First published in the United States of America by Viking Penguin,
a member of Penguin Group (USA) Inc. 2007
Published in Penguin Books 2008

1 3 5 7 9 10 8 6 4 2

Illustrations by Bill Mudron and Dylan Meconis

Grateful acknowledgment is made to Agatha Christie Limited (A Chorion Company) for reference
to *They Do It with Mirrors* © Agatha Christie (A Chorion Company). All rights reserved.

THE LIBRARY OF CONGRESS HAS CATALOGED THE HARDCOVER EDITION AS FOLLOWS:
Fforde, Jasper.
Thursday next in first among sequels / Jasper Fforde.
p. cm.
ISBN 978-0-670-03871-8 (hc.)
ISBN 978-0-14-311356-0 (pbk.)
1. Next, Thursday (Fictitious character)—Fiction. 2. Characters and characteristics
in literature—Fiction.
3. Women detectives—Great Britain—Fiction. 4. Books and reading—Fiction.
5. Time travel—Fiction.
I. Title. II. Title: First among sequels.
PR6106.F67T475 2007
823'.914—dc22 2007014615

Printed in the United States of America
Set in Berkeley Oldstyle Medium Designed by Francesca Belanger

For Cressida,

the bestest sister in the world

Contents

Author's Note

This book has been bundled with **Special Features**, including *The Making of . . .* wordamentary, deleted scenes, alternative endings and much more.

To access all these free bonus features, log on to www.jasperfforde.com/features.html and follow the on-screen instructions.

The year is 2002. It is fourteen years since Thursday almost pegged out at the 1988 Croquet SuperHoop, and life is beginning to get back to normal. . . .

1.

Breakfast

The Swindon that I knew in 2002 had a lot going for it. A busy financial center coupled with excellent infrastructure and surrounded by green and peaceful countryside had made the city about as popular a place as you might find anywhere in the nation. We had our own forty-thousand-seat croquet stadium, the recently finished Cathedral of St. Zvlkx, a concert hall, two local TV networks and the only radio station in England dedicated solely to mariachi music. Our central position in southern England also made us the hub for high-speed overland travel from the newly appointed Clary-LaMarr Travelport. It was little wonder that we called Swindon "the Jewel on the M4."

The dangerously high level of the stupidity surplus was once again the lead story in *The Owl* that morning. The reason for the crisis was clear: Prime Minister Redmond van de Poste and his ruling Commonsense Party had been discharging their duties with a reckless degree of responsibility that bordered on inspired sagacity. Instead of drifting from one crisis to the next and appeasing the nation with a steady stream of knee-jerk legislation and headline-grabbing but arguably pointless initiatives, they had been resolutely building a raft of considered long-term plans that concentrated on unity, fairness and tolerance. It was a state of affairs deplored by Mr. Alfredo Traficcone, leader of the opposition Prevailing Wind Party, who wanted to lead the nation back onto the safer grounds of uninformed stupidity.

"How could they let it get this bad?" asked Landen as he walked into the kitchen, having just dispatched our daughters off to school. They walked themselves, naturally; Tuesday was twelve and took great pride in looking after Jenny, who was now ten.

"Sorry?" I said, my mind full of other matters, foremost among them the worrying possibility that Pickwick's plumage might *never* grow back, and that she would have to spend the rest of her life looking like a supermarket oven-ready chicken.

"The stupidity surplus," repeated Landen as he sat down at the kitchen table, "I'm all for responsible government, but storing it up like this is bound to cause problems sooner or later—even by acting sensibly, the government has shown itself to be a bunch of idiots."

"There are a lot of idiots in this country," I replied absently, "and they deserve representation as much as the next man."

But he was right. Unlike previous governments that had skillfully managed to eke out our collective stupidity all year round, the current administration had decided to store it all up and then blow it on something *unbelievably* dopey, arguing that one major balls-up every ten years or so was less damaging than a weekly helping of mild political asininity. The problem was, the surplus had reached absurdly high levels, where it had even surpassed the "monumentally dumb" mark. Only a blunder of staggering proportions would remove the surplus, and the nature of this mind-numbing act of idiocy was a matter of considerable media speculation.

"It says here," he said, getting into full rant mode by adjusting his glasses and tapping at the newspaper with his index finger, "that even the government is having to admit that the stupidity surplus is a far, far bigger problem than they had first imagined."

I held the striped dodo cozy I was knitting for Pickwick against her pink and blotchy body to check the size, and she puffed herself up to look more alluring, but to no avail. She then made an indignant plocking noise, which was the only sound she ever uttered.

"Do you think I should knit her a party one as well? Y'know, black, off the shoulder and with sparkly bits in it?"

"But," Landen went on in a lather of outrage, "the prime minister has poured scorn on Traficcone's suggestion to offload our unwanted stupidity to Third World nations, who would be only too happy to have it in exchange for several sacks of cash and a Mercedes or two."

"He's right," I replied with a sigh. "Idiocy offsets are bullshit; stupidity is our own problem and has to be dealt with on an individual 'stupidity footprint' basis—and landfill *certainly* doesn't work."

I was thinking of the debacle in Cornwall, where twenty thousand tons of half-wittedness was buried in the sixties, only to percolate to the surface two decades later when the residents started to do inexplicably dumb things, such as using an electric mixer in the bath and parting their hair in the center.

"What if," Landen continued thoughtfully, "the thirty million or so inhabitants of the British Archipelago were to all simultaneously fall for one of those e-mail 'tell us all your bank details' phishing scams or—I don't know—fall down a manhole or something?"

"They tried the mass walking-into-lamppost experiment in France to see if they could alleviate *la dette idiote*," I pointed out, "but the seriousness under which the plan was undertaken made it de facto sensible, and all that was damaged was the proud Gallic forehead."

Landen took a sip of coffee, unfolded the paper and scanned the rest of the front page before remarking absently, "I took up your idea and sent my publisher a few outlines for self-help books last week."

"Who do they think you should be helping?"

"Well . . . *me* . . . and them, I suppose—isn't that how it's meant to work? It looks really easy. How about this for a title: *Men Are from Earth, Women Are from Earth—Just Deal with It.*"

He looked at me and smiled, and I smiled back. I didn't love him just because he had a nice knee, was tall and made me laugh, but because we were two parts of one, and neither of us could imagine life without the other. I wish I had a better way to describe it, but I'm not a poet. Privately he was a husband and father to our three mostly wonderful kids, but professionally he was a writer. Unfortunately, despite winning the 1988 Armitage Shanks Fiction Award for *Bad Sofa,* a string of flops had left the relationship with his publisher a bit strained. So strained, in fact, that he was reduced to penning point-of-sale nonfiction classics such as *The Little Book of Cute Pets That You Really Like to Hug* and *The Darndest Things Kids Say.* When he wasn't working on these, he was looking after our children and attempting to rekindle his career with a seriously good blockbuster—his magnum opus. It wasn't easy, but it was what he loved, and I loved *him,* so we lived off my salary, which was about the size of Pickwick's brain—not that big, and unlikely to become so.

"This is for you," said Landen, pushing a small parcel wrapped in pink paper across the table.

"Sweetheart," I said, *really* annoyed and *really* pleased all at the same time, "I don't do birthdays."

"I know," he said without looking up, "so you'll just have to humor me."

I unwrapped the package to find a small silver locket and chain. I'm not a jewelry person, but I am a *Landen* person, so held my hair out of the way while he fastened the clasp, then thanked him and gave him a kiss, which he returned. And then, since he knew all about my abhorrence of birthdays, dropped the matter entirely.

"Is Friday up?"

"At this hour?"

Friday, it should be noted, was the eldest of our three children and the only boy. He was now sixteen, and instead of gearing himself up for a successful career with the time industry's elite operatives known as the ChronoGuard, he was a tedious teenage cliché—grunting, sighing at any request no matter how small and staying in bed until past midday, then slouching around the house in a state of semiconsciousness that would do credit to a career zombie. We might not have known he was living with us if it weren't for the grubby cereal bowls that mysteriously appeared in the vague vicinity of the sink, a muffled heavy metal beat from his bedroom that Landen was convinced kept the slugs from the garden and a succession of equally languid no-hopers who called at the door to mumble, "Is Friday at home?"—something that I couldn't resist answering with, "It's a matter of some conjecture."

"When does he go back to school?" asked Landen, who did most of the day-to-day kidwork but, like many men, had trouble remembering specific dates.

"Next Monday," I replied, having gone to retrieve the mail that had just fallen through the door. "Exclusion from school was better than he deserved—it's a good thing the cops didn't get involved."

"All he did was throw Barney Plotz's cap in a muddy puddle," said Landen reflectively, "and then stomp on it."

"Yes, but Barney Plotz was *wearing* it at the time," I pointed out, thinking privately that the entire Plotz family stomped on in a muddy puddle might be a very good idea indeed. "Friday shouldn't have done what he did. Violence never solved anything."

Landen raised an eyebrow and looked at me.

"Okay, *sometimes* it solves things—but not for him, at least not yet."

"I wonder," mused Landen, "if we could get the nation's teenagers to go on a serious binge of alcohol-inspired dopiness to use up the excess stupidity?"

"It's a surplus of stupidity we have, not stereotypical dreariness," I replied, picking up an envelope at random and staring at the postmark. I still received at least half a dozen fan letters every day, even though the march of time had, fortunately, reduced my celebrity to what the Entertainments Facilitation Department termed Z-4, which is the kind of celebrities who appear in "Whatever happened to . . . ?" articles and only ever get column inches if arrested, divorced, in rehab or, if the editor's luck is really in, all three at the same time—and have some tenuous connection to Miss Corby Starlet, or whoever else happens to be the *célébrité du jour.*

The fan mail was mostly from die-hard fans who didn't care that I was Z-4, bless them. They usually asked obscure questions about my many adventures that were now in print, or something about what crap the movie was, or why I'd given up professional croquet. But for the most part, it was from fans of *Jane Eyre,* who wanted to know how Mrs. Fairfax could have been a ninja assassin, whether I *had* to shoot Bertha Rochester and if it was true I'd slept with Edward Rochester—three of the more persistent and untrue rumors surrounding the factually dubious first novel of my adventures, *The Eyre Affair.*

Landen grinned. "What's it about? Someone wanting to know whether Lola Vavoom will play you in the next Thursday film?"

"There won't be one. Not after the disaster of the first. No, it's from the World Croquet Federation. They want me to present a video entitled *The Fifty Greatest Croquet Sporting Moments.*"

"Is your SuperHoop fifty-yard peg-out in the top ten?"

I scanned the list. "They have me at twenty-six."

"Tell them ballocks."

"They'll pay me five hundred guineas."

"Cancel the ballocks thing—tell them you'll be honored and overjoyed."

"It's a sellout. I don't do sellouts. Not for *that* price anyway."

I opened a small parcel that contained a copy of the third book in my series: *The Well of Lost Plots.* I showed it to Landen, who made a face.

"Are they still selling?" he asked.

"Unfortunately."

"Am I in that one?"

"No, sweetheart—you're only in number five." I looked at the covering letter. "They want me to sign it."

I had a stack of form letters in the office that explained why I *wouldn't* sign it—the first four Thursday Next books were about as true to real life as a donkey is to a turnip, and my signature somehow gave a credibility that I didn't want to encourage. The only book I *would* sign was the fifth in the series, *The Great Samuel Pepys Fiasco,* which, unlike the first four, had my seal of approval. The Thursday Next in *The Great Samuel Pepys Fiasco* was much more of a caring and diplomatic heroine—unlike the Thursday in the previous four, who blasted away at everything in sight, drank, swore, slept around and generally kicked butt all over the BookWorld. I wanted the series to be a thought-provoking romp around literature; a book for people who like stories or a story for people who like books. It wasn't to be. The first four in the series had been less a lighthearted chronicling of my adventures and more of a "Dirty Harry meets Fanny Hill," but with a good deal more sex and violence. The publishers managed to be not only factually inaccurate but dangerously slanderous as well. By the time I'd regained control of the series for *The Great Samuel Pepys Fiasco,* the damage to my reputation had been done.

"Oh!" said Landen, reading a letter. "A rejection from my publisher. They didn't think *Fatal Parachuting Mistakes and How to Avoid Making Them Again* was what they had in mind for self-help."

"I guess their target audience doesn't include dead people."

"You could be right."

I opened another letter. "Hang on," I said, scanning the lines thoughtfully. "The Swindon Dodo Fanciers Society is offering us thirty grand for Pickers."

I looked across at Pickwick, who had started to do that almost-falling-over thing she does when she goes to sleep standing up. I had built her myself when home-cloning kits were all the rage. At almost twenty-nine and with the serial number D-009, she was the oldest dodo in existence. Because she was an early Version 1.2, she didn't have any wings, as the gene sequence wasn't complete at that time, but then she didn't have built-in cell redundancy either. It was likely she'd outlive . . . well, everything. In any event, her value had grown considerably as interest in the seventies home-cloning unextincting revolution had suddenly become fashionable. A 1978 V1.5.6 mammoth recently changed hands for sixty thousand, great auks in any condition could be worth up to five grand each, and if you had a pre-1972 trilobite of any order, you could pretty much name your price.

"Thirty grand?" echoed Landen. "Do they know she's a bit challenged in the brain and plumage department?"

"I honestly don't think they care. It would pay off the mortgage."

Pickwick was suddenly wide awake and looking at us with the dodo equivalent of a raised eyebrow, which is indistinguishable from the dodo equivalent of sniffing a raw onion.

"And buy one of those new diesel-molasses hybrid cars," said Landen.

"Or a holiday."

"We could send Friday off to the Swindon Home for Dreary Teenagers," added Landen.

"And Jenny could have a new piano."

It was too much for Pickwick, who fainted dead away in the middle of the table.

"Doesn't have much of a sense of humor, does she?" said Landen with a smile, returning to his paper.

"Not really," I replied, tearing up the letter from the Swindon Dodo Fanciers Society. "But, you know, for a bird of incalculably little brain, I'm sure she understands almost everything we say."

Landen looked at Pickwick, who had by now recovered and was staring suspiciously at her left foot, wondering if it had *always* been there and, if not, what it might be doing creeping up on her.

"It's not likely."

"How's the book going?" I asked, returning to my knitting.

"The self-help stuff?"

"The magnum opus."

Landen looked thoughtful for a moment and then said, "More opus than magnum. I'm trying to figure out whether the lack of progress is writer's block, procrastination, idleness or just plain incompetence."

"Well, now," I said, feigning seriousness, "with such an excellent range of choices, it's hard to put my finger on it. Have you considered that it might be a mixture of all four?"

"By gad!" he said, slapping his palm on his forehead. "You could be right!"

"Seriously, though?"

He shrugged. "It's so-so. Although the story is toodling along, there's no real bite to it—I think I need to inject a new plot twist or character."

"Which book are you working on?"

"Bananas for Edward."

"You'll think of something, sweetheart—you usually do."

I dropped a stitch on my knitting, rehooked it, checked the wall clock and then said, "Mum texted me earlier."

"Has she got the hang of it yet?"

"She said, 'L&Ks4DnRNXT-SNDY??' "

"Hmm," said Landen, "one of the most coherent yet. That's probably code for 'I've forgotten how to text.' Why does she even bother to try to use new technology at her age?"

"You know what she's like. I'll nip over and see what she wants on my way to work."

"Don't forget about Friday and the ChronoGuard 'If You've Got Time for Us, We've Got Time for You' careers presentation this evening."

"How could I forget?" I replied, having tried to cajole Friday into this for weeks.

"He's behind with his homework," added Landen, "and since you're at least six times more scary than I am, would you do phase one of the teenager-waking procedure? Sometimes I think he's actually glued to the bed."

"Considering his current level of personal hygiene," I mused, "you're probably right."

"If he doesn't get up," added Landen with a smile, "you could always threaten him with a bar of soap and some shampoo."

"And traumatize the poor lad? Shame on *you*, Mr. Parke-Laine."

Landen laughed, and I went up to Friday's room.

I knocked on his door, received no reply and opened it to a fetid smell of old socks and unwashed adolescence. Carefully bottled and distilled, it would do sterling work as a shark repellent, but I didn't say so. Teenage sons react badly to sarcasm. The room was liberally covered with posters of Jimi Hendrix, Che Guevara and Wayne Skunk, lead guitar and vocals of Strontium Goat. The floor was covered with discarded clothes, deadline-expired schoolwork and side plates with hardened toast crusts on them. I *think* the room had once been carpeted, but I couldn't be sure anymore.

"Hiya, Friday," I said to an inert object wrapped up in a duvet. I sat on the bed and prodded a small patch of skin I could see.

"Grunt," came a voice from somewhere deep within the bedclothes.

"Your father tells me that you're behind with your homework."

"Grunt."

"Well, *yes,* you might be suspended for two weeks, but you still need to do your coursework."

"Grunt."

"The time? It's nine right now, and I need you to be sitting up with your eyes open before I leave the room."

There was another grunt and a fart. I sighed, prodded him again, and eventually something with unwashed dark hair sat up and stared at me beneath heavy lids.

"Grunt," it said. "Grunt-grunt."

I thought of making some sarcastic remark about how it helps to open your mouth when talking but didn't, as I desperately needed his compliance, and although I couldn't actually speak teenage Mumblegrunt, I could certainly understand it.

"How's the music going?" I asked, as there is a certain degree of consciousness that you have to bring teenagers toward before leaving them to get up on their own. Fall even a few degrees below the critical threshold and they go back to sleep for eight hours—sometimes more.

"Mumble," he said slowly. "I've grunt-mumble formed a band grunty-mutter."

"A band? What's it called?"

He took a deep breath and rubbed his face. He knew he wouldn't get rid of me until he'd answered at least three questions. He looked at me with his bright, intelligent eyes and sniffed before announcing in a rebellious tone, "It's called the Gobshites."

"You can't call it that!"

Friday shrugged. "All right," he grumbled in a slovenly manner, "we'll go back to the original name."

"Which is?"

"The Wankers."

"Actually, I think Gobshites is a terrific name for a band. Pithy and degenerate all at the same time. Now, listen, I know you're not keen on this whole 'career in the time industry' stuff, but you did promise. I'll expect you to be all bright-eyed, alert and bushy-tailed, washed, showered, scrubbed and all homework finished by the time I get back."

I stared at the picture of slovenly teenagerhood in front of me. I'd have settled for "awake and/or coherent"—but I always aim high.

"Allrightmum," he said in a long slur.

As soon as I had closed the door behind me I heard him flop back. It didn't matter. He was awake, and his father could do the rest.

"I expect he's raring to go?" suggested Landen when I came downstairs. "Had to lock him in his room to curb his enthusiasm?"

"Champing at the bit," I replied wearily. "We'd get a more dynamic response from a vapid slug on tranquilizers."

"*I* wasn't so dreary when I was a kid," said Landen thoughtfully, handing me my tea. "I wonder where he gets it from?"

"Modern living, but don't worry. He's only sixteen—he'll snap out of it."

"I hope so."

And that was the problem. This wasn't just the usual worries of concerned parents with grunty and unintelligible teenagers; he *had* to snap out of it. I'd met the future Friday several times in the past, and he'd risen to the lofty heights of ChronoGuard director-general with absolute power over the Standard History Eventline, a job of awesome responsibilities. He was instrumental in saving my life, his own—and the planet from destruction no fewer than 756 times. By his fortieth birthday, he would be known as "Apocalypse" Next. But that hadn't happened yet. And with Friday's chief interest in life at present being Strontium Goat, sleeping, Che Guevara, Hendrix and more sleeping, we were beginning to wonder how it ever would.

Landen looked at his watch.

"Isn't it time you were off to work, wifey darling? The good folk of Swindon would be utterly lost and confused without you to take the burden of floor-covering decision making from them."

He was right. I was already ten minutes late, and I kissed him several times, just in case something unexpected occurred that might separate us for longer than planned. By "unexpected" I was thinking of the time he was eradicated for two years by the Goliath Corporation. Although the vast multinational was back in business after many years in the financial and political doldrums, they had not yet attempted any of the monkey business that had marked our relationship in the past. I hoped they'd learned their lesson, but I'd never quite freed myself of the idea that a further fracas with them might be just around the corner, so I always made quite sure that I'd told Landen everything I needed to tell him.

"Busy day ahead?" he asked as he saw me to the garden gate.

"A large carpet to install for a new company in the financial center—bespoke executive pile, plus the usual quotes. I think

Spike and I have a stair carpet to do in an old Tudor house with uneven treads, so one of those nightmare jobs."

He paused and sucked his lower lip for a moment.

"Good, so . . . no . . . no . . . SpecOps stuff or anything?"

"Sweetheart!" I said, giving him a hug. "That's all past history. I do carpets these days—it's a lot less stressful, believe me. Why?"

"No reason. It's just that what with *Diatrymas* being seen as far north as Salisbury, people are saying that the old SpecOps personnel might be recalled into service."

"Six-foot-tall carnivorous birds from the late Paleocene would be SO-13 business if they were real, which I doubt," I pointed out. "I was SO-27. The Literary Detectives. When copies of *Tristram Shandy* are threatening old ladies in dark alleys, I just *might* be asked for my opinion. Besides, no one's reading books much anymore, so I'm fairly redundant."

"That's true," said Landen. "Perhaps being an author isn't such a great move after all."

"Then write your magnum opus for *me,*" I told him tenderly. "I'll be your audience, wife, fan club, sex kitten and critic all rolled into one. It's me picking up Tuesday from school, right?"

"Right."

"And you'll pick up Jenny?"

"I won't forget. What shall I do if Pickwick starts shivering in that hopelessly pathetic way that she does?"

"Pop her in the airing cupboard—I'll try and get her cozy finished at work."

"Not *so* busy, then?"

I kissed him again and departed.

2.

Mum and Polly and Mycroft

My mother's main aim in life was to get from the cradle to the grave with the minimum of fuss and bother and the maximum of tea and Battenberg. Along the way she brought up three children, attended a lot of Women's Federation meetings and managed to squeeze a few severely burned meals somewhere in between. It wasn't until I was six that I realized that cake wasn't meant to be 87 percent carbon and that chicken actually tasted of something. Despite all this, or perhaps even because *of it, we all loved her a great deal.*

My mother lived less than a mile away and actually on the route to work, so I often dropped in just to make sure she was okay and wasn't about to embark on some harebrained scheme, as was her habit. A few years ago she had hoarded tinned pears on the principle that once she'd cornered the market, she could "name her price," a flagrant misunderstanding of the rules of supply and demand that did no damage to the tinned-fruit producers of the world but condemned her immediate family and friends to pears at every meal for almost three years.

She was the sort of parent you would want to have living close by, but only on the grounds that she would then never come to stay. I loved her dearly, but in small doses. A cup of tea here, a dinner there—and as much child care as I could squeeze out of her. The text excuse I gave Landen was actually something of a mild fib, as the *real* reason for my popping around was to pick something up from Mycroft's workshop.

"Hello, darling!" said Mum as soon as she opened the door. "Did you get my text?"

"Yes. But you must learn how to use the backspace and delete keys—it all came out as nonsense."

"'L&Ks4DnRNXT-SNDY??'" she repeated, showing me her cell phone. "What else *could* that mean but 'Landen and kids for dinner next Sunday?' Really, darling, how you even *begin* to communicate with your children, I have no idea."

"That wasn't *real* text shorthand," I said, narrowing my eyes suspiciously. "You just made it up."

"I'm barely eighty-two," she said indignantly. "I'm not on the scrap heap yet. Made up the text indeed! Do you want to come back for lunch?" she added, without seeming to draw breath. "I've got a few friends coming around, and after we've discussed who is the most unwell, we'll agree volubly with one another about the sorry state of the nation and then put it all to rights with poorly thought-out and totally impractical ideas. And if there's time after that, we might even play cribbage."

"Hello, Auntie," I said to Polly, who hobbled out of the front room with the aid of a stick, "If I texted you 'L&Ks4DnRNXT-SNDY??' what would you think I meant?"

Polly frowned and thought for a moment, her prunelike forehead rising in a folding ripple like a festoon curtain. She was over ninety and looked so unwell that she was often mistaken for dead when asleep on the bus. Despite this she was totally sound upstairs, with only three or four fair-to-serious medical ailments, unlike my mother, who had the full dozen—or so she claimed.

"Well, do you know I'd be a bit confused—"

"Hah!" I said to Mum. "You see?"

"—because," Polly carried on, "if *you* texted me asking for Landen and the kids to come over for Sunday dinner, I'd not know why you hadn't asked him yourself."

"Ah . . . I see," I mumbled, suspicious that the two of them had been colluding in some way—as they generally did. Still, I never knew why they made me feel as though I were an eighteen-year-old when I was now fifty-two and myself in the sort of respectable time of life that I thought they should be. That's the thing about hitting fifty. All your life you think the half century is death's adolescence, but actually it's really not that bad, as long as you can remember where you left your glasses.

"Happy birthday, by the way," said my mother. "I got you something—look."

She handed me the most hideous sweater you could possibly imagine.

"I don't know what to say, Mum, and I really mean that—a short-sleeved lime green sweater with a hood and mock-antler buttons."

"Do you like it?"

"One's attention is drawn to it instantly."

"Good! Then you'll wear it straightaway?"

"I wouldn't want to ruin it," I replied hastily. "I'm just off to work."

"Ooh!" said Polly. "I've only now remembered." She handed me a CD in a plain sleeve. "This is a preproduction copy of *Hosing the Dolly*."

"It's what?"

"*Please* try to keep up with the times, darling. *Hosing the Dolly*. The new album by Strontium Goat. It won't be out until November. I thought Friday might like it."

"It's really totally out there, man," put in my mother. "Whatever that means. There's a solo guitar riff on the second track that reminded me of Friday's playing and was so good it made my toes tingle—although that might just have been a pinched nerve. Wayne Skunk's granny is Mrs. Arbuthnot—you know, the funny old lady with the large wart on her nose and the elbows that bend both ways. He sent it to her."

I looked at the CD. Friday *would* like it, I was certain of that.

"And," added Polly, leaning closer and with a conspiratorial wink, "you don't have to tell him it was from us—I know what teenagers are like, and a bit of parental kudos counts for a lot."

"Thank you," I said, and meant it. It was more than a CD—it was currency.

"Good!" said my mother. "Have you got time for a cup of tea and a slice of Battenberg?"

"No, thank you—I'm going to pick something up from Mycroft's workshop, and then I'll be on my way."

"How about some Battenberg to go, then?"

"I've just had breakfast."

The doorbell rang.

"Ooooh!" said Polly, peering furtively out the window. "What fun. It looks like a market researcher!"

"Right," said my mother in a very military tone. "Let's see how long we can keep him before he runs out screaming. I'll pretend to have mild dementia, and you can complain about your sciatica in German. We'll try to beat our personal Market-Researcher Containment record of two hours and twelve minutes."

I shook my head sadly. "I wish you two would grow up."

"You are *so* judgmental, daughter dear," scolded my mother. "When you reach our age and level of physical decrepitude, you'll take your entertainment wherever you can find it. Now, be off with you."

And they shooed me into the kitchen while I mumbled something about how remedial basket weaving, whist drives or daytime soaps would probably suit them better. Mind you, inflicting mental torture on market researchers kept them busy, I suppose.

I walked out the back door, crossed the back garden and quietly entered the wooden outhouse that was my uncle Mycroft's laboratory. I switched on the light and walked to my Porsche, which was looking a little forlorn under a dust sheet. It was still unrepaired from the accident five years before. The damage hadn't been that severe, but 356 parts were getting pricey these days, and we couldn't spare the cash. I reached into the cockpit, pulled the release and opened the hood. It was here that I kept a tote bag containing twenty thousand Welsh tocyns. On this side of the border pretty worthless, but enough to buy a three-bedroom house in Merthyr. I wasn't planning to move to the Welsh Socialist Republic, of course—I needed the cash for a Welsh cheese deal I had cooking that evening. I checked that the cash was all still there and was just replacing the sheet on the car when a noise made me turn. Standing at the workbench in the half-light was my uncle Mycroft. An undeniable genius, with his keen mind he had pushed the frontiers in a range of disciplines that included genetics, fusion power, abstract geometry, perpetual motion and romantic fiction. It was he who had ushered in the home-cloning revolution, he who may have developed a memory-erasure machine and he who had invented the Prose Portal that had catapulted me into fiction. He was dressed in his trademark wool three-piece suit but without the jacket, his shirtsleeves were rolled up, and he was in what we all called his "inventing mode." He seemed to be concentrating on a delicate mechanism, the function of which was impossible to guess. As I watched him in silence and with a growing sense of wonder, he suddenly noticed me.

"Ah!" he said with a smile. "Thursday! Haven't seen you for a while—all well?"

"Yes," I replied a bit uncertainly, "I think so."

"Splendid! I just had an idea for a cheap form of power: by bringing pasta and antipasta together, we could be looking at the utter annihilation of ravioli and the liberation of vast quantities of energy. I safely predict that an average-size cannelloni would be able to power Swindon for over a year. Mind you, I could be wrong."

"You're not often wrong," I said quietly.

"I think I was wrong to start inventing in the first place," he replied after a moment's reflection. "Just because I *can* do it, it doesn't follow that I *should*. If scientists stopped to think about their creations more, the world might be a better—"

He broke off talking and looked at me in a quizzical manner.

"You're staring at me in a strange way," he said, with uncharacteristic astuteness.

"Well, yes," I replied, trying to frame my words carefully. "You see . . . I think . . . that is to say . . . I'm *very* surprised to see you."

"Really?" he said, putting down the device he was working on. "Why?"

"Well," I replied with greater firmness, "I'm surprised to see you because . . . you died six years ago!"

"I did?" inquired Mycroft with genuine concern. "Why does no one tell me these things?"

I shrugged, as there was really no good answer to this.

"Are you sure?" he asked, patting himself on the chest and stomach and then taking his pulse to try to convince himself I might be mistaken. "I know I'm a bit forgetful, but I'm certain I would have remembered *that*."

"Yes, quite sure," I replied. "I was there."

"Well, goodness," murmured Mycroft thoughtfully, "if what you say is correct and I *am* dead, it's entirely possible that this isn't me at all, but a variable-response holographic recording of some sort. Let's have a look for a projector."

And so saying, he began to ferret through the piles of dusty machinery in his lab. And with nothing better to do and faintly curious, I joined in.

We searched for a good five minutes, but after finding nothing even vaguely resembling a holographic projector, Mycroft and I sat down on a packing case and didn't speak for some moments.

"Dead," muttered Mycroft with a resigned air. "Never been that before. Not even once. Are you quite sure?"

"Quite sure," I replied. "You were eighty-seven. It was expected."

"Oh, yes," he said, as though some dim memory were stirring. "And Polly?" he added, suddenly remembering his wife. "How is she?"

"She's very well," I told him. "She and Mum are up to their old tricks."

"Annoying market researchers?"

"Among other things. But she's missing you dreadfully."

"And I her." He looked nervous for a moment. "Has she got a boyfriend yet?"

"At ninety-two?"

"Damn good-looking woman—smart, too."

"Well, she hasn't."

"Hmm. Well, If you see someone suitable, O favorite niece, push him her way, won't you? I don't want her to be lonely."

"I'll do that, Uncle, I promise."

We sat in silence for a few seconds more, and I shivered.

"Mycroft," I said, suddenly thinking that perhaps there wasn't a scientific explanation for his appearance after all, "I'm going to try something."

I put out my fingertips to touch him, but where they should have met the firm resistance of his shirtsleeve, there was none—my fingers just melted into him. He wasn't there. Or if he was, he was something insubstantial—a phantom.

"Ooooh!" he said as I withdrew my hand. "That felt odd."

"Mycroft . . . you're a *ghost*."

"Nonsense! Scientifically proven to be completely impossible." He paused for thought. "Why would I be one of those?"

I shrugged. "I don't know—perhaps there's something you hadn't finished at your death and it's been bothering you."

"Great Scott! You're right. I never did finish the final chapter of *Love Among the Begonias*."

In retirement Mycroft had spent his time writing romantic novels, all of which sold surprisingly well. So well, in fact, that he had attracted the lasting enmity of Daphne Farquitt, the indisputable leader in the field. She fired off an accusatory letter accusing him of "wanton" plagiarism. A barrage of claims and counterclaims followed, which ended only when Mycroft died. It was so venomous, in fact, that conspiracy theorists claimed he was poisoned by crazed Farquitt fans. We had to publish his death certificate to quell the rumors.

"Polly finished *Love Among the Begonias* for you," I said.

"Ah," he replied, "maybe I've come back to haunt that loathsome cow Farquitt."

"If that were the case, you'd be over at her place doing the wooo-wooo thing and clanking chains."

"Hmm," he said disdainfully, "that doesn't sound very dignified."

"How about some last-minute inventing? Some idea you never got around to researching?"

Mycroft thought long and hard, making several bizarre faces as he did so.

"Fascinating!" he said at last, panting with the effort. "I can't do original thought anymore. As soon as my brain stopped functioning, that was the end of Mycroft the inventor. You're right: I must be dead. It's *most* depressing."

"But no idea why you're here?"

"None," he said despondently.

"Well," I said as I got up, "I'll make a few inquiries. Do you want Polly to know you've reappeared in spirit form?"

"I'll leave it to your judgment," he said. "But if you do tell her, you might mention something about how she was the finest partner any man could have. Two minds with but a single thought, two hearts that beat as one."

I snapped my fingers. That's how I wanted to describe Landen and me. "That was good—can I use it?"

"Of course. Have you any idea how much I miss Polly?"

I thought of the two years Landen had been eradicated. "I do. And she misses you, Uncle, every second of every day."

He looked up at me, and I saw his eyes glisten.

I tried to put my hand on his arm, but it went through his phantom limb and instead landed on the hard surface of the workbench.

"I'll have a think about why I might be here," said Mycroft in a quiet voice. "Will you look in on me from time to time?" He smiled to himself and began to tinker with the device on the workbench again.

"Of course. Good-bye, Uncle."

"Good-bye, Thursday."

And he slowly began to fade. I noticed as he did so that the room grew warmer again, and within a few more seconds he had vanished entirely. I retrieved the bag of Welsh cash and walked thoughtfully to the door, turning to have one last look. The workshop was empty, dusty and forgotten. Abandoned as it was when Mycroft died, six years before.

3.

Acme Carpets

The Special Operations Network was instituted in 1928 to handle policing duties considered either too unusual or too specialized to be tackled by the regular force. Amongst the stranger departments were those that dealt with vampires (SO-17), time travel (SO-12), literary crime (SO-27) and the Cheese Enforcement Agency (SO-31). Notoriously secretive and with increased accusations of unaccountability and heavy-handedness, 90 percent of the service was disbanded during the winter of 1991–92. Of the thirty-two departments, only five were retained. My department, the Literary Detectives, was not among them.

The name Acme Carpets was a misnomer, to be honest. We didn't just do carpets—we did tiles, linoleum and wooden flooring, too. Competitive, fast and reliable, we had been trading in Swindon for ten years, ever since the SpecOps divisions were disbanded in '92. In 1996 we moved to bigger premises on the Oxford Road trading estate. If you needed any sort of floor covering in the Swindon area, you could come to us for the most competitive quote.

I pushed open the front doors and was surprised that there was no one around. Not that there was a lack of customers, as Mondays before ten were generally pretty light, but that there was no staff—not even in the office or skulking next to the spotlessly clean complimentary-tea area. I walked to the back of the store, past quality rolls of carpet and a varied selection of samples piled high on the light and spacious showroom floor. I opened the heavy swinging doors that led to the storerooms and froze. Standing next to a pile of last year's sample books was a flightless bird about four feet high and with an unfeasibly large and rather nastily serrated beak. It stared at me suspiciously with two small black eyes. I looked around. The stockroom staff were all dutifully standing still, and behind the *Dyatrima* was a stocky figure in an Acme Carpets uniform, a man with a large, brow-ridged head and deeply sunken brown eyes. He had a lot in common with the Paleocene anomaly that faced me—he, too, had once been extinct and was here not by the meanderings of natural selection but from the inconsiderate meddling of a scientist who never stopped to ask whether if a thing *could* be done, that it *should*. His name was Stig, and he was a reengineered neanderthal, ex–SO-13 and a valued colleague from the old days of SpecOps. He'd saved my butt on several occasions, and I'd helped him and his fellow extinctees to species self-determination.

"Don't move," said Stig in a low rumble. "We don't want to hurt it."

He never did. Stig saw any renegade unextinctees as something akin to family and always caught them alive, if possible. On the other hand, chimeras, a hodgepodge of the hobby sequencer's art, were another matter—he dispatched them without mercy, and without pain.

The *Diatryma* made a vicious jab toward me; I jumped to my left as the beak snapped shut with the sound of oversize castanets. Quick as a flash, Stig leaped forward and covered the creature's head with an old flour sack, which seemed to subdue it enough for him to wrestle it to the floor. I joined in, as did the entire storeroom staff, and within a few moments we had wrapped some duct tape securely around its massive beak, rendering it harmless.

"Thanks," said Stig, securing a leash around the bird's neck.

"Salisbury?" I asked as we walked past the rolls of Wilton shag and cushioned linoleum in a wide choice of colors.

"Devizes," replied the neanderthal. "We had to run for eight miles across open farmland to catch it."

"Did anyone see you?" I asked, mindful of any rumors getting out.

"Who'd believe them if they did?" he replied. "But there're more *Diatrymas*—we'll be out again tonight."

Acme Carpets, as you might have gathered, was just the cover story. In truth it was the old SpecOps under another name. The service hadn't really been disbanded in the early nineties—it just went underground, and freelance. All *strictly* unofficial, of course. Luckily, the Swindon chief of police was Braxton Hicks, my old divisional boss at SpecOps. Although he suspected what we got up to, he told me he would feign ignorance unless "someone gets eaten or something." Besides, if we didn't mop up all the bizarrer elements of modern living, his regular officers would have to, and Braxton might then have a demand of bonus payments for "actions beyond the call of duty." And Hicks loved his budget almost as much as he loved his golf. So the cops didn't bother us and we didn't bother them.

"We have a question," said Stig. "Do we have to mention the possibility of being trampled by mammoths on our Health and Safety Risk-Assessment Form?"

"No—that's the part of Acme we don't want anyone to know about. The safety stuff only relates to carpet laying."

"We understand," said Stig. "What about being shredded by a chimera?"

"Just carpets, Stig."

"Okay. By the way," he added, "have you told Landen about all your SpecOps work yet? You said you were going to."

"I'm . . . building up to it."

"You should tell him, Thursday."

"I know."

"And have a good anniversary of your mother giving birth to you."

"Thank you."

I bade Stig good day and then walked to the store offices, which were situated in a raised position halfway between the storeroom and the showroom floor. From there you could see pretty much everything that went on in the building.

As I walked in, a man looked up from where he was crouched under the desk.

"Have you captured it?" he asked in a quavering voice.

"Yes."

He looked relieved and clambered out from his hiding place. He was in his early forties, and his features were just beginning to show the shades of middle age. Around his eyes were fine lines, his dark hair now flecked with gray. Even though he was management, he also wore an Acme Carpets uniform. Only his looked a lot better on him than mine did on me. In fact, he looked a lot better in his than *anyone* in the establishment, leading us to accuse him of having his professionally tailored, something he strenuously denied but, given his fastidious nature, not outside the bounds of possibility. Bowden Cable had been my partner at the Swindon branch of the Literary Detectives, and it seemed only natural that he would have the top admin job at Acme Carpets when we were all laid off from SpecOps.

"Are we busy today?" I asked, pouring myself a cup of coffee.

Bowden pointed to the newspaper. "Have you read this?"

"The stupidity surplus?"

"Part of it, I guess," he replied despondently. "Incredibly enough, reality TV has just gotten *worse*."

"Is that possible?" I asked. "Wasn't *Celebrity Trainee Pathologist* the pits?" I thought for a moment. "Actually, *Whose Life Support Do We Switch Off?* was worse. Or maybe *Sell Your Granny*. Wow, the choice these days makes it all so tricky to decide."

Bowden laughed.

"I'll agree that *Granny* lowered the bar for distasteful program makers everywhere, but RTA-TV, never one to shrink from a challenge, has devised *Samaritan Kidney Swap*. Ten renal-failure patients take turns trying to convince a tissue-typed donor—and the voting viewers—which one should have his spare kidney."

I groaned. Reality TV was to me the worst form of entertainment—the modern equivalent of paying sixpence to watch lunatics howling at the walls down at the local madhouse. I shook my head sadly.

"What's wrong with a good book?" I asked.

Bowden shrugged. In these days of junk TV, short attention spans and easy-to-digest sound bites, it seemed that the book, the noble device to which both Bowden and I had devoted much of our lives, was being marginalized into just another human storytelling experience also-ran, along with the epic poem, Greek theater, Jackanory, Beta and Tarzanagrams.

"How's the family?" asked Bowden, trying to elevate the mood.

"They're all good," I replied. "Except Friday, who is still incapable of any human activity other than torpidity."

"And Pickwick? Feathers growing back?"

"No—listen, can you knit?"

"No. . . . Why?"

"No reason. What's on the books for us today?"

Bowden picked up a clipboard and thumbed through the pages. "Spike's got a brace of undead to deal with and a possible pack of howlers in the Savernake. Stig's still on the path of those *Diatrymas.* The Taste Division has got an outbreak of stonecladding to deal with in Cirencester, and the Pampas Squad will be busy on a slash 'n' burn in Bristol. Oh, yes—and we've an outbreak of doppelgängers in Chippenham."

"Any literary stuff?" I asked hopefully.

"Only Mrs. Mattock and her stolen first editions—*again.* Face it, Thurs, books just don't light anyone's candle these days. It's as good that they don't—add the sixteen or so carpets to be laid and the twenty-eight quotes needed yesterday, and we're kind of stretched. Do we pull Spike off zombies to do stair runners?"

"Can't we just drag in some freelance installers?"

"And pay them with what? An illegal *Diatryma* each?"

"It's that bad, is it?"

"Thursday, it's *always* that bad. We're nuzzling up to the overdraft limit again."

"No problem. I've got a seriously good cheese deal going down this evening."

"I don't want to know about it. When you're arrested, I need *deniability*—and besides, if you actually sold carpets instead of gallivanting around like a lunatic, you wouldn't need to buy and sell on the volatile cheese market."

"That reminds me," I said with a smile. "I'll be out of my office today, so don't put any calls through."

"Thursday!" he said in an exasperated tone. "*Please* don't vanish today of *all* days. I really need you to quote for the new lobby carpet in the Finis, I've got the Wilton rep popping in at four-thirty to show us their new line, and the Health and Safety Inspectorate is coming in to make sure we're up to speed."

"On safety procedures?"

"Good Lord no! On how to fill the forms in properly."

"Listen," I said, "I've got to take Friday to the ChronoGuard career night at five-thirty, so I'll try to get back a couple of hours before then and do some quotes. Have a list ready for me."

"Already done," he said, and before I could make up an excuse, he passed me a clipboard full of addresses and contact names.

"Good," I muttered, "very efficient—nice job."

I took my coffee and walked to my own office, a small and windowless room next to the forklift-recharging point. I sat at my desk and stared despondently at the list Bowden had given me, then rocked back and forth on my chair in an absent mood. Stig had been right. I *should* tell Landen about what I got up to, but life was better with him thinking I was working at Acme. Besides, running several illegal SpecOps departments wasn't all I did. It was . . . well, the tip of a very large and misshapen iceberg.

I got up, took off my jacket and was about to change into more comfortable clothes when there was another tap at the door. I opened it to reveal a large and muscular man a few years younger than myself and looking even more incongruous in his Acme Carpets uniform than I looked in mine—although I doubted that anyone would ever try to tell him so. He had long dreadlocks that reached almost to his waist and were tied back in a loose hair band, and he was wearing a liberal amount of jewelry, similar to the sort that Goths are fond of—skulls, bats, things like that. But it wasn't for decoration—it was for protection. This was ex–SO-17 operative "Spike" Stoker, the most successful vampire staker and werewolf hunter in the Southwest, and although no friend of the undead, he was a friend of mine.

"Happy birthday, bookworm," he said genially. "Got a second?"

I looked at my watch. I was late for work. Not carpet work, of course, since I was already there, but *work* work.

"Is it about health and safety?"

"No, this is important and relevant."

He led the way to the other side of the storeroom, just next to where we kept the adhesive, tacks and grippers. We entered a door hidden behind a poster for Brinton's Carpets and took a small flight of steps down to the level below. Spike opened a sturdy door with a large brass key, and we stepped into what I described as the "Containment Suite" but what Spike referred to as the "Weirdshitorium." His appraisal was better. Our work took us to the very limits of credibility—to a place where even the most stalwart conspiracy theorists would shake their heads and remark sarcastically, "Oh, yeah . . . right." When we were SpecOps, we had secrecy, manpower, budget and unaccountability to help us do the job. Now we had just secrecy, complimentary tea and cookies and a big brass key. It was here that Stig kept his creatures until he decided what to do with them and where Spike incarcerated any of the captured undead for observation—in case they were thinking of becoming either *nearly* dead or *mostly* dead. Death, I had discovered long ago, was available in varying flavors, and none of them particularly palatable.

We passed a cell that was full of gallon-size glass jars containing captured Supreme Evil Beings. They were small, wraithlike objects about the size and texture of well-used dish cloths, only less substantial, and they spent most of the time bickering over who was the *most* supreme Supreme Evil Being. But we weren't here to bother with SEBs; Spike led me on to a cell right at the end of the corridor and opened the door. Sitting on a chair in the middle of the room was a man in jeans and a plain leather jacket. He was staring at the floor with the light on above, so I couldn't at first see his face, and his large and well-manicured hands were clenched tightly in front of him. I also noticed that his ankle was attached to the floor by a sturdy chain. I winced. Spike would have to be right about this one—imprisonment of something actually *human* was definitely illegal and could be seriously bad for business.

"Hey!" said Spike and the figure slowly raised his head to look at me. I recognized him instantly and not without a certain degree of alarm. It was Felix8, Acheron Hades' henchman from way back in the days of the *Jane Eyre* adventure. Hades had taken the face from the first Felix when he died and implanted it on a suitable stranger who'd been bent to his evil will. Whenever a Felix died, which was quite often, he just swapped the face. Felix8's real name was Danny Chance, but his freewill had been appropriated by Hades—he was merely an empty vessel, devoid of pity or morals. His life had no meaning other than to do his master's bidding. The point now was, his master had died sixteen years ago, and the last time I saw Felix8 was at the Penderyn Hotel in Merthyr, the capital of the Welsh Socialist Republic.

Felix8 looked at me with a slight sense of amusement and gave a subtle nod of greeting.

"Where did you find him?" I asked.

"Outside your place half an hour ago. He had this on him."

Spike showed me an ugly-looking machine pistol with a delicately carved stock. "There was a single round in the chamber."

I bent down to Felix8's level and stared at him for a moment. "Who sent you?"

Felix8 smiled, said nothing and looked at the chain that was firmly clasped around his ankle.

"What do you want?"

Still Felix8 said nothing.

"Where have you been these past sixteen years?"

All my questions were met with blank insolence, and after five minutes of this I walked back outside the cell block, Spike at my side.

"Who reported him?" I asked.

"Your stalker—what's his name again?"

"Millon."

"Right. He thought Felix8 might have been *another* stalker and was going to warn him off, but when he noticed the absence of notebooks, cameras or even a duffel coat, he called me."

I thought for a moment. If Felix8 was back on my trail, then somebody in the Hades family was looking for revenge—and they were big on revenge. I'd had run-ins with the Hades family before, and I thought they'd learned their lesson by now. I had personally defeated Acheron, Aornis and Cocytus, which left only Lethe and Phlgethon. Lethe was the "white sheep" of the family and spent most of his time doing charity work, which left only Phlgethon, who had dropped off the radar in the mid-nineties, despite numerous manhunts by SO-5 and myself.

"What do you suggest?" I asked. "He doesn't fall into any of the categories that might ethically give us a reason to keep him under lock and key without trial of some sort. After all, he's only wearing the *face* of Felix—under there he's an erased Danny Chance, married father of two who went missing in 1985."

"I agree we can't keep him," replied Spike, "but if we let him go he'll just try to kill you."

"I live to be over a hundred," I murmured. "I know—I've met the future me."

It was said without much conviction. I'd seen enough of time's paradoxical nature to know that meeting the future me wasn't any guarantee of a long life.

"We'll keep him for twenty-four hours," I announced. "I'll make a few inquiries and see if I can figure out which Hades is involved—if any. He might be simply trying to carry out the last order he was given. After all, he was under orders to kill me, but no one said anything about *when*."

"Thursday . . . ?" began Spike in a tone that I recognized and didn't like.

"No," I said quickly. "Out of the question."

"The only reason he'd mind being killed," said Spike in an annoyingly matter-of-fact way, "is that it would mean he failed to carry out his mission—to kill you."

"I hear you, Spike, but he's done nothing wrong. Give me a day, and if I can't find anything, we'll hand him over to Braxton."

"Okay, then," replied Spike, with a sulky air of disappointment.

"Another thing," I said as we returned to the carpet storeroom. "My uncle Mycroft has returned as a ghost."

"It happens," replied Spike with a shrug. "Did he seem substantial?"

"As you or I."

"How long was he materialized for?"

"Seven minutes, I guess."

"Then you got him at first haunting. First-timers are always the most solid."

"That might be so, but I'd like to know *why*."

"I'm owed a few favors by the Realm of the Dead," he said offhandedly, "so I can find out. By the way, have you told Landen about all this crazy SpecOps shit?"

"I'm telling him this evening."

"Sure you are."

* * *

I walked back to my office, locked the door and changed out of the less-than-appealing Acme Carpets uniform and put on something more comfortable. I would have to speak to Aornis Hades about Felix8, but she would probably tell me to go and stick it in my ear—after all, she was seven years into a thirty-year enloopment based on my testimony, and yours truly was unlikely to fill her evil little soul with any sort of heartwarming benevolence.

I finished lacing my boots, locked the door, refilled my water bottle and placed it in the shoulder bag. Acme Carpets might have been a cover for my clandestine work at SpecOps, but this itself was cover for *another* job that only Bowden knew about. If Landen found out about SpecOps, he'd be annoyed—if he found out about Jurisfiction, he'd go bonkers. Not long after the Minotaur's attack following the '88 SuperHoop, Landen and I had a heart-to-heart where I told him I was giving up Jurisfiction—my primary duty being wife and mother. And so it was agreed. Unfortunately, my *other* primary duty was to fiction—the make-believe. Unable to reconcile the two, I did both and lied a bit—well, a lot, actually—to plaster over the gaping crack in my loyalties. It wasn't with an easy or light heart, but it had worked for the past fourteen years. The odd thing was, Jurisfiction didn't earn me a penny and was dangerous and wildly unpredictable. There was another reason I liked it, too—it brought me into close contact with *story*. It would have been easier to get a registered cheesehead off a five-times-a-day Limburger habit than to keep me away from fiction. But, hey—I could handle it.

I sat down, took a deep breath and opened the TravelBook I kept in my bag. It had been given to me by Mrs. Nakajima many years before and was my passport in and out of the world on the other side of the printed page. I lowered my head, emptied my mind as much as possible and read from the book. The words echoed about me with a resonance that sounded like wind chimes and looked like a thousand glowworms. The room around me rippled and stretched, then returned with a *twang* to my office at Acme. Blast. This happened more and more often these days. I had once been a natural bookjumper, but the skill had faded with the years. I took a deep breath and tried again. The wind chimes and glow-worms returned, and once more the room distorted around me like a barrel, then faded from view to be replaced by a kaleidoscope of images, sounds and emotions as I jumped through the boundary that separates the real from the written, the actual from the fable. With a rushing sound like distant waterfalls and a warm sensation that felt like hot rain and kittens, I was transported from Acme Carpets in Swindon to the entrance hallway of a large Georgian country house.

4.

Jurisfiction

Jurisfiction is the name given to the policing agency *within* books. Working with the intelligence-gathering capabilities of Text Grand Central, the Prose Resource Operatives at Jurisfiction work tirelessly to maintain the continuity of the narrative within the pages of all the books ever written, a sometimes thankless task. Jurisfiction agents live mostly on their wits as they attempt to reconcile the author's original wishes and the reader's expectations against a strict and largely pointless set of bureaucratic guidelines laid down by the Council of Genres.

It was a spacious hallway, with deep picture windows that afforded a fine view of the extensive parklands beyond the gravel drive and perfectly planted flower beds. Inside, the walls were hung with delicate silks, the woodwork shone brightly, and the marble floor was so polished I could see myself in it. I quickly drank a pint of water, as the bookjumping process could leave me dangerously dehydrated these days, and dialed TransGenre Taxis on my mobilefootnoterphone to order a cab in a half hour's time, since they were always busy and it paid to book ahead. I then looked around cautiously. Not to check for impending danger, as this was the peaceful backstory of Jane Austen's *Sense and Sensibility*. No, I was making quite sure my current Jurisfiction Cadet wasn't anywhere in sight. My overriding wish at present was not to have to deal with her until roll call had finished.

"Good morning, ma'am!" she said, appearing in front of me so abruptly I almost cried out. She spoke in the overeager manner of the terminally keen, a trait that began to annoy soon after I'd agreed to assess her suitability, twenty-four hours before.

"Do you have to jump in so abruptly?" I asked her. "You nearly gave me a heart attack!"

"Oh! I'm sorry. But I did bring you some breakfast."

"Well, in that case . . ." I looked into the bag she handed me and frowned. "Wait a minute—that doesn't look like a bacon sandwich."

"It isn't. It's a crispy lentil cake made with soy milk and bean curd. It cleanses the bowels. Bacon definitely *will* give you a heart attack."

"How thoughtful of you," I remarked sarcastically. "The body is a temple, right?"

"Right. And I didn't get you coffee because it raises blood pressure. I got you this beetroot-and-edelweiss energy drink."

"What happened to the squid ink and hippopotamus milk?"

"They were out."

"Look," I said, handing back the lentil animal-feed thing and the drink, "tomorrow is the third and last day of your assessment, and I haven't yet made up my mind. Do you want to be a Jurisfiction agent?"

"More than anything."

"Right. So if you want me to sign you out for advanced training, you're going to have to do as you're told. If that means killing a grammasite, recapturing an irregular verb, dressing Quasimodo or even something as simple as getting me coffee and a bacon roll, then that's what you'll do. Understand?"

"Sorry," she said, adding as an afterthought, "Then I suppose you don't want this?" She showed me a small lump of quartz crystal.

"What do I do with it?"

"You wear it. It can help retune your vibrational energy system."

"The only energy system I need right now is a bacon roll. You might be a veggie, but I'm not. I'm not *you*—you're a version of *me*. You might be into tarot and yogurt and vitamins and standing naked in the middle of crop circles with your eyes closed and your palms facing skyward, but don't think that I am as well, okay?"

She looked crestfallen, and I sighed. After all, I felt kind of responsible. Since I'd made it into print, I'd been naturally curious about meeting the fictional me, but I'd never entertained the possibility that she might want to join Jurisfiction. But here she was—the Thursday Next from *The Great Samuel Pepys Fiasco.* It was mildly spooky at first, because she wasn't similar just in the way that identical twins are similar, but physically *indistinguishable* from me. Stranger still, despite *Pepys Fiasco*'s being set six years before, she looked as old as my fifty-two years. Every crag and wrinkle, even the flecks of gray hair I pretended I didn't care about. For all intents and purposes, she *was* me. But only, I was at pains to point out, in facial appearance. She didn't act or dress like me; her clothes were more earthy and sustainable. Instead of my usual jeans, shirt and jacket, she wore a naturally dyed cotton skirt and a homespun crocheted pullover. She carried a shoulder bag of felt instead of my Billingham, and in place of the scarlet scrunchie holding my ponytail in place, hers was secured with a strip of hemp cloth tied in a neat bow. It wasn't by accident. After I had endured the wholly unwarranted aggression of the first four Thursday books, I'd insisted that the fifth reflect my more sensitive nature. Unfortunately, they took me a little too seriously, and Thursday5 was the result. She was sensitive, caring, compassionate, kind, thoughtful—and unreadable. *The Great Samuel Pepys Fiasco* sold so badly it was remaindered within six months and never made it to paperback, something I was secretly glad of. Thursday5 might have remained in unreadable retirement, too, but for her sudden wish to join Jurisfiction and "do her bit," as she called it. She'd passed her written tests and basic training and was now with me for a three-day assessment. It hadn't gone that well—she was going to have to do something pretty dramatic to redeem herself.

"By the way," I said as I had an unrelated thought, "can you knit?"

"Is this part of my assessment?"

"A simple yes or no will suffice."

"Yes."

I handed her Pickwick's half-knitted sweater. "You can finish this. The dimensions are on that piece of paper. It's a cozy for a pet," I added as Thursday5 stared at the oddly shaped stripy piece of knitting.

"You have a deformed jellyfish for a pet?"

"It's for Pickwick."

"Oh!" said Thursday5. "I'd be delighted. I have a dodo, too—she's called Pickwick5."

"You don't say."

"Yes—how did yours lose her plumage?"

"It's a long story that involves the cat next door."

"I have a cat next door. It's called . . . now, what *was* her name?"

"Cat Next Door5?" I suggested.

"That's right," she said, astonished at my powers of detection. "You've met her, then?"

I ignored her and pushed open the doors to the ballroom. We were just in time. The Bellman's daily briefing was about to begin.

Jurisfiction's offices were in the disused ballroom of Mr. and Mrs. John Dashwood's residence of Norland Park, safely hidden in the backstory of Jane Austen's *Sense and Sensibility.* Wagging and perhaps jealous tongues claimed that it was for "special protection," but I'd never seen any particular favors shown myself. The room was painted pale blue, and the walls, where not decorated with delicate plaster moldings, were hung with lavish gold-framed mirrors. It was here that we ran the policing agency that functioned *within* books to keep order in the dangerously flexible narrative environment. We called it Jurisfiction.

The offices of Jurisfiction had long been settled at Norland. It had been many years since they had been used as a ballroom. The floor space was liberally covered with tables, chairs, filing cabinets and piles of paperwork. Each desk had its own brass-horned footnoterphone, a typewriter and an in-tray that always seemed larger than the out. Although electronics were a daily part of life in the real world, here in fiction there was no machine so complicated that it couldn't be described in a line or two. It was a different story over in nonfiction, where they had advanced technology coming out of their ears—it was a matter of some pride that we were about eight times more efficient with half the workforce. I paused for a moment. Even after sixteen years, walking into the Jurisfiction offices always gave me a bit of a buzz. Silly, really, but I couldn't help myself.

"Just in time!" barked Commander Bradshaw, who was standing on a table so as to be more easily seen. He was Jurisfiction's longest-serving member and onetime star of the Commander Bradshaw colonial ripping adventure stories for boys. His jingoistic and anachronistic brand of British Empire fiction wasn't read at all these days, which he'd be the first to admit was no great loss and freed him up to be the head of Jurisfiction, or Bellman, a post he was unique in having held twice. He and Mrs. Bradshaw were two of the best friends I possessed. His wife, Melanie, had been Friday and Tuesday's au pair, and even though Jenny was now ten and needed less looking after, Mel was still around. She loved our kids as if they were her own. She and Bradshaw had never had children. Not surprisingly, really, since Melanie was, and had always been, a gorilla.

"Is everyone here?" he asked, carefully scanning the small group of Jurisfiction agents.

"Hamlet's dealing with a potentially damaging outbreak of reasonable behavior inside *Othello,*" said Mr. Fainset, a middle-aged man dressed in worn merchant navy garb. "He also said he needed to see Iago about something."

"That'll be about their Shakespeare spin-off play *Iago v. Hamlet,*" said the Red Queen, who was actually not a real queen at all but an anthropomorphized chess piece from *Through the Looking Glass*. "Does he really think he's going to get the Council of Genres to agree to a thirty-ninth Shakespeare play?"

"Stranger things have happened." Bradshaw sighed. "Where are Peter and Jane?"

"The new feline in *The Tiger Who Came to Tea* got stage fright," said Lady Cavendish, "and after that they said they needed to deal with a troublesome brake van in *The Twin Engines*."

"Very well," said Bradshaw, tingling a small bell. "Jurisfiction meeting number 43,369 is now in session. Item One: The number of fictioneers trying to escape into the real world has increased this month. We've had seven attempts, all of them rebuffed. The Council of Genres has made it abundantly clear that this will not be tolerated without a Letter of Transit, and anyone caught moving across or *attempting* to move across will be reduced to text on sight."

There was silence. I was the only one who crossed over on a regular basis, but no one liked the idea of reducing people to text, whether they deserved it or not. It was irreversible and the closest thing there was to death in the written world.

"I'm not saying you *have* to do that," continued Bradshaw, "and I want you to pursue all other avenues before lethal force. But if it's the only way, then that's what you'll do. Item Two: It's been six months, and there's still no sign of the final two volumes of *The Good Soldier Švejk*. If we don't hear anything more, we'll just bundle up the four volumes into one and reluctantly call it a day. Thursday, have you seen anything around the Well that might indicate they were stolen to order to be broken up for scrap?"

"None at all," I replied, "but I spoke with our opposite number over at Jurisfiktivní, and he said they'd lost it over there, too."

"That's wonderful news!" breathed Bradshaw, much relieved.

"It is?"

"Yes—it's someone else's problem. Item Three: The inexplicable departure of comedy from the Thomas Hardy novels is still a cause for great concern."

"Hadn't we put a stop to that?" asked Emperor Zhark.

"Not at all," replied Bradshaw. "We tried to have the comedy that was being leached *out* replaced by fresh comedy coming *in*, but because misery has a greater natural affinity for the Wessex novels, it always seems to gain the ascendancy. Hard to believe *Jude the Obscure* was once the most rip-roaringly funny novel in the English language, eh?"

I put up my hand.

"Yes, Thursday?"

"Do you think the Comedy genre might be mining the books for laughs? You know how those guys will happily steal and modify from anything and everywhere for even the most perfunctory of chuckles."

"It's possible, but we need hard evidence. Who wants to have a trawl around Comedy for a Thomas Hardy funnyism we can use to prove one way or the other?"

"I will," said the Red Queen, before I could volunteer.

"Better get busy. If they *are* sucking the comedy out of *Jude*, we don't have much time. Now that the farce, rib-cracking one-liners and whimsical asides have all been removed, a continued drain on the novel's reserves of lightheartedness will place the book in a state of negative funniness. Insufferably gloomy—miserable, in fact."

We thought about it for a moment. Even until as little as thirty years ago, the whole Thomas Hardy series was actually very funny—pointlessly frivolous, in fact. As things stood at the moment, if you wanted a happy ending to anything in Hardy, you'd be well advised to read it backward.

"Item Four," continued Bradshaw, "a few genre realignments."

There was an audible sigh in the air, and a few agents lost interest. This was one of those boring-but-important items that, while of little consequence to the book in question, subtly changed the way in which it was policed. We had to know what novel was in what genre—sometimes it wasn't altogether obvious, and when a book stretched across two genres or more, it could open a jurisdictional can of worms that might have us tied up for years. We all reached for our notepads and pencils as Bradshaw stared at the list.

"Erich von Däniken's *Chariots of the Gods?* has been moved from nonfiction to fiction," he began, leaving a pause so we could write it down, "and Orwell's *1984* is no longer *truly* fiction, so has been reallocated to nonfiction. Vonnegut's *The Sirens of Titan* is no longer Sci-Fi but Philosophy."

This was actually good news; I'd thought the same for years.

"The subgenre of Literary Smut has finally been disbanded, with *Fanny Hill* and *Moll Flanders* being transferred to Racy Novel and *Lady Chatterley's Lover* to Human Drama."

We diligently wrote it all down as Bradshaw continued:

"*The History of Tom Jones* is now in Romantic Comedy, and *The Story of O* is part of the Erotic Novel genre, as are *Lolita* and *The Autobiography of a Flea*. As part of a separate genre reappraisal, Orwell's *Animal Farm* belongs not just to the Allegorical and Political genres but has expanded to be part of Animal Drama and Juvenilia as well."

"Four genres bad, two genres good," murmured Mr. Fainset.

"I'm sorry?"

"Nothing."

"Good," said Bradshaw, stroking his large white mustache. "Item Five: The entire works of Jane Austen are down in the maintenance bay for a refit. We've diverted all the Outlander readings through a book-club boxed set, and I want someone to patrol the series until the originals are back online. Volunteers?"

"I will," I said.

"You're on cadet assessment, Thursday. Anyone else?"

Lady Margaret Cavendish put up her hand. Unusually for a resident of fiction, she had once been real. Originally a flamboyant seventeenth-century aristocratic socialite much keen on poetry, women's issues and self-publicity, our Lady Cavendish hailed from an unfair biography. Annoyed by the slurs committed, as so often to the defamed dead, she took flight to the bright lights of Jurisfiction, in which she seemed to excel, especially in the poetry form, which no one else much liked to handle.

"What would you have me do?" she asked.

"Nothing, really—just maintain a presence to make sure any mischievous character understudies think twice before they do their own dialogue or try to 'improve' anything."

Lady Cavendish shrugged and nodded her agreement.

"Item Six," said Bradshaw, consulting his clipboard again, "Falling Outlander ReadRates."

He looked at us all over his glasses. We all knew the problem but saw it more as a systemic difficulty rather than something we could deal with on a book-to-book policing basis.

"The Outlander Reading Index has dropped once again for the 1,782nd day running," reported Bradshaw, "and although there are certain books that will always be read, we are finding that more and more minor classics and a lot of general fiction are going for long periods without even being opened. Because of this, Text Grand Central is worried that bored characters in lesser books might try to move to more popular novels for work, which will doubtless cause friction."

We were all silent, and the inference wasn't lost on any of us: The fictional characters in the BookWorld could be a jittery bunch, and it didn't take much to set off a riot.

"I can't say any more at this point," concluded Bradshaw, "as it's only a *potential* problem, but be aware of what's going on. The last thing we need right now is a band of disgruntled bookpeople besieging the Council of Genres demanding the right to be read. Okay, Item Seven: The MAWk-15H virus has once again resurfaced in Dickens, particularly in the death of Little Nell, which is now so uncomfortably saccharine that even our own dear, gentle, patient, noble Nell complained. I need someone to liaise with the BookWorld Communicable Textual Diseases Unit to deal with this. Volunteers?"

Foyle reluctantly put up his hand. Working for the BCTD on

Bookviruses was never popular, as it required a lengthy quarantine on completion; most of Victorian melodrama was to some degree infected with MAWk-15H, and it was often blamed on Jurisfiction agents with poor hygiene.

"Item Eight: Jurisfiction recruitment. The percentage of recruits making it to full agent status is currently eight percent, down from twenty-two percent three years ago. I'm not saying that standards need to slip or anything, but Senator Jobsworth has threatened to force agents upon us if we can't recruit, and we don't want that."

We all muttered our agreement. Just recently a few cadets had been making themselves conspicuous by their poor performance. None of us wanted to be understaffed, but then neither did we want the service swamped with knuckleheads.

"So," continued Bradshaw, "on the basis that poor training makes failed cadets, I want you all to think about giving them all a little more of your time."

He put down his clipboard.

"That's it for now. Do the best you can, keep me informed as to progress and, as regards health and safety, we've had the welcome news that you can ignore safety practices to save time, but you *must* complete the paperwork. Good luck, and . . . let's be *careful* out there."

Everyone started to talk among themselves, and after I told Thursday5 to wait at my desk, I threaded my way through the small gathering to speak to Bradshaw. I caught up with him as he was heading back to his desk.

"You want me to report on the Jane Austen refit?" I asked him. "Any particular reason?"

Bradshaw was dressed as you might expect a colonial white hunter to dress: in a safari suit with shorts, pith helmet and a revolver in a leather holster. He didn't need to dress like that anymore, of course, but he was a man of habit.

"That was mostly misdirection," he asserted. "I *do* want you to take a gander, but there's something else I'd like you to look at—something I don't want Senator Jobsworth to know about, or at least not yet."

Senator Jobsworth was the head of the Council of Genres and a powerful man. Politics within Jurisfiction could be tricky at times, and I had to be particularly diplomatic as far as Jobsworth was concerned—I often had to cross swords with him in the debating chamber. As the only real person in fiction, my advice was often called for—but rarely welcomed.

"What do you want me to do?"

Bradshaw rubbed his mustache thoughtfully. "We've had a report of something that sounds *transfictional*."

"Another one?"

It was the name given to something that had arrived from the real world—the Outland, as it was known. I was a transfictional, of course, but the term was more usually used to refer to something or somebody that had crossed over unexpectedly.

Bradshaw handed me a scrap of paper with the title of a book on it. "I feel happier with you handling it, because you're an Outlander. Appreciate a woman who's proper flesh and blood. By the way, how's Thursday5 doing?"

"She isn't," I replied. "Her timidity will end up getting her killed. We had a run-in with a grammasite inside *Lord of the Flies* while dealing with the glasses problem, and she decided to give the Verbisoid the benefit of the doubt and a very large hug."

"What type of Verbisoid? Intransitive?"

I shook my head sadly. "Nope. *Ditransitive*."

Bradshaw whistled low. He hadn't been kidding over recruitment troubles or Senator Jobsworth's involvement. Even I knew there were at least three totally unsuitable candidates Jobsworth was pressuring us to "reappraise."

"She's lucky to have a single verb left in her body," said Bradshaw after a pause. "Give her the full three days before firing her, yes? It has to be by the book, in case she tries to sue us."

I assured him I would and moved back to my desk, where Thursday5 was sitting on the floor in the lotus position. I had a quick rummage through my case notes, which were now stacked high on my desk. In a rash moment I'd volunteered to look at Jurisfiction "cold cases," thinking that there would only be three or four. As it turned out, there were over a hundred infractions of sorts, ranging from random plot fluctuations in the *Gormenghast* trilogy to the inexplicable and untimely death of Charles Dickens, who had once lived long enough to finish *Edwin Drood*. I did as much as I had time for, which wasn't a lot.

"Right," I said, pulling on my jacket and grabbing my bag, "we're off. Stick close to me and do *exactly* as I say—even if that means killing grammasites. It's them or us."

"Them or us," repeated Thursday5 halfheartedly, slinging her felt handbag over her shoulder in exactly the same way as I did. I stopped for a moment and stared at my desk. It had been rearranged.

"Thursday?" I said testily. "Have you been doing feng shui on my desk again?"

"It was more of a *harmonization*, really," she replied somewhat sheepishly.

"Well, don't."

"Why not?"

"Just . . . just *don't*."

5.

Training Day

The BookWorld was a minefield for the unwary, so apprenticeships were essential. We'd lost more agents through poor training than were ever taken by grammasites. A foot wrong in the imaginatively confusing world of fiction could see the inexperienced Jurisfiction Cadet mispelled, conjugated or reduced to text. My tutor had been the first Miss Havisham, and I like to think it was her wise counsel that had allowed me to survive as long as I did. Many cadets didn't. The average life expectancy for a raw recruit in BookWorld was about forty-seven chapters.

We stepped outside the colonnaded entrance of Norland Park and basked in the warmth of the sunshine. The story had long ago departed with the Dashwood family to Devon, and this corner of *Sense and Sensibility* was quiet and unused. To one side a saddled horse was leaning languidly against a tree with a hound sitting on the ground quite near it. Birds sang in the branches, and clouds moved slowly across the heavens. Each cloud was identical, of course, and the sun didn't track across the sky as it did back home, and, come to think of it, the birdsong was on a twenty-second loop. It was what we called "narrative economics," the bare amount of description necessary to create a scene. The BookWorld was like that—mostly ordered, and without the rich texture that nature's randomness brings to the real world.

We sat in silence for a few minutes to wait for my taxi. I was thinking about the mostly bald Pickwick, Friday's ChronoGuard presentation, Felix8's return and my perfidy to Landen. Thursday5 had no such worries—she was reading the astrology section of the BookWorld's premier newspaper, *The Word.*

After a while she said, "It's my birthday today."

"I know."

"You do? How?"

"Never mind."

"Listen to what it says in the horoscopes: 'If it is your birthday, there may be an increased amount of mail. Expect gifts, friendly salutations from people and the occasional surprise. Possibility of cake.' That's so weird—I wonder if any of it will come true?"

"I've no idea. Have you noticed the amount of Mrs. Danvers you see wandering around these days?"

I mentioned this because a pair of them had been seen at Norland Park that morning. They were becoming a familiar sight in fiction, hanging around popular books out of sight of the reader, looking furtive and glaring malevolently at anyone who asked what they were up to. The excess of Mrs. Danvers in the BookWorld was easily explained. Generics, or characters-in-waiting, are created blank, without any personality or gender, and are then billeted in novels until called up for training in character schools. From there they are sent either to populate the books being built or to replace characters who are due for retirement or replacement. The problem is, generics have a chameleonic habit of assimilating themselves to a strong leading character, and when six thousand impressionable generics were lodged inside *Rebecca,* all but eight became Mrs. Danvers, the creepy housekeeper of Manderley. Since creepy housekeepers are not much in demand these days, they were mostly used as expendable drones for the Mispeling Vyrus Farst Respons Groop or, more sinisterly, for riot control and any other civic disturbances. At Jurisfiction we were concerned that they were becoming another layer of policing, answerable only to the Council of Genres, something that was stridently denied.

"Mrs. Danvers?" repeated Thursday5, studying a pullout guide to reading tea leaves. "I've got one or two in my books, but I think they're meant to be there."

"Tell me," I said by way of conversation, "is there any aspect of the BookWorld that you'd like to learn about as part of your time with me?"

"Well," she said after a pause, "I'd like to have a go and see what it's like inside a story during a recitation in the oral tradition—I've heard it's really kind of *buzzing*."

She was right. It was like sweaty live improv theater—anything could happen.

"No way," I said, "and if I hear that you've been anywhere near OralTrad, you'll be confined to *The Great Samuel Pepys Fiasco.* It's not like books where everything's laid out and orderly. The oral tradition is *dynamic* like you've no idea. Change anything in there and you will, quite literally, give the narrator an aneurysm."

"A *what*?"

"A brain hemorrhage. The same can be said of Poetry. You don't want to go hacking around in there without a clear head on your shoulders."

"Why?"

"It's like a big emotion magnifier. All feelings are exacerbated to a dangerous level. You can find things out about yourself that you never knew—or never wanted to know. We have a saying: 'You can lose yourself in a book, but you find yourself in Poetry.' It's like being able to see yourself when drunk."

"Aha," she said in a quiet voice.

There was a pause.

"You've never been drunk, have you?"

She shook her head. "Do you think I should try it?"

"It's overrated."

I had a thought. "Have you ever been up to the Council of Genres?"

"No."

"A lamentable omission. That's where we'll go first."

I pulled out my mobilefootnoterphone and called TransGenre

Taxis to see where my cab had gone. The reason for a taxi was not altogether obvious to Thursday5, who, like most residents of the BookWorld, could bookjump to any novel previously visited with an ease I found annoying. My *intra*fictional bookjumping was twenty times better than my *trans*fictional jumps, but even then a bit ropey. I needed to read a full paragraph to get in, and if I didn't have the right section in my TravelBook, then I had to walk via the Great Library or get a taxi—as long as one was available.

"Wouldn't it be quicker just to bookjump?" asked Thursday5 with annoying directness.

"You young things are always in a hurry, aren't you?" I replied. "Besides, it's more dignified to walk—and the view is generally better. However," I added with a sense of deflated ego, "in the absence of an available cab, we shall."

I pulled out my TravelBook, turned to the correct page and jumped from *Sense and Sensibility* to the Great Library.

6.

The Great Library and Council of Genres

The Textual Sieve was designed and constructed by JurisTech, the technological arm of Jurisfiction. The Textual Sieve is a fantastically useful and mostly unexplained device that allows the user to "sieve" or "strain" text in order to isolate a specified search string. Infinitely variable, a well-tuned Textual Sieve on "full opaque" can rebuff an entire book, but set to "fine" can delicately remove a spiderweb from a half-million-word novel.

I found myself in a long, dark, wood-paneled corridor lined with bookshelves that reached from the richly carpeted floor to the vaulted ceiling. The carpet was elegantly patterned, and the ceiling was decorated with rich moldings that depicted scenes from the classics, each cornice supporting the marble bust of an author. High above me, spaced at regular intervals, were finely decorated circular apertures through which light gained entry and reflected off the polished wood, reinforcing the serious mood of the library. Running down the center of the corridor was a long row of reading tables, each with a green-shaded brass lamp. In both directions the corridor vanished into darkness with no definable end.

I had first entered the Great Library sixteen years ago, and the description of it hadn't altered by so much as a word. Hundreds of miles of shelves containing not every single book but every single *edition* of every book. Anything that had been published in the real world had a counterpart logged somewhere within its endless corridors.

Thursday5 was nearby and joined me to walk along the corridor, making our way toward the crossover section right at the heart of the library. But the thing to realize was that it wasn't in any sense of the word *real*, any more than the rest of the BookWorld was. The library was as nebulous as the books it contained; its form was decided not only by the base description but my *interpretation* of what a Great Library might look like. Because of this the library was as subtly changeable as my moods. At times dark and somber, at others light and airy. Reading, I had learned, was as creative a process as writing, sometimes more so. When we read of the dying rays of the setting sun or the boom and swish of the incoming tide, we should reserve as much praise for ourselves as for the author. After all, the reader is doing all the work—the writer might have died long ago.

We approached another corridor perpendicular to the one we had just walked down. In the middle of the crossway was a large, circular void with a wrought-iron rail and a spiral staircase bolted securely to one side. We walked over to the handrail and peered down. Not more than thirty feet below us, I could see another floor, exactly like this one. In the middle of that floor was another circular void through which I could see another floor, and another and another, and so on to the depths of the library. It was the same above us.

"Twenty-six floors for the published works," replied Thursday5 as I caught her eye and raised an eyebrow quizzically, "and twenty-six subbasements where books are actually constructed—the Well of Lost Plots."

I beckoned her to the ornate wrought-iron elevator and pressed the call button. We got into the elevator, I drew the gates shut with a clatter, and the electric motors whined as we headed upward. Because there are very few authors whose names begin with

Q, *X* and *Z*, floors seventeen, twenty-four and twenty-six were relatively empty and thus free for other purposes. The seventeenth floor housed the Mispeling Vyrus Farst Respons Groop, the twenty-fourth floor was used essentially for storage, and the twenty-sixth was where the legislative body that governs the BookWorld had taken up residence: the Council of Genres.

This was a floor unlike any other in the Great Library. Gone were the dark wood, molded plaster ceilings and busts of long-dead writers, and in their place was a light, airy working space with a roof of curved wrought iron covered in glass through which we could see the clouds and sky. I beckoned Thursday5 to a large picture window in an area to one side of the corridor. There were a few chairs scattered about, and it was a restful spot, designed so that overworked CofG employees could relax for a moment. I had stood here with my own mentor, the first Miss Havisham, almost sixteen years previously.

"The Great Library looks smaller from the outside," observed Thursday5, staring out the window at the rain-streaked exterior.

She was right. The corridors in the library below could be as long as two hundred miles in each direction, expandable upon requirements, but from the outside the library looked more akin to the Chrysler Building, liberally decorated with stainless-steel statuary and measuring less than two hundred yards along each face. And even though we were only on the twenty-sixth floor, it looked a great deal higher. I had once been to the top of the 120-story Goliath Tower at Goliathopolis, and this seemed easily as high as that.

"The other towers?" she asked, still staring out the window. Far below us were the treetops of a deep forest flecked with mist, and scattered around at varying distances were other towers just like ours.

"The nearest one is German," I said, "and behind those are French and Spanish. Arabic is just beyond them—and that one over there is Welsh."

"Oh," said Thursday5, staring at the green foliage far below.

"The Council of Genres looks after the Fictional Legislature," I said, walking down the corridor to the main assembly chamber. It had become busier since we'd arrived, with various clerks moving around holding file folders, reports and so forth. I had thought red tape was bad in the real world, but in the paper world it was everything. I'd come to realize over the years that anything created by mankind had error, mischief and bureaucratic officialdom hardwired at inception, and the fictional world was no different.

"The council governs dramatic conventions, strictly controls the use of irony, legislates on word use and, through the Book Inspectorate, decides which novels are to be published and which ones scrapped."

We had arrived at a viewing gallery overlooking the main debating chamber, which was a spacious hall of white marble with an arched roof suspended by riveted iron girders. There was a raised dais at the back surmounted by a central and ornately carved chair flanked on each side by four smaller ones. A lectern for the speaker was in front of that, and facing both the lectern and the dais was a horseshoe pattern of desks for the representatives of the various genres. The back wall of the chamber was decorated with a vast mosaic representing the theoretical positions of the genres as they hung in the Nothing. The only other item of note in the debating chamber was the Read-O-Meter, which gave us a continually updated figure of just how many books had been read over the previous twenty-four hours. This instrument was a constant reminder of the falling ReadRates that had troubled the BookWorld over the past five years, and every time the numbers flopped over—and they did every five seconds—the number went *down*. Sometimes in depressingly large amounts. There was someone speaking volubly at the lectern, and the debating chamber was less than a third full.

"The main genres are seated at the front," I explained, "and the subgenres radiate out behind them, in order of importance and size. Although the CofG oversees broad legislative issues, each individual genre can make its own decision on a local level. They all field a senator to appear before the council and look after their own interests—sometimes the debating chamber resembles something less like a seat of democracy and more like plain old horse trading."

"Who's talking now?" she asked as a new member took the podium. He looked as though he hadn't brushed his hair that morning, was handsome if a bit dim-looking, had no shoes and was wearing a shirt split open to the waist.

"That'll be Speedy Muffler, the senator from the Racy Novel genre, although I suspect that might not be his real name."

"They have a senator?"

"Of course. Every genre has at least one, and depending on the popularity of subgenres, they might have several. Thriller which is subgenred into Political, Spy and Adventure, has three. Comedy at the last count had six; Crime has twelve."

"I see. So what's Racy Novel's problem?"

"It's a border dispute. Although each book exists on its own and is adrift in the intragenre space known as the Nothing, the books belonging to the various genres clump together for mutual protection, free trade of ideas and easy movement of characters."

"I get it. Books of a feather flock together, yes?"

"Pretty much. Sensibly, Thriller was placed next door to Crime, which itself is bordered by Human Drama—a fine demonstration of inspired genreography for the very best mutual improvement of both."

"And Racy Novel?"

"Some idiot placed it somewhat recklessly between Ecclesiastical and Feminist, with the tiny principality of Erotica to the far north and a buffer zone with Comedy to the south comprising the subcrossover genre of Bedroom Farce/Bawdy Romp. Racy Novel gets along with Comedy and Erotica fine, but Ecclesiastical and Feminist really don't think Racy Novel is worthy of a genre at all and often fire salvos of long-winded intellectual dissent across the border, which might do more damage if anyone in Racy Novel could understand them. For its part, Racy Novel sends panty-raiding parties into its neighbors, which wasn't welcome in Feminist and even less in Ecclesiastical—or was it the other way around? Anyway, the whole deal might have escalated into an all-out genre war without the Council of Genres stepping in and brokering a peace deal. The CofG would guarantee Racy Novel's independence as long as it agreed to certain . . . sanctions."

"Which were?"

"An import ban on metaphor, characterization and competent description. Speedy Muffler is a bit of a megalomaniac, and both Feminist and Ecclesiastical thought containment was better than out-and-out conflict. The problem is, Racy Novel claims that this is worse than a slow attritional war, as these sanctions deny it the potential of literary advancement beyond the limited scope of its work."

"I can't say I'm very sympathetic to that cause."

"It's not important that you are—your role in Jurisfiction is only to defend the status—"

I stopped talking, as something seemed to be going on down in the debating chamber. In a well-orchestrated lapse of protocol, delegates were throwing their ballot papers around, and among the jeering and catcalls Muffler was struggling to make himself heard. I shook my head sadly.

"What is it?"

"Something that Racy Novel has been threatening for some time—they've claimed to have developed and tested a . . . dirty bomb."

"A what?"

"It's a tightly packed mass of inappropriate plot devices, explicit suggestions and sexual scenes of an expressly gratuitous nature. The 'dirty' elements of the bomb fly apart at a preset time and attach themselves to any unshielded prose. Given the target, it has the potential for untold damage. A well-placed dirty bomb could scatter poorly described fornication all across drab theological debate or drop a wholly unwarranted scene of a sexually exploitative nature right into the middle of *Mrs. Dalloway.*"

Even Thursday5 could see this was not a good thing. "Would he do that?"

"He just might. Senator Muffler is as mad as a barrel of skunks, and the inclusion of Racy Novel in the Council of Genres' definition of the 'Axis of Unreadable' along with Misery Memoirs and Pseudointellectual Drivel didn't help matters a bit. It'll be all over the BookWorld by nightfall, mark my words—the papers love this kind of combative, saber-rattling crap."

"Ms. Next!" came an annoying, high-pitched voice.

I turned to find a small weasel of a man with pinched features, dressed in robes and with a goodly retinue of self-important assistants stacked up behind him.

"Good morning, Senator," I said, bowing as protocol demanded. "May I introduce my apprentice, Thursday5? Thursday5, this is Senator Jobsworth, director-general of the CofG and head of the Pan-Genre Treaty Organization."

"Sklub," gulped Thursday5, trying to curtsy, bob and bow all at the same time. The senator nodded in her direction, then dismissed everyone before beckoning me to join him at the large picture window.

"Ms. Next," he said in a quiet voice, "how are things down at Jurisfiction?"

"Underfunded as usual," I replied, well used to Jobsworth's manipulative ways.

"It needn't be so," he replied. "If I can count on your support for policy direction in the near future, I am sure we can rectify the situation."

"You are too kind," I replied, "but I will judge my decisions on what is best for the BookWorld as a whole, rather than the department I work in."

His eyes flashed angrily. Despite his being the head of the council, policy decisions still had to be made by consensus—and it annoyed the hell out of him.

"With Outlander ReadRates almost in free fall," continued Jobsworth with a snarl, "I'd have thought you'd be willing to compromise on those precious scruples of yours."

"I don't compromise," I told him resolutely, repeating, "I base my decisions on what is best for the BookWorld."

"Well," said Jobsworth with an insincere smile, "let's hope you don't regret any of your decisions. Good day."

And he swept off with his entourage at his heels. His threats didn't frighten me; he'd been making them—and I'd been ignoring them—for almost as long as we'd known each other.

"I didn't realize you were so close to Senator Jobsworth," said Thursday5 as soon as she had rejoined me.

"I have a seat at the upper-level policy-directive meetings as the official LBOCS. Since I'm an Outlander, I have powers of abstract and long-term thought that most fictioneers can only dream about. The thing is, I don't generally toe the line, and Jobsworth doesn't like that."

"Can I ask a question?" asked Thursday5 as we took the elevator back down into the heart of the Great Library.

"Of course."

"I'm a little confused over how the whole imaginotransference technology works. I mean, how do books *here* get to be read out *there*?"

I sighed. Cadets were supposed to come to me for assessment when they already knew the basics. This one was as green as *Brighton Rock*. The elevator stopped on the third floor, and I pulled open the gates. We stepped out into one of the Great Library's endless corridors, and I waved a hand in the direction of the bookshelves.

"Okay: imaginotransference. Did any of your tutors tell you even vaguely how the reader-writer thing actually *works*?"

"I think I might have been having a colonic that morning."

I moved closer to the shelves and beckoned her to follow. As I came to within a yard of the books, I could feel their influence warm me like a hot radiator. But it wasn't heat I was feeling; it was the warmth of a good story, well told. A potpourri of jumbled narrative, hovering just above of the books like morning mist on a lake. I could actually feel the emotions, hear the whispered snatches of conversation and see the images that momentarily broke free of the gravity that bound them to the story.

"Can you feel that?" I whispered.

"Feel what?"

I sighed. Fictional people were less attuned to *story;* it was rare indeed that anyone in the BookWorld actually read a book—unless the narrative called for it.

"Place your hands gently against the spines."

She did as I asked, and after a moment's puzzlement she smiled.

"I can hear voices," she whispered back, trying not to break the moment, "and a waterfall. And joy, betrayal, laughter—and a young man who has lost his hat."

"What you're feeling is the raw imaginotransference energy, the method by which all books are dispersed into the reader's imagination. The books we have in the Outland are no more similar to these than a photograph is to the subject—these books are *alive,* each one a small universe unto itself—and by throughputting some of that energy from here to their counterparts in the real world, we can transmit the story direct to the reader."

Thursday5 took her hand from the books and experimented to see how far out she had to go before losing the energy. It was barely a few inches.

"Throughputting? Is that where Textual Sieves come into it?"

"No. I've got to go and look at something for Bradshaw, so we'll check out core containment—it's at the heart of the imaginotransference technology."

We walked a few yards up the corridor, and after carefully consulting the note Bradshaw had given me, I selected a book from the bewildering array of the same title in all its various incarnations. I opened the volume and looked at the stats page, which blinked up a real-time Outland ReadRate, a total of the editions still in existence and much else besides.

"The 1929 book-club deluxe leather-bound edition with nine copies still in circulation from a total of twenty-five hundred," I explained, "and with no readers actually making their way through it. An ideal choice for a bit of training."

I rummaged in my bag and brought out what looked like a large-caliber flare pistol.

Thursday5 regarded me nervously.

"Are you expecting trouble?"

"I *always* expect trouble."

"Isn't that a TextMarker?" she asked, her confusion understandable, because this wasn't officially a weapon at all. These were generally used to mark the text of a book from within so an agent could be extracted in an emergency. Once an essential piece of equipment, they were carried less and less as the mobilefootnoterphone had made such devices redundant.

"It was," I replied, breaking open the stubby weapon and taking a single brass cartridge from a small leather pouch. "But I've modified it to take an eraserhead."

I slipped the cartridge in, snapped the pistol shut and put it back in my bag. The eraserhead was just one of the many abstract technologies that JurisTech built for us. Designed to sever the bonds between letters in a word, it was a devastating weapon to anyone of textual origin—a single blast from one of these and the unlucky recipient would be nothing but a jumbled heap of letters and a bluish haze. Its use was strictly controlled—Jurisfiction agents only.

"Gosh," said Thursday after I'd explained it to her. "I don't carry any weapons at all."

"I'd so love not to have to," I told her, and with the taxi still nowhere in sight, I passed the volume across to her. "Here," I said, "let's see how good you are at taking a passenger into a book."

She accepted the novel without demur, opened it and started to read. She had a good speaking voice, fruity and expressive, and she quickly began to fade from view. I grabbed hold of her cuff so as not to be left behind, and she instantly regained her solidity; it was the library that was now faded and indistinct. Within a few more words, we had traveled into our chosen book. The first thing I noticed as we arrived was that the chief protagonist's feet were on fire. Worse still, *he* hadn't noticed.

7.

A Probe Inside *Pinocchio*

Although the idea of using footnotes as a communication medium was suggested by Dr. Faustus as far back as 1622, it wasn't until 1856 that the first practical footnoterphone was demonstrated. The first transgenre trunk line between Human Drama and Crime was opened in 1915, and the network has been expanded and improved ever since. Although the system is far from complete, with many books still having only a single payfootnoterpayphone, on the outer reaches of the known BookWorld many books are without any coverage at all.

It was Pinocchio, of course, I'd know that nose anywhere. As we jumped into the toy workshop on page 26, the wooden puppet—Geppetto's or Collodi's creation, depending on which way you looked at it—was asleep with his feet on a brazier. The workbench was clean and tidy. Half-finished wooden toys filled every available space, and all the woodworking tools were hung up neatly upon the wall. There was a cot in one corner, a sideboard in another, and the floor was covered with curly wood shavings, but there was no sawdust or dirt. The fictional world was like that, a sort of narrative shorthand that precluded any of the shabby grottiness and *texture* that gives the real world its richness.

Pinocchio was snoring loudly. Comically, almost. His feet were smoldering, and within a few lines it would be morning and he would have nothing left but charred stumps. He wasn't the only person in the room. On the sideboard were two crickets watching the one-day test match on a portable TV. One was wearing a smoking jacket and a pillbox hat and held a cigarette in a silver holder, and the other had a broken antennae, a black eye and one leg in a sling.

"The name's Thursday Next," I announced to them both, holding up my Jurisfiction badge, and this is . . . Thursday Next."

"Which is the real one?" asked the cricket in the pillbox hat—somewhat tactlessly, I thought.

"I am," I replied through gritted teeth. "Can't you tell?"

"Frankly, no," replied the cricket, looking at the pair of us in turn. "So . . . which is the one that does naked yoga?"

"That would be me," said Thursday5 brightly.

I groaned audibly.

"What's the matter?" she asked, amused by my prudishness. "You should try it someday. It's relaxing and very empowering."

"I don't do yoga," I told her.

"Take it up and drop the bacon sandwiches and it will put ten years on your life."

The cricket, who spoke in a clipped accent reminiscent of Noël Coward's, folded up his paper and said, "We don't often get visitors, you know—the last lot to pass through this way was the Italian Translation Inspectorate making sure we were keeping to the spirit of the original."

The cricket had a sudden thought and indicated the damaged cricket sitting next to him. "How rude could I be? This is Jim 'Bruises' McDowell, my stunt double."

Bruises looked as though the stunt sequence with the mallet hadn't gone quite as planned.

"Hello," said the stunt cricket with an embarrassed shrug. "I had an accident during training. Some damn fool went and moved the crash mat." As he said it, he looked at the other cricket, who did nothing but puff on his cigarette and preen his antennae in a nonchalant fashion.

"I'm sorry to hear that," I said by way of conversation—a good relationship with the characters within the BookWorld was essential in our work. "Have you been read recently?"

The cricket in the pillbox hat suddenly looked embarrassed.

"The truth is," he said awkwardly, "we've *never* been read. Not once in seventy-three years. Deluxe book-club editions are like that—just for show. But if we *did* have a reading, we'd all be primed and set to go."

"I can do a lot more than the 'being hit with the mallet' stunt," added Bruises excitedly. "Would you like me to set myself on fire and fall out of a window? I can wave my arms very convincingly."

"No thanks."

"Shame," replied Bruises wistfully. "I'd like to broaden my skills to cover car-to-helicopter transfers and being dragged backwards by a horse—whatever that is."

"When the last of the nine copies of this book have gone," pointed out the cricket, "we can finally come off duty and be reassigned. I'm studying for the lead in *Charlotte's Web*."

"Do you know of any other books that require stunt crickets?" asked Bruises hopefully. "I've been practicing the very dangerous and not-at-all-foolhardy leap over seventeen motorcycles in a double-decker bus."

"Isn't it meant to be the other way around?"

"I told you it seemed a bit rum," said the cricket as Bruises' shoulders sagged. "But never mind all that," he added, returning his attention to me. "I suppose you're here about . . . the *thing*?"

"We are, sir. Where is it?"

The cricket pointed with three of his legs at a pile of half-finished toys in the corner and, thus rendered lopsided, fell over. His stunt double laughed until the cricket glared at him dangerously.

"It appeared unannounced three days ago—quite ruined my entrance."

"I thought you'd never been read?"

"*Rehearsals,* dahling. I do like to keep the thespian juices fresh—and Bruises here likes to practice his celebrated 'falling from the wall after being struck by a mallet' stunt—and then the leg twitching and death throes, which he does *so* well."

Bruises said nothing and studied the tips of his antennae modestly.

I cautiously approached the area of the room the cricket had indicated. Half hidden behind a marionette with no head and a hobby horse in need of sanding was a dull metallic sphere about the size of a grapefruit. It had several aerials sticking out of the top and an array of lenses protruding from the front. I leaned closer and sniffed at it cautiously. I could smell the odor of corrosion and see the fine pits on the heat-streaked surface. This wasn't an errant space probe from the Sci-Fi canon; it was too well described for that. Bradshaw had been right—it was transfictional.

"Where do you think it's from?" asked the cricket. "We get scraps of other books blowing in from time to time when there's a WordStorm, but nothing serious. Bottom from *A Midsummer Night's Dream* sheltered here for a while during the textphoon of '32 and picked up a thing or two from Lamp-Wick, but only the odd verb or two otherwise. Is it important?"

"Not really," I replied. It was a lie, of course—but I didn't want a panic. This was anything *but* unimportant. I gently rotated the probe and read the engraved metal plate on the back. There was a serial number and a name that I recognized only too well—the Goliath Corporation. My least favorite multinational and a thorn in my side for many years. I was annoyed and heartened all at the same time. Annoyed that they had developed a machine for hurling probes inside fiction, but heartened that this was all they had managed to achieve. As I peered closer at the inert metallic ball, there was a warning chirp from my bag. I quickly dug out a small instrument and tossed it to Thursday5.

"A reader?" she said with surprise. "In here?"

"So it seems. How far away?"

She flipped the device open and stared at the flickering needle blankly. Technology was another point she wasn't that strong on. "We're clear. The reader is . . . er, two paragraphs ahead of us."

"Are you sure?"

She looked at the instrument again. It was a Narrative Proximity Device, designed to ensure that our intrafictional perambulations couldn't be seen by readers in the Outland. One of the odd things about the BookWorld was that when characters weren't being read, they generally relaxed and talked, rehearsed, drank coffee, watched cricket or played mah-jongg. But as soon as a reading loomed, they all leaped into place and did their thing. They could sense the reading approaching out of long experience, but we couldn't—hence the Narrative Proximity Device. Being caught up in a reading wasn't particularly desirable for a Jurisfiction agent, as it generally caused a certain degree of confusion in the reader. I was spotted once myself—and once is once too often.

"I think so," replied Thursday, staring at the meter again. "No, wait—yes."

"A positive echo means the reader is ahead of us, a negative means . . . ?"

"Bother," she muttered. "Paragraphs *behind* and coming this way— Ma'am, I think we're about to be *read*."

"Is it a fast reader?"

She consulted the meter once more. If the reader was fast—a fan on a reread or a bored student—then we'd be fine. A slow reader searching every word for hidden meaning and subtle nuance and we might have to jump out until whoever it was had passed.

"Looks like a 41.3."

This was faster than the maximum throughput of the book, which was pegged at about sixteen words per second. It was a speed-reader, as likely as not reading every fifth word and skimming over the top of the prose like a stone skipping on water.

"They'll never see us. Press yourself against the wall until the reading moves through."

"Are you sure?" asked Thursday5, who had done her basic

training with the old Jurisfiction adage "Better dead than read" ringing in her ears.

"You should know what a reading looks like if you're to be an asset to Jurisfiction. Besides," I added, "overcaution is for losers."

I was being unnecessarily strict. We could quite easily have jumped out or even hopped back a few pages and followed the narrative *behind* the reading, but cadets need to sail close to the wind a few times. Both the crickets were in something of a tizzy at the prospect of their first-ever reading and tried to run in several directions at once before vanishing off to their places.

"Stand still," I said as we pressed ourselves against the least-well-described part of the wall and looked again at the NPD. The needle was rising rapidly and counting off the words to what we termed "Read Zero"—the actual time and place, the comprehension singularity, where the story was actually being *read*.

There was a distant hum and a rumble as the reading approached. Then came a light buzz in the air like static and an increased heightening of the senses as the reader took up the descriptive power of the book and translated it into his or her own unique interpretation of the events—channeled from here through the massive imaginotransference Storycode Engines back at Text Grand Central and into the reader's imagination. It was a technology of almost incalculable complexity, which I had yet to fully understand. But the beauty of the whole process was that the reader in the Outland never suspected there was any sort of process at all—the act of reading was to most people, myself included, as natural as breathing.

Geppetto's woodworking tools started to jiggle on the workbench, and a few of the wood shavings started to drift across the floor, gaining more detail as they moved. I frowned. Something wasn't right. I had expected the room to gain a small amount of increased reality as the reader's imagination bathed it in the power of his or her own past experiences and interpretations, but as the trembling and warmth increased, I noticed that this small section of Collodi's eighteenth-century allegorical tale was being raised into an unprecedented level of descriptive power. The walls, which up until then had been a blank wash of color, suddenly gained texture, a myriad of subtle hues and even areas of damp. The window frames peeled and dusted up, the floor moved and undulated until it was covered in flagstones that even I, as an Outlander, would not be able to distinguish from real ones. As Pinocchio slept on, the reading suddenly swelled like a breaking ocean roller and crossed the room in front of us, a crest of heightened reality that moved through us and imparted a warm feeling of well-being. But more than that, a rare thing in fiction, a delicate potpourri of *smells*. Freshly cut wood, cooking, spice, damp—and Pinocchio's scorched legs, which I recognized were carved from cherry. There was more, too—a strange jumble of faces, a young girl laughing and a derelict castle in the moonlight. The smells grew stronger, to the point where I could taste them in my mouth, the dust and grime in the room seemingly accentuated until there was a faint hiss and a *ploof* sound and the enhanced feelings dropped away in an instant. Everything once more returned to the limited reality we had experienced when we arrived—the bare description necessary for the room to be Geppetto's workshop. I nudged Thursday5, who opened her eyes and looked around with relief.

"What was *that*?" she asked, staring at me in alarm.

"We were *read*," I said, a little rattled myself. Whoever it was could not have failed to see us.

"I've been read many times," murmured Thursday5, "from perfunctory skim to critical analysis, and nothing ever felt like *that*."

She was right. I'd stood in for GSD knows how many characters over the years, but even I'd never felt such an in-depth reading.

"Look," she said, holding up the Narrative Proximity Device. The read-through rate had peaked at an unheard-of 68.5.

"That's not possible," I muttered. "The imaginotransference bandwidth doesn't support readings of that depth at such a speed."

The reading suddenly swelled like a breaking ocean roller
and crossed the room in front of us.

"Do you think they saw us?"

"I'm sure of it," I replied, my ears still singing and a strange woody taste still in my mouth. I consulted the NPD again. The reader was now well ahead of us and tearing through the prose toward the end of the book.

"Goodness!" exclaimed the cricket, who looked a little flushed and spacey when he reappeared along with his stunt double a few minutes later. "That was every bit as exhilarating as I thought it would be—and I didn't dry. I was excellent, wasn't I?"

"You were just *wonderful,* darling," said his stunt double. "The whole of Allegorical Juvenilia will be talking about you—one for the envelope, I think."

"And you, sir," returned the cricket, "that fall from the wall—*simply* divine."

But self-congratulatory crickets didn't really concern me right now, and even the Goliath probe was momentarily forgotten.

"A *Superreader,*" I breathed. "I've heard the legends but thought they were nothing more than that, tall tales from burned-out text jockeys who'd been mainlining on irregular verbs."

"Superreader?" echoed Thursday5 inquisitively, and even the crickets stopped congratulating each other on a perfect performance and leaned closer to listen.

"It's a reader with an unprecedented power of comprehension, someone who can pick up every subtle nuance, all the inferred narrative and deeply embedded subtext in one-tenth the time of normal readers."

"That's good, right?"

"Not really. A dozen or so Superreads could strip all the meaning out of a book, leaving the volume a tattered husk with little characterization and only the thinnest of plots."

"So . . . most Daphne Farquitt novels have been subjected to a Superreader?"

"No, they're just bad."

I thought for a moment, made a few notes in the pad I kept in my pocket and then picked up the Outlander probe. I tried to call

Bradshaw to tell him but got only his answering machine. I placed the probe in my bag, recalled that I was also here to tell Thursday5 something about the imaginotransference technology and turned to the crickets.

"Where's the core-containment chamber?"

"Cri-cri-cri," muttered the cricket, thinking hard. "I think it's one of the doors off the kitchen."

"Right."

I bade farewell to the crickets, who had begun to bicker when the one with the pillbox hat suggested it was high time he did his own stunts.

"I say, do you mind?" inquired Pinocchio indolently, neither opening his eyes nor removing his feet from the brazier. "Some of us are trying to get some shut-eye."

8.

Julian Sparkle

Standard-issue equipment to all Jurisfiction agents, the dimensionally ambivalent TravelBook contains information, tips, maps, recipes and extracts from popular or troublesome novels to enable speedier intrafiction travel. It also contains numerous JurisTech gadgets for more specialized tasks, such as an MV Mask, TextMarker and Eject-O-Hat. The TravelBook's cover is read-locked to each individual operative and contains a standard emergency alert and autodestruct mechanism.

We entered the kitchen of Geppetto's small house. It had a sort of worthy austerity about it but was clean and functional. A cat was asleep next to a log basket, and a kettle sang merrily to itself on the range. But we weren't the only people in the kitchen. There were two other doors leading off, and in front of each was a bored-looking individual sitting on a three-legged stool. In the center of the room was what appeared to be a quiz-show host dressed in a gold lamé suit. He had a fake tan that was almost orange, was weighed down with heavy gold jewelry, and had a perfectly sculpted hairstyle that looked as though it had been imported from the fifties.

"Ah!" he said as soon as he saw us. "Contestants!"

He picked up his microphone.

"Welcome," he said with faux bonhomie, showing acres of perfect white teeth, "to *Puzzlemania,* the popular brain game. I'm your host, Julian Sparkle."

He smiled at us and an imaginary audience and beckoned Thursday5 closer, but I indicated for her to stay where she was.

"I can do this!" she exclaimed.

"No," I whispered. "Sparkle might *seem* like an innocuous game-show host, but he's a potential killer."

"I thought you said overcaution was for losers?" she returned, attempting to make up for the bacon-roll debacle. "Besides, I can look after myself."

"Then be my guest," I said with a smile. "Or, rather, you can be *his* guest."

My namesake turned to Sparkle and walked up to a mark on the floor that he had indicated. As she did so, the lights in the room dimmed, apart from a spotlight on the two of them. There was a short blast of applause, seemingly from nowhere.

"So, Contestant Number One, what's your name, why are you in Geppetto's kitchen, and where do you come from?"

"My name's Thursday Next–5, I want to visit the core-containment chamber as part of a training mission, and I'm from *The Great Samuel Pepys Fiasco.*"

"Well, then, if you can *contain* your excitement, you could have a prize *visited* upon you—fail and it might well be a *fiasco.*"

Thursday5 blinked at him uncomprehendingly.

"*Contain* your excitement . . . prize *visited* . . . not a *fiasco*?" repeated Sparkle, trying to get her to understand his appalling attempts at humor.

She continued to stare at him blankly.

"Never mind. All righty, then. Ms. Next who wants to visit core containment, today we're going to play . . . Liars and Tigers."

He indicated the two doors leading off the kitchen, each with a bored-looking individual staring vacantly into space in front of it.

"The rules are very simple: You have two identical doors. Behind one is the core-containment chamber you seek, and behind the other . . . is a tiger."

The confident expression dropped from Thursday5's face, and I hid a smile.

"A what?" she asked.

"A tiger."

"A real one or a written one?"

"It's the same thing. Guarding each door is an individual, one who always tells the truth and another who always lies. You can't know which is which, nor which door is guarded by whom—and you have one question, to one guard, to discover the correct door. Ms. Next, are you ready to play Liars and Tigers?"

"A *tiger*? A real tiger?"

"All eight feet of it." Julian smiled, enjoying himself again. "Teeth one end, tail the other, claws at all four corners. Are you ready?"

"If it's just the same to you," she said politely, "I'll be getting on my way."

In a flash, Sparkle had pulled out a shiny automatic and pressed it hard into her cheek.

"You're going to play the game, Next," he growled. "Get it right and you win today's super-duper prize. Get it wrong and you're tiger poo. Refuse and I play the Spread the Dopey Cow All Over the Kitchen game."

"Can't we form a circle of trust, have a cup of herbal tea and then discuss our issues?"

"That," said Sparkle softly, a maniacal glint in his eyes, "was the *incorrect* answer."

His finger tightened on the trigger, and the two guards both covered their heads. This had gone far enough.

"Wait!" I shouted.

Sparkle stopped and looked at me. "What?"

"I'll take her place."

"It's against the rules."

"Not if we play the Double-Death Tiger-Snack game."

Sparkle looked at Thursday5, then at me. "I'm not fully conversant with that one," he said slowly, eyes narrowed.

"It's easy," I replied. "I take her place, and if I lose, then you get to feed us *both* to the tiger. If I win, we both go free."

"Okay," said Sparkle, and he released Thursday5, who ran and hid behind me.

"Shoot him," she said in hoarse whisper.

"What about the herbal tea?"

"*Shoot him.*"

"That's *not* how we do things," I said in a quiet voice. "Now, just watch and listen and *learn*."

The two guards donned steel helmets, and Sparkle himself retreated to the other side of the room, where he could escape if the tiger was released. I walked up to the two individuals, who looked at me with a quizzical air and started to rub some tiger repellent on themselves from a large tube. The doors were identical, and so were the guards. I scratched my head and thought hard, considering my question. Two doors, two guards. One guard always told the truth, one always lied—and one question to one guard to find the correct door. I'd heard of this puzzle as a kid but never thought my life might depend upon it. But hey, this was fiction. Strange, unpredictable—and *fun*.

9.

Core Containment

For thousands of years, OralTrad was the only Story Operating System and indeed is still in use today. The *recordable* Story Operating Systems began with ClayTablet V2.1 and went through several competing systems (WaxTablet, Papyrus, VellumPro) before merging into the award-winning SCROLL, which was upgraded eight times before being swept aside by the all new and clearly superior BOOK V1. Stable, easy to store and transport, compact and with a workable index, BOOK has led the way for nearly eighteen hundred years.

I turned to the guard on the left.

"If I asked the *other* guard," I said with some trepidation, "which was the door to the core-containment chamber, which one would he say?"

The guard thought for a moment and pointed to one of the doors, and I turned back to look at Sparkle and the somewhat concerned face of Thursday5, who was rapidly coming to terms with the idea that there was a lot of weird shit in the BookWorld that she'd no idea how to handle—such as potential tiger attacks inside *Pinocchio*.

"Have you chosen your door, Ms. Next?" asked Julian Sparkle. "Remember, if you win, you get through to core containment—and if you lose, there is a high probability of being eaten. Choose your door . . . wisely."

I gave a smile and grasped the handle—not on the door that

had been indicated by the guard but the *other* one. I pulled it open to reveal . . . a flight of steps leading downward.

Sparkle's eyebrow twitched, and he grimaced momentarily before breaking once more into an insincere grin. The two guards breathed a sigh of relief and removed their helmets to mop their brows—it was clear that dealing with tigers wasn't something they much liked to do—and the tiger, itself a bit miffed, growled from behind the other door.

"Congratulations," muttered Sparkle. "You have chosen . . . correctly."

I nodded to Thursday5, who joined me at the doorway, leaving Sparkle and the two guards arguing over what my super-duper prize should be.

"How did you know which guard was which?" she asked in a respectful tone.

"I didn't," I replied, "and still don't. But I assumed that the guards would know who told the truth and who didn't. Since my question would *always* show me the wrong door irrespective of whom I asked, I just took the opposite of the one indicated."

"Oh!" she said, trying to figure it out. "What were they doing there anyway?"

"Sparkle and the others are what we call 'anecdotals.' Brain teasers, puzzles, jokes, anecdotes and urban legends that are in the oral tradition but not big enough to exist on their own. Since they need to be instantly retrieved, they have to be flexible and available at a moment's notice—so we billet them unseen around the various works of fiction."

"I get it," replied Thursday5. "We had the joke about the centipede playing rugby with us at *Fiasco* for a while. Out of sight of the readers, of course. Total pest—we kept on tripping over his boots."

We stopped at the foot of the stairs. The room was about the size of a double garage and seemed to be constructed of riveted brass that was green with oxidization. The walls were gently curved, giving the impression that we were inside a huge barrel, and there was a hollow, cathedral-like quality to our voices. In the center of the room was a circular, waist-high bronze plinth about the size and shape of a ship's capstan, upon which two electrodes sprouted upward and then bent gently outward until they were about six inches apart. At the end of each electrode was a carbon sphere no bigger than a Ping-Pong ball, and between the two of them a languid blue arc of electricity crackled quietly to itself.

"What's that?" asked Thursday5 in a deferential whisper.

"It's the spark, the notion, the *core* of the book, the central nub of energy that binds a novel together."

We watched for a few moments as the arc of energy moved in a lazy wave between the poles. Every now and then, it would fizzle as though somehow disturbed by something.

"It moves as the crickets talk to each other upstairs," I explained. "If the book were being read, you'd really see the spark flicker and dance. I've been in the core of *Anna Karenina* when it was going full bore with fifty thousand simultaneous readings, and the effect was better than any fireworks display—a multistranded spark in a thousand different hues that snaked and arced out into the room and twisted around one another. A book's reason for being is to be read; the spark reflects this in a shimmering light show of dynamic proportions."

"You speak as though it were alive."

"Sometimes I think it is," I mused, staring at the spark. "After all, a story is born, it can evolve, replicate and then die. I used to go down to core containment quite a lot, but I don't have as much time for it these days."

I pointed at a pipe about the width of my arm that led out from the plinth and disappeared into the floor.

"That's the throughput pipe that takes all the readings to the Storycode Engine Floor at Text Grand Central and from there to the Outland, where they're channeled direct to the reader's imagination."

"And . . . all books work this way?"

"I wish. Books that are *not* within the influence of Text Grand Central have their own onboard Storycode Engines, as do books being constructed in the Well of Lost Plots and most of the vanity publishing genre."

Thursday5 looked thoughtful. "The readers are everything, aren't they?"

"Now you've got it," I replied. "*Everything.*"

We stood in silence for a moment.

"I was just thinking about the awesome responsibility that comes with being a Jurisfiction agent," I said at last. "What were you thinking about?"

"Me?"

I looked around the empty room. "Yes, you."

"I was wondering if extracting aloe vera hurt the plant. What's that?"

She was pointing at a small round hatch that was partially hidden behind some copper tubing. It looked like something you might find in the watertight bulkhead of a submarine. Riveted and of robust construction, it had a large central lever and two locking devices farther than an arm span apart, so it could never be opened accidentally by one person.

"That leads to . . . *Nothing*," I murmured.

"You mean a blank wall?"

"No, a blank wall would be something. This is not *a* nothing but *the* Nothing, the Nothing by which all Somethings are defined."

She looked confused, so I beckoned her to a small porthole next to the hatch and told her to look out.

"I can't see anything," she said after a while. "It's completely black. . . . No, wait, I can see small pinpoints of light—like stars."

"Not stars," I told her. "*Books*. Each one adrift in the firmament and each one burning not just with the light that the author gave it upon creation but with the warm glow of being read and appreciated. The brighter ones are the most popular."

"I can see *millions* of them," she murmured, cupping her hands around her face to help her eyes penetrate the inky blackness.

"Every book is a small world unto itself, reachable only by bookjumping. See how some points of light tend to group near others?"

"Yes?"

"They're clumped together in genres, attracted by the gravitational tug of their mutual plotlines."

"And between them?"

"An abstraction where all the laws of literary theory and storytelling conventions break down—the Nothing. It doesn't support textual life and has no description, form or function."

I tapped the innocuous-looking hatch.

"Out there you'd not last a second before the text that makes up your descriptive existence was stripped of all meaning and consequence. Before bookjumping was developed, every character was marooned in his or her own novel. For many of the books outside the influence of the Council of Genres and Text Grand Central, it's still like that. *Pilgrim's Progress* and the Sherlock Holmes series are good examples. We know roughly where they are, due to the literary influence they exert on similar books, but we still haven't figured out a way in. And until someone does, a bookjump is impossible."

I switched off the light, and we returned to Geppetto's kitchen.

"Here you go," said Julian Sparkle, handing me a cardboard box. Any sort of enmity he might have felt toward us had vanished.

"What's this?"

"Why, your prize, of course! A selection of Tupperware™ containers. Durable and with ingenious spillproof lids, they're the ideal way to keep food fresh."

"Give them to the tiger."

"He doesn't like Tupperware—the lids are tricky to get off with paws."

"Then *you* have them."

"I didn't win them," replied Sparkle with a trace of annoyance, but then he added after a moment's thought, "However, if you would like to play our Super Wizzo Double Jackpot game, we can double your prize the next time you play!"

"Good, fine—whatever," I said as a phone on the kitchen table started jangling. Julian picked it up.

"Hello? Two doors, one tiger, liar/nonliar puzzle speaking." He raised his eyebrows and grabbed a handy pen to scribble a note. "We'll be onto it right away."

He replaced the phone and addressed the two guards, who were watching him expectantly. "Scramble, lads. We're needed on a boring car journey on the M4 westbound near Lyneham."

The room was suddenly a whirl of activity. Each guard removed his door, which seemed to be on quick-release hinges, and then held it under his arm. The first guard placed his hand on the shoulder of Sparkle, who had turned his back, and the second on the shoulder of his compatriot. The tiger, now free, stood behind the second guard and placed one paw on his shoulder and with the other lifted the telephone off the table.

"Ready?" called out Sparkle to the odd line that had formed expertly behind him.

"Yes," said the first guard.

"No," said the second.

"Growl," said the tiger, and turned to wink at us.

There was a mild concussion as they all jumped out. The fire blazed momentarily in the grate, the cat ran out of the room, and loose papers were thrown into the air. Phone call to exit had taken less then eight seconds. These guys were professionals.

Thursday5 and I, suitably impressed and still without a taxi, jumped out of *Pinocchio* and were once again in the Great Library.

She replaced the book on the shelf and looked up at me.

"Even if I *had* played Liars and Tigers," she said with a

mournful sigh, "I wouldn't have been able to figure it out. I'd have been eaten."

"Not necessarily," I replied. "Even by guessing, your chances were still fifty-fifty, and that's thought favorable odds at Jurisfiction."

"You mean I have a fifty percent chance of being killed in the service?"

"Consider yourself lucky. Out in the real world, despite huge advances in medical science, the chance of death remains unchanged at a hundred percent. Still, there's a bright side to the human mortality thing—at least, there is for the BookWorld."

"Which is?"

"A never-ending supply of new readers. Come on, you can jump me back to the Jurisfiction offices."

She stared at me for a moment and then said, "You're not so good at bookjumping anymore, are you?"

"Not really—but that's between you and me, yes?"

"Do you want to talk about it?"

"No."

10.

The Well of Lost Plots

Due to the specialized tasks undertaken by Prose Resource Operatives, JurisTech is permitted to build gadgets deemed outside the usual laws of physics—the only department (aside from the SF genre) licensed to do so. Aside from the famed TravelBook, JurisTech is also responsible for the Textual Sieve, an extremely useful device that can do almost anything—even though its precise use, form and function are never fully explained.

As soon as we were back at the Jurisfiction offices in Norland Park, I gave Thursday5 an hour off for lunch so I could get some work done. I pulled all the files on potential transfictional probe appearances and discovered I had the only solid piece of evidence—all the rest had merely been sightings. It seemed that whenever a Goliath probe appeared, it was gone again in under a minute. The phenomenon had begun seven years ago, reached a peak eight months before and now seemed to be ebbing. Mind you, this was based on only thirty-six sightings and so couldn't be considered conclusive.

I took the information to Bradshaw, who listened carefully to my report and to what I knew about Goliath, which was quite a lot and none of it good. He nodded soberly as I spoke and, when I had finished, paused for a moment before observing, "Goliath is Outlander and well beyond our jurisdiction. I'm loath to take it to

Senator Jobsworth, as he'll instigate some daft 'initiative' or something with resources that we just don't have. Is there any evidence that these probes do anything other than observe? Throwing a metal ball into fiction is one thing; moving a person between the two is quite another."

"None at all," I replied. "But it must be their intention, even if they haven't managed it yet."

"Do you think they will?"

"My uncle could do it. And if he could, then it's possible."

Bradshaw thought for a moment. "We'll keep this to ourselves for now. With our plunging ReadRates, I don't want to needlessly panic the CofG into some insane knee-jerk response. Is there a chance you could find out something from the real world?"

"I could try," I replied reflectively, "but don't hold your breath—I'm not exactly on Goliath's Christmas-card list."

"On the contrary," said Bradshaw, passing me the probe, "I'm sure they'd be overjoyed to meet someone who can travel into fiction. Can you check up on the Jane Austen refits this afternoon? Isambard was keen to show us something."

I told him I'd go down there straightaway, and he thanked me, wished me good luck and departed. I had a few minutes to spare before Thursday5 got back, so I checked the card-index databases for anything about Superreaders, of which there was frustratingly little. Most Superreader legends had their base in the Text Sea, usually from word fishermen home on leave from scrawltrawlers. The issue was complicated by the fact that one Superread is technically identical to a large quantity of simultaneous reads, so only an examination of a book's maintenance log would identify whether it had been a victim or not.

Thursday5 returned exactly on time, having spent the lunch hour in a mud bath, the details of which she felt compelled to tell me—at length. Mind you, she was a lot more relaxed than I was, so something was working. We stepped outside, and after I argued with TransGenre Taxis' dispatch for five minutes, we read ourselves to the Great Library, then took the elevator and descended in silence to the subbasements, which had been known colloquially as the Well of Lost Plots for so long that no one could remember their proper name—if they'd ever had one. It was here that books were actually *constructed*. The "laying of the spine" was the first act in the process, and after that a continuous series of work gangs would toil tirelessly on the novel, embedding plot and subtext within the fabric of the narrative. They carefully lowered in the settings and atmosphere before the characters, fresh from dialogue training and in the presence of a skilled imaginator, would record the book onto an ImaginoTransferoRecordingDevice ready for reading in the Outland. It was slow, manpower-intensive and costly—any Supervising Book Engineer who could construct a complex novel in the minimum of time and on budget was much in demand.

"I was thinking," said Thursday5 as the elevator plunged downward, "about being a bit more proactive. I *would* have been eaten by that tiger, and it was, I must confess, the seventh time you've rescued me over the past day and a half."

"Eighth," I pointed out. "Remember you were attacked by that adjectivore?"

"Oh, yes. It didn't really take to my suggestion of a discussion group to reappraise the passive role of grammasites within the BookWorld, now, did it?"

"No. All it wanted was to tear the adjectives from your still-breathing body."

"Well, my point is that I think I need to be more aggressive."

"Sounds like a good plan," I replied. "If a situation arises, we'll see how you do."

The elevator stopped, and we stepped out. Down here in the Well, the subbasements looked more like narrow Elizabethan streets than corridors. It was here that purveyors of book-construction-related merchandise could be found displaying their wares in a multitude of specialty shops that would appeal to any genre, style or setting. The corridors were alive with the bustling activity of artisans moving hither and thither in the gainful pursuit of book building. Plot traders, backstoryists, hole stitchers, journeymen and generics trotted purposefully in every direction, and cartloads of prefabricated sections for protobooks were being slowly pulled down the center of the street by Pitman ponies, which are a sort of shorthand horse that doesn't take up so much room.

Most of it was salvage. In the very lowest subbasement was the Text Sea, and it was on the shores of this ocean that scrapped books were pulled apart by work gangs using nothing more refined than hammers, chains and muscle. The chunks of battered narrative were then dismantled by cutters, who would remove and package any salvageable items to be resold. Any idea, setting or character that was too damaged or too dull to be reused was unceremoniously dumped in the Text Sea, where the bonds within the sentences were loosened until they were nothing but words, and then these, too, were reduced to letters and punctuation, the meaning burning off into a bluish mist that lingered near the foreshore before evaporating.

"Who are we going to see?" asked Thursday5 as we made our way through the crowded throng.

"Bradshaw wanted me to cast an eye over the Jane Austen refit," I replied. "The engineer in charge is Isambard Kingdom Buñuel, the finest and most surreal book engineer in the WOLP. When he constructed *War and Peace,* no one thought that anything of such scale and grandeur *could* be built, let alone launched. It was so large an entire subbasement had to be constructed to take it. Even now a permanent crew of twenty is needed to keep it going."

Thursday5 looked curiously around as a gang of riveters walked past, laughing loudly and talking about a spine they'd been working on.

"So once the book is built, it's moved to the Great Library?" she asked.

"If only," I replied. "Once completed and the spark has been ignited, it undergoes a rigorous twelve-point narrative safety-and-compliance regime before being studiously and penetratively test-read on a special rig. After that, the book is taken on a trial reading by the Council of Genres Book Inspectorate before being passed—or not—for publication."

We walked on and presently saw the Book Maintenance Facility hangars in the distance, rising above the low roofs of the street like the airship hangars I knew so well back home. They were always full; book maintenance carried on 24/7. After another five minutes' walk and with the street expanding dramatically to be able to encompass the vast size of the complex, we arrived outside the Book Maintenance Facility.

11.

The Refit

Books suffer wear and tear, just the same as hip joints, cars and reputations. For this reason all books have to go into the maintenance bay for a periodic refit, either every thirty years or every million readings, whichever comes first. For those books that suffer a high initial readership but then lose it through boredom or insufficient reader intellect, a partial refit may be in order. Salmon Thrusty's intractable masterpiece *The Demonic Couplets* has had its first two chapters rebuilt six times, but the rest is relatively unscathed.

Ever since the ProCaths had mounted a guerrilla-style attack on *Wuthering Heights* during routine maintenance, security had been increased, and tall cast-iron railings now separated the Book Maintenance Facility from the rest of the Well. Heathcliff—possibly the most hated man inside fiction—had not been harmed, partly due to the vigilance of the Jurisfiction agents who were on Heathcliff Protection Duty that day but also due to a misunderstanding of the word "guerrilla," a woeful lexicological lapse that had left five confused apes dead and the facility littered with bananas. There was now a guardhouse, too, and it was impossible to get in unless on official business.

"Now, here's an opportunity," I whispered to Thursday5, "to test your aggressiveness. These guys can be tricky, so you need to be firm."

"Firm?"

"Firm."

She took a deep breath, steeled herself and marched up to the guardhouse in a meaningful manner.

"Next and Next," she announced, passing our IDs to a guard who was sitting in a small wooden shed at the gates of the facility. "And if you cause us any trouble, we'll . . . not be happy. And then *you'll* not be happy, because we can do unhappy things . . . to people . . . *sometimes*."

"I'm sorry?" said the guard, who had a large white mustache and seemed to be a little deaf.

"I said . . . ah, how are you?"

"Oh, we're fine, thank you, missy," replied the guard amiably. Thursday5 turned to me and gave me the thumbs-up sign, and I smiled. I actually quite liked her, but there was a huge quantity of work to be done before she might be considered Jurisfiction material. At present I was planning on assessing her "potential with retraining" and sending her back to cadet school.

I looked around as the guard stared at our identification and then at us. Above the hangars I could see tall chimneys belching forth clouds of smoke, while in the distance we could hear the ring of hammers and the rumble of machinery.

"Which one is Thursday Next?" asked the guard, staring closely at the almost identical IDs.

"Both of us," said Thursday5. "I'm Thursday5, and she's the Outlander."

"An Outlander?" repeated the guard with great interest. I glared at Thursday5. My Outlander status wasn't something I liked to bandy about.

"Hey, Bert!" he said to the other guard, who seemed to be on permanent tea break. "We've got an Outlander here!"

"No!" he said, getting up from a chair that had its seat polished to a high shine. "Get out of here!"

"What an honor!" said the first guard. "Someone from the *real* world." He thought for a moment. "Tell me, if it rains on a really hot day, do sheep shrink?"

"Is that a security question?"

"No, no," replied the guard quickly. "Bert and I were just discussing it recently."

This wasn't unusual. Characters in fiction had a very skewed view of the real world. To them the extreme elements of human experience were commonplace, as they were generally the sorts of issues that made it into books, which left the mundanities of real life somewhat obscure and mysterious. Ask a resident of the BookWorld about terminal diseases, loss, gunshot trajectories, dramatic irony and problematic relatives and he'd be more expert than you or me—quiz him on paintbrushes and he'd spend the rest of the week trying to figure out how the paint stays on the bristles until it touches another surface.

"It's *woolens* that shrink," I explained, "and it has to be *very* hot."

"I told you so," said Bert triumphantly.

"Thank you," I said, taking the security badges from the guard while I signed the ledger. He admitted us both to the facility, and almost from nowhere a bright yellow jeep appeared with a young man dressed in blue overalls and a cap sporting the BMF logo.

"Can you take us to Isambard Kingdom Buñuel?" I said as we climbed in the back.

"Yes," replied the driver without moving.

"Then would you?"

"I suppose."

The jeep moved off. The hangars were, as previously stated, of gigantic proportions. Unlike the real world, where practical difficulties in civil engineering might be a defining factor in the scale of a facility, here it was not a consideration at all. Indeed, the size of the plant could expand and contract depending on need, a little like Mary Poppins's suitcase, which was hardly surprising, as they were designed by the same person. We drove on for a time in silence.

"What's in Hangar One at the moment?" I asked the driver.

"*The Magus.*"

"Still?"

Even the biggest refit never took more than a week, and John Fowles's labyrinthine-plotted masterpiece had been in there nearly five.

"It's taking longer than we thought—they removed all the plot elements for cleaning, and no one can remember how they go back together again."

"I'm not sure it will make a difference," I murmured as we pulled up outside Hangar Eight. The driver said nothing, waited until we climbed out and then drove off without a word.

To say that the interior of the hangar was vast would have been pointless, as the Great Library, Text Grand Central and the CofG *also* had vast interiors, and continued descriptions of an increasingly hyperbolic nature would be insufferably repetitious. Suffice it to say that there was room on the hangar floor for not only Darcy's country home of Pemberley but also Rosings, Netherfield *and* Longbourn as well. They had all been hoisted from the book by a massive overhead crane so the empty husk of the novel could be checked for fatigue cracks before being fumigated for nesting grammasites and then repainted. At the same time, an army of technicians, plasterers, painters, carpenters and so forth were crawling over the houses, locations, props, furnishings and costumes, all of which had been removed for checking and maintenance.

"If this is *Pride and Prejudice,*" said Thursday5 as we walked toward the Bennets' property of Longbourn, "then what are people reading in the Outland?"

The house was resting incongruously on wooden blocks laid on the hangar floor but without its grounds—they were elsewhere being tended to by a happy buzz of gardeners.

"We divert the readings to a lesser copy on a standby Storycode Engine, and people read that," I replied, nodding a greeting to the various technicians who were trying to make good the damage wrought by the last million readings or so. "The book is never *quite* as good, but the only people who might see a difference are the Austen enthusiasts and scholars. They would notice the slight dulling and lack of vitality, but, unable to come to a satisfactory answer as to why this might be so, they will simply blame themselves—a reading later in the week will once again renew their confidence in the magnificence of the novel."

We stepped inside the main doorway of Longbourn, where a similar repair gang was working on the interior. They had only just gotten started, and from here it was easier to see the extent of the corrosion. The paintwork was dull and lifeless, the wallpaper hung off the wall in long strips, and the marble fireplace was stained and darkened by smoke. Everything we looked at seemed tired and worn.

"Oh, mercy!" came a voice behind us, and we turned to find Mrs. Bennet dressed in a threadbare poke bonnet and shawl. Following her was a construction manager, and behind him was Mr. Bennet.

"This will *never* be ready in time," she lamented, looking around the parlor of her house unhappily, "and every second not spent looking for husbands is a second wasted."

"My dear, you must come and have your wardrobe replaced," implored Mr. Bennet. "You are *quite* in tatters and unsuited for being read, let alone receiving gentlemen—potential husbands or otherwise."

"He's quite right," urged the manager. "It is only a refit, nothing more; we will have you back on the shelf in a few days."

"On the shelf?" she shrieked. "Like my daughters?"

And she was about to burst into tears when she suddenly caught sight of me.

"You there! Do you have a single brother in possession of a good fortune who is in want of a wife?"

"I'm afraid not," I replied, thinking of Joffy, who failed on all three counts.

"Are you sure? I've a choice of five daughters; one of them *must* be suitable—although I have my doubts about Mary being acceptable to anyone. Ahhhhh!"

She had started to scream.

"Good lady, calm yourself!" cried Mr. Bennet. "Whatever is the matter?"

"My nerves are so bad I am now seeing double!"

"You are *not*, madam," I told her hastily. "This is my . . . twin sister."

At that moment a small phalanx of seamstresses came in holding a replacement costume. Mrs. Bennet made another sharp cry and ran off upstairs, quickly followed by the wardrobe department, who would doubtless have to hold her down and undress her—like the last time.

"I'll leave it in your capable hands," said Mr. Bennet to the wardrobe mistress. "I am going to my library and don't wish to be disturbed."

He opened the door and found to his dismay that it, too, was being rebuilt. Large portions of the wall were missing, and plasterers were attempting to fill the gaps to the room beyond. There was the flickering light of an arc welder and a shower of sparks. He harrumphed, shrugged, gave us a wan smile and walked out.

"Quite a lot of damage," I said to the construction manager, whose name we learned was Sid.

"We get a lot of this in the classics," he said with a shrug. "This is the third P^2 refit I've done in the past fifteen years—but it's not as bad as the *Lord of the Rings* trilogy; those things are *always* in for maintenance. The fantasy readership really gives it a hammering—and the fan fiction doesn't help neither."

"The name's Thursday Next," I told him, "from Jurisfiction. I need to speak to Isambard."

He led us outside to where the five Bennet sisters were running through their lines with a wordsmith holding a script.

"But you are not entitled to know mine; nor will such behavior ever induce me to be explicit," said Elizabeth.

"Not *quite* right," replied the wordsmith as she consulted the script. "You dropped the 'as this,' from the middle of the sentence."

"I did?" queried Lizzie, craning over to look at the script. "Where?"

"It still sounded *perfect* to me," said Jane good-naturedly.

"This is all just so *boring*," muttered Lydia, tapping her foot impatiently and looking around. Wisely, the maintenance staff had separated the soldiers and especially Wickham from Kitty and Lydia—for their own protection, if not the soldiers'.

"Lydia dearest, do *please* concentrate," said Mary, looking up from the book she was reading. "It is for your own good."

"Ms. Next!" came an authoritarian voice that I knew I could ignore only at my peril.

"Your ladyship," I said, curtsying neatly to a tall woman bedecked in dark crinolines. She had strongly marked features that might once have been handsome but now appeared haughty and superior.

"May I present Cadet Next?" I said. "Thursday5, this is the Right Honorable Lady Catherine de Bourgh, widow of Sir Lewis de Bourgh."

Thursday5 was about to say something, but I caught her eye and she curtsied instead, which Lady Catherine returned with a slight incline of her head.

"I must speak to you, Ms. Next," continued her ladyship, taking my arm to walk with me, "upon a matter of considerable concern. As you know, I have a daughter named Anne, who is unfortunately of a sickly constitution, which has prevented her from making accomplishments she otherwise could not have failed. If good health had been hers, she would have joined Jurisfiction many years ago and about now would begin to accrue the benefits of her age, wisdom and experience."

"Doubtless, your ladyship."

Lady Catherine gave a polite smile. "Then we are agreed. Miss Anne should join Jurisfiction on the morrow with a rank, salary and duties commensurate with the standing that her ill health has taken from her—shall we say five thousand guineas a year and light work only with mornings off and three servants?"

"I will bring it to the attention of the relevant authorities," I told her diplomatically. "My good friend and colleague Commander Bradshaw will attend to your request personally."

I sniggered inwardly. Bradshaw and I had spent many years attempting to drop each other in impossible situations for amusement, and he'd never top this.

"Indeed," said Lady Catherine in an imperious tone. "I spoke to Commander Bradshaw, and he suggested I speak to *you*."

"Ah."

"Shall we say Monday?" continued Lady Catherine. "Jurisfiction can send a carriage for my daughter, but be warned—if it is unfit for her use, it shall be returned."

"Monday would be admirable," I told her, thinking quickly. "Miss Anne's assumed expertise will be much in demand. As you have no doubt heard, *Fanny Hill* has been moved from Literary Smut to the Racy Novel genre, and your daughter's considerable skills may be required for character retraining."

Lady Catherine was silent for a moment.

"Quite impossible," she said at last. "Next week is the busiest in our calendar. I shall inform you as to when and where she will accept her duties—good day!"

And with a harrumph of a most haughty nature, she was gone.

I rejoined Thursday5, who was waiting for me near two carriages that were being rebuilt, and then we made our way toward the engineer's office. As we passed a moth-eaten horse, I heard it say to another shabby old nag, "So what's this *Pride and Prejudice* all about, then?"

"It's about a horse who pulls a carriage for the Bennets," replied his friend, taking a mouthful from the feed bucket and munching thoughtfully.

"Please come in," said the construction manager, and we entered the work hut. The interior was a neat and orderly drawing office with a half dozen octopi seated at draftsmen's desks and dressed in tartan waistcoats that made them all look like oversize bagpipes—apart from one, who actually *was* an oversize set of bagpipes. They were all studying plans of the book, consulting damage reports and then sketching repair recommendations on eight different notepads simultaneously. The octopi blinked at us curiously as we walked in, except for one who was asleep and muttering something about his "garden being in the shade," and another who was playing a doleful tune on a bouzouki.

"How odd," said Thursday5.

"You're right," I agreed. "Bruce usually plays the lute."

In the center of the room was Isambard Kingdom Buñuel. He was standing in shirtsleeves over the blueprints of the book and was a man in healthy middle age who looked as if he had seen a lot of life and was much the better for it. His dark wool suit was spattered with mud, he wore a tall stovepipe hat, and moving constantly in his mouth was an unlit cigar. He was engaged in animated conversation with his three trusty engineering assistants. The first could best be described as a mad monk who was dressed in a coarse habit and had startling, divergent eyes. The second was a daringly sparkly drag queen who it seemed had just hopped off a carnival float in Rio, and the third was more ethereal—he was simply a disembodied voice known only as Horace. They were all discussing the pros and cons of balancing essential work with budgetary constraints, then about Loretta's choice of sequins and the available restaurants for dinner.

"Thursday!" said Isambard as we walked in. "What a very fortuitous happenstance—I trust you are wellhealthy?"

"Wellhealthy indeedly," I replied.

Buñuel's engineering skills were without peer—not just from a simple mechanistic point of view but also from his somewhat surreal method of problem solving that made lesser book engineers pale into insignificance. It was he who first thought of using custard as a transfer medium for speedier throughput from the books to the Storycode Engines and he who pioneered the hydroponic growth of usable dramatic irony. When he wasn't working toward the decriminalization of class-C grammatical abuses, such as starting a sentence with "and," he was busy designing new and interesting plot devices. It was he who suggested the groundbreaking twist in *The Murder of Roger Ackroyd*, and also the "Gally Threepwood memoirs" device in the Blandings series. Naturally, he'd had other, lesser ideas that didn't find favor, such as the discarded U-boat–*Nautilus* battle sequence in *Mysterious Island*, a new process for distilling quotation marks from boiled mice, a method of making books grammasite-proof by marinating them in dew, and a whole host of farcical new words that only he used. But his hits were greater than the sum of his misses, and such is the way with greatness.

"I hope we are not in any sort of troublesome with Jurisfiction?"

"Not at all," I assured him. "You spoke to Bradshaw about something?"

"My memory is *so* stringbagness these days," he said, slapping his forehead with his palm. "Walk with me."

We left the work hut at a brisk pace and walked toward the empty book, Thursday5 a few steps behind.

"We've got another seventeen clockchimes before we have to click it all back onwise," he said, mopping his brow.

"Will you manage it?"

"We should be dokey," replied Isambard with a laugh. "Always supposeding that Mrs. Bennet doesn't do anything sensible."

We walked up a set of wooden stairs and stepped onto the novel. From our vantage point, we could see the empty husk of the book laid out in front of us. Everything had been removed, and it looked like an empty steel barge several hundred acres in size.

"What's happening over there?" asked Thursday5, pointing to a group of men working in an area where several girders joined in a delicate latticework of steel and rivets.

"We're checklooking for fatigue splitcracks near the irony-expansion slot," explained Isambard. "The ceaseless flexiblations of a book as readers of varying skill make their way through it can set up a harmonic that exacts stresstications the book was never blueprinted to take. I expect you heard about the mid-read fractsplosion of *Hard Times* during the postmaintenance testification in 1932?"

Thursday5 nodded.

"We've had to be more uttercarefulness since then," continued Isambard, "which is why classics like this come in for rebuildificance every thirty years whether they require it or not."

There was a crackle of bright blue light as the work gang effected a repair, and a subengineer supervising the gang waved to Isambard, who waved back.

"Looks like we found a fatigue crevicette," he said, "which goes to show that one can never be too carefulphobic."

"Commander Bradshaw told me you had something you wanted to say?"

"That's true," replied Buñuel. "I've done enough rebuildificances to know when something's a bit squiddly. It's the Council of Genres. They've been slicedicing budgets for years, and now they ask us to topgrade the imaginotransference conduits."

He pointed at a large pipe that looked like a water main. A conduit that size would take a lot of readers—far more than we had at present. Although in itself a good move, with falling ReadRates it seemed a little . . . well, *odd*.

"Did they give a reason?"

"They said *Pride and Prejudice* has been added to twenty-eight more teachcrammer syllabuses this year, and there's another silverflick out soon."

"Sounds fair to me."

"Posstruthful, but it makes nonsense. It's potentious *new* books we should be cashsquandering on, not the stalnovelwarts who will be read no matter what. Besides, the costcash of the extra conduits is verlittle compared to the amount of custard needed to fillup all."

"I'll make some inquiries," I told him.

We watched as the overhead crane gently lowered Darcy's stately home of Pemberley back into its position in the book, where it was then securely bolted by a group of men in overalls wielding wrenches as big as they were.

"Spot-on-time-tastic," murmured Isambard, consulting a large gold pocketwatch. "We might make the deadule after all."

"Mr. Buñuel?" murmured a disembodied voice that sounded as though it came from everywhere at once.

"Yes, Horace?"

"Sorry to trouble you, sir," came the voice again, "but Mrs. Bennet and Lady Catherine de Bourgh have locked antlers in the living room and are threatening to kill each other. What do you want to do?"

"No time to lose!" exclaimed Buñuel, reaching into his pocket. "I'll have five guineas on Mrs. Bennet."

Thursday5 and I walked out of the maintenance facility and back to the busy corridors of the Well of Lost Plots. I called TransGenre Taxis and was told that my cab was "stuck in a traffic jam in Mrs. Beeton's" but would "be with you shortly," so we walked toward the elevators. Buñuel had a point about the extra conduiting—but equally it could be just another of the bizarre accounting anomalies that abound at the council—they once refused to allocate funds for maintenance on *Captain Corelli's Mandolin,* despite an almost unprecedented burst of popularity. By the time they agreed to some remedial construction work, it was too late—the first few chapters suffered permanent damage. On the other side of the coin, they had no problem issuing the Danvers with new black uniforms and designer dark glasses so they "looked nice on parade."

"Is it true you have a chair at the Council of Genres?" asked Thursday5 with a sense of wholly unwarranted awe in her voice.

"And a table, too. As an Outlander I don't have the strictures of the narrative to dictate my actions, so I'm quite good at forward planning and— Hang on a moment."

Recalling Landen's writer's block, I ducked into a bric-a-brac store full of plot devices, props, backstories and handy snatches of verbal banter for that oh-so-important exchange. I made my way past packing cases full of plot twists and false resolutions and walked up to the counter.

"Hello, Murray."

"Thursday!" replied the owner of the store, a retired gag-and-groan man who had worked the Comedy genre for years before giving it all up to run a used-plot shop. "What can I do you for?"

"A plot device," I said somewhat vaguely. "Something exciting that will change a story from the mundane to the fantastic in a paragraph."

"Budget?"

"Depends on what you've got."

"Hmm," said the shopkeeper, thinking hard and staring at the wall of small drawers behind him, which made it look a little like an apothecary's shop. On each drawer there was a painted label denoting some exciting and improbable plot-turning device. "Tincture of breathlessness," said one, and "Paternal root," read another.

"How about a *Suddenly a shot rang out*? That's always a safe bet for mysteries or to get you out of a scrape when you don't know what to do next."

"I think I can afford something better than that. Got anything a bit more . . . complex?"

Murray looked at the labels on the drawers again. "I've got a *And that, said Mr. Wimple, was when we discovered . . . the truth.*"

"Too vague."

"Perhaps, but it's cheap. Okay. How about a *Mysterious stranger arriving during a thunderstorm*? We've got a special on this week. Take the stranger and you can have a corrupt local chief of police and an escaped homicidal lunatic at no extra charge."

But I was still undecided.

"I was thinking of something more character- than plot-led."

"I hope you've got deep pockets," said the shopkeeper ominously and with a trace of annoyance, as the line behind me was becoming longer by the second.

"How about the arrival of a distant and *extremely* eccentric ex-military uncle upsetting the delicate balance of the ordered household?"

"That sounds like just the thing. How much?"

"He was pulled out complete and unused a few days ago. Took a lot of skill to pluck him out of the narrative without damage, and with all ancillary props and walk-ons—"

"Yes, okay, okay, I get the picture—*How much?*"

"To you, a thousand guineas."

"I get the uncle fully realized for that, yes?"

"He's over there."

I turned to see a slender and very jovial-looking gentleman sitting on a packing case on the other side of the shop. He was dressed in a suit of outrageously loud green and yellow checks and was resting his gloves on the top of a cane. He inclined his head in greeting when he saw us looking at him and smiled impishly.

"Perfect. I get a full backstory as well, yes?"

"It's all here," said Murray, placing on the counter a glass jar that seemed to be full of swirling colored mist.

"Then it's a deal."

We shook hands, and I gave him my BookWorld ChargeCard. I was just standing there in that blank sort of way you do while waiting for a shopkeeper to complete a transaction, when the hair on the back of my neck suddenly rose. It was a sixth sense, if you like—something you acquire in the BookWorld, where jeopardy is sometimes never more than a line away. I surreptitiously slipped my hand into my bag and clasped the butt of my pistol. I looked cautiously from the corner of my eye at the customer to my left. It was a freelance imaginator buying powdered kabuki—no problem there. I looked to the right and perceived a tall figure dressed in a trench coat with a fedora pulled down to hide his face. I tensed as the faint odor of bovine reached my nostrils. It was the Minotaur, the half-man, half-bull son of Queen Pasiphaë of Crete. He'd killed one Jurisfiction agent and tried the same with me several times, so consequently he had an "erase on sight" order across sixteen genres—there were few these days who would dare harbor him. I stayed calm and turned toward Thursday5, who was looking at a pair of toucans that were a job lot from a scrapped bird-identification handbook. I caught her eye and showed her three fingers, which was a prearranged signal of imminent danger, then gave an almost imperceptible nod in the Minotaur's direction. Thursday5 looked bewildered, I gave up and turned slowly back.

"Soon be done!" muttered Murray, filling out the credit form. I stole a look toward the Minotaur again. I could have erased him there and then, but it was always possible that this wasn't the Minotaur we were hunting. After all, there were thousands of Minotaurs dotted around the BookWorld, and they all looked pretty much alike. Admittedly, not many wore trench coats and fedoras, but I wasn't going to dispatch anyone without being sure.

"Would you like that frying pan wrapped, Mr. Johnson?" asked the lady serving the Minotaur. I required nothing more. He'd been using the "Mr. Johnson" pseudonym for many years—and the frying pan? Well, we'd darted him once with SlapStick as a tracking device, and it seemed to have crept into his modus operandi of assassination. Steamrollers, banana skins, falling pianos—he'd used them all. In the pantheon of SlapStick, the close-quarters hand weapon of choice was . . . a frying pan. Without waiting another second, I drew my pistol. The Minotaur, with a speed out of all proportion to his bulk, flipped the frying pan to his other hand and swiped it in my direction, catching the pistol and sending it clattering to the other side of the room. We paused and stared at each other. The frying pan had a two-foot handle, and he brandished it at me in a threatening manner. He removed his hat, and as the other customers realized who he was, there was a cry of fear and a mass exodus from the shop. He had the body of a man but the head of a bull, which had a kind of *humanness* about it that was truly disturbing. His yellow eyes gleamed at me with malevolence, and his horns, I noticed, had been sharpened to wickedly fine points.

"We can talk about this," I said in a quiet tone, wondering if Thursday5 had the wits to try to distract him.

"No talk," said the Minotaur in a basso profundo. "My job is to kill you, and yours . . . is to *die*."

I tried to stall him. "Let's talk for a minute about job descriptions."

But the Minotaur wasn't in the talking vein. He took a pace forward and made another swipe at me with the frying pan. I took a step backward but even so felt the breeze of the pan as it just missed my head. I grabbed the object nearest to hand, which was a golf club, and tried to hit him with it, but he was faster, and the wooden shaft of the club was reduced to splinters and sawdust with the ferocity of his blow. He gave out another deep, hearty laugh and took a further step toward me.

"I say," came a voice that sounded like crumpets and tea at four o'clock sharp. "You, sir—with the horns."

The Minotaur looked to where the voice had come from but still kept me within his vision. The interloper, of course, was the eccentric relative I'd just purchased for Landen's book. He had left his packing case and stood facing the beast armed with nothing more than his walking stick.

"Now, run along, there's a good chap," he said, as though he were talking to a child.

The Minotaur curled a lip and breathed a threatening, *"Begone!"*

"Look here," replied the character in the green and yellow checks. "I'm not sure I care for the tone of your voice."

The Minotaur was suddenly a whirling mass of demonic destruction. He swung the frying pan toward the gentleman in an arc that could never have missed. But he *did* miss. There was a flash of silver, a blur of green and yellow, and the frying pan clattered to the floor—with the Minotaur's hand still clutching it. The Minotaur looked at the frying pan, at the severed hand, then at his stump. He grimaced, gave out a deafening yell that shattered the windows of the shop and then evaporated into nothing as he jumped off and away.

"By gad, what a to-do," exclaimed the gentleman as he calmly cleaned his sword-stick and returned it to his sheath. "Anyone know who he was?"

"The Minotaur."

"Was he, by George?" exclaimed the gentleman in surprise. "Would have expected a better fight than that. Are you quite well?"

"Yes," I answered, "thanks to you. That was a nifty piece of sword-work."

"My dear girl, think nothing of it," he replied with the ghost of a smile. "I was captain of the fencing team at Rugby."

He was a handsome man in his mid-forties, and everything he did and said was liberally iced with a heavy coating of stiff British reserve. I couldn't imagine what book he had come from or even why he'd been offered up as salvage.

"Thursday Next," I said, putting out my hand.

"The pleasure is all mine, Ms. Next," he replied. "Wing Commander Cornelius Scampton-Tappett at your service."

The customers were slowly coming back to peer into the store, but Murray was already placing Closed signs on the doors.

"So," said Scampton-Tappett, "now that you've bought me, what would you have me do?"

"Oh . . . yes . . . right."

I dug a calling card from my pocket, wrote down the title of Landen's latest novel—*Bananas for Edward*—and handed it to him.

"Do what you can, would you? And if you need anything, you can contact me over at Jurisfiction."

Scampton-Tappett raised an eyebrow, told me he would do the very best he could, tucked the jar containing his backstory under his arm and vanished.

I breathed a sigh of relief and glanced around. Thursday5 was regarding me with such a sense of abject loss and failure on her face that I thought at first she'd been hurt.

"Are you all right?"

She nodded and looked down. I followed her gaze. Lying at her feet was my pistol.

"Is that where it ended up after it was knocked from my grasp?"

She nodded miserably, her eyes brimming with tears of self-anger.

I sighed. She and I both knew that this was the end of the road when it came to her cadetship. If Scampton-Tappett hadn't intervened, I might well be dead—and she'd done nothing to prevent it.

"You don't have to say it," she said. "I'm manifestly not cut out for this work and never shall be. I'd try to apologize, but I can't think of words that could adequately express my shame."

She took a deep breath, pulled the bow out of her hair, put it in her mouth and then gathered up her hair in a ponytail again before retying it. It was just the way I did it, and I suddenly felt a pang of guilt. After all, she only acted in her morbidly peaceable way because that's how she was *written,* as an antidote to the rest of the Thursday series. The thing was, the sex-and-violence nature of the first four books had been my fault, too. I'd sold the character rights in order to fund Acme Carpets.

"I'd best be getting back to my book now," she said, and turned to go.

"Did I say you could leave?" I asked in my stoniest voice.

"Well, that is to say . . . no."

"Then until I *say* you can go, you stay with me. I'm still undecided as to your fate, and until that happens—Lord help me—you'll stay as my cadet."

We returned to Jurisfiction, and Thursday5 went and did some Pilates in the corner, much to the consternation of Mrs. Dashwood, who happened to be passing. I reported the Minotaur's appearance and the state of the Austen refit to Bradshaw, who told me to have the Minotaur's details and current whereabouts texted to all agents.

After returning to my desk, dealing with some paperwork and being consulted on a number of matters, I drew out Thursday5's assessment form, filled it in and then checked the "Failed" box on the last page before I signed it. I folded it twice, slid it into the envelope and wavered for a moment before eventually placing it in the top drawer of my desk.

I looked at my watch. It was time to go home. I walked over to Thursday5, who had her eyes closed and was standing on one leg. "Same time tomorrow?"

She opened her eyes and stared into mine. I got the same feeling when staring into the mirror at home. The touchy-feely New Age stuff was all immaterial. She was me, but me as I *might* have been if I'd never joined the police, army, SpecOps or Jurisfiction. Perhaps I wouldn't have been any happier if I'd connected with the side of me that was her, but I'd be a lot more relaxed and a good deal healthier.

"Do you mean it?" she asked.

"Wouldn't say it if I didn't. But remember one thing: It's coffee and a bacon roll."

She smiled. "Right. Coffee and bacon roll it is." She handed me a paper bag. "This is for you."

I peered inside. It contained Pickwick's blue-and-white knitted cozy—finished.

"Good job," I murmured, looking at the delicate knitting enviously. "Thank—"

But she'd gone. I walked to the corridor outside and dug out my TravelBook, turned to the description of my office at Acme Carpets and read. After a few lines, the air turned suddenly colder, there was the sound of crackling cellophane, and I was back in my small office with a dry mouth and a thirst so strong I thought I would faint. I kept a pitcher of water close by for just these moments, and thus I spent the next ten minutes drinking water and breathing deeply.

12.

Kids

Landen and I had often talked about it, but we never had a fourth. When Jenny came along, I was forty-two, and that, I figured, was it. On the occasion of our last attempt to induct Friday into the ChronoGuard's Academy of Time, he was the eldest at sixteen, Tuesday was twelve, and Jenny, the youngest, was ten. I resisted naming Jenny after a day of the week; I thought at least one of us should have the semblance of normality.

I arrived at Tuesday's school at ten to four and waited patiently outside the math room. She'd shown a peculiar flair for the subject all her life but had first achieved prominence when aged nine. She'd wandered into the sixth-form math room and found an equation written on the board, thinking it was homework. But it wasn't. It was Fermat's Last Theorem, and the math master had written it down to demonstrate how this simple equation could not be solved. The thing was, Tuesday had *found a solution,* thus rendering a proof of the unworkability of the equation both redundant and erroneous.

When the hunt was on for the person who had solved it, Tuesday thought they were angry with her for spoiling their fun, so she wasn't revealed as the culprit for almost a week. Even then she had to be cajoled into explaining the answer. Professors of mathematics had tubed in from every corner of the globe to see how such a simple solution could have been staring them in the face without any of them noticing it.

At four on the button, Tuesday came out of the math class looking drained and a bit cross.

"Hi, sweetheart," I said. "How was school?"

"S'okay," she said with a shrug, handing me her Hello Kitty school bag, pink raincoat and half-empty Winnie-the-Pooh lunch box. "Do you have to pick me up in your Acme uniform? It's, like, soooooo embarrassing."

"I certainly do," I replied, giving her a big smoochy kiss to embarrass her further, something that didn't really work, as the pupils in her math class were all grown up and too obsessed with number sets and parameterized elliptic curves to be bothered by a daughter's embarrassment over her mother.

"They're all a bit *slow*," she said as we walked to the van. "Some of them can barely count."

"Sweetheart, they are the finest minds in mathematics today; you should be happy that they're coming to you for tutoring. It must have been a bit of a shock to the mathematics fraternity when you revealed that there were sixteen more odd numbers than even ones."

"Seventeen," she corrected me. "I thought of another one on the bus this morning. The odd-even disparity is the easy bit," she explained. "The hard part is trying to explain that there actually *is* a highest number, a fact that tends to throw all work regarding infinite sets into a flat spin."

Clearly, the seriously smart genes that Mycroft had inherited from *his* father had bypassed my mother and me but appeared in Tuesday. It was odd to think that Mycroft's two sons were known collectively as "the Stupids"—and it wasn't an ironic title either.

Tuesday groaned again when she saw we were driving home in the Acme Carpets van but agreed to get in when I pointed out that a long walk home was the only alternative. She scrunched down in her seat so as not to be spotted.

We didn't go straight home. I'd spoken to Spike before leaving work, and he mentioned that he had some news about Mycroft's haunting and agreed to meet me at Mum's. When I arrived, she and Polly were in the kitchen bickering about something pointless, such as the average size of an orange, so I left Tuesday with them: Mother to burn her a cake and Polly to discuss advanced Nextian Geometry.

"Hiya," I said to Spike, who'd been waiting in his car.

"Yo. Thought about what to do with Felix8?"

"Not yet. I'll interview him again later this evening."

"As you wish. I made a few inquiries on the other side. Remember my dead partner, Chesney? He said Mycroft's spooking was what we call a Nonrecurring Informative Phantasm."

"You have them categorized?"

"Sure. The A-list contains Pointless Screamer, Crisis Warner, Murder Avenger and Recurrent Dreary. From there it's all downhill: poltergeists, faceless orbs, quasi-religious visions and phantom smells—more usually associated with recently departed pet Labradors."

We walked up the garden path to Mycroft's workshop.

"I get the picture. So what does it all mean?" I asked.

"It means that Mycroft had something he wanted to say before he died—but didn't manage to. It was obviously important enough for him to be given a license to come back, if only for a few hours. Turn off your cell phone."

I reached into my pocket and did as he asked.

"Radio waves scramble their energy field," he explained. "Spooking's dropped big-time since the cell-phone network kicked in. I'm amazed there are any ghosts left at all. Ready?"

"Ready."

We had arrived at my uncle's workshop, and Spike grasped the handle and gently pushed the door open. If we were hoping to find Mycroft standing there in all his spectral glory, we were disappointed. The room was empty.

"He was just over there."

Spike closed his eyes, sniffed the air and touched the workbench. "Yeah," he said, "I can feel him."

"Can you?"

"No, not really. Where was he again?"

"At the worktop. Spike, what exactly *is* a ghost?"

"A phantom," said my uncle Mycroft, who had just materialized, "is essentially a heteromorphic wave pattern that gains solidity when the apparition converts thermal energy from the surroundings to visible light. It's a fascinating process, and I'm amazed no one has thought of harnessing it—a holographic TV that could operate from the heat given off by an average-size guinea pig."

I shivered. Mycroft was right—the temperature *had* dropped—and there he was, but a lot less solid than the previous time. I could easily see the other side of the workshop through him.

"Hello again, Thursday," he said. "Good afternoon, Mr. Stoker."

"Good afternoon, sir," replied Spike. "Word in the Realm of the Dead says you've got something to tell us."

"I have?" asked Mycroft, looking at me.

"Yes, Uncle," I told him, "You're a Nonrecurring . . . um—"

"Nonrecurring Informative Phantasm," put in Spike helpfully. "An NIP, or what we call in the trade Speak Up and Shut Down."

"It means, Uncle," I said, "that you've got something *really* important to tell us."

Mycroft looked thoughtful for so long that I almost nudged him before I realized it would be useless.

"Like what?" he said at last.

"I don't know. Perhaps a . . . philosophy of life or something?"

Mycroft looked at me doubtfully and raised an eyebrow. "The only thing that springs to mind is, 'You can never have too many chairs.'"

"That's it? You returned from the dead to give me advice on furniture distribution?"

"I know it's not much of a philosophy," said Mycroft with a shrug, "but it can pay dividends if someone unexpectedly pops around for dinner."

"Uncle, *please* try to remember what it is you have to tell us!"

"Was I murdered or anything?" he asked in a dreamy fashion. "Ghosts often come back if they've been killed or something—at least, Patrick Swayze did."

"You definitely weren't murdered," I told him. "It was a long illness."

"Then this *is* something of a puzzle," murmured Mycroft, "but I suppose I've got the greater part of eternity to figure it out."

That's what I liked about my uncle—always optimistic. But that was it. In another moment he had gone.

"Thirty-three seconds," said Spike, who had put a stopwatch on him, "and about fifty-five percent opacity." He flicked through a small book of tables he had with him. "Hmm," he said at last, "almost certainly a trivisitation. You've got him one more time. He'll be down at fifteen to twenty percent opacity and will only be around for about fifteen seconds."

"Then I could miss him?"

"No," said Spike with a smile, "he appeared to you twice out of twice. The final appearance will be to you, too. Just have a proper question ready for him when you next come here—Mycroft's memory being what it is, you can't rely on him remembering what he came back for. It's up to you."

"Thanks, Spike," I said as I closed the door of the workshop. "I owe you."

Tuesday and I were home in a few minutes. The house felt warm and comfy, and there was the smell of cooking that embraced me like an old friend.

"Hi, darling!" I called out. Landen stopped his typing and came out of the office to give me a hug.

"How was work?" he asked.

I thought of what I'd been doing that day. Of firing and not firing my drippy alter ego, of a Superreader loose somewhere in the BookWorld, of Goliath's unwelcome intrusion and of Mycroft as a ghost. Then there was the return of Felix8, the Minotaur, and my bag of Welsh cash. The time for truth was now. I *had* to tell him.

"I . . . I had to do a stair carpet over in Baydon. Hell on earth; the treads were all squiffy, none of the stair rods would fit, and Spike and I spent the whole afternoon on it—how's the book going?"

He kissed me on the forehead and tousled Tuesday's hair affectionately, then took me by the hand and led me into the kitchen, where there was a stew on the stove.

"Kind of okay, I guess," he replied, stirring the dinner, "but nothing really spectacular."

"No ideas?" I prompted. "An odd *character*, perhaps?"

"No—I was mostly working on pace and atmosphere."

This was strange. I'd specifically told Scampton-Tappett to do his best. I had a sudden thought.

"What book are you working on, sweetheart?"

"The Mews of Doom."

Aha.

"I thought you said you'd be rewriting *Bananas for Edward*?"

"I got bored with it. Why do you ask?"

"No reason. Where's Friday?"

"In his room. I made him have a shower, so he's in a bit of a snot."

"Plock."

"A clean snot is better than a dirty snot I suppose. And Jenny?"

"Watching TV."

I called out, "Hey, Jenny!" but there was no answer.

"Plock."

"She's upstairs in her room."

I looked at the hall clock. We still had a half hour until we had to go to the ChronoGuard's career-advisory presentation.

"PLOCK!"

"Yes, yes, hello, Pickwick—how's this?"

I showed her the finished blue-and-white sweater, and before she could even think of complaining, I had slipped it over her featherless body. Landen and I stared at her this way and that, trying to figure out if it was for the better or the worse.

"It makes her look like something out of the Cornish Blue pottery catalog," said Landen at last.

"Or a very large licorice allsort," I added.

Pickwick glared at us sullenly, then realized she was a good deal warmer and hopped off the kitchen table and trotted down the corridor to try to look in the mirror, which was unfortunately just too high, so she spent the next half hour jumping up and down trying to catch a glimpse of herself.

"Hi, Mum," said Friday, looking vaguely presentable as he walked down the stairs.

"Hello, Sweetpea," I said, passing him the CD Polly had given me. "I got this for you. It's an early release of *Hosing the Dolly*. Check out the guitar riff on the second track."

"Cool," replied Friday, visibly impressed in a "nothing impresses me" sort of way. "How did you get hold of it?"

"Oh, you know," I said offhandedly. "I have friends in the recording industry. I wasn't always just a boring mum, you know."

"Polly gave it to you, didn't she?"

I sighed. "Yes. Ready to go?"

Landen joined us, and he and I moved toward the door. Friday stood where he was.

"Do I have to?"

"You promised. And there isn't another ChronoGuard career-advisory meeting in Swindon for another six months."

"I don't want to work in the time industry."

"Listen," I said, my voice rising as I finally lost patience, "get your lazy butt out the door—okay?"

He knew better than to argue with angry-determined Mum. Landen knocked on the partition wall, and a minute later our neighbor Mrs. Berko-Boyler was on the doorstep wearing a pink quilted dressing gown, her hair in curlers.

"Good evening, Mrs. Berko-Boyler," I said.

"Is it?" she said with a snarl. "Is it *really*?"

"We'll be about an hour," explained Landen, who was more skilled at dealing with our volatile yet oddly helpful neighbor.

"Do you know the last time Mr. Berko-Boyler took me out anywhere?" she asked, scowling at all three of us.

"I've no idea."

"Saturday."

"Well, that's not *that* long ago—"

"Saturday, October the sixth, 1983," she said with a contemptuous sniff, and shuffled past us into the living room. "Nineteen years ago. Makes me sick, I tell you. Hello, Tuesday," she said in a kindlier tone. "Where's your sister?"

We walked down to the tram stop in silence. Friday's lack of interest in the ChronoGuard was a matter not only of annoyance but *surprise.* The Standard History Eventline had him joining the industry three years ago on their Junior Time Scout program, something that he had failed to do despite our efforts and those of the ChronoGuard, which was as concerned as we were. But we couldn't force him either—time was the glue of the cosmos and had to be *eased* apart—push destiny too hard and it had an annoying habit of pushing back. He had to join the ChronoGuard, but it had to be his decision. Every way you looked at it, time was out of joint.

14.

The ChronoGuard

SpecOps-12 is the ChronoGuard, the governmental department dealing with Temporal Stability. Its job is to maintain the integrity of the Standard History Eventline (SHE) and police the time stream against any unauthorized changes or usage. Its most brilliant work is never noticed, as changes in the past always seem to have been that way. Planet-destroying cataclysms generally happen twice a week but are carefully rerouted by skilled ChronoGuard operatives. The citizenry never notices a thing—which is just as well, really.

The ChronoGuard had its regional offices in the old SpecOps building where I had worked at SO-27, the Literary Detectives. It was a large, no-nonsense Germanic design that had certainly seen better days. Landen and I walked into what had once been the main debriefing room, Friday shuffling in behind us, hands thrust deeply in his pockets and head nodding to the beat of his Walkman. Of course, this being the ChronoGuard, they already had a list of attendees from the forms we'd filled out at the end of the evening, which seemed to work quite well until a couple with a spotty kid in front of us found they weren't on the list.

"Oh, dear," said the woman at the registration desk in an apologetic tone. "But it seems that you don't stay until the end of the presentation, so we've been unable to include you in the registration process. You're going to have to come to the next careers presentation in six months' time."

The father of the group scratched his head for a moment, stopped to say something, thought better of it and then departed, arguing with his wife.

"Mr. and Mrs. Parke-Laine-Next and their son, Friday," I said to the woman, who blinked for a few seconds, looked at Friday, gave a shy smile and then started to chatter and gush in a most unseemly manner.

"Mr. Next—Friday—how do you do? I've wanted to meet you again for the first time. May I shake you by the hand and congratulate you on—"

She stopped, realized she was being a bit previous and making a fool of herself, so coughed in an embarrassed manner before smoothing her skirt absently and sitting down again.

"Sorry. Welcome to the presentation. Here are your badges and your information pack. If you would like to go in, Captain Scintilla will join you soon."

We dutifully took our seats, and Friday slouched in a very obvious don't-give-a-monkey's manner until I told him to sit up straight, which he didn't like but sat up nonetheless.

"What are we doing here?" he asked in a bored voice. "And why the time industry? What about plumbing or something?"

"Because your grandfather was a time operative."

"Yeah," he grunted, "and look what happened to him."

Landen and I exchanged glances. Friday was right. Ending up not having existed wasn't a terrific end to a promising career.

"Well!" said a youthful-looking man in the pale blue uniform of the ChronoGuard who up until now had been helping escort the previous group out of the room. "My name is Captain Bendix Scintilla, and I am head of ChronoGuard Recruitment. I'd like to welcome all of you to this ChronoGuard careers presentation and hope that this short talk might go some way toward explaining what it is that we done. Did. *Do.* Anyhow, my aims are twofold: secondly, to try to demonstrate to the young people here that a career in the time industry is a very exciting prospect indeed and, firstly, to lift the lid on the Temporal Trade and explode a few common myths and misunderstandings. As I'm about to say, did say or would say, my name is Bendix Scintilla, and I was died on March sixteenth, 3291. I'm twenty-three years old in my own personal time, seven hundred and twenty-six in my elapsed work time, and you meet me twenty-seven percent through my life."

He smiled, unaware that he was making very little sense. I was used to it, but by the manner in which the rest of the audience members were scratching their heads and looking at one another, they weren't. Bendix picked up a solid bar of yellow plastic that was about three feet long, two inches wide and domed at either end.

"Does anyone know what this is?" he asked. There was silence, so he passed it to the nearest family and told them to pass it on. "Anyone who can guess wins a prize."

The first family shrugged and passed it to us. Friday gave it the most cursory of glances, and I passed it on.

"Yes, sir?" asked Bendix, pointing to a man in the front row who was with his painfully thin wife and a pair of geeky-looking twins.

"Me?" said the man in a confused voice.

"Yes. I understand you have a question? Sorry, I should have explained. To save time I thought I'd ask you *before* you actually raised your hand."

"Oh!" said the man, and then he shrugged and said, "I was wondering, since we were told this was the only open day for six months, just who the previous group filing out of the door was—and why were they looking at us in that extremely inquisitive manner?"

"Why, that was *you* good people, of course! In order not to keep you from your busy schedules, this meeting actually takes no time at all. The moment you arrived was precisely the time you left, only out the other entrance so you wouldn't meet yourselves."

As soon as he said it, a twitter of understanding and wonderment went through the small group. I'd experienced the ChronoGuard in the past, so these sorts of cheap parlor tricks didn't impress me, but for many of the people present, to whom time was immutable, it was something new and exciting. Scintilla had been doing this show for many years and knew how to get an audience's attention.

"Time is odd," said Bendix, "*very* odd. It's odder than almost anything you can think of. What you *consider* the usual march of time—effect rather quaintly following cause and so forth—is actually a useful illusion, impressed upon you by rules of physics so *very* benign that we consider them devised by Something Awfully Friendly indeed; if it weren't for time, everything would happen at the same instant and existence would become tiresomely frenetic and be over very quickly. But before we get into all that, let's have a show of hands to see who is actually considering a career in time?"

Quite a few hands went up, but Friday's was not among them. I noticed Scintilla staring in our direction as he asked, and he seemed put out by Friday's intransigence.

"Yes, miss, you have a question?"

He pointed to a young girl sitting in the back row with her expensive-looking parents.

"How did you know I was going to ask a question?"

"That was your question, wasn't it?"

"Um . . . yes."

"Because you've already asked it."

"I haven't."

"Actually, you *have*. Everything that makes up what you call the present is in reality the long distant past. The *actual* present is in what you regard as the far-distant future. All of this happened a long time ago and is recorded in the Standard History Eventline, so we know what will happen and can see when things happen that weren't *meant* to. You and I and everything in this room are actually ancient history—but if that seems a bit depressing, let me assure you that these really *are* the good old days. Yes, madam?"

A woman just next to us hadn't put up her hand, of course, but was clearly thinking of it.

"So how is it possible to move through time?"

"The force that pushes the fabric of time along is the past attempting to catch up with the future in order to reach an equilibrium. Think of it as a wave—and where the past starts to break over the future in front of it, that's the present. At that moment of temporal instability is a vortex—a *tube,* in surfing parlance—that runs perpendicular to the arrow of time but leads to everything that has ever happened or ever will happen. Of course, that's greatly simplified, but with skill, training, a really good uniform and a bit of aptitude, you'll learn to ride the tube as it ripples through the fabric of space-time. Yes, sir?"

A young lad in the front row was the next to ask a question.

"How can you surf a time wave that is squillions of years in the future?"

"Because it isn't. It's everywhere, all at once. Time is like a river, with the source, body and mouth all existing at the same time."

Friday turned to me and said in a very unsubtle whisper, "Is this going to take long?"

"Keep quiet and pay attention."

He looked heavenward, sighed audibly and slouched deeper in his chair.

Scintilla carried on, "The time industry is an equal-opportunity employer, has its own union of Federated Timeworkers and a pay structure with overtime payments and bonuses. The working week is forty hours, but each hour is only fifty-two minutes long. Time-related holidays are a perk of the service and can be undertaken after the first ten years' employment. And also, to make it *really* attractive, we will give each new recruit a Walkman and vouchers to buy ten CDs of your—"

He stopped talking, because Friday had put up his hand. We noticed that the other members of the ChronoGuard were staring in dumb wonderment at Friday. The reason wasn't altogether clear until it suddenly struck me: *Scintilla hadn't known that Friday was going to ask a question.*

"You . . . have a question?"

"I do. The question is, 'Tell me the question I'm going to ask.'"

Scintilla gave a nervous laugh and looked around the audience in an uncomfortable manner. Eventually he hazarded a guess:

"You . . . want to know where the toilet is?"

"No. I wanted to know if everything we do is preordained."

Scintilla gave out another shrill, nervous laugh. Friday was a natural, and they all knew it. The thing was, I think Friday did, too—but didn't care.

"A good point and, as you just demonstrated, not at all. Your question was what we call a 'free radical,' an anomalous event that exists independent of the Standard History Eventline, or SHE. Generally, SHE is the one that must be obeyed, but time also has an annoying propensity for random flexibility. Like rivers, time starts and finishes in generally the same place. Certain events—like gorges and rapids—tend to stay the same. However, on the flat temporal plain, the timestream can meander quite considerably, and when it moves toward danger, it's up to us to change something in the event-past to swing the timestream back on course. It's like navigation on the open seas, really, only the ship stays still and you navigate the storm."

He smiled again. "But I'm getting ahead of myself. Apocalypse avoidance is only one area of our expertise. Patches of bad time that open spontaneously need to be stitched closed, ChronoTheft is very big in the seventh millennium, and the total eradication of the Dark Ages by a timephoon is requiring a considerable amount of effort to repair, and—"

He stopped talking, because Friday had inexplicably raised his hand once again.

"Why don't you tell us about the downside?" asked Friday in a sullen voice from beneath a curtain of hair. "About time aggregations and leaks in the gravity suits that leave cadets a molecule thick?"

"That's why we're here," explained Scintilla, attempting to make light of the situation, "to clear up any small matters of misrepresentation that you might have heard. I won't try to convince you that accidents haven't happened, but like all industries we take health and safety very seriously."

"Son," I said, laying a hand on his arm, "hear what he has to say first."

Friday turned and parted his long hair so I could see his eyes. They were intelligent, bright—and *scared.*

"Mum, you told me about the accidents—about Dad's eradication and Filbert Snood. Why do you want me to work for an industry that seems to leave its workers dead, nonexistent or old before their time?"

He got up and made for the exit, and we followed him as Scintilla attempted to carry on his talk, although firmly rattled. But as we tried to leave, a ChronoGuard operative stood in our way.

"I think you should stay and listen to the presentation," he said, addressing Friday, who told him to get stuffed. The Chrono took exception to this and made a grab for him, but I was quicker and caught the guard's wrist, pulled him around and had him on the floor with his arm behind his back.

"Muumm!" whined Friday, more embarrassed than outraged. "Do you have to? People are *watching*!"

"Sorry," I said, letting go of the guard. Scintilla had excused himself from his talk and came over to see what was going on.

"If we want to leave, we leave," growled Landen.

"Of course!" agreed Scintilla, motioning with a flick of his head for the Chrono to move off. "You can go whenever you want." He looked at me; he knew how important it was to get Friday inducted, and knew I knew it, too.

"But before you go," he said, "Friday, I want you to know that we would be very happy to have you join the time industry. No minimum academic qualifications, no entrance exam. It's an unconditional offer—the first we've ever made."

"And what makes you think I'd be any good at it?"

"You can ask questions that aren't already lodged in the SHE. Do you think just *anyone* can do that?"

He shrugged. "I'm not interested."

"I'm just asking for you to stay and hear what we have to say."

"I'm . . . not . . . interested," replied Friday more forcefully.

"Listen," said Scintilla, after looking around furtively and lowering his voice, "this is a bit unofficial, but I've had a word with Wayne Skunk, and he's agreed to let you play a guitar riff on the second track of *Hosing the Dolly*."

"It's too late," said Friday, "it's already been recorded."

Bendix stared at him. "Yes—and by *you*."

"I never did anything of the sort!"

"No, but you *might*. And since *that* possibility exists, you did. Whether you *actually* do is up to you, but either way you can have that one on us. It's your solo in any case. Your name is already in the liner notes."

Friday looked at Scintilla, then at me. I knew how much he loved Strontium Goat, and Scintilla knew, too. He had Friday's complete service record, after all. But Friday wasn't interested. He didn't like being pushed, cajoled, bullied or bribed. I couldn't blame him—I hated it, too, and he was my son, after all.

"You think you can *buy* me?" he said finally, and left without another word.

"I'll catch up," I said as he walked out with Landen.

While the swinging doors shut noisily behind them, Scintilla said to me, "Do I need to emphasize how important it is that Friday joins the ChronoGuard as soon as possible? He should have signed up three years ago and be surfing the timestream by now."

"You may have to wait a little longer, Bendix."

"That's just it," he replied. "We don't have much time."

"I thought you had all the time there was."

He took me by the arm, and we moved to a corner of the room.

"Thursday—can I call you Thursday?—we're facing a serious crisis in the time industry, and as far as we know, Friday's leadership several trillion bang/crunch cycles from now is the only thing that we can depend on—his truculence at this end of time means his desk is empty at the other."

"But there's *always* a crisis in time, Bendix."

"Not like this. This isn't a crisis *in* time—it's a crisis *of* time. We've been pushing the frontiers of time forward for trillions upon trillions of years, and in a little over four days we'll have reached the . . . End of Time."

"And that's bad, right?"

Bendix laughed. "Of course not! Time has to end *somewhere.* But there's a problem with the very mechanism that controls the way we've been scooting around the here and now for most of eternity."

"And that is?"

He looked left and right and lowered his voice. "*Time travel has yet to be invented!* And with the entire multiverse one giant hot ball of superheated gas contracting at incalculable speed into a point one trillion-trillionth the size of a neutron, it's not likely to be."

"Wait, wait," I said, trying to get this latest piece of information into my head. "I know that the whole time travel thing makes very little logical sense, but you must have machines that enable you to move through time, right?"

"Of course—but we've got no idea how they work, who built them or when. We've been running the entire industry on something we call 'retro-deficit-engineering.' We use the technology *now,* safe in the assumption that it will be invented in the *future.* We did the same with the Gravitube in the fifties and the microchip ten years ago—neither of them actually gets invented for over ten thousand years, but it helps us more to have them *now.*"

"Let me get this straight," I said slowly. "You're using technology you don't have—like me overspending on my credit card."

"Right. And we've searched every single moment in case it *was* invented and we hadn't noticed. Nothing. Zip. Nada. *Rien.*"

His shoulders slumped, and he ran his fingers through his hair.

"Listen, if Friday doesn't retake his seat at the head of the ChronoGuard and use his astonishing skills to somehow save us, then everything that we've worked toward will be undone as soon as we hit Time Zero."

"I think I get it. Then why is Friday not following his destined career?"

"I've no idea. We always had him down as dynamic and aggressively inquisitive when he was a child—what happened?"

I shrugged. "All kids are like that today. It's a modern thing, caused by too much TV, video games and other instant-gratification bullshit. Either that—or kids are *exactly* the same and I'm getting crusty and intolerant in my old age. Listen, I'll do what I can."

Scintilla thanked me, and I joined Friday and Landen outside.

"I don't want to work in the time industry, Mum. I'd only break some dumb rule and end up eradicated."

"My eradication was pretty painless," reflected Landen. "In fact, if your mother hadn't told me about it, I never would have known it happened."

"That doesn't help, Dad," grumbled Friday. "You were reactualized—what about Granddad? No one can say whether he exists or not—not even him."

I rested my hand on his shoulder. He didn't pull away this time.

"I know, Sweetpea. And if you don't want to join, no one's going to make you."

He was quiet for a while, then said, "Do you *have* to call me Sweetpea? I'm sixteen."

Landen and I looked at each other, and then we took the tram back home. True to his word, Bendix had slipped us back a few minutes to just before we went in, and as we rattled home in silence, we passed ourselves arriving.

"You know that yellow rod Bendix showed us?" said Friday, staring out the window.

"Yes?"

"It was a half second of snooker ball."

15.

Home Again

Noting with dismay that most cross-religion bickering occurred only because all the major religions were convinced they were the *right* one and every other religion was the *wrong* one, the founders of the Global Standard Deity based their fledgling "portmanteau" faith on the premise that most religions want the same thing once all the shameless, manipulative power play had been subtracted: peace, stability, equality and justice—the same as the nonfaiths. As soon as they found that centralizing thread that unites all people and made a dialogue of sorts with a Being of Supreme Moral Authority mostly optional, the GSD flourished.

Friday went to his room in a huff as soon as we got in. Mrs. Berko-Boyler told us that the girls were fine and that she had folded all the washing, cleaned the kitchen, fed Pickwick and made us all cottage pie. This wasn't unusual for her, and she scoffed at any sort of payment, then shuffled off home, muttering darkly about how if she'd killed her husband when she'd first thought of it, she'd be "out of prison by now."

"Where's Jenny?" I asked Landen, having just gone upstairs to check. "She's not in her room."

"She was just in the kitchen."

The phone rang, and I picked it up.

"Hello?"

"It's Millon," came a soft voice, "and I'm sorry to call you at home."

"Where are you?"

"Look out the window."

I did as he asked and saw him wave from his usual spot between the compost heap and the laurels. Millon de Floss, it should be explained, was my official stalker. Even though I had long ago dropped to the bottom of the Z-class celebrity list, he had insisted on maintaining his benign stalkership because, as he explained it, "we all need a retirement hobby." Since he had shown considerable fortitude during a sojourn into the Elan back in '88, I now counted him as a family friend, something that he always denied, when asked. "Friendship," he intoned soberly, "always damages the pest factor that is the essence of the bond between stalker and stalkee." None of the kids were bothered by him at all, and his early-warning capabilities were actually very helpful—he'd spotted Felix8, after all. Not that stalking was his sole job, of course. Aside from fencing cheese to the east of Swindon, he edited *Conspiracy Theorist* magazine and worked on my official biography, something that was taking longer than we had both thought.

"So what's the problem? You still up for the cheese buy this evening?" I asked him.

"Of course—but you've got visitors. A car on the street with two men in it and another man climbing over the back wall."

I thanked him and put the phone down. I'd made a few enemies in the past, so Landen and I had some prearranged contingency measures.

"Problems?" asked Landen.

"It's a code yellow."

Landen understood and without a word dashed off toward the front of the house. I opened the back door and crept out into the garden, took the side passage next to the dustbins and slipped behind the summerhouse. I didn't have to wait long, as a man wearing a black coverall and a balaclava helmet came tiptoeing up the path toward where I was hidden. He was carrying a sack and a bag of marshmallows. I didn't waste any time on pleasantries; I simply whacked him hard on the chin with my fist, and when he staggered, momentarily stunned, I thumped him in the chest, and he fell over backward with a grunt. I pulled off the balaclava to reveal a man I recognized—it was Arthur Plunkett of the Swindon Dodo Fanciers Guild.

"For GSD's sake, Arthur," I said, "how many times do I have to tell you that Pickwick's not for sale?"

"Uuuuh," he said, groaning and wheezing as he tried to regain his wind.

"Come on, idiot," I said as I heaved him up and rested him against the back of the summerhouse. "You know better than to break into my house—I can be dangerously protective of my family. Why do you think I'm the only one in Swindon able to leave my car unlocked at night?"

"Ooooooh."

"Wait here," I said to him, and trotted back indoors. I could be dangerous, but then so could Landen, even with one leg. The front door was open, and I could see him hiding behind the privet hedge. I ran low across the lawn and joined him.

"It's only dodo fanciers," I hissed.

"Again?" he replied. "After what happened last time?"

I nodded. Clearly, Pickwick's Version 1.2 rarity was a prize worth risking a lot for. I looked across the road to where a Buick was parked by the curb. The two men inside were wearing dark glasses and making a lot of effort to be inconspicuous.

"Shall we stop them?"

"No," giggled Landen. "They won't get far."

"What have you done?" I asked in my serious voice.

"You'll see."

As we watched, Arthur Plunkett decided to make a run for it—well, a hobble for it, actually—and came out through the gate and limped across the road. The driver of the car started up the engine, waited until Plunkett had thrown himself in the back, then pulled rapidly away from the curb. They got about twenty feet before the cable that Landen had tied around their rear axle whipped tight and, secured to a lamppost at the other end and far too strong to snap, it tore the axle and most of the suspension clear from the back of the car, which then almost pitched up onto its nose before falling with a crunch in the middle of the road. After a short pause, the three men climbed shakily out of the car and then legged it off down the street, Plunkett behind.

"Was that *really* necessary?" I asked.

"Not at all," admitted Landen through a series of childish giggles. "But I'd always wanted to try it."

"I wish you two would grow up."

We looked up. My brother Joffy and his partner, Miles, were staring at us over the garden gate.

"I don't know what you mean," I said, getting up from where we'd been crouched behind the hedge and giving Landen a heave to get him on his feet. "It's just a normal evening in Swindon." I looked around, as the neighbors had come out to gawk at the wreck of the Buick and motioned Joffy and Miles inside. "Come on in for a cup of tea."

"No tea," said Joffy as we walked into the house. "We've just had a tankerful at Mum's—can't you hear me slosh as I walk?"

"And enough Battenberg cake to fill the Grand Canyon," added Miles in a stuffed-with-cake sort of voice.

"How's the carpet business, Doofus?" asked Joffy as we stood in the hall.

"Couldn't be better—how's the faith-unification business?"

"We've *nearly* got everyone," said Joffy with a smile. "The atheists came on board last week. Once we'd suggested that 'god' could be a set of essentially beneficent physical rules of the cosmos, they were only too happy to join. In fact, apart from a few scattered remnants of faith leaders who can't quite come to terms with the loss of their power, influence and associated funny hats, it's all looking pretty good."

Joffy's nominal leadership of the British Archipelago Branch of the Global Standard Deity was a matter of considerable import within the Next family. The GSD was proposed by delegates of the 1978 Global Interfaith Symposium and had gathered momentum since then, garnering converts from all the faiths into one diverse religion that was flexible enough to offer something for everyone.

"I'm amazed you managed to convert them all," I said.

"It wasn't a *conversion*," he replied, "it was a *unification*."

"And you are here now because . . . ?"

"Landen said he'd videotape *Dr. Who* for me, and the Daleks are my favorite."

"I'm more into the Sontarans myself," said Miles.

"Humph!" said Joffy. "It's what I would expect from someone who thinks Jon Pertwee was the best Doctor."

Landen and I stared at him, unsure of whether we should agree, postulate a different theory—or what.

"It was Tom Baker," said Joffy, ending the embarrassed silence. Miles made a noise that sounded like "conventionalist," and Landen went off to fetch the tape.

"Doofus?" whispered Joffy when Landen had gone.

"Yes?"

"Have you told him?"

"No," I whispered back.

"You can't *not* tell him, Thursday—if you don't tell him the truth about the BookWorld and Acme Carpets, it's like you're—I don't know—lying to him."

"It's for his own good," I hissed. "It's not like I'm having an affair or something."

"Are you?"

"No, of course not!"

"It's still a lie, sister dearest. How would you like it if he lied to you about what he did all day?"

"I daresay I'd not like it. Leave it to me, Joff—I'll be fine."

"I hope so. Happy birthday—and in case you hadn't noticed, there's some Camembert on fire in the hood of your Acme Carpets van."

"Some what?"

"Camembert. On fire."

"Here it is," said Landen, returning with a video. "'Remembrance of the Daleks.' Where did Thursday go?"

"Oh, she just nipped out for something. Well, must be off! People to educate, persuade and unify—hopefully in that order. Ha-ha-ha."

"Sorry about that," I said, coming back from outside. "I thought I saw Pickwick make faces at the cat next door—you know how they hate each other."

"But she's over there," said Landen, pointing to where Pickwick was still struggling to look at herself and her blue-and-white stripy sweater in the mirror.

I shrugged. "Must have been another dodo."

"*Is* there another bald dodo in the neighborhood with a blue stripy cardigan? And can you smell burning cheese?"

"No," I said innocently. "What about you, Joff?"

"I've got to go," he repeated, staring at his watch. "Remember what I said, sister dearest!"

And he and Miles walked off toward the crowd that had started to gather around the wrecked car.

"I swear I can smell burning cheese," said Landen as I shut the front door.

"Probably Mrs. Berko-Boyler cooking next door."

Outwardly I was worry-free, but inside I was more nervous. A chunk of burning Camembert on your doorstep meant only one thing: a warning from the Swindon Old Town Cheese Mafia—or, as they liked to be known, the Stiltonistas.

16.

Cheese

The controversial Milk Levy from which the unpopular Cheese Duty is derived was imposed in 1970 by the then Whig government, which needed to raise funds for a potential escalation of war in the Crimea. With the duty now running at 1,530 percent on hard and 1,290 percent on smelly, illegal cheese making and smuggling had become a very lucrative business indeed. The Cheese Enforcement Agency was formed not only to supervise the licensing of cheese but also to collect the tax levied on it by an overzealous government. Small wonder that there was a thriving underground cheese market.

"Thanks for tipping us the wink about the dodo fanciers," I said as we drove through the darkened streets of Swindon two hours later. A tow truck had removed the wreckage of the fanciers' car, and the police had been around to collect statements. Despite its being a busy neighborhood, no one had seen anything. They had, of course, but the Parke-Laine-Nexts were quite popular in the area.

"Are you sure we weren't followed?" asked Millon as we pulled up outside an empty industrial unit not a stone's throw from the city's airship field.

"Positive," I replied. "Have you got buyers for it?"

"The usual cheeseheads are all champing at the bit, recipes at the ready. The evening air will be rich with the scent of Welsh rarebit tonight."

A large seventy-seat airship rose slowly into the sky behind the factory units. We watched while its silver flanks caught the colors of the late-evening sun as it turned and, with its four propellers beating the still air with a rhythmic hum, set course for Southampton.

"Ready?" I asked.

"Ready," said Millon.

I beeped the horn twice, and the steel shutters were slowly raised on the nearest industrial unit.

"Tell me," said Millon, "why do you think the Old Town Stiltonistas gave you the flaming Camembert?"

"A warning, perhaps. But we've never bothered them, and they've never bothered us."

"Our two territories don't even overlap," he observed. "Do you think the Cheese Enforcement Agency is getting bolder?"

"Perhaps."

"You don't seem very worried."

"The CEA is underfunded and knows nothing. Besides, we have customers to attend to—and Acme needs the cash. Think you can liberate five grand by tomorrow morning?"

"Depends what they've got," he said after a moment's reflection. "If they're trying to peddle common-or-garden Cheddaresque or that processed crap, then we could be in trouble. But if they've got something exotic, then no problem at all."

The roller shutter was high enough to let us in by now, and we drove inside, the shutter reversing direction to close behind us.

We climbed out of the van. The industrial unit was empty except for a large Welsh-registered Griffin-V8 truck, a long table with leather sample cases lying on it and four men wearing black suits with black ties and sunglasses and looking vaguely menacing. It was all bravado, of course—Scorsese movies were big in the Welsh Republic. I tried to see by the swing of their jackets if any of them were packing heat and guessed that they weren't. I'd only carried a gun once in the real world since SpecOps was disbanded and hoped I never had to again. Cheese smuggling was still a polite undertaking. As soon as it turned ugly, I was out.

"Owen Pryce the Cheese," I said in a genial manner, greeting the leader of the group with a smile and a firm handshake, "good to see you again. I trust the trip across the border was uneventful?"

"It's getting a lot harder these days," he replied in a singsong Welsh accent that betrayed his roots in the south of the republic, probably Abertawe. "There are dutymen everywhere, and the bribes I have to pay are reflected in the price of the goods."

"As long as it's fair price, Pryce," I replied pleasantly. "My clients love cheese, but there's a limit to what they'll pay."

We were both lying, but it was the game we played. My clients would pay good money for high-quality cheese, and as likely as not he didn't bribe anyone. The border with Wales was 170 miles long and had more holes than a hastily matured Emmentaler. There weren't enough dutymen to cover it all, and to be honest, although it was illegal, no one took cheese smuggling that seriously.

Pryce nodded to one of his compatriots, and they opened the sample cases with a flourish. It was all there—every single make of cheese you could imagine, from pure white to dark amber. Crumbly, hard, soft, liquid, gas. The rich aroma of well-matured cheese escaped into the room, and I felt my taste buds tingle. This was top-quality shit—the best available.

"Smells good, Pryce."

He said nothing and showed me a large slab of white cheese. "Caerphilly," he said, "the best. We can—"

I put up a hand to stop him. "The punks can deal with the mild stuff, Pryce. We're interested in Level 3.8 and above."

He shrugged, set the Caerphilly down and picked up a small chunk of creamy-colored cheese.

"Quintuple Llanboidy," he announced, "a 5.2. It'll play on your taste buds like the plucked strings of a harp."

"We'll have the usual of that, Pryce," I muttered, "but my clients are into something a little stronger. What else you got?"

We always went through this charade. My specialty was the volatile cheese market, and when I say volatile, I don't mean the market—I mean the cheese.

Pryce nodded and showed me a golden yellow cheese that had veins of red running through it.

"Quadruple-strength Dolgellau Veinclotter," he announced. "It's a 9.5. Matured in Blaenafon for eighteen years and not for the fainthearted. Good on crackers but can function equally well as an amorous-skunk repellent."

I took a daringly large amount and popped it on my tongue. The taste was extraordinary; I could almost *see* the Cambrian Mountains just visible in the rain, low clouds, gushing water and limestone crags, frost-shattered scree and—

"Are you all right?" said Millon when I opened my eyes. "You passed out for a moment there."

"Kicks like a mule, doesn't it?" said Pryce kindly. "Have a glass of water."

"Thank you. We'll take all you have—what else you got?"

"Mynachlog-ddu Old Contemptible," said Pryce, showing me a whitish crumbly cheese. "It's kept in a glass jar because it will eat through cardboard or steel. Don't leave it in the air too long, as it will start dogs howling."

"We'll have thirty kilos. What about this one?" I asked, pointing at an innocuous-looking ivory-colored soft cheese.

"Ystradgynlais Molecular Unstable Brie," announced Pryce, "a soft cheese we've cloned from our cheese-making brethren in France—but every bit as good. Useful as a contact anesthetic or a paint stripper, it can cure insomnia and ground to dust is a very useful self-defense against muggers and wandering bears. It has a half-life of twenty-three days, glows in the dark and can be used as a source of X-rays."

"We'll take the lot. Got anything *really* strong?"

Pryce raised an eyebrow, and his minders looked at one another uneasily. "Are you sure?"

"It's not for me," I said hastily, "but we've got a few serious cheeseheads who can take the hard stuff."

"We've got some Machynlleth Wedi Marw."

"What the hell's that?"

"It's what you asked for—*really* strong cheese. It'll bring you up in a rash just by looking at it. Denser than enriched plutonium, two grams can season enough macaroni and cheese for eight hundred men. The smell alone will corrode iron. A concentration in air of only seventeen parts per million will bring on nausea and unconsciousness within twenty seconds. Our chief taster ate a half ounce by accident and was dead to the world for six hours. Open only out of doors, and even then only with a doctor's certificate and well away from populated areas. It's not really a cheese for eating—it's more for encasing in concrete and dumping in the ocean a long way from civilization."

I looked at Millon, who nodded. There was *always* someone stupid enough to experiment. After all, no one had ever died from cheese ingestion. Yet.

"Let us have a half pound, and we'll see what we can do with it."

"Very well," said Pryce. He nodded to a colleague, who opened another suitcase and gingerly took out a sealed lead box. He laid it gently on the table and then took a hurried step backward.

"You won't attempt to open it until we're at least thirty miles away, will you?" Pryce asked.

"We'll do our best."

"Actually, I'd advise you not to open it at all."

"Thanks for the advice."

The trading went on in this manner for another half hour, and with our order book full and the cost totted up, we transported the cheese from their truck to the Acme van, whose springs groaned under the weight.

"What's that?" I asked, pointing at a wooden crate in the back of their truck. It was securely fixed to the floor with heavy chains.

"That's nothing," Pryce said quickly, his henchmen moving together to try to block my view.

"Something you're not showing us?"

Pryce took me by the arm as they slammed the rear doors and threw the latch.

"You've always been a good customer, Ms. Next, but we know what you will and won't do, and this cheese is not for you."

"Strong?"

He wouldn't answer me.

"It's been nice doing business with you, Ms. Next. Same time next month?"

"Yes," I said slowly, wondering just how strong a cheese has to be before you've got to keep it chained down. More interestingly, the box was stenciled with the code X-14.

I handed over the Welsh cash, it was swiftly counted, and before I knew it, Owen Pryce and his marginally threatening flunkies had revved up the truck and vanished into the night, off to sell cheese to the Stiltonistas in the Old Town. I always got first dibs—that was probably what the flaming Camembert was all about.

"Did you see that cheese chained up in the back?" I asked Millon as we got back into the van.

"No—what cheese?"

"Nothing."

I started the van, and we drove out of the industrial estate. This was the point at which the CEA would have pounced if they'd have known what was going on, but they didn't. All was quiet in the town, and within a few minutes Millon had dropped me off at home, taking the Acme van himself to start peddling the cheese.

I had only just opened the garden gate when I noticed a figure standing in the shadows. I instinctively moved to grab my pistol, before remembering that I didn't carry one in the Outland anymore. I needn't have worried: It was Spike.

"You made me jump!"

"Sorry," he replied soberly. "I came to ask you if you wanted any help disposing of the body."

"I'm sorry?"

"The body. The ground can be hard this time of year."

"*Whose* body?"

"Felix8. You did him in, right?"

"No."

"Then how did he escape? You, me and Stig have the only keys."

"Wait a moment," I said nervously. "Felix8 has *gone*?"

"Completely. Are you *sure* you didn't kill him?"

"I think I would have remembered."

"Well," said Spike, handing me a spade, "you better give this back to Landen, then." I must have looked horrified, because he added, "I told him it was to plant some garlic. Listen, you get inside and keep the doors and windows locked—I'll be in my car across the street if you need me."

I went into the house and locked the door securely behind me. Felix8 was a worry, but not tonight—I had a complimentary block of Llangloffan, and nothing was going to come between me and Landen's unbeatable macaroni and cheese.

17.

Breakfast Again

Commonsense Party leader Redmond van de Poste, MP, succeeded Chancellor Yorrick Kaine in the hastily called elections of 1988, changed the job title back to "prime minister" and announced a series of innovative policies. For a start he insisted that democracy, while a good idea for a good idea, was potentially vulnerable to predation by the greedy, egotistical and insane, so his plan to *democratize* democracy was ruthlessly implemented. There were initial issues regarding civil liberties, but now, fourteen years later, we were beginning to accrue the benefits.

The news on the radio that morning was devoted—once again—to the ongoing crisis of the week—namely, where the nation's stupidity surplus could be discharged safely. Some suggested a small war in a distant country against a race of people we weren't generally disposed toward, but others thought this too risky and favored crippling the efficiency of the public services by adding a new layer of bureaucracy at huge expense and little benefit. Not all suggestions were sensible: Fringe elements of the debate maintained that the nation should revitalize the stupendously costly Anti-Smite Shield project. Designed to protect mankind—or at least England—against the potential threat by an enraged deity eager to cleanse a sinful race with a rain of fire, the shield project would have the twin benefits of profligate waste of good cash plus the possibility that other European nations could be persuaded to join and thus deal with Europe's combined stupidity excess in one fell swoop.

Prime Minister Redmond van de Poste took the unusual step of speaking on live radio to not only reject all the suggestions but also to make the inflammatory statement that despite the escalating surplus they would continue the Commonsense approach to government. When asked how the stupidity surplus might be reduced, Van de Poste replied that he was certain something would come along that "would be fantastically dim-witted but economical," and added that as a conciliatory dumb measure to appease his critics they would be setting fire to a large quantity of rubber tires for no very good purpose. This last remark was met with a cry of "too little, too late" from Mr. Alfredo Traficcone of the opposition Prevailing Wind Party, which was gradually gaining ground promoting policies of "immediate gain," something that Mr. Traficcone said was "utterly preferable to the hideously long-sighted policies of cautious perceptiveness."

"What a load of old poo," said Landen, giving Tuesday a boiled egg for breakfast and putting one in front of Jenny's place, then yelling up the stairs to her that breakfast was on the table.

"What time did Friday get in last night?" I asked, since I had gone to bed first.

"Past midnight. He said he was making noise with his mates."

"The Gobshites?"

"I think so, but they might as well be called the Feedbacks and working on the single 'Static' from the *White Noise* album."

"It's only because we're old and fuddy-duddy," I said, resting an affectionate hand on his. "I'm sure the music we listened to was as much crap to our parents as his music is to us."

But Landen was elsewhere. He was composing an outline for a self-help book for dogs, called *Yes, You CAN Open the Door Yourself,* and was thus functionally deaf to everything.

"Land, I'm sleeping with the milkman."

He didn't look up, but said, "That's nice, darling."

Tuesday and I laughed, and I turned to look at her with an expression of faux shock and said, "What are you laughing about? You shouldn't know anything about milkmen!"

"Mum," she said with a mixture of precocity and matter-of-factness, "I have an IQ of two hundred and eighty and know more about everything than you do."

"I doubt it."

"Then what does the ischiocavernosus muscle do?"

"Okay, you *do* know more than I do. Where is Jenny? She's *always* late for breakfast!"

I took the tram toward the old SpecOps Building to do some investigations. The escape of Felix8 was fresh in my mind, and several times I saw someone who I thought was him, but on each occasion it was a harmless passerby. I still had no idea how he had escaped, but one thing I *did* know was that the Hades family had some pretty demonic attributes, and they looked after their friends. Felix8, loathsome cur that he was, would have been considered a friend. If he was still in their pay, then I would have to speak to a member of the Hades family. It had to be Aornis: the only one in custody.

I got off the tram at the Town Hall and walked down the hill to the SpecOps Building. It was eerily deserted as I stepped in, a strong contrast to the hive of activity that I had known. I was issued a visitor's badge and headed off down the empty corridors toward the ChronoGuard's office. Not the briefing hall we had visited the previous evening but a small room on the second floor. I'd been here on a number of occasions, so knew what to expect—as I watched, the decor and furniture changed constantly, the ChronoGuard operatives themselves jumping in and out, their speed making them into little more than smears of light. There was one piece of furniture that remained unchanged while all about raced, moved and blurred in a never-ending jumble. It was a small table with an old candlestick telephone upon it, and as I put out my hand, it rang. I picked up the phone and held the earpiece to my ear.

"Mrs. Parke-Laine-Next?" came a voice.

"Yes?"

"He'll be right down."

And in an instant he was. The room stopped moving from one time to the next and froze with a decor that looked vaguely contemporary. There was a figure at the desk who smiled when he saw me. But it wasn't Bendix or my father—it was *Friday*. Not the mid-twenties Friday I'd met at my wedding bash or the old Friday I'd met during the Samuel Pepys Fiasco but a young Friday—almost indistinguishable from the one who was still fast asleep at home, snoring loudly in the pit of despair we called his bedroom.

"Hi, Mum!"

"Hi, Sweetpea," I said, deeply confused and also kind of relieved. This was the Friday I thought I was meant to have—clean-cut, well presented, confident and with an infectious smile that reminded me of Landen. And he probably bathed more than once a fortnight, too.

"How old are you?" I asked, placing a hand on his chin to make sure he was real, and not a phantasm or something, like Mycroft. He *was* real. Warm and still needing to shave only once a week.

"I'm sixteen, Mum, the same age as the lazy slob asleep at home. In a context that you'd understand, I'm a *Potential* Friday. I started with the Junior Time Scouts at thirteen and popped my first tube at fifteen—the youngest ever to do so. The Friday you know is the Friday *Present*. The older me that will hopefully be the director-general is the Friday *Last*, and because he's indisposed due to a mild temporal ambiguity caused by the younger alternative me not joining the Time Scouts, Bendix reconstituted me from the echoes of the might-have-been. They asked me to see what I can do."

"Nope," I replied in some confusion, "didn't understand a word."

"It's a split-timeline thing, Mum," explained Friday, "in which two versions of the same person can exist at the same time."

"So can't *you* become the director-general at the other end of time?"

"Not that easy. The alternative timelines have to be in concurrence to go forward to a mutually compatible future."

I understood—sort of.

"I guess this means you haven't invented time travel yet?"

"Nope. Any idea why the other me is such a slouch?"

"I asked you to join the Time Scouts three years ago, but you couldn't be bothered," I murmured by way of explanation. "You were too busy playing on computer games and watching TV."

"I don't blame you or Dad. Something's seriously out of joint, but I don't know what. Friday Present seems to have the intelligence but not the pizzazz to want to do anything."

"Except play the guitar in the Gobshites."

"If you can call it playing," said Friday with an unkind laugh.

"Don't be so—" I checked myself. If this wasn't self-criticism, I didn't know what was.

All of a sudden, there was *another* Friday standing next to Potential Friday. He was identical, except he was carrying a manila folder. They looked at each other curiously. The newest Friday said "Sorry" in an embarrassed fashion and walked a little way down the corridor, where he pretended to be interested in the carved wood around the doorframe.

"This morning I only had one son," I muttered despondently. "Now I've got three!"

Friday glanced at the second Friday over his shoulder, who was caught staring at us and quickly looked the other way. "You've only got one, Mum. Don't worry about him."

"So what's gone wrong?" I asked. "Why is Friday Present so unlike Potential Friday?"

"It's difficult to tell. This 2002 isn't like the one in the Standard History Eventline. Everyone seems introspective and lacking in any sort of charisma. It's as though a heavy sky is forcing lassitude on the population—in a word, a *grayness* seems to have spread across the land."

"I know what you mean," I said, shaking my head sadly. "We've seen a sixty percent drop in book readership; it seems no one can be bothered to invest their time in a good novel."

"That would figure," replied Friday thoughtfully. "It's not supposed to be like this, I assure you—the best minds have it as the beginning of the Great Unraveling. If what we suspect is true and time travel isn't invented in the next three and a half days, we might be heading toward a spontaneously accelerated inverse obliteration of all history."

"Can you put that into a carpet metaphor I might understand?"

"If we can't secure our existence right at the beginning, time will start to roll up like a carpet, taking history with it."

"How fast?"

"It will begin slowly at 22:03 on Friday with the obliteration of the earliest fossil record. Ten minutes after that, all evidence of ancient hominids will vanish, swiftly followed by the sudden absence of everything from the middle Holocene. Five minutes later all megalithic structures will vanish as if they'd never been. The pyramids will go in another two minutes, with ancient Greece vanishing soon after. In the course of another minute, the Dark Ages will disappear, and in the next twenty seconds the Norman Conquest will never have happened. In the final twenty-seven seconds, we will see modern history disappear with increased rapidity, until at 22:48 and nine seconds the end of history will catch up with us and there will be nothing left at all, nor any evidence that there was—to all intents and purposes, we won't ever have existed."

"So what's the cause?"

"I've no idea, but I'm going to have a good look around. Did you want something?"

"Oh—yes. I need to speak to Aornis. One of her family's old henchmen is on the prowl—or was."

"Wait a moment."

And in an instant he was gone.

"Ah!" said the other Friday, returning from just up the corridor.

"Sorry about that. Enloopment records are kept in the twelfth millennium, and being accurate to the second on a ten-thousand-year jump is still a bit beyond me."

He opened the manila file and flicked through the contents.

"She's done seven years of a thirty-year looping for unlawful memory distortion," he murmured. "We had to hold her trial in the thirty-seventh century, where it actually *is* a crime. The dubious legality of being tried outside one's own time zone would have been cause for an appeal, but she never lodged one."

"Perhaps she forgot."

"It's possible. Shall we go?"

We stepped outside the SpecOps Building, turned left and walked the short distance to the Brunel Shopping Centre.

"Have you seen anything of my father?" I asked. I hadn't seen him for over a year, not since the last potential life-extinguishing Armageddon anyway.

"I see him flash past from time to time," replied Friday, "but he's a bit of an enigma. Sometimes we're told to hunt him down, and the next moment we're working under him. Sometimes he's even *leading* the hunt for himself. Listen, I'm ChronoGuard and even I can't figure it out. Ah! We're here."

I looked up and frowned. We didn't seem to be "here" anywhere in particular—we were outside T.J. Maxx, the discount clothes store.

18.

Aornis Hades

They called it being "in the loop," but the official name was Closed Loop Temporal Field Containment. It was used only for criminals where there was little hope of rehabilitation, or even contrition. It was run by the ChronoGuard and was frighteningly simple. They popped the convict in an eight-minute repetitive time loop for five, ten, twenty years. The prisoner's body aged but never needed sustenance. It was cruel and unnatural—yet cheap and required no bars, guards or food.

We walked into the Swindon T.J. Maxx, threaded our way through the busy morning bargain hunters and found the manager, a well-dressed woman with an agreeable manner who had been in my class at school but whose name I had forgotten—we always gave polite nods to each other, but nothing more than that. Friday showed her his ID. She smiled and led us to a keypad mounted on the wall. The manager punched in a long series of numbers, and then Friday punched an even *longer* series of numbers. There was a shift in the light to a greeny blue, the manager and all the customers stopped dead in their tracks as time ground to a halt, and a faint buzz replaced the happy murmur of shoppers.

Friday looked at the manila folder he was carrying and then around the store. The illumination was similar to the cool glow you get from underwater lights in a swimming pool, with reflections that danced on the ceiling. Within the bluey greenness of the store's interior, I could see spheres of warm light, and within these there seemed to be some life. We walked past several of these spheres, and I noted that while most of the people inside were dark and indistinct, at least one was more vivid than the rest and looking very much alive—the prisoner.

"She should be at Checkout Six," said Friday, leading the way past a ten-foot-wide translucent yellow sphere that was centered on the chair outside the changing rooms. "That's Reginald Danforth," murmured Friday. "He assassinated Mahatma Winston Smith al Wazeed during his historic speech to the citizens of the World State in 3419. Looped for seven hundred and ninety-eight years in an eight-minute sliver of time where he's waiting for his girlfriend, Trudi, to try on a camisole."

"Does he know he's looped?"

"Of course."

I looked at Danforth, who was staring at the floor and clenching and unclenching his fists in frustration.

"How long's he been in?"

"Thirty-four years. If he tells us who his co-conspirator was, we'll enlarge his loop from eight minutes to fifteen."

"Do you loop people just in stores?"

"We used to use dentists' waiting rooms, bus stops and cinemas during Merchant-Ivory films, as these tended to be natural occurrences of slow time, but there were too many prisoners, so we had to design our own. Temporal-J, Maximum Security—why, what did you think T.J. Maxx was?"

"A place to buy designer-label clothing at reasonable prices?"

He laughed. "The very idea! Next you'll be telling me that IKEA just sells furniture you have to build yourself."

"Isn't it?"

"Of course not. Here she is."

We had approached the checkout, where a sphere of warm light about eighteen feet wide encompassed most of the till and a line of bored-looking shoppers. Right at the back of the queue was a familiar face: Aornis Hades, younger sister of Acheron. She was a Mnemonomorph—someone with the ability to control memories. I'd defeated her good and proper, twice in the real world and once in my head. She was slim, dark and attractive and dressed in the very latest fashion—but only from when she was looped seven years ago. Mind you, because of the vague meanderings of the fashion industry, she'd been in and out of high style twenty-seven times since then and was currently in—although she'd never know it. To a looped individual, time remains the same.

"You know she can control coincidences?"

"Not anymore," replied Friday, with a grimness that I found disconcerting in one so young.

"Who are they?" I asked, pointing at the other women in the line for the checkout.

"They're not prisoners—just real shoppers doing real shopping at the time of her enloopment; Miss Hades is stuck in an eight-minute zone waiting to pay for goods, but she never does. If it's true what they say about her love of shopping, this punishment is *particularly* apt."

"Do I have anything to bargain with?"

Friday looked at the file. "You can stretch her loop by twenty minutes."

"How do I get to talk to her?"

"Just step inside the sphere of influence."

I took a deep breath and walked into the globe of yellow light. All of a sudden, normality returned with a jerk. I was back in what seemed like real life. It was raining outside, which was what must have been happening when she was looped. Aornis, well used to the monotonous round of limited dialogue during her eight-minute existence, noticed me immediately.

"Well, well," she murmured sarcastically, "is it visitors' day already?"

"Hello, Aornis," I said with a smile. "Remember me?"

"Very funny. What do you want, Next?"

I offered her a small vanity case with some cosmetics in it that I had picked off a shelf earlier. She didn't take it.

"Information," I said.

"Is there a deal in the offing?"

"I can give you another ten minutes. It's not much, but it's something."

She looked at me, then all around her. She knew that people were outside the sphere looking in, but not how many and who. She had the power to wipe memories but not read minds. If she could, she'd know how much I hated her. Mind you, she probably knew that already.

"Next, please!" said the checkout girl, and Aornis put two dresses and a pair of shoes on the counter.

"How's the family, Thursday—Landen and Friday and the girls?"

"Information, Aornis."

She took a deep breath as the loop jumped back to the beginning of her eight minutes and she was once more at the rear of the line. She clenched her fists so tightly her knuckles went white. She'd been doing this for ten years without respite. The only thing worse than a loop was a loop in which one suffered a painful trauma, such as a broken leg. But even the most sadistic judges could never find it in themselves to order that.

Aornis calmed herself, looked up at me and said, "Give me twenty minutes and I'll tell you what you want to know."

"I want to know about Felix8."

"That's not a name I've heard for a while," replied Aornis evenly. "What's your interest in that empty husk?"

"He was hanging around my house with a loaded gun yesterday," I told her, "and I can only assume he was wanting to do me harm."

Aornis looked mildly perturbed. "You saw him?"

"With my own eyes."

"Then I don't understand. After Acheron's untimely end, Felix8 seemed rather at a loss. He came around to the house and was making a nuisance of himself, very like an abandoned dog."

"So what happened?"

"Cocytus put him down."

"I'm assuming you don't mean in the sense of 'to humiliate.'"

"You think correct."

"And when was this?"

"In 1986."

"Did you witness the murder? Or see the body?" I stared at her carefully, trying to determine if she was telling the truth.

"No. He just *said* he had. You could have asked him yourself, but you killed him, didn't you?"

"He was evil. He brought it upon himself."

"I wasn't being serious," replied Aornis. "It's what passes for humor in the Hades family."

"This doesn't really help me," I murmured.

"That's nothing to do with me," replied Aornis. "You wanted intel, and I gave it to you."

"If I find out you've lied," I said, getting ready to leave, "I'll be back to take away the twenty minutes I gave you."

"If you've seen Felix8, how could you think otherwise?" pointed out Aornis with impeccable logic.

"Stranger things have happened."

I stepped out of the loop cell and was back in the bluey greenness of T.J. Maxx among the time-frozen customers, with Friday at my side.

"Think she's telling the truth?" he asked.

"If she is, it makes no sense at all, which is a point in her favor. If she'd told me what I wanted to hear, I'd have been more suspicious. Did she say anything else to me she might have made me forget?"

Aornis, with her power of memory distortion and erasure, was wholly untrustworthy—she could tell you everything, only to make you forget it a few seconds later. At her trial the judge and jury were merely actors—the real judge and jury watched it all on CCTV. To this day the actors in the courtroom still have no idea why that "frightfully pleasant girl" was in the dock at all. Friday ran over what he had witnessed her saying, and we managed to find an exchange that she'd erased from my recollection: that she was going to bust out of T.J. Maxx with the help of someone "on the outside."

"Any idea who that might be?" I asked. "And why did she shield it from me?"

"No idea—and it's probably just her being manipulative; my guess is the recollection will be on time release—it'll pop into your head in a few hours."

I nodded. She'd done something similar to me before.

"But I wouldn't worry," added Friday. "Temporal Enloopment has a hundred percent past-present-future escape-free record; she'd have to bend the Standard History Eventline to get out."

I left Aornis to her never-ending wait at the checkout, and Friday powered down the visitors' interface. The manager popped back into life as time started up again.

"Did you get all you need?" she asked pleasantly.

"I hope so," I replied, and followed Friday from the store. "Thanks," I said, giving him a motherly hug and a kiss.

"Mum," he said in a serious tone.

"What?"

"There's something I need to suggest to you, and you're going to have to think really carefully before you reply."

"What is it?"

"It's Friday. The *other* Friday. We've got two and a half days to the End of Time. Does it seriously look like he's going to join the ChronoGuard?"

"It's possible."

"Mum—truthfully?"

"No."

"We're running out of options fast. My director-general older self is still absent at the End of Time, so I had a word with Bendix, and he suggested we try . . . *replacement*."

"What do you mean?"

"That your Friday is removed and I take his place."

"Define 'removed.' "

Friday scratched his head.

"We've run several timestream models, and it looks good. I'm precisely the same age as him, and I'm what he *would* be like if he hadn't gone down the bone-idle route. If 'replacement' isn't a good word for you, why not think of it as just rectifying a small error in the Standard History Eventline."

"Let me get this straight," I said. "You want to murder my son and replace him with yourself? I only met you ten minutes ago."

"*I'm* your son, Mum. Every memory, good or bad is as much a part of me as it is the Friday at home. You want me to prove it? Who else knows about the BookWorld? One of your best friends is Melanie Bradshaw, who's a gorilla. It's true she let me climb all over the furniture and swing from the light fixtures. I can speak **Courier Bold** and Lorem Ipsum and even unpeel a banana with my feet—want me to show you?"

"No," I said. "I accept that you're my son. But you can't kill the other Friday—he's done nothing wrong. I won't let you."

"Mum! Which Friday would you rather have? The feckless, lazy ass or me?"

"You don't understand what it is to be a mother, Friday. The answer's no. I'll take the Friday I'm dealt."

"I thought you might say that," he said in a harsher manner. "I'll report back to Scintilla, but if the ChronoGuard feels there's no alternative, we might decide to go ahead anyway—with or without your permission."

"I think we've spoken enough," I said, keeping my anger at bay. "Do one thing for me: Tell me how long you think I have until they might take that action."

He shrugged. "Forty-eight hours?"

"Promise?"

"I promise," said Friday. "By the way, have you told Dad about all your Jurisfiction work? You said you were going to."

"I will—soon, I promise. Good-bye, darling."

And I kissed him again and walked away, boiling with inner rage. Fighting with the ChronoGuard was like fighting city hall. You couldn't win. Every way I looked at it, Friday's days were numbered. But, paradoxically, they weren't—the Friday I had just spoken to was the one I was meant to have and the one I'd met in the future, the one who made sure he escaped Landen's eradication and the one who whipped up the timephoon in the Dark Ages to cover up St. Zvlkx's illegal time fraud. I rubbed my head. Time travel was like that—full of impossible paradoxes that defied explanation and made theoretical physicists' brains turn to something resembling guacamole. But at least I still had two days to figure out a way to save the lazy good-for-nothing loafer that was my son. Before then, though, I needed to find out just how Goliath had managed to send a probe into fiction.

19.

The Goliath Corporation

The Isle of Man had been an independent corporate state within England since it was appropriated for the greater fiscal good in 1963. It had hospitals and schools, a university, its own fusion reactor and also, leading from Douglas to Kennedy Graviport in New York, the world's only privately run Gravitube. The Isle of Man was home to almost two hundred thousand people who did nothing but support, or support the support, of the one enterprise that dominated the small island: the Goliath Corporation.

I hopped on the Skyrail at the Brunel Shopping Centre and went the three stops to Swindon's Clary-LaMarr Travelport, where I caught the bullet train to Saknussemm International. From there I jumped on the next Overmantle Gravitube with seconds to spare and was at James Tarbuck Graviport in Liverpool in a journey time of just over an hour. The country's hyperefficient public transport network was the Commonsense Party's greatest achievement so far. Very few people used cars for journeys over ten miles these days. The system had its detractors, of course—the car-parking consortiums were naturally appalled, as was the motorway service industry, which had taken the extraordinary step of producing decent food in order to win back customers.

I made good use of the time by calling Landen and telling him all about the alternative Friday's offer: to replace our idle and mostly bedridden headbanger of a son with a well-groomed, upright and responsible member of society, and Landen had agreed with me—that we'd keep the smelly one we had, thank you very much. Once I'd tubed to Tarbuck, I took the high-speed Ekranoplane all the way to the distinctly unimaginatively titled Goliathopolis on what had once been the Isle of Man. Despite losing nearly everything during the dramatic St. Zvlkx adventure back in 1988, the vast multinational had staged an impressive comeback—mostly, it was said, by hiding its net worth and filing for bankruptcy on a subsidiary company that conveniently emerged from the distant past to take a lot of the flak. Timefoolery was suggested, but despite an investigation by the ChronoGuard's Fiscal Chronuption Unit, which looked very closely at such matters, no wrongdoing had been found—or could be proved. After that it didn't take long for the corporation to reestablish itself, and Goliathopolis was once again the Hong Kong of the Western Hemisphere, a forest of glassy towers striding up the hillside toward Snaefell.

Even before we left the dock at Tarbuck International, I had the idea that I was being watched. As the Goliath ground-effect transport jetted across the Irish Sea, several of the Goliath employees on the craft looked at me cautiously, and when I sat down in the coffee shop, the people near me moved away. It was kind of flattering, really, but since I had trounced the corporation in the very biggest way possible at least once, they clearly regarded me as something of a threat. How big a threat was revealed to me when we docked at Goliathopolis forty minutes later. There was a welcoming committee already waiting for me. But I don't mean "welcoming committee" in the ironic sense of large men with no necks and blackjacks—they had laid out the red carpet, bedecked the jetty with bunting and put on a baton-twirling demonstration by the Goliathopolis Majorettes. More important, the entire upper echelons of Goliath management had turned out to greet me, which included the president, John Henry Goliath V, and a dozen or so of his executive officers, all of whom had a look of earnest apprehension etched upon their pasty faces. As someone who'd cost the company dearly over the past two decades, I was clearly feared—and possibly even revered.

"Welcome back to Goliathopolis," said John Henry politely, shaking my hand warmly. "I hope that your stay is a happy one and that whatever brings you here can be a matter of mutual concern. I hardly need to stress the respect in which we hold you and would hate that you might find reason to act upon us without first entertaining the possibility of a misunderstanding."

He was a large man. It looked as though someone had handed his parents a blueprint of a baby and told them to scale it up by a factor of one and a quarter.

"This is a joke, right?"

"On the contrary, Ms. Next. Based on past experiences, we have decided that complete and utter disclosure is the only policy worth pursuing as far as your good self is concerned."

"You'll excuse me if I remain unconvinced by your perceived honesty."

"It's not honesty, Ms. Next. You *personally* cost us over a hundred billion pounds in lost revenue, so we regard our openness as a sound business strategy—albeit of an abstract nature. Because of this, there is no door closed to you, no document unreadable, no member to whom you may not speak. I hope I am candid?"

"Very," I replied, put off my guard by the corporation's attitude. "I have a matter I'd like to discuss with you."

"Naturally," replied John Henry. "The majorettes would like to perform, if that's all right with you?"

"Of course."

So we watched the majorettes march up and down for twenty minutes to music of the Goliath Brass Band, and when it was over, I was driven in John Henry's Bentley toward the Goliath head office, a mighty 110-story building right at the heart of Goliathopolis.

"Your son and family are well?" asked John Henry, who aside from a few more gray hairs didn't seem to have aged a great deal since we last met. He fixed me with his piercing green eyes and poured on the natural charm he'd been blessed with.

"I expect you know full well they are," I replied, "and everything else about me."

"On the contrary," protested John Henry. "We thought that if even the sniff of surveillance was detected, you might decide to take action, and action from you, as we have seen to our cost, is never less than devastating to our interests."

"Ah," I murmured, suddenly realizing why there had been a deafening silence from Goliath over the years.

"So how can we help?" asked John Henry. "If," he added, "we can help at all."

"I want to find out what advances you have made in transfictional travel."

John Henry raised his eyebrows and smiled genially. "I never thought it would remain a secret from you forever."

"You've been leaving Outlander probes scattered all over the BookWorld."

"The research and development on the Book Project has been somewhat hit or miss, I'll admit that," replied John Henry candidly. "To be honest, I had expected you to call on us sooner than you have."

"I've been busy."

"Of course. And since you are here, perhaps you would grace us with your comments on the technical aspects of our project."

"I promise nothing, but I'd certainly like to see what you're up to."

The car drove toward the glassy modern towers of the corporate center of the multinational and past well-tailored executives going about their administrative business. A few minutes later, we pulled up outside the front entrance of the Goliath headquarters, which was comfortably nestled into the hillside.

"I don't suppose that you would want to freshen up or anything before we show you around?" asked John Henry hopefully.

"And miss something you might try and hide from me?" I answered. "No, if it's all the same to you, I'd really like to see how far you've gotten."

"Very well," said John Henry without any sense of concern, "come with me."

We walked into the expansive lobby and crossed not to the elevators or the Apologarium, where I'd been last time, but to where a golf cart was at the ready. A curious crowd of Goliath employees had gathered to watch our progress with undisguised inquisitiveness. I couldn't think it was just me—I don't suppose many of them had ever seen John Henry Goliath either.

We drove out of the lobby and into a tunnel that led directly back into the hillside. It was crudely utilitarian after the simple elegance of the entrance vestibule, with roughly concreted walls and lit by overhead track lights. The roadway was smooth concrete, and there were cable conduits attached to the walls. The subterranean vaults of Goliath R&D were at least half a mile inside the hill, and on the journey, John Henry and I chatted amiably about national politics and global economics. Surprisingly, a more intelligent and well-informed conversation about current affairs I have yet to have. I might even have liked him, but for the utter ruthlessness and singularity of purpose that ran through his speech. Excusable in a person of little or no power, but potentially devastating in one such as John Henry Goliath.

We encountered three different levels of security on the way, each of them waved aside by John Henry. Beyond the third security checkpoint was a large set of steel blast doors, and after abandoning the golf cart we proceeded on foot. John Henry had his tie knot scanned to confirm his identity, and the doors slid open to let us in. I gasped at the sight that met my eyes. Their technology had gone beyond the small metal probe I'd already seen. It had gone further—*much* further.

20.

The *Austen Rover*

I had been aware for many years of Goliath's endeavors to enter fiction. Following their abortive attempt to use the fictional world to "actualize" flawed technology during the Plasma Rifle debacle of '85, they had embarked upon a protracted R&D project to try to emulate Mycroft's Prose Portal. Until the appearance of the probe, the furthest I thought they'd gotten was to synthesize a form of stodgy grunge from volumes one to eight of *The World of Cheese.*

In the center of the room and looking resplendent in the blue-and-yellow livery of some long-forgotten bus company was a flat-fronted single-decker bus that to my mind dated from the fifties. Something my mother, in her long-forgotten and now much-embellished youth, might have boarded for a trip to the seaside, equipped with hampers of food and gallons of ice cream. Aside from the anachronistic feel, the most obvious feature of the bus was that the wheels had been removed and the voids covered over to give the vague appearance of streamlining. Clearly, it wasn't the only modification. The vehicle in front of me now was probably the most advanced piece of transport technology known to man.

"Why base it on an old bus?" I asked.

John Henry shrugged. "If you're going to travel, do it in style. Besides, a Rolls-Royce Phantom II doesn't have enough seats."

We walked down to the workshop floor, and I took a closer

look. On both sides at the rear of the bus and on the roof were small faired outriggers that each held a complicated engine with which I was not familiar. The tight-fitting cowlings had been removed, and the engines were being worked on by white-coated technicians who had stopped what they were doing as soon as we walked in but now resumed their tinkering with a buzz of muted whispers. I moved closer to the front of the bus and ran my fingers across the Leyland badge atop the large and very prominent radia.................glass-covered panel that once told prospective passengers the ultimate destination of the bus. I expected it to read BOURNEMOUTH or PORTSMOUTH but it didn't. It read NORTHANGER ABBEY.

I looked at John Henry Goliath, who said, "This, Ms. Next, is the *Austen Rover*—the most advanced piece of transfictional technology in the world!"

"Does it work?" I asked.

"We're not entirely sure," remarked John Henry. "It's the prototype and has yet to be tested."

He beckoned to the technician who seemed to be in charge and introduced us.

"This is Dr. Anne Wirthlass, the project manager of the *Austen Rover.* She will answer any questions you have—I hope perhaps you will answer some of ours?"

I made a noncommittal noise, and Wirthlass gave me a hand to shake. She was tall, willowy and walked with a rolling gait. Like everyone in the lab, she wore a white coat with her Goliath ID badge affixed to it, and although I could not see her precise laddernumber, she was certainly within four figures—the top 1 percent. *Seriously* important.

"I'm pleased to meet you at last," she said in a Swedish accent. "We have much to learn from your experience."

"If you know *anything* about me," I responded, "you'll know exactly why it is that I don't trust Goliath."

"Ah!" she said, somewhat taken aback. "I thought we'd left those days behind us."

"I'll need convincing," I returned without malice. It wasn't her fault, after all. I indicated the tour bus. "How does it work?"

She looked at John Henry, who nodded his permission.

"The *Austen Rover* is a standard Leyland Tiger PS2/3 under a Burlingham body," she began, touching the shiny coachwork fondly, "but with a few . . . modifications. Come aboard."

She stepped up into the bus, and I followed her. The interior had been stripped and replaced with the very latest technology, which she attempted to explain in the sort of technical language where it is possible to understand only one word in eight, if you're lucky. I came off the bus ten minutes later having absorbed not much more than the fact that it had twelve seats, carried a small thirty-megawatt fusion device in the rear and couldn't be tested—its first trip would be either an utter failure or a complete success, nothing in between.

"And the probes?"

"Yes, indeed," replied Wirthlass. "We've been using a form of gravity-wave inducer to catapult a small probe into fiction on a one-minute free-return trajectory—think of it as a very large yo-yo. We aimed them at the Dune series, because it was a large and very wordy target that was probably somewhere near the heart of Science Fiction, and after seven hundred and ninety-six subfictional flights we hit pay dirt: The probe returned with a twenty-eight-second audiovisual recording of Paul Atreides riding a sandworm."

"When was this?" I asked.

"In 1996. We fared better after that and by a system of trial and error have managed to figure out that individual books seem to be clumped together in groups. We've started plotting a map—I'll show you if you like."

We walked into a room next door that seemed to be filled to capacity with computers and their operators.

"How many probe missions have you sent?"

"About seventy thousand," said John Henry, who had followed us. "Most come back without recording anything, and over eight thousand never return at all. In total we have had four hundred and twenty successful missions. As you can see, getting into fiction for us is at present a somewhat haphazard affair. The *Austen Rover* is ready for its first trip—but by simple extrapolation of the probe figures, every journey has a one-in-eight chance of not returning, and only a one-in-one-hundred-and-sixty possibility of hitting something."

I could see what they were up against—and why. They were hurling probes into a BookWorld that was 80 percent Nothing. The thing was, I could pretty much draw from memory a genre map of the BookWorld. With my help they might actually make it.

"This is the BookWorld as we think it exists," explained John Henry, laying out a large sheet of paper on a desk. It was patchy in the extreme and full of errors. It was a bit like throwing Ping-Pong balls into a dark furniture store and then trying to list the contents by the noises they made.

"This will take you a long time to figure out," I murmured.

"Time that we don't really have, Ms. Next. Despite my position as president, even I have to concede that the amount spent will never be recouped. All funding for this project will be withdrawn in a week."

It was the first time I'd felt any sort of relief since I arrived. The idea of Goliath's even setting so much as a toe inside fiction filled me with utter dread. But one question still niggled at me.

"Why?"

"I'm sorry?" said John Henry.

"Why are you trying to get into fiction at all?"

"Book tourism," he replied simply. "The *Austen Rover* was designed to take twelve people around the high points of Jane Austen's work. At five hundred pounds for a twenty-minute hop around the most-loved works, we thought at the time it would be quite profitable. Mind you, that was nine years ago, when people were still reading books."

"We thought it might reinvigorate the classics," added Wirthlass.

"And your interest in the classics?"

It was John Henry who answered. "We feel that publishing in general and books in particular are well worth hanging on to."

"You'll excuse me if I'm not convinced by your supposed altruism."

"No altruism, Ms. Next. The fall in revenue of our publishing arm has been dramatic, and since we own little in the way of computer games or consoles, the low ReadRate is something that affects us financially. I think you'll find that we're together on this one. What we want is what *you* want. Even though our past associations have not been happy and I understand your distrust, Goliath in its reborn shape is not quite the all-devouring corporation that you think it is."

"I haven't been in the BookWorld since the days of *The Eyre Affair.*"

John Henry coughed politely. "You knew about the probes, Ms. Next."

Damn.

"I have . . . contacts over there."

I could tell they didn't believe me, but that was tough. I'd seen enough.

"Looks like you've wasted a lot of money," I said.

"With or without you, we're going to test it on Friday evening," announced Wirthlass. "I and two others have decided to risk all and take her out for a spin. We may not return, but if we do, then the data gained would be priceless!"

I admired her courage, but it didn't matter—I wasn't going to tell them what I knew.

"Just explain one thing," said Wirthlass. "Is the force of gravity entirely normal in the BookWorld?"

"What about the universality of physical laws?" piped up a second technician, who'd been watching us.

"And communication between books—is such a thing possible?"

Before long there were eight people, all asking questions about the BookWorld that I could have answered with ease—had I any inclination to do so.

"I'm sorry," I said as the questions reached a crescendo. "I can't help you!"

They were all quiet and stared at me. To them this project was everything, and to see its cancellation without fruition was clearly a matter of supreme frustration—especially as they suspected I had the answers.

I made my way toward the exit and was joined by John Henry, who had not yet given up trying to charm me.

"Will you stay for lunch? We have the finest chefs available to make whatever you want."

"I run a carpet shop, Mr. Goliath, and I'm late for work."

"A carpet shop?" he echoed with incredulity. "That sells carpets?"

"All sorts of floor coverings, actually."

"I would offer you discounted carpets for life in order for you to help us," he said, "but from what I know of you, such a course would be unthinkable. My private Dakota is at Douglas Graviport if you want to use it to fly straight home. I ask for nothing but say only this: We are doing this for the preservation and promotion of books and reading. Try to find it in your heart to consider what we are doing here in an objective light."

We had by now walked outside the building, and John Henry's Bentley pulled up in front of us.

"My car is yours. Good day, Ms. Next."

"Good day, Mr. Goliath."

He shook my hand and then departed. I looked at the Bentley and then at the ranks of cabs a little way down the road. I shrugged and climbed in the back of the Bentley.

"Where to, madam?" asked the driver.

I thought quickly. I had my TravelBook on me and could jump to the Great Library from here—as long as I could find a quiet spot conducive to bookjumping.

"The nearest library," I told him. "I'm late for work."

"You're a librarian?" he inquired politely.

"Let's just say I'm really into books."

21.

Holmes

I don't know what it was about traveling to and from the BookWorld that dehydrated me so much. It had gotten progressively worse, almost without my noticing, a bit like a mildly increased girth and skin that isn't as elastic as it used to be. On the upside, however, the textual environment kept all the aches and pains at bay. I hardly noticed my bad back in the BookWorld and was never troubled by headaches.

A few minutes and several pints of rehydrating water later, I walked into the Jurisfiction offices at Norland Park. Thursday5 was waiting for me by my desk, looking decidedly pleased with herself.

"Guess what!" she enthused.

"I have no idea."

"Go on, guess!"

"I don't want to guess," I told her, hoping the tedium in my voice would send out a few warning bells. It didn't.

"No, you *must* guess!"

"Okay," I sighed. "You've got some new beads or something."

"Wrong," she said, producing a paper bag with a flourish. "I got you the bacon roll you wanted!"

"I never would have guessed *that*," I replied, sitting before a desk that seemed to be flooded with new memos and reports, adding, in an unthinking moment, "How are things with you?"

"I didn't sleep very well last night."

I rubbed my forehead as she sat down and stared at me intently, hands clasped nervously in front of her. I didn't have the heart to tell her that my inquiry over her health was merely politeness. I didn't actually want to know. Quite the reverse, in fact.

"Really?" I said, trying to find a memo that might be vaguely relevant to something.

"No. I was thinking about the Minotaur incident yesterday, and I want to apologize—again."

"It's past history. Any messages?"

"So I'm sorry."

"Apology accepted. Now: Any messages?"

"I wrote you a letter outlining my apology."

"I won't read it. The matter is closed."

"Yes . . . well . . . right," she began, flustered that we weren't going to analyze the previous day at length and trying to remember everything she'd been told that morning. "Mr. Buñuel called to say that he'd completed the refit of *Pride and Prejudice* and it was online again this morning. He's got *Northanger Abbey* in the maintenance bay at the moment, and it should be ready on time as long as Catherine stops attempting to have the book 'Gothicized.'"

"Good. What else?"

"The Council of Genres," she announced, barely able to control her excitement. "Senator Jobsworth's secretary *herself* called to ask you to appear in the debating chamber for a policy-directive meeting at three this afternoon!"

"I wonder what the old bore wants now? Anything else?"

"No," replied Thursday5, disappointed that I didn't share her unbridled enthusiasm over an appearance at the CofG. I couldn't. I'd been there so many times I just saw it as part of my duties, nothing more.

I opened my desk drawer to take out a sheet of letterhead and noticed Thursday5's assessment letter where I'd put it the night before. I thought for a moment and decided to give her one more chance. I left it where it was, pulled out a sheet of paper and wrote a letter to Wing Commander Scampton-Tappett, telling him to get out of *Bananas for Edward,* since Landen wasn't currently working on it, and move instead to *The Mews of Doom,* which he was. I folded up the letter, placed it in an envelope and told Thursday5 to deliver it to Scampton-Tappett in person. I could have asked her to send it by courier, but twenty minutes' peace and quiet had a great deal of appeal to it. Thursday5 nodded happily and vanished.

I had just leaned back in my chair and was thinking about Felix8, the possible End of Time and the *Austen Rover* when a hearty bellow of "Stand to!" indicated the imminence of Bradshaw's daily Jurisfiction briefing. I dutifully stood up and joined the other agents who had gathered in the center of the room.

After the usual apologies for absence, Bradshaw climbed on to a table, tinkled a small bell and said, "Jurisfiction meeting number 43370 is now in session. But before all that we are to welcome a new agent to the fold: Colonel William Dobbin!"

We all applauded as Colonel Dobbin gave a polite bow and remarked in a shy yet resolute manner that he would do his utmost to further the good work of Jurisfiction.

"Jolly good," intoned Bradshaw, eager to get on. "Item One: An active cell of bowdlerizers has been at work again, this time in Philip Larkin and 'This Be the Verse.' We've found several editions with the first line altered to read 'They tuck you up, your mum and dad,' which is a gross distortion of the original intent. Who wants to have a go at this?"

"I will," I said.

"No. What about you, King Pellinore?"

"Yes-yes what-what hey-hey?" said the white-whiskered knight in grubby armor.

"You've had experience dealing with bowdlerizers in Larkin before—cracking the group that altered the first line of 'Love Again' to read: 'Love again: thanking her at ten past three' was great stuff—fancy tackling them again?"

"What-what to go a mollocking for the bowlders?" replied Pellinore happily. " 'Twill be achieved happily and in half the time."

"Anyone want to go with him?"

"I'll go," I said.

"Anyone else?"

The Red Queen put up her hand.

"Item Two: The Two Hundred Eighty-seventh Annual BookWorld Conference is due in six months' time, and the Council of Genres has insisted we need to have a security review after last year's . . . problems."

There was a muttering from the assembled agents. BookCon was the sort of event that was too large and too varied to keep all factions happy, and the previous year's decision to lift the restriction on Abstract Concepts attending as delegates opened the floodgates to a multitude of Literary Theories and Grammatical Conventions who spent most of the time pontificating loftily and causing trouble in the bar, where fights broke out at the drop of a participle. When Poststructuralism got into a fight with Classicism, they were all banned, something that upset the Subjunctives no end, who complained bitterly that if *they* had been fighting, they would have won.

"Are the Abstracts allowed to attend this year?" asked Lady Cavendish.

"I'm afraid so," replied Bradshaw. "Not to invite them would be seen as discriminatory. Volunteers?"

Six of us put up our hands, and Bradshaw diligently scribbled down our names.

"Top-notch," he said at last. "The first meeting will be next week. Now, Item Three, and this one is something of a corker: We've got a Major Narrative Flexation brewing in *The Memoirs of Sherlock Holmes*."

"Is it the Watson bullet-wound problem again?" asked Mr. Fainset.

"No, it's more serious than that. Sherlock Holmes . . . *has been murdered!*"

There was a spontaneous cry of shock and outrage from the assembled agents. The Holmes series was a perennial favorite and thus of particular concern—textual anomalies in unread or unpopular books were always lower priority, or ignored altogether. Bradshaw handed a stack of papers to Lady Cavendish, who distributed them.

"It's in 'The Final Problem.' You can read it yourself, but essentially Sherlock travels to Switzerland to deal with Professor Moriarty. After the usual Holmesian escapades, Watson follows Sherlock to the Reichenbach Falls, where he discovers that Holmes has apparently fallen to his death—and the book ends twenty-nine pages before it was meant to."

There was a shocked silence as everyone took this in. We hadn't had a textual anomaly of this size since Lucy Pevensie refused to get into the wardrobe at the beginning of *The Lion, the Witch and the Wardrobe.*

"But *The Memoirs of Sherlock Holmes* was the fourth volume," observed Mrs. Tiggy-Winkle, looking up from her ironing. "With Sherlock dead at the Reichenbach, it would render the remaining five volumes of stories narratively unsustainable."

"Partly right," replied Bradshaw. "*The Hound of the Baskervilles* was written after *Memoirs* but is set earlier—I think we can keep hold of that one. But yes, the remaining four in the series will start to spontaneously unravel unless we do something about it. And we will, I assure you—erasure is not an option."

This was not as easy as it sounded despite Bradshaw's rhetoric, and we all knew it. The entire Sherlock Holmes series was closed books, unavailable to enter until someone had actually booksplored his or her way in—and the Holmes canon had continuously resisted exploration. Gomez was the first Jurisfiction booksplorer to try by way of Conan Doyle's *The Lost World,* but he mistakenly became involved in the narrative and was shot dead by Lord Roxton. Harris Tweed tried it next and was nearly trampled by a herd of angry *Stegosauri.*

"I want everyone in on this problem. The Cat Formerly Known as Cheshire will be keeping a careful eye on the narrative corruption of the series up at Text Grand Central, and I want Beatrice, Benedict, Zhark and Tiggy-Winkle to try to find a way of using the other books in the Conan Doyle oeuvre—I suggest the Professor Challenger stories. Fainset and Foyle, I want you to explore the possibility of *communication* with anyone inside the Holmes series—they may not even know they have a problem."

"They're well outside the footnoterphone network," said Mr. Fainset. "Any suggestions?"

"I'm relying on Foyle's ingenuity. If anyone sees Hamlet or Peter and Jane before I do, send them immediately to me. Any questions?"

"What do you want me to do?" I asked, wondering why I had been left out of everything important so far.

"I'll speak to you later. Okay, that's it. Good luck, and . . . let's be *careful* out there."

The collected agents instantly started chattering. We hadn't had anything like this for years, which made it seem even more stupid that Bradshaw wasn't including me on the assignment. I caught up with him as he sat at his desk.

"What's going on?" I asked. "You need me on this."

"Hello, my dear! Not like you to nearly miss a session—problems in the Outland?"

"I was up at Goliath."

He raised an eyebrow. "How do things look?"

I explained at length what I had seen, ending with the observation that it wasn't likely they'd perfect a transfictional machine anytime soon, if at all—but we needed to keep our eyes on them.

Bradshaw nodded sagely, and I reiterated my feeling that I was being somehow "left out" of the Holmes inquiry.

"How's Friday? Still a bed slug?"

"Yes—but nothing I can't handle."

"Have you told Landen about us yet?"

"I'm building up to it. Bradshaw, you're flanneling—*why aren't I on the Holmes case?*"

He gestured for me to sit and lowered his voice. "I had a call from Senator Jobsworth this morning. He's keen to reinstate a certain cadet that we recently . . . had to let go."

I knew the cadet he was referring to. There was a sound reason for her rejection—she'd been euphemistically entitled "unsuitable." Not in the way that my nice-but-a-bit-dopey cadet was unsuitable, but unsuitable as in obnoxious. She'd gone through five tutors in as many days. Even Emperor Zhark said that he'd preferred to be eaten alive by the Snurgg of Epsilon-7 than spend another five minutes in her company.

"Why has Jobsworth requested her? There are at least ten we rejected that are six times better."

"Because we're light on agents in contemporary fiction, and the CofG thinks she checks all the genre boxes."

"He's wrong, of course," I said quite matter-of-factly, but people like Jobsworth are politicians and have a different set of rules. "I can see his point, though. The question is, what are you going to do about it? She's exhausted all the agents licensed to take apprentices."

Bradshaw said nothing and stared at me. In an instant I understood.

"Oh, no," I said, "not me. Not in a thousand years. Besides, I've already got a cadet on assessment."

"Then get rid of her. You told me yourself that her timidity would get her killed."

"It will—but I feel kind of responsible. Besides, I've already got a full caseload. The Mrs. Danvers that went berserk in *The God of Small Things* still needs investigating, the Minotaur tried to kill me—not to mention about thirty or so cold cases, some of which are potentially solvable—especially the Drood case. I think it's possible Dickens was . . . *murdered*."

"In the Outland? And for what reason?"

"To silence Edwin Drood—or someone else in the book."

I *wasn't* sure about this, of course, and any evidence was already over a hundred years old, but I would do anything not to get stuck with this apprentice. Sadly, Bradshaw wasn't taking no for an answer or softening to my pleas.

"Don't make me order you, old girl. It will embarrass us both.

Besides, if you fail her—as I'm sure you shall—then we really *have* run out of tutors, and I can tell Jobsworth we did everything in our power."

I groaned. "How about I take her next week? That way I can come to grips with the Holmes death thing."

"Senator Jobsworth was *most* insistent," added Bradshaw. "He's been on the footnoterphone three times this morning already."

I knew what he meant. When Jobsworth got his teeth into something, he rarely let go. The relationship between us was decidedly chilly, and we were at best only cordial. The crazy thing was, we both wanted the best for the BookWorld—we just had different methods of trying to achieve it.

"Very well," I said finally. "I'll give her a day—or a morning, if she lasts that."

"Good lass!" exclaimed Bradshaw happily. "Appreciate a woman who knows when she's being coerced. I'll get her to meet you outside Norland."

"Is that all?" I asked somewhat crossly.

"No. It seems someone's made an ass of themselves over at Resource Management regarding maintenance schedules, and we've got a— Well, see for yourself."

He handed me a report, and I flicked through the pages with a rising sense of despair. It was always the same. Someone at admin screws up and we have to pick up the pieces.

"The Piano Squad has been on the go for eight hours straight," he added, "so I'd like you to step in and relieve them for a rest period. Take your cadets with you. Should be a useful training session."

My heart sank.

"I've got to appear at the CofG later this afternoon," I explained, "and if I've a second cadet to nursemaid—"

"I'll make it up to you," interrupted Bradshaw. "It'll be a doddle—a walk in the park. How much trouble can anyone get into with pianos?"

22.

Next

TransGenre Taxis was one of several BookWorld taxi companies and the only firm that could boast an accident rate that was vaguely acceptable. Taxis were a good way to get around the BookWorld if you weren't that good at jumping or had lots of luggage, but in comparison to the instantaneous bookjump they were like snails. They didn't so much jump as creep. Getting all the way across the BookWorld—from Philosophy to Poetry, for instance—could take as long as an hour.

"You're kidding me?" I said into my mobilefootnoterphone twenty minutes later. I was outside the main entrance to Norland Park as the sun began its downward slope from midday heat into the rare beauty of an Austen literary afternoon. The warm rural environment was rich with the sounds of the plowhorse's bridles jingling in the fields, the bees buzzing merrily in the hedgerows and young ladies atwitter with gossip regarding the genteel ensnarement of monied husbands.

"Well," I added crossly, "just send it as soon as you can."

I snapped the phone shut.

"Problems?" asked Thursday5, who had been making daisy chains while sitting cross-legged on the warm grass.

"Those twits at TransGenre Taxis," I replied. "More excuses. They claim there are long backups due to a traffic accident inside *The Great Gatsby* and our cab will be at least an hour."

"Can't we just jump straight to wherever it is we're going?" She stopped and thought for a moment. "Where *are* we going?"

"The Piano Squad. But we're waiting for someone."

"Who?"

"We're waiting," I said, unsure of how to break the news, "for a cadet who is under reappraisal."

"*Another* cadet?" repeated Thursday5, who seemed vaguely miffed at first but soon recovered. "If only I'd known, I could have baked a welcome cake."

"I don't think she's a cake sort of person," I murmured, as a noise like the scrunching of cellophane heralded her arrival. She appeared looking somewhat out of breath, and we all three stared at one another for some moments in silence until both cadets said at precisely the same time:

"What's *she* doing here?"

"Listen," I said to them both, "I know this is an awkward situation—and a little weird, too, if you want to know my opinion, and if either of you doesn't like it, you can just go straight back to your respective books."

My latest apprentice glared at me, then at Thursday5, then at me again before saying with a forced smile, "In that case I should probably introduce myself and say what an *incredible* honor it is to be apprenticed to the *great* Thursday Next."

"Why don't you save your breath—and your sarcasm?" I retorted. I liked a challenge, but this was probably one or two challenges too far. For this, of course, was the *other* Thursday Next, the one from the first four books in the series—the violent ones full of death and gratuitous sex.

"Well, whoop-de-do," she said quietly, looking at us both. "If this is how the day starts, it can only get better."

Thursday5 and I stared at the newcomer with a curious kind of fascination. Unlike Thursday5, who always dressed in fair-trade cotton and woolens, this Thursday preferred aggressive black leather. Leather trousers, jacket and a greatcoat that swept to the floor. So much, in fact, that she squeaked when she walked. Her hair was the same length as ours but was pulled back into a ponytail more sharply, and her eyes were hidden by small dark glasses. Attached to her belt were two automatic pistols with the butts facing in so she could cross-draw—heaven knows why. Aside from this and despite being featured in books that were set between 1985 and 1988, she looked exactly as I did—even to the flecks of gray hair that I *still* pretended I didn't care about.

But she wasn't me. She was less like me, in fact, than the talking-to-flowers version, if such a thing was possible. I'd read the books and although she *attempted* to do things for the right reason, her methods could best be described as dubious and her motivations suspect. Thursday5 was mostly thought with very little action; Thursday1–4 was mostly action with very little thought. The series had sacrificed characterization for plot, and humor for action and pace. All atmosphere had evaporated, and the books were a parade of violent set pieces interspersed with romantic interludes, and when I say "romantic," I'm stretching the term. Most famous was her torrid affair with Edward Rochester and the stand-up catfight with Jane Eyre. I had thought it couldn't get any worse until Mrs. Fairfax turned out to be a ninja assassin and Bertha Rochester was abducted by aliens. And all that was just in the first book. It got more far-fetched after that. By book four it felt as though the first draft had been torn apart by wolves and then stuck back together at random before publication.

I took a deep breath, inwardly cursed Commander Bradshaw and said, "Thursday . . . meet Thursday."

"Hello!" said Thursday5 brightly, offering a hand in reconciliation. "*So* pleased to meet you, and happy birthday—for yesterday."

Thursday looked at Thursday's outstretched hand and raised an eyebrow.

"I've had the misfortune to read *The Great Samuel Pepys Fiasco,*" she said in an unfriendly tone. "If you took the 'Samuel Pepys' out of the title, it would be a lot more honest. A bigger crock of shit I've yet to find. I kept on waiting for the shoot-outs to begin, and there weren't any—just a load of hugging, vitamins and people saying they love one another."

"There's nothing wrong with hugging," retorted Thursday5 defensively. "Perhaps if you were to try . . . ?"

She put out her arms but was met with the curt response, "Lay your muesli-smelling paws on me and I'll break your nose."

"Well!" said Thursday5 in an indignant huff. "I'm almost sorry I wished you a happy birthday—and I'm *very* glad I didn't bake you a cake."

"I'm devastated."

"Listen," I said before this descended into blows, "I'm not going to *ask* you to get along, I'm *telling* you to get along. Okay?"

Thursday1–4 gave a lackadaisical shrug.

"Right," I began, addressing Thursday1–4. "There are three simple rules if you want to train with me. Rule One: You do exactly as I tell you. Rule Two: You speak when you're spoken to. Rule Three: I shall call you 'Thursday1–4' or 'Thur1–4' or Onesday or . . . anything I want, really. You will call me 'ma'am.' If I summon you, you come running. Rule Four: You give me any crap and you're history."

"I thought you said there were only three rules."

"I make it up as I go along. Do you have any problem with that?"

"I suppose not."

"Good. Let's start at the beginning. How much classroom theory have you done?"

"Six weeks. Took my finals last Tuesday and came in third."

"That's not bad."

"How many in the class?" asked Thursday5, who was still smarting over the possibility that her hands smelled of muesli, let alone the threat of a broken nose.

Thursday1–4 glared at her and mumbled, "Three, and two percent above the minimum pass mark, before you ask. But I scored ninety-nine percent on the range. Pistols, rifle, machine gun, grenade launcher—you name it."

This was the main reason I didn't like the Thursday Next series—far, far too many guns and a body count that would be the envy of the cinematic Rambo. Thursday1–4 unholstered an aggressive-looking automatic and showed it to us both.

"Glock nine-millimeter," she said proudly. "Sixteen in the clip and one up the spout. *Severe* stopping power. I carry two to make quite sure."

"Only two?" I murmured sarcastically.

"No, since you're asking." She lifted up the back of her leather greatcoat to show me a large, shiny revolver stuffed down the back of her trousers.

"What do you carry?" she asked. "Beretta? Browning? Walther?"

"None," I said. "Charge into a room with a gun and someone ends up dead."

"Isn't that how it's supposed to work?"

"In *your* books, perhaps. If someone dies during an assignment, then the assignment was a failure. No exceptions."

"Diplomacy and using your head," put in Thursday5 bravely, "are better than waving a gun around."

"And what would you know about it, your supreme bogusness?"

"You don't have to insult me *all* the time," she replied, visibly upset. "And besides, I'm not sure 'bogusness' is a word."

"Well, listen here, veggieburger," said the leather-clad Thursday in a sneering tone of voice, "I *do* have to insult you all the time. Firstly because it's fun, and secondly because . . . No, I don't need a second reason."

"Jeez," I said, shaking my head sadly as all patience left me. "You're still revolting, aren't you?"

"Revolting?" she retorted. "Perhaps. But since I'm mostly you, I guess you're partly to blame, right?"

"Get this straight in your head," I said, moving closer. "The only thing you share with me is a name and a face. You can have a go at *The Great Samuel Pepys Fiasco* all you want, but at least it's not a constant orgy of comic-book violence and abundant, meaningless sex."

"Oh, I'm sorry—is that a criticism? Or just wishful thinking on your part? Because I was having a look at the figures the other day and I'm still selling strongly." She turned to the *Pepys* Thursday. "How many books have *you* sold in the past five years?"

It was a pointed yet strictly rhetorical remark. *The Great Samuel Pepys Fiasco* had been remaindered less than six months after publication.

"You don't hate *me*," said Thursday1–4 to Thursday5. "You secretly want to be like me. If you want to hate anyone, hate *her*." She directed this comment at me.

"Why would I?" asked Thursday5, close to tears.

With a creaking of leather, Thursday1–4 moved closer to her and said in a low voice, "Because she insisted that your book was full of touchy-feely family values—pet dodo, gardening, a husband, two lovely kids—"

"Three."

"Whatever. They asked me to do book five, but I took one look at the script and told them to stick it." She pointed a gloved finger at me. "Her personal vanity condemned you to the slow death of being unread, unreviewed, undiscussed and out of print. The real Thursday is as single-minded as I am—even to the ultimate vanity of rewriting herself into the guise of little Miss Granola Tree-Hugger here—with no other reason than to protect her own fragile vanity, Z-class celebrity status and inconsequential public opinion. She and I are more alike than she thinks."

She stopped talking with a triumphant smile on her face. The other Thursday looked at me with tears in her eyes, and I was feeling hotly indignant myself, mostly because what she was saying was *true*. The only reason I'd taken on Thursday5 at all was that I felt responsible. Not just because she *was* an insufferable drip, but because she was an unread one as well.

"Oh, no!" said Thursday5, giving out a heavy sob. "Now all my chakras are *completely* unaligned—can I have the rest of the day off?"

"Good idea," said Thursday1–4 with an unpleasant chuckle. "Why not go and meditate? After all, it's better than doing nothing the whole day."

Thursday gave another cry of indignation, I told her she could leave, and she did so with a faint *pop*.

"Listen," I said, also lowering my voice, "you can do your character-assassination crap all day if you want, but that's not important. What *is* important is that the CofG in all its misguided wisdom seems to think you might be good enough for Jurisfiction. Five previous tutors don't agree. *I* don't agree. I think you're a viper. But it's not up to me. It's up to you. For you to join Jurisfiction, you need to learn how to survive in the hostile and dynamic textual environment. You and I are going to spend the next few days together whether I like it or not, and since my conduct review of you is the only thing that counts toward your final acceptance at Jurisfiction, you need to try *really* hard not to piss me off."

"Ahh!" she murmured patronizingly. "She does speeches. Listen, sister, you may be a big cheese at Jurisfiction *today,* but if I were you, I'd show a keen sense of diplomacy. I'll have the Bellman's job one day—and I'll be looking out only for my friends. Now, are you going to be a friend or not?"

"Good Lord," I said in a quiet voice, "the Cheshire Cat was right—you really are *completely* obnoxious. Is that your final word?"

"It is."

"Then you can piss off back to your boxed set right now. Give me your badge."

She seemed perturbed for an instant. Her all-consuming arrogance had not even *once* entertained the notion she might actually be fired. But, true to form, instead of even attempting conciliation, she went into more threats:

"The CofG cadet selection subcommittee won't be happy."

"Screw *them*. Your badge?"

She stared at me with a sense of rising confusion. "You'd fire . . . *me*?"

"Just have. Give me your badge or I'll place you under arrest."

She took the Jurisfiction Cadet's shield from her pocket and slapped it into my open palm. Without that or a travel permit, she was technically a PageRunner and could be erased on sight.

"Good day," I said. "I won't say it's been a pleasure, because it hasn't."

And I walked away, pulling out my mobilefootnoterphone as I did so.

"Hello, Bradshaw? I've just fired Thursday1–4. I'm amazed anyone lasted more than ten minutes with her—I didn't."[1]

"Yes, already. Tell Jobsworth we did our best."[2]

"Too bad. I'll take the flak for it. This one's a serious piece of—"

"Wait, wait!" yelled Thursday, holding her head in a massive display of self-control. "That was my last chance, wasn't it?"

"Yes."

She massaged her temples. "I can do this. I'm sor— I'm sor— *Soooor*—"

"You can say it."

"I can't."

"*Try*."

She screwed up her face and forced the word out. "I'm . . . *soorry*. I'll be your apprentice. Jurisfiction has need of people like me, and I am willing to run the gauntlet of your overbearing mediocrity in order to achieve that."

I stared at her for a moment. "Vague apology accepted."

[1] "Goodness! Already?"

[2] "This is really awkward. Jobsworth just called—he's overjoyed that you're taking Thursday and said that if we do a *really* good job, he would give Jurisfiction's extra funding his special attention."

I moved away so Thursday1–4 couldn't hear me and spoke into my mobilefootnoterphone again.

"Bradshaw, how badly do we need to suck up to Jobsworth right now?"[3]

I told Bradshaw to rely on me. He thanked me profusely, wished me well and rang off. I snapped the phone shut and placed it back in my bag.

"Right," I said, tossing Thursday1–4's badge back at her. "For your first assignment, you are to get Thursday5 back here, chakras realigned or not, and apologize to her."

Thursday1–4 stared at me for a moment, then dialed her own cell phone. I turned away and walked down the gravel drive, trying to relax. What a start.

I sat on an ornamental lion at the foot of the entrance steps and watched from a distance as Thursday5 reappeared and, after the briefest of altercations, they shook hands. There was a pause and then a few raised voices until finally, incredibly, and with Thursday1–4 as stiff as a poker, she allowed herself to be hugged. I smiled to myself, got up and walked back to where the pair of them were standing, Thursday5 looking optimistically positive and Thursday1–4 brooding stonily.

"Have you two sorted yourselves out?"

They both nodded.

"Good," I said, consulting my watch. "We've got a few hours before we attend the Council of Genres' policy-directive meeting, but before that—"

"*We* are attending the CofG meeting?" asked Thursday5 with eyes like saucers.

"Yes, but only in the sort of 'we' that means you stand at the back and say nothing."

"Wow! What will they be discussing?"

[3] "Bundles, old girl. Do this as a favor to old Bradders, eh? Just until the end of the day."

"BookWorld policy. Such as whether we should be supplying characters to video games to give them added depth. It's particularly relevant, as publishing these days doesn't necessarily restrict books to being just books. It's said that Harry Potter will make a rare appearance. Now, we've got to—"

"Will we really meet Harry Potter?" she asked in a soft whisper, her eyes going all dewy at the mention of the young wizard. Thursday1–4 looked to heaven and stood, arms crossed, waiting for us to get on with the day's work.

"It depends," I sighed. "If you pay attention or not. Now for this afternoon's assignment: relieving the staff who are dealing with the BookWorld's ongoing piano problem. And for that we need to go to Text Grand Central."

23.

The Piano Problem

The piano was thought to have been invented by Bartolomeo Cristofori in the early eighteenth century and was originally called the *gravicembalo col piano e forte,* which was fortunately reduced to *pianoforte,* then more simply to *piano.* Composed of 550 pounds of iron, wood, strings and felt, the eighty-eight-key instrument is capable of the subtlest of melodies, yet stored up in the tensioned strings is the destructive power of a subcompact moving at twenty miles per hour.

If Jurisfiction was the policing agency inside books and the Council of Genres was the political arm, Text Grand Central was the bureaucracy that bridged the two. Right up until the Ultraword™ debacle, TGC had remained unimpeachably honest, but after that, the Council of Genres—on my advice—took the harsh but only possible course of action to ensure that Text Grand Central would be too inefficient and unimaginative to pose a threat. They appointed a committee to run it.

As we walked onto one of the main Storycode Engine floors, I heard Thursday5 gasp. The proportions of the room were more in keeping with a factory that made Very Large Things, and the stone walls, vaulted ceiling and flickering gas lamps betrayed the room's provenance as something borrowed from an unpublished Gothic Horror novel. Laid in serried ranks across the echoing vastness of the space were hundreds of Storycode Engines, each one the size of a bus and built of shiny brass, mahogany and cast iron. A convoluted mass of pipes, valves and gauges, they looked like a cross between an espresso machine, a ship's engine and a euphonium on acid. They were so large there was a catwalk running around the upper section for easy maintenance, with a cast-iron spiral staircase at one end for access.

"These are Imaginotransference Storycode Engines. The most important piece of technology we possess. Remember the pipe leading out of core containment in *Pinocchio*?"

Thursday5 nodded.

"The throughput is radiated across the intragenre Nothing and ends up here, where they are then transmitted into the reader's imagination."

I knew why it worked but not *how*. Indeed, I was suspicious that perhaps there wasn't an explanation at all—or indeed any need for one. It was something we called an "abstract narrative imperative": They work solely because it's expedient that they do. The BookWorld is like that. Full of wholly improbable plot devices that are there to help grease the storytelling cogs.

I paused so they could both watch the proceedings for a moment. Thursday5 made no secret of her fascination, but Thursday1–4 stifled a faux yawn. Despite this, she still looked around. It was hard not to be impressed—the machines stretched off into the hazy distance almost as far as you could see. Technicians scurried like ants over the whirring machinery checking dials, oiling, venting off steam and filling out reports on clipboards. Others moved between machines with trolleys full of papers to be filed, and the air was full of the smell of hot oil and steam. Above our heads a series of clanking shafts and flapping leather belts brought power to the engines, and the combined clatter and hum in the vast chamber sounded like a cascading waterfall.

"Five hundred machines on each floor!" I shouted above the tumult. "With each one capable of handling up to fifty thousand concurrent readings. The ones in the blue overalls are the storycode technicians, known affectionately as 'word monkeys.' They keep the engines running smoothly, clean out the dialogue injectors and make sure there isn't a buildup of irony on the compressors. The man dressed in the white lab coat is the 'text collector.' There is a reader echo that pings back to the engine to throughput the next word, so we can use that to check if the book is running true to the author's original wishes. Any variance is termed a 'textual anomaly' and is caught in the waste gate of the echo skimmers, which are those large copper things on the top."

"This is all *really* fascinating technological stuff," observed Thursday1–4 drily, "but I'm waiting to see how it relates to pianos."

"It doesn't, O sarcastic one. It's called ed-u-cation."

"Pointless exposition, if you ask me."

"She's not asking you," retorted Thursday5.

"Exactly," I replied, "and some people enjoy the techie stuff. Follow me."

I opened an arched oak door that led off the engine floor and into the administrative section of Text Grand Central, a labyrinth of stone corridors lit by flaming torches affixed to the walls. It was insufferably gloomy but economical—part of the unfinished Gothic Horror novel from which all of TGC was fashioned. As soon as the door closed, the noise from the main engine floor ceased abruptly.

"I was just trying to explain," I said, "how we find out about narrative flexations. Most of the time, the anomalies are just misreads and lazy readers getting the wrong end of the stick, but we have to check everything, just in case."

"I can get this on the Text Grand Central tour for twenty shillings and with better company," said Thursday1–4, looking pointedly at Thursday5.

"*I'm* interested, ma'am."

"Creep."

"Slut."

"What did you call me?"

"Hey!" I shouted. "*Cut it out!*"

"She started it," said Thursday1–4.

"I don't care who started it. You'll *both* be fired if you carry on like this."

They fell silent, and we walked along the echoing corridors, past endless oak doors, all relating to some textual activity such as word meanings, idea licensing and grammasite control.

"The problem with pianos," I began, "is that there aren't enough to go around. Lots of people in the BookWorld play them, they frequently appear in the narrative, and they're often used as plot devices. Yet for an unfathomable reason that no one can fully explain, there are only fifteen to cover the entire BookWorld."

"Fifteen?" snorted Thursday1–4, who was lagging behind in a petulant manner. "How do they manage that, then?"

"With a lot of difficulty. Have a look."

I opened a door off the corridor. The room was much like a psychiatrist's office, full of bookshelves and with diplomas on the wall. There were two chairs, a desk and a couch. Two men were sitting in the chairs: A beard and pipe identified the first man immediately as a psychiatrist, and the second, who seemed desperately nervous, was obviously the patient.

"So, Mr. Patient," began the psychiatrist, "what can I do for you?"

"Well, Doc," muttered the patient unhappily, "I keep on thinking I'm a dog."

"I see. And how long has this been going on?"

"Since I was a puppy."

"Excuse me," I interrupted, "I'm looking for the Piano Squad."

"This is Very Old Jokes," explained the psychiatrist apologetically. "Pianos are down the corridor, first on the left."

"Sorry," I muttered somewhat sheepishly, and quietly closed the door. "I keep on doing that," I murmured. "They should really label these doors better."

We walked along the corridor, found the correct door and opened it to reveal a room about fifty feet square. The walls were roughly plastered, and the vaulted stone ceiling was supported in the center of the room by a sturdy pillar. Set into the wall to our right was an aperture the size of a single garage, painted bright white and illuminated from within by several hundred lightbulbs. As we watched, there was a faint buzz, a flicker, and an ornate cabinet piano suddenly appeared in the aperture. Almost instantly a workman dressed in brown overalls and with a flat cap moved forward to wheel it out on well-oiled castors. Facing the bright white opening was a control desk that looked like a recording studio's mixing console, and behind this were two men of youthful countenance, dressed in linen suits. They were wearing headsets and had the harried look of people under great pressure.

"Upright rosewood returned from *Sons and Lovers*," whispered the one who was standing. "Stand by to send the Goetzmann into *Villette*."

"Check!" shouted the other man as he adjusted the knobs and sliders on the console. The workman pushed a Goetzmann grand into the empty aperture, stepped back, called "Clear," and with another buzz, the piano vanished.

They looked at us as soon as we entered, and I nodded a greeting. They nodded one back and returned to their work.

"Observe," I said to the Thursdays, pointing to a large indicator panel on the wall behind the men. The fifteen pianos were listed down the left-hand side, and in columns next to them were indicator lights and illuminated panels that explained what was happening to each. The uppermost piano on the list we noted was a "generic" grand and was currently inside *Bleak House*. It would be available in a few minutes and was next due to appear in *Mill on the Floss*, where it would stay for a number of scenes until departing for *Heart of Darkness*. While we watched, the indicator boards clicked the various changes as the two operators expertly moved the pianos back and forth across fiction. Below the indicator boards were several other desks, a watercooler and a kitchenette and coffee bar. There were a few desultory potted plants kicking around, but aside from several rusty filing cabinets, there was not much else in the room.

"Fifteen pianos is usually ample," I explained, "and when all pianos are available for use, the Piano Squad just trots along merrily to a set timetable. There are a few changes here and there when a new book requires a piano, but it generally works—eighty-six percent of pianos appear in nineteenth- and early-twentieth-century literature."

I pointed to the indicator board.

"But if you notice, eight pianos are 'status unavailable,' which means that they have been pulled out of frontline service for maintenance." I waved the report Bradshaw had handed me. "There was an administrative mix-up; we usually have one piano offline at a time, but some clot had them all refitted at once to save costs."

The Thursdays looked at the two operators again, and as we watched, the upright piano made of rosewood and with inlaid brass was moved from *Sons and Lovers* to *The Mayor of Casterbridge* and then on to *The Turn of the Screw.*

"That's right," I said, "Charles and Roger are having to spread seven pianos around the entire canon of English fiction. Hang on, it looks as though we're coming to a break."

They did indeed seem to be about to stop work for a few minutes. The two operators relaxed, stopped what they were doing, removed their headsets and stretched.

"Hello, Thursday," said the younger of the two in a quiet whisper. "Brought your family in to work?"

"Not a chance," I laughed. "Jurisfiction Cadets Thursday5 and Thursday1–4, meet Charles and Roger of the Piano Squad."

"Hello!" yelled Roger, who appeared not to be able to converse at anything less than a shout. "Come up and have a look-see!"

The Thursdays went to join Roger at the console, Thursday5 because she was genuinely interested and Thursday1–4 because Roger was actually quite attractive.

"Just how many piano mentions are there in fiction?" asked Thursday5.

"Thousands," he replied, "but in varying degrees. Much of nineteenth-century literature—the Brontës, Hardy and Dickens in particular—is literally *awash* with pianos, but they're rarely played. Those are the easy ones to deal with. Our pianos one to seven are nonfunctioning and are for description only. They are simply on an automatic circuit of the BookWorld, appearing momentarily in the text before flashing off to appear elsewhere." He turned to the indicator board. "If you look at the panel, our trusty old P-6 Broadwood upright is currently on page three hundred and thirty-nine of *The Lost World,* where it occupies a space near the standard lamp in the Pottses' villa in Streatham. In a few moments, it will jump automatically to the subbasement on page ninety-one of *Howards End,* where it will sit beneath a Maud Goodman painting. A moment later it will jump off to page one hundred and sixty-one of *Huckleberry Finn* and the Grangerford parlor."

"However," added Charles in a whisper, "Eliot, Austen and Thackeray are not only knee-deep in pianos, but working ones which in many instances are the linchpin of a scene. And *those* are the ones we have to be most careful about regarding supply and demand. Amelia Sedley's piano in *Vanity Fair* is sold at auction and repurchased by Dobbin to be given to her as a gift, and the singing and accompaniment within Austen do much to add to the general atmosphere."

Thursday5 nodded enthusiastically, and Thursday1–4, for the first time that day, actually expressed a vague interest and asked a question: "Can't someone just make some more pianos?"

"There is a measure of economy that runs throughout the BookWorld," he replied. "We count ourselves lucky—pianos are positively *bountiful* compared to the number of real dusty gray and wrinkly elephants."

"How many of those are there?"

"One. If anyone needs a herd, the Pachyderm Supply Division has to make do with cardboard cutouts and a lot of off-page trumpeting."

The Thursdays mused upon this for a moment, as Charles and

Roger donned their jackets and prepared to take a few hours off while I took over. I'd done it before, so it wasn't a problem.

"Everything's pretty much set on automatic," explained Charles as they headed out the door, "but there are a few manual piano movements you'll need to do—there's a list on the console. We'll be back in two hours to take care of the whole *Jude the Obscure* letter-in-the-piano plot-device nonsense and to somehow juggle the requirements of a usable piano in *Three Men in a Boat* with the destruction of a Beulhoff grand in *Decline and Fall*."

"Sooner you than me," I said. "Enjoy your break."

They assured me that they would and departed with the man in overalls, whose name, we learned, was Ken.

"Right," I said, sitting down and putting my feet up on the console. "Get the coffee on, Thursday."

Neither of them budged an inch.

"She gave *you* an order," said Thursday1–4. "And I take mine black and strong."

"Humph!" muttered Thursday5, but she went off to put the kettle on nonetheless.

Thursday1–4 took off her greatcoat, hung it on a peg and sat down in one of the other chairs.

"So . . . we just sit here and watch pianos move around the BookWorld?" she asked in a somewhat sneering tone of voice. Mind you, she usually spoke like that, so it was nothing unusual.

"That's *exactly* what we do. Much of Jurisfiction's work is like this. Boring but essential. Without an uninterrupted supply of pianos, much essential atmosphere would be lost. Can you imagine *The Woman in White* without Laura's playing?"

Thursday1–4 looked blank.

"You don't know what I'm talking about, do you?"

"The classics are too slow for me," she replied, idly taking one of her automatics from its holster and removing the clip to stare at the shiny rounds. "Not enough action. I'm more into David Webb."

"You've read Robert Ludlum?" I asked in surprise. Most bookpeople didn't read. It was too much like a busman's holiday.

"Nope. It's Dave I like, *especially* when he's Jason Bourne. Knows how to show a lady a good time and can pop a head shot from a thousand yards."

"Is there anyone in fiction you *haven't* slept with?"

"I love *The Woman in White,*" put in Thursday5, who had returned with a tray of coffees—but with a glass of water for herself, I noticed. "All that Mozart to express her love for Hartright—dreamy!"

I took my coffee, and we watched the lights flicker on the console as a nonfunctioning Bösendorfer was moved from *Our Mutual Friend* to *Persuasion,* where it jumped rapidly between the twelve different scenes in which it was mentioned before vanishing off into *Wives and Daughters.*

"I think atmosphere in novels is overrated," said Thursday1–4, taking a sip of coffee before she added patronizingly, "Good coffee, Thursday—jolly well done."

"That's put my mind at rest," replied Thursday5 sarcastically, something that Thursday1–4 missed.

"Are there any cookies?" I asked.

"Yes," echoed Thursday1–4, "are there any?"

Thursday5 huffed, got up, found some Jaffa cakes and placed them on the console in front of me, glaring at Thursday1–4 as she did so.

"Don't underestimate atmosphere," I said slowly, helping myself to a Jaffa cake. "The four opposing forces in any novel are atmosphere, plot, character and pace. But they don't have to be in equilibrium. You can have a book without any plot or pace at all, but it has to make up for it in character and a bit of atmosphere—like *The Old Man and the Sea.* Most thrillers are plot and pace and nothing else, such as *Where Eagles Dare.* But it doesn't matter; each to a reader's own—"

I stopped talking, because a warning light was flashing on the console in front of us.

"Hmm," I murmured as I leaned closer, "they're overrunning

in *The Dubliners*, and *Ulysses* needs an upright piano for Mr. Dedalus to comment upon at the Ormond Hotel in less than a minute's time."

"Isn't there a spare piano at Norland Park?" asked Thursday5.

"No—Marianne took it with her to Devon, and it's currently one of those being overhauled."

I scanned the knobs and switches of the console, looking for a spare piano that could be redirected. I eventually found one in *Peter Pan*. It was only referred to in a line of dialogue, so I redirected it to *Ulysses* as quickly as I could. Too quickly, to be honest, and I fumbled the interchange.

"Shit," I muttered under my breath.

"What?"

"Nothing," I replied, knowing full well that no one would notice. I'd placed it in the wrong part of the Ormond Hotel. I didn't have time to worry about this, however, as another warning light was flashing. This was to alert us that the first manual piano movement that Roger and Charles had left us with was approaching. I picked up the handwritten note and read it.

"We've got the Goetzmann grand returning from *Villette*, and it has to be sent with piano stool 87B into Agatha Christie's *They Do It with Mirrors*. Who can see a piano stool anywhere?"

Neither of the Thursdays moved an inch. Thursday5 eventually tapped Thursday1–4 on the arm and said, "Your turn. I did the coffee."

"In that case," replied Thursday1–4 with impeccable twisted logic, "it must have been *my* turn to do the Jaffa cakes."

"I suppose."

"Then, since you very kindly undertook that task on *my* behalf, it's *your* turn to do something again—so find the sodding piano stool and stop bothering me with your bleating."

I laid a hand on Thursday1–4's arm and said, "Find the piano stool, Thursday."

She tutted haughtily in a manner that Friday would have

approved of but got up and had a look around the room, eventually finding it near a heap of sheet music, a few music stands and a dusty bassoon.

"Here," she said in a bored tone, lifting the lid to look inside. Just at that moment, there was a buzzing noise, and the Goetzmann grand appeared in the brightly lit aperture in the wall.

"Right on time."

I twiddled a few knobs to set its onward journey, told Thursday1–4 to put the piano stool with it, which she did, and then, with yet another buzz, I sent it on to the great hall of Stonygates inside Agatha Christie's *They Do It with Mirrors.*

"Good," I muttered, crossing that first task off the list. "We've got nothing else for a half hour."

But my troubles weren't nearly over, as Thursday5 had sat in the chair recently vacated by Thursday1–4.

"You're in my seat."

"It's not your seat."

"I sat in it first, so it's mine."

"You can't do dibs on seats, and besides, you don't *own* it."

"Listen," growled Thursday1–4, "do you like doing crochet?"

"Yes, so . . . ?"

"Then perhaps you can imagine how tricky that might be . . . *with broken fingers.*"

Thursday5's lip trembled for a moment. "I'm . . . I'm . . . sure we can discuss this like rational adults before resorting to anything so crude as violence."

"Perhaps we could," returned Thursday1–4, "but it's far easier with me telling you how it's going to be. Now, get your tie-dyed butt out of my seat."

"Thursday?" I said.

"I can deal with this," snapped Thursday5 in a rare show of annoyance. "I don't need to be rescued like a child every single time Miss Slagfest here opens her trap!"

"I'm not meddling," I replied. "All I want to know is where Thursday1–4 got that pistol."

"This?" she said, holding up the small black automatic that I'd suddenly noticed she was holding. "It's really cool, isn't it? A Browning twenty-six-caliber standard single-action automatic with slide and grip safety."

"Where did you get it?"

"I found it," she retorted defensively, "so I'm keeping it."

I didn't have time for this.

"Tell me where you found it, or you'll be its next victim."

She paused, then said, "It was . . . in that piano stool."

"Idiot!" I yelled, getting up and demanding she hand it over, which she did. "That's an essential plot point in *They Do It with Mirrors!* Why can't you just leave things alone?"

"I thought—"

"That's the problem. You don't. Stay here while we sort this out, and don't touch anything. I repeat: Touch *nothing*. Do you understand?"

"Yes, yes, of course I understand—what do you think I am, a child?"

I didn't have time to argue, so after telling Thursday5 to follow me closely, I jumped out of the Piano Squad to the Great Library, and from there we made our way into Agatha Christie's *They Do It with Mirrors*.

We arrived at Stonygates in the short length of dimly lit corridor that connected the square lobby with the great hall. We pressed ourselves into the shadows, and I looked inside the hall. It was a large room that oozed Victorian Gothic gloominess, with dark wood and minimal lighting. There were a half dozen or so people chattering, but more important, directly ahead of us was the Goetzmann grand that we had dispatched not two minutes before. And in front of this, the piano stool to which the weapon had to be returned. I was about to chance my luck and sneak in but had not gotten two paces when a young man came and sat on the piano stool and began to play. I retreated into the shadows and felt Thursday5 grip my arm nervously as the lights flickered and went out, leaving the house in semidarkness. We backed farther into the shadows as a large man with a sulky expression came out of the door and vanished into the gloom, muttering about the fuses. A few minutes later, an elderly woman tottered to the dining room and back to retrieve something, and almost immediately the front door was pushed violently open and a young man strode into the hall in an overdramatic manner. This was followed by an argument, the sound of the study door opening and closing, more muffled shouting and eventually two shots. With the characters in the room thus distracted, I padded softly to the man seated at the piano and tapped him lightly on his shoulder. He looked up with some surprise, and I showed him my Jurisfiction badge. I raised my eyebrows, placed a finger to my lips and gestured him to join the people on the other side of the room. He did as I asked, and once his back was turned, I slipped the small automatic into the piano stool, between a copy of Handel's Largo and Chopin's Preludes.

I quickly and noiselessly retraced my steps to where Thursday5 was waiting for me, and within a few minutes we had returned to the Piano Squad's headquarters.

As we reentered, the squad room was in chaos. Warning lights were flashing, klaxons were going off, and the control console was a mass of flickering indicator lights. I was relieved to see—if such a word could be used in such uproar—that Roger and Charles had both returned and were trying to bring some sort of semblance of order back to the piano-distribution network.

"I need the Thürmer back from *Agnes Grey*!" yelled Roger. "And I'll swap it for a nonworking Streicher—"

"What the hell's going on, Thursday?"

It was Commander Bradshaw, and he didn't look very happy.

"I don't know. When I left everything was fine."

"You *left*?" he echoed incredulously. "You left the piano room unattended?"

"I left—"

But I stopped myself. I was responsible for any cadet's actions or inactions, irrespective of what they were and where they happened. I'd made a mistake. I should have called Bradshaw to cover for me or to get someone to go into *Mirrors*.

I took a deep breath. "No excuses, sir—I screwed up. I'm sorry."

"*Sorry?*" repeated Bradshaw, "That's it? You're *sorry*? I've got a dead Holmes on my hands, one of the Outland's most favorite series is about to unravel, and I really don't need one of your idiot cadets suddenly thinking that she's god of all the pianos."

"What did she do?"

"If you'd been supervising properly, you'd know!"

"Okay, okay," I retorted, seriously beginning to get pissed off, "this one's down to me, and I'll face the music, but I'd like to know what she's done before I wipe the smirk off her face for good."

"She decided," he said slowly and with great restraint, "to do her own thing with piano supply in your absence. Every single piano reference has been deleted from Melville, Scott and Defoe."

"*What?*" I said, looking around the room and finally catching sight of Thursday1–4 on the other side of the room, where she was standing arms folded and apparently without a care in the world.

"As I said. And we don't have the time or the pianos to replace them. But that's not the worst bit."

"It gets worse?"

"Certainly. For some reason known only to herself, she dropped an upright Broadwood straight into Miss Bates's drawing room inside Austen's *Emma*."

"Have they noticed?"

"Pianos aren't generally the sort of thing one can miss. As soon as it arrived, speculation began on where it might have come from. Miss Bates agrees with Mrs. Cole that it's from Colonel Campbell, but Emma thinks it's from Mrs. Dixon. Mrs. Weston is more inclined to think it was from Mr. Knightley, but Mr. Knightley believes it's from Frank Churchill. Quite a mess, wouldn't you agree?"

"Can we get it out?"

"It's embedded itself now. I'm going to get Churchill to take the rap, and it shouldn't inflict too much damage. But this is down to you, Thursday, and I've got no choice but to suspend you from Jurisfiction duties pending a disciplinary inquiry."

"Let's keep a sense of perspective on this, Bradshaw. I know I'm responsible, but it's not my fault—besides, you told me to do this, and I said I couldn't."

"It's my fault, is it?"

"Partly."

"Humph," replied Bradshaw, bristling his mustache in anger. "I'll take it under advisement—but you're still suspended."

I jerked a thumb in the direction of Thursday1–4. "What about her?"

"She's your cadet, Thursday. *You* deal with it."

He took a deep breath, shook his head, softened for a moment to tell me to look after myself and departed. I told Thursday5 to meet me up at the CofG and beckoned Thursday1–4 into the corridor.

"What the *hell* did you think you were doing?"

"Oh, c'mon," she said, "don't be such a hard-ass. There's no seriously lasting damage. So I dropped a piano into *Emma*—it's not like it landed on anyone."

I stared at her for a moment. Even allowing for Thursday1–4's supreme arrogance, it still didn't make any sense.

"You're not stupid. You *knew* it would get you fired once and for all, so why do it?"

She stared at me with a look of cold hatred. "You were going to fire me anyway. There wasn't a ghost's chance I'd have made it."

"The chance was slim," I admitted, "but it was there."

"I don't agree. You hate me. Always have. From the moment I was first published. We could have been friends, but you never even *visited.* Not once in four entire books. Not a postcard, a footnote, nothing. I'm closer to you than family, Thursday, and you treated me like crap."

And then I understood.

"You put the piano into *Emma* to stitch me up, didn't you?"

"After what you've done to me, you deserve far worse. You had it in for me the moment I arrived at Jurisfiction. You all did."

I shook my head sadly. She was consumed by hate. But instead of trying to deal with it, she just projected it onto everyone around her. I sighed.

"You did this for revenge over some perceived slight?"

"That wasn't revenge," said Thursday1–4 in a quiet voice. "You'll know revenge when you see it."

"Give me your badge."

She dug it from her pocket and then tossed it onto the floor rather than hand it over.

"I quit," she spat. "I wouldn't join Jurisfiction now if you *begged* me."

It was all I could do not to laugh at her preposterous line of reasoning. She couldn't help herself. She was written this way.

"Go on," I said in an even tone, "go home."

She seemed surprised that I was no longer angry.

"Aren't you going to yell at me or hit me or try to kill me or something? Face it: This isn't much of a resolution."

"It's all you're going to get. You really don't understand me at all, do you?"

She glared at me for a moment, then bookjumped out.

I stood in the corridor for a few minutes, wondering if there was anything else I might have done. Aside from not trusting her an inch, not really. I shrugged, tried and failed to get TransGenre Taxis to even *answer* the footnoterphone and then, checking the time so I wouldn't be late for the policy-directive meeting, made my way slowly toward the elevators.

24.

Policy Directives

The Council of Genres is the administrative body that looks after all aspects of BookWorld regulation, from making policy decisions in the main debating chamber to the day-to-day running of ordinary BookWorld affairs, from furnishing plot devices to controlling the word supply coming in from the Text Sea. They oversee the Book Inspectorate, which governs which books are to be published and which to be demolished, and also Text Grand Central and Jurisfiction—but only regarding policy. For the most part, they are evenhanded but need to be watched, and that's where I come into the equation.

I didn't go straight to either Jurisfiction or the Council of Genres but instead went for a quiet walk in Wainwright's *Pictorial Guide to the Lakeland Fells*. I often go there when in a thoughtful or pensive mood, and although the line drawings that I climbed were not as beautiful nor as colorful as the real thing, they were peaceful and friendly, imbued as they were with a love of the fells that is seldom equaled or surpassed. I sat on the warm sketched grass atop Haystacks, threw a pebble into the tarn and watched the drawn ripples radiate outward. I returned much refreshed an hour later.

I found Thursday5 still waiting for me in the seating area near the picture window with the view of the other towers. She stood up when I approached.

"I'm sorry," she said.

"Why?" I responded. "It wasn't your fault."

"But it certainly wasn't yours."

"That's the thing," I replied. "It was. She's a cadet. She has no responsibility. Her faults are mine."

I stopped to think about what I'd just said. Thursday 1–4 was impetuous, passionate and capable of almost uncontrollable rage. Her faults really *were* mine.

I took a deep breath and looked at my watch. "Showtime," I murmured despondently. "Time for the policy-directive meeting."

"Oh!" exclaimed Thursday5, and then searched through her bag until she found a small yellow book and a pen.

"I hope that's not what I think it is."

"What do you think it is?"

"An autograph book."

She said nothing and bit her lip.

"If you even *think* about asking Harry Potter for an autograph, your day ends right now."

She sighed and dropped the book back into her bag.

The policy meeting was held in the main debating chamber. Jobsworth's chair was the large one behind the dais, with the seats on either side of him reserved for his closest aides and advisers. We arrived twenty minutes early and were the first ones there. I sat down in my usual seat to the left of where the genres would sit, and Thursday5 sat just behind me. The Read-O-Meter was still clicking resolutely downward, and I looked absently around the chamber, trying to gather my thoughts. Along the side walls were paintings of various dignitaries who had distinguished themselves in one way or another during the Council of Genres' rule—my own painting was two from the end, sandwiched between Paddington Bear and Henry Pooter.

"So what's on the agenda?" asked Thursday5.

I shrugged, having become somewhat ticked off with the whole process. I just wanted to go home—somewhere away from fiction and the parts of me I didn't much care for.

"Who knows?" I said in a nonchalant fashion. "Falling ReadRates, I imagine—fundamentally, it's all there is."

At that moment the main doors were pushed open and Jobsworth appeared, followed by his usual retinue of hangers-on. He saw me immediately and chose a route that would take him past my desk.

"Good afternoon, Next," he said. "I heard you were recently suspended?"

"It's an occupational hazard when you're working in the front line," I replied pointedly—Jobsworth had always been administration. If he understood the remark, he made no sign of it. I added, "Are you well, sir?"

"Can't complain. Which one's that?" he asked, pointing to Thursday5 in much the same way as you'd direct someone to the toilet.

"Thursday5, sir."

"You're making a mistake to fire the other one," said Jobsworth, addressing me. "I'd ask for a second or third opinion about her if there was anyone left to ask. Nevertheless, the decision was yours, and I abide by it. The matter is closed."

"I was down in the maintenance facility recently," I told him, "and Isambard told me that the CofG had insisted on upgrading all the throughput conduits."

"Really?" replied Jobsworth vaguely. "I do wish he'd keep himself to himself."

He walked to the raised dais, sat in the central chair and busied himself with his notes. The room fell silent, aside from the occasional click of the Read-O-Meter as it heralded another drop in the Outland ReadRate.

The next delegate to arrive was Colonel Barksdale, head of the CofG Combined Forces. He sat down four desks away without looking at me. We had not seen eye to eye much in the past, as I disliked his constant warmongering. Next to arrive was Baxter, the senator's chief adviser, who flicked a distasteful look in my direction. In fact, all eight members of the directive panel, except for the Equestrian senator Black Beauty, didn't much like me. It wasn't surprising. I wasn't just the only Outlander member on the panel, I was the LBOCS and consequently wielded the weapon that committees always feared—the veto. I tried to discharge my duties as well as I could, despite the enmity it brought.

I could see Thursday5 move expectantly every time the door opened, but apart from the usual ten members of the committee and their staff, no one else turned up.

"Good afternoon, everyone," said Jobsworth, standing up to address us. There weren't many of us in the debating chamber, but it was usually this way—policy meetings were closed-door affairs.

"Sadly, I have to advise you that Mr. Harry Potter is unable to attend due to copyright restrictions, so we're going to leave the 'supplying characters from video games' issue for another time."

There was a grumbling from the senators, and I noticed one or two put their autograph books back into their bags.

"Apologies for absence," continued Jobsworth. "Jacob Marley is too alive to attend, the Snork Maiden is at the hairdresser's, and Senator Zigo is once more unavailable. So we'll begin. Item One: the grammasite problem. Mr. Bamford?"

Senator Bamford was a small man with wispy blond hair and eyes that were so small they almost weren't there. He wore a blue coverall very obviously under his senatorial robes and had been in charge of what we called "the grammasite problem" for almost four decades, seemingly to no avail. The predations of the little parasitical beasts upon the books on which they fed was damaging and a constant drain on resources. Despite culling in the past, their numbers were no smaller now than they'd ever been. Mass extermination was often suggested, something the Naturalist genre was violently against. Pests they might be, but the young were cute and cuddly and had big eyes, which was definitely an evolutionary edge to secure survival.

"The problem is so well known that I will not outline it here again, but suffice it to say that numbers of grammasites have risen dramatically over the years, and in order to keep the naturalists happy I suggest we undertake a program of textualization, whereby representative specimens of the seven hundred or so species will be preserved in long-winded accounts in dreary academic tomes. In that way we can preserve the animal and even, if necessary, bring it back from extinction—yet still exterminate the species."

Bamford sat down again, and Jobsworth asked for a show of hands. We all agreed. Grammasites were a pest and needed to be dealt with.

"Item Two," said Jobsworth. "Falling readership figures. Baxter?"

Baxter stood up and addressed the room, although, to be honest, the other delegates—with the possible exception of Beauty—generally went with Jobsworth on everything. The person Baxter really needed to address was me. As the holder of the only veto, I was the one he would have to swing.

"The falling readership figures have been a matter of some concern for a number of years now, and increased expenditure in the Well of Lost Plots to construct thrilling new books has failed to grasp the imagination of the reading public. As head of the Readership Increasement Committee, I have been formulating some radical ideas to rekindle interest in novels."

He turned over a paper and coughed before continuing.

"After a fact-finding mission conducted in the real world, I have decided that 'interactivity' is the keyword of the new generation. For many readers books are too much of a one-sided conduit of information, and a new form of novel that allows its readers to choose where the story goes is the way forward."

"Isn't that the point of books?" asked Black Beauty, stamping his hoof angrily on the table and upsetting an inkwell. "The pleasure lies in the *unfolding* of the plots. Even if we know what must happen, how one *arrives* there is still entertaining."

"I couldn't agree with you more," remarked Baxter, "but our

core readership is aging, and the world's youth is growing up without being in the habit of reading books."

"So what's your suggestion?" asked Jobsworth.

"To create a new form of book—an *interactive* book that begins blank except for ten or so basic characters. Then, as it is written, chapter by chapter, the readers are polled on whom they want to keep and whom they want to exclude. As soon as we know, we write the new section, and at the end of the new chapter we poll the readers again. I call it a 'reality book show'—life as it *really* is, with all the human interactions that make it so rich."

"And the boring bits as well?" I asked, recalling my only experience with reality TV.

"I don't suggest that *every* book should be this way," added Baxter hurriedly, "but we want to make books hip and appealing to the youth market. Society is moving on, and if we don't move with it, books—and we—will vanish."

As if to reinforce his argument, he waved a hand at the Read-O-Meter, which dropped another seventeen books by way of confirmation.

"Why don't we just write better books?" I asked.

"Because it's expensive, it's time-consuming, and there's no guarantee it will work," said Senator Aimsworth, speaking for the first time. "From what I've seen of the real world, interactivity is a sure-fire hit. Baxter is right. The future is reality book shows based on democratic decision making shared by the creators and the readers. Give people what they want and in just the way they want it."

"Once the ball starts rolling downhill, it can't be stopped," I remarked. "This is the wrong route—I can feel it."

"Your loyalty is misplaced, Ms. Next. What could be wrong with offering readers choice? I say we vote on it. All those in favor of directing funds and resources to an interactive reality-book project?"

They all raised their hands—except me and Senator Beauty.

Me because I didn't agree with them and Beauty because he had a hoof. It didn't matter. He was against it.

"As usual," growled Aimsworth, "the contrarian amongst us knows better. Your objections, Ms. Next?"

I took a deep breath. "The point is, ladies and gentlemen, that we're *not* in the book industry. This isn't a publishing meeting with sales targets, goals, market research and focus groups. The book may be the delivery medium, but what we're actually peddling here is *story*. Humans like stories. Humans *need* stories. Stories are good. Stories *work*. Story clarifies and captures the essence of the human spirit. Story, in all its forms—of life, of love, of knowledge—has traced the upward surge of mankind. And story, you mark my words, will be with the last human to draw breath, and we should be there, too, supporting that one last person. I say we place our faith in good stories well told and leave the interactivity as the transient Outlander fad that it is. Instead of being subservient to reader opinion, we should be leading it."

I paused for a moment and stared at the sea of unconvinced faces. The Read-O-Meter clicked down another twenty-eight books.

"Listen, I'm as worried about falling ReadRates as anyone, but wild and desperate measures are not the answer. We've got to go back to the root cause and figure out why people prefer watching *Samaritan Kidney Swap* to reading a good book. If we *can't* create better books, then we should be doing a lot more than simply dreaming up gimmicks to pander to the lowest common denominator."

There was silence. I meant about 75 percent of it but needed to get the message across. There should be room on this planet for *Dr. Zhivago* and *Extreme Spatula Makeover,* but the scales had tipped far enough—and I didn't want them to go any further. They all stared at me in silence as Jobsworth drummed his fingers on the desk.

"Does this mean you are exercising your veto?"

"It does."

There was a collective groan from the other delegates, and I suddenly wondered if I'd gone too far. After all, they had the good of the BookWorld as their priority, as did I—and it wasn't as though I could come up with anything better.

"I'd like to conduct my own study group," I said, hoping that by using their own corporate-buzzword language I might get them to go for it, "and see if I can throw up any strategies to pursue. If I can't, we'll go with your interactivity idea, no matter how dumb it sounds."

"I see," intoned Jobsworth as they all exchanged annoyed looks. "Since I know you too well to expect you to change your mind, we'll reappraise the situation in a week's time and move on. Next item?"

Colonel Barksdale stood up and looked at us all in the somber manner in which he always imparted bad news. He never had anything else. In fact, I think he *engineered* bad news in order to have the pleasure of giving it. He'd been head of BookWorld Defense for the past eight years and clearly wanted to increase his game to include an intragenre war or two. A chance to achieve greatness, if you like.

"I expect you've all heard about Speedy Muffler's recent threat to the stability of the BookWorld?"

We all mumbled our agreement.

"Good. Well, as security is my province, I want you all to agree to a plan of action that is both decisive and *final*. If Muffler can deploy a dirty bomb, then none of us are safe. Hard-liners in Ecclesiastical and Feminist are ready to mobilize for war to protect their ideologies, and it is my opinion that a preemptive strike will show those immoral bastards that we mean business. I've three brigades of Danverclones ready and waiting to stream across the border. It won't take long—Racy Novel is a ramshackle genre at best."

"Isn't war a bit hasty?" I persisted. "Muffler will try anything to punch above his weight. And even if he *has* developed a dirty bomb, he still has to deliver it. How's he going to smuggle something like that into Feminist? It's got one of the best-protected frontiers in the BookWorld."

"We have it on good authority that they might disguise it as a double entendre in a bedroom farce and deliver it up the rear entrance at Comedy."

"Pure conjecture. What about good old-fashioned diplomacy? You could offer Muffler some Well-surplus subtext or even dialogue to dilute the worst excesses of the genre—he'd probably respond favorably to it. After all, they merely want to develop as a genre."

Colonel Barksdale drummed his fingers impatiently and opened his mouth to speak, but Jobsworth beat him to it.

"That's the worry. Ecclesiastical is concerned that Racy Novel wants to undertake an expansionist policy—there's talk of their wanting to reoccupy the dehumorized zone. Besides," he added, "subtext and dialogue are up to almost seven hundred and fifty guineas a kilo."

"Do we know if they even *have* a dirty bomb?" I asked. "It might all be a bluff."

Jobsworth signaled to Colonel Barksdale, who handed me a dossier marked 'Terribly Secret.'

"It's no bluff. We've been sent some rather disturbing reports regarding outbreaks of incongruous obscenity from as far away as Drama—Charles Dickens, no less."

"*Bleak House,*" I read from the sheet of paper I'd been handed, "and I quote: 'Sir Leicester leans back in his chair, and breathlessly ejaculates.' "

"You see?" said Barksdale as the rest of the delegates muttered to themselves and shook their heads in a shocked manner. "And what about this one?"

He handed me another sheet of paper, this time from Thomas Hardy's *Mayor of Casterbridge.*

" '. . . the Mayor beheld the unattractive exterior of Farfrae's erection.' "

"And," he added decisively, "we've got a character named 'Master Bates' turning up all over *Oliver Twist*."

"Master Bates has always been called that," I pointed out. "We used to giggle over the name at school."

"Despite that," replied Colonel Barksdale with no loss of confidence, "the other two are quite enough to have this taken *extremely* seriously. The Danverclones are ready. I only need your approval—"

"It's called 'word drift.'"

It was Thursday5. The meeting had never seen such a flagrant lapse of protocol, and I would have thrown her out myself—but for the fact she had a point.

"I'm sorry," said Senator Jobsworth in a sarcastic tone. "I must have missed the meeting where the other Thursday was elected to the Security Council. Jurisfiction Cadets must train, so I will overlook it this once. But one more word . . . !"

Unabashed, Thursday5 added, "Did Senator Muffler send those examples to you?"

Senator Jobsworth wasted no time and called over his shoulder to one of the many Danverclones standing close by. "Security? See that Thursday with the flower in her hair? She is to be returned to her—"

"She's with me," I said, staring at Jobsworth, who glared back dangerously, "and I vouch for her. She has opinions that I feel are worth listening to."

Jobsworth and Barksdale went silent and looked at each other, wondering if there wasn't some sort of rule they could invoke. There wasn't. And it was for precisely these moments that the Great Panjandrum had given me the veto—to slow things down and make the Council of Genres think before it acted.

"Well?" I said. "*Did* Speedy Muffler send those examples to you?"

"Well, not perhaps . . . as such," replied Colonel Barksdale with a shrug, "but the evidence is unequivocally compelling and totally, absolutely without doubt."

"I contend," added Thursday5, "that they are simply words whose meanings have meandered over the years, and those books were written with *precisely* the words you quoted us now. Word drift."

"I hardly think that's likely, my dear," replied Jobsworth patronizingly.

"Oh, no?" I countered. "Do you mean to tell me that when Lydia from *Pride and Prejudice* thinks of Brighton and '. . . the glories of the camp—its tents stretched forth in beauteous uniformity of lines, crowded with the young and the gay,' that she might possibly mean something else?"

"Well, no, of course not," replied the senator, suddenly feeling uncomfortable under the combined baleful stares of Thursday5 and me.

There was a mumbling among the other delegates, and I said, "Words change. Whoever sent these examples to you has an agenda, which is more about confrontation than a peaceful outcome to the crisis. I'm going to exercise my veto again. I suggest that a diplomatic resolution be attempted until we have irrefutable evidence that Muffler really has the capabilities he claims."

"This is bad judgment," growled Jobsworth with barely controlled rage as he rose from his seat and gathered his papers together. "You're on morally tricky ground if you side with Racy Novel."

"I'm on morally *trickier* ground if I don't," I replied. "I will not sanction a war on misplaced words in a few of the classics. Show me a blatantly unsubtle and badly written sex scene in *To the Lighthouse* and I will personally lead the battle myself."

Jobsworth stared at me, and I stared back angrily.

"By then the damage will have been done. We want to stop them before they even get started," he insisted.

He paused and composed himself.

"Two vetoes in one day," he added. "You must be particularly pleased with yourself. I hope you have as many smart answers when smutty innuendo is sprinkled liberally across *The Second Sex*."

And without another word, he stormed from the meeting, closely followed by Barksdale, Baxter and all the others, each of them making tut-tut noises and shaking their heads in a sickening display of inspired toadying. Only Senator Beauty wasn't with them. He shook his own head at me in a gesture meaning "better you than me" and then trotted out.

We were left in silence, aside from the Read-O-Meter, which ominously dropped another thirty-six books.

"That word-drift explanation was really very good," I said to Thursday5 when we were back in the elevator.

"It was nothing, really."

"Nothing?" I echoed. "Don't sell yourself short. You probably just averted a genre war."

"Time will tell. I meant to ask. You said you were the 'LBOCS.' What does that mean?"

"It means I'm the council's Last Bastion of Common Sense. Because I'm from the Outland, I have a better notion of independent thought than those in the generally deterministic BookWorld. Nothing happens without my knowledge or comment."

"That must make you unpopular sometimes."

"No," I replied, "it makes me unpopular *all* the time."

We went back down to the Jurisfiction offices for me to formally hand over my badge to Bradshaw, who took it from me without expression and resumed his work. I returned despondently to where Thursday5 was waiting expectantly at my desk. It was the end of her assessment, and I knew she wanted to be put out of her misery one way or another.

"There are three recommendations I can make," I began, sitting back in my chair. "One: for you to be put forward for further training. Two: for you to be returned to basic training. And three: for you to leave the service entirely."

I looked across at her and found myself staring back at me. It was the look I usually gave to the mirror, and it was disconcerting.

But I had to be firm and make my decision based on her performance and suitability.

"You were nearly eaten by a grammasite, and you would have let the Minotaur kill me," I began, "but on the plus side, you came up with the word-drift explanation, which was pretty cool."

She looked hopeful for a moment.

"But I have to take all things under consideration and without bias—either in your favor or against. The Minotaur episode was too important a failing for me to ignore, and much as I like your mildly eccentric ways, I'm sorry, but I'm going to have to recommend that you do not join Jurisfiction, either now or in the future."

She didn't say anything for a while and looked as though she was about to cry, which she did a second or two later. She might have made a decent Jurisfiction agent, but the chances of her getting herself killed were just too high for me to risk. On my graduation assignment, I was almost murdered by a bunch of emotion junkies inside *Shadow the Sheepdog.* Given the same situation, Thursday5 wouldn't have survived, and I wasn't going to have that on my conscience. She wasn't just a version of me, she was something closer to *family,* and I didn't want her coming to any harm.

"I understand," she said between sniffs, dabbing at her nose with a lacy handkerchief.

She thanked me for my time, apologized again for the Minotaur, laid her badge on my desk and vanished off into her book. I leaned back in my chair and sighed—what with firing both Thursdays, I'd really been giving myself a hard time today. I wanted to go home, but the power required for a transfictional jump to the Outland might be tricky on an empty stomach. I looked at my watch. It was only four, and Jurisfiction agents at that time liked to take tea. And to take tea, they generally liked to go to the best tearooms in the BookWorld—or anywhere else, for that matter.

25.

The Paragon

There are three things in life that can make even the worst problems seem just that tiniest bit better. The first is a cup of tea—loose-leaf Assam with a hint of Lapsang and poured before it gets too dark and then with a dash of milk and the smallest hint of sugar. Calming, soothing and almost without peer. The second, naturally, is a hot soaking bath. The third is Puccini. In the bath with a hot cup of tea and Puccini. Heaven.

It was called the Paragon and was the most perfect 1920s tearoom, nestled in the safe and unobserved background fabric of P. G. Wodehouse's *Summer Lightning.* To your left and right upon entering through the carved wooden doors were glass display cases containing the most sumptuous homemade cakes and pastries. Beyond these were the tearooms proper, with booths and tables constructed of a dark wood that perfectly matched the paneled interior. This was itself decorated with plaster reliefs of Greek characters disporting themselves in matters of equestrian and athletic prowess. To the rear were two additional and private tearooms, the one of light-colored wood and the other in delicate carvings of a most agreeable nature. Needless to say, it was inhabited by the most populous characters in Wodehouse's novels. That is to say it was full of voluble and opinionated aunts.

There were two Jurisfiction agents sitting at the table we usually reserved for our three-thirty tea and cakes. The first was tall and dressed in jet black, high-collared robes buttoned tightly up to his throat. He had a pale complexion, prominent cheekbones and a small and very precise goatee. He sat with his arms crossed and was staring at all the other customers in the tearooms with an air of haughty superiority, eyebrows raised imperiously. This was truly a tyrant among tyrants, a ruthless leader who had murdered billions in his never-ending and inadequately explained quest for the unquestioned obedience of every living entity in the known galaxy. The other, of course, was a six-foot-tall hedgehog dressed in a multitude of petticoats, an apron and bonnet, and carrying a wicker basket of washing. There was no more celebrated partnership in Jurisfiction either then or now—it was Mrs. Tiggy-Winkle and Emperor Zhark. The hedgehog from Beatrix Potter and the emperor from the Zhark series of bad science-fiction novels.

"Good afternoon, Thursday," intoned the emperor when he saw me, a flicker of a smile attempting to crack through his imperialist bearing.

"Hi, Emperor. How's the galactic-domination business these days?"

"Hard work," he replied, rolling his eyes heavenward. "Honestly, I invade peaceful civilizations on a whim, destroy their cities and generally cause a great deal of unhappy mayhem—and then they turn against me for absolutely no reason at all."

"How senselessly irrational of them," I remarked, winking at Mrs. Tiggy-Winkle.

"Quite," continued Zhark, looking aggrieved and not getting the sarcasm. "It's not as though I put them *all* to the sword anyway—I magnanimously decided to spare several hundred thousand as slaves to build an eight-hundred-foot-high statue of myself striding triumphantly over the broken bodies of the vanquished."

"That's probably the reason they don't like you," I murmured.

"Oh?" he asked with genuine concern. "Do you think the statue will be too small?"

"No, it's the 'striding triumphantly over the broken bodies of the vanquished' bit. People generally don't like having their noses rubbed in their ill fortune by the person who caused it."

Emperor Zhark snorted. "That's the problem with inferiors," he said at last. "No sense of humor."

And he lapsed into a sullen silence, took an old school exercise book from within his robes, licked a pencil stub and started to write.

I sat down next to him.

"What's that?"

"My speech. The Thargoids graciously accepted me as god-emperor of their star system, and I thought it might be nice to say a few words—sort of thank them, really, for their kindness—but underscore the humility with veiled threats of mass extermination if they step out of line."

"How does it begin?"

Zhark read from his notes. "'Dear Worthless Peons—I pity you your irrelevance.' What do you think?"

"Well, it's definitely to the point," I admitted. "How are things on the Holmes case?"

"We've been trying to get into the series all morning," said Zhark, laying his modest acceptance speech aside for a moment and taking a spoonful of the pie that had been placed in front of him, "but to no avail. I heard you got suspended. What was that about?"

I told him about the piano and *Emma,* and he whistled low.

"Tricky. But I shouldn't sweat it. I saw Bradshaw writing up the duty rosters for next week, and you're still on them. One moment." He waved a carefully manicured hand at the waitress and said, "Sugar on the table, my girl, or I'll have you, your family and all your descendants put to death."

The waitress bobbed politely, ignored his manner entirely and said, "If you killed me, Your Imperial Mightiness, I wouldn't have any descendants, now would I?"

"Yes, well, *obviously* I meant the ones yet living, girl."

"Oh!" she said. "Just so we're clear on the matter," and with a cute bob she was gone.

"I keep on having trouble with that waitress," muttered Zhark after she had departed. "Do you think she was . . . mocking me?"

"Oh, no," said Mrs. Tiggy-Winkle, hiding a smile, "I think she was terrified of you."

"Has anyone thought of redirecting the Sherlock Holmes throughput feeds from the Outland?" I asked. "With a well-positioned Textual Sieve, we could bounce the series to a Storycode Engine at TGC and rewrite the ending with the Holmes and Watson from *The Seven-Per-Cent Solution*. It will hold things together long enough to give us time to effect a permanent answer."

"But where *exactly* to put the sieve?" inquired Zhark, not unreasonably.

"What exactly *is* a Textual Sieve?" asked Mrs. Tiggy-Winkle.

"It's never fully explained," I replied.

The waitress returned with the sugar.

"Thank you," said Zhark kindly. "I have decided to . . . spare your family."

"Your Highness is overly generous," replied the waitress, humoring him. "Perhaps you could just torture one of us—my younger brother, for instance?"

"No, my mind is made up. You're to be spared. Now begone or I will— Oh, no. You don't trick me that way. Begone or I will *never* torture your family."

The waitress bobbed again, thanked him and was gone.

"Perky, that one, isn't she?" said Zhark, staring after her. "Do you think I should make her my wife?"

"You're considering getting married?" asked Mrs. Tiggy-Winkle, almost scorching a collar in her surprise.

"I think it's high time that I did," he said. "Slaughtering peaceful civilizations on a whim is a lot more fun when you've got someone to do it with."

"Does your mother know about this?" I asked, fully aware of the power that the Dowager Empress Zharkina IV wielded in his books. Emperor Zhark might have been the embodiment of terror across innumerable star systems, but he lived with his mum—and if the rumors were correct, she still insisted on bathing him.

"Well, she doesn't know *yet*," he replied defensively. "But I'm big enough to make my *own* decisions, you know."

Mrs. Tiggy-Winkle and I exchanged knowing looks. Nothing happened in the imperial palace without the empress's agreement.

Zhark chewed for a moment, winced and then swallowed with a look of utter disgust on his face. He turned to Mrs. Tiggy-Winkle.

"I think you've got my pie."

"Have I?" she replied offhandedly. "Now you come to mention it, I thought these slugs tasted sort of funny."

They swapped pies and continued eating.

"Ms. Next?"

I looked up. A confident middle-aged woman was standing next to the table. She had starburst wrinkles around the eyes and graying brown hair, a chicken-pox scar above her left brow, and asymmetric dimples. She was a well-realized character but I didn't recognize her—at least not at first.

"Can I help?" I asked.

"I'm looking for the Jurisfiction agent named Thursday Next."

"That's me."

Our visitor seemed relieved at this and allowed herself a smile. "Pleased to meet you. My name's Dr. Temperance Brennan."

I knew who she was, of course: the heroine of her own genre—that of the forensic anthropologist.

"Very pleased to meet you," I said, rising to shake her hand. "Perhaps you'd care to join us?"

"Thank you, I shall."

"This is Emperor Zhark," I said, "and the one with the spines is Mrs. Tiggy-Winkle."

"Hello," said Zhark, sizing her up for matrimony as he shook her hand. "How would you like the power of life or death over a billion godless heathens?"

She paused for a moment and raised an eyebrow. "Montreal suits me just fine."

She shook Mrs. Tiggy-Winkle's claw, and they exchanged a few pleasantries over the correct method to wash linens. I ordered her some coffee, and after I'd asked about her Outlander book sales, which were impressively large compared to mine, she admitted to me that this wasn't a social call.

"I've got an understudy covering for me, so I'll come straight to the point," she said, looking with apparent professional interest at Zhark's high cheekbones. "Someone's trying to kill me."

"You and I have much in common, Dr. Brennan," I replied. "When did this happen?"

"Call me Tempe. Have you read my latest adventure?"

"*Grave Secrets*? Of course."

"Near the end I'm captured after being slipped a Mickey Finn. I talk my way out of it, and the bad guy kills himself."

"So?"

"Thirty-two readings ago, I was drugged for *real* and nearly didn't make it. It was all I could do to stay conscious long enough to keep the book on its tracks. I'm first-person narrative so everything's up to me."

"Yeah," I murmured, "that first-person thing can be a drag. Did you report it to Text Grand Central?"

She pushed the hair away from her face and said, "Naturally. But since I kept the show going, it was never logged as a textual anomaly, so according to TGC there's no crime. You know what they told me? 'Come back when you're dead, and *then* we can do something.'"

"Hmm," I said, drumming my fingers on the desk. "Who do you think is behind it?"

She shrugged. "No one in the book. We're all on very good terms."

"Any skeletons in the closet? If you'll excuse the expression."

"Plenty. In Crime there's always at least one seriously bad guy to deal with per book—sometimes more."

"*Narratively* speaking, that's how it appears," I pointed out. "But with you dead, everyone else in your books would become redundant overnight—and with the possibility of erasure looming over them, your former enemies actually have some of the best reasons to keep you alive."

"Hmm," said Dr. Brenann thoughtfully, "I hadn't thought of it that way."

"The most likely person to want to kill you is someone outside your book—any thoughts?"

"I don't know anyone outside my books—except Kathy and Kerry, of course."

"It won't be them. Leave it with me," I said after a moment's pause, "and I'll see what I can do. Just keep your eyes and ears open, yes?"

Dr. Brennan smiled and thanked me, shook my hand again, said good-bye to Zhark and Mrs. Tiggy-Winkle and was gone, muttering that she had to relieve the substandard and decidedly bone-idle understudy who was standing in for her.

"What was that all about?" asked Zhark.

"No idea," I replied. "It's kind of flattering that people bring their problems to me. I just wish there were another Thursday to deal with it."

"I thought there was."

"Don't even joke about it, Emperor."

There was a crackle in the air, and Commander Bradshaw suddenly appeared just next to us. Zhark and Tiggy-Winkle looked guilty all of a sudden, and the hedgepig washerwoman made a vain attempt to hide the ironing she was doing.

"I thought I would find you here," he said, mustache all atwitch, as it was when he was a bit peeved. "That wouldn't be moonlighting, would it, Agent Tiggy-Winkle?"

"Not at all," she replied. "I spend so much time at Jurisfiction I can hardly get through the ironing I need to do for my own book!"

"Very well," said Bradshaw slowly, turning to me. "I thought I'd find *you* here, too. I have a job that only you can handle."

"I thought I was suspended?"

He passed me my badge. "The suspension was purely for the CofG's benefit. The disciplinary paperwork was accidentally eaten by snails. Most perplexing."

I smiled. "What's up?"

"A matter of great delicacy. There were a few minor textual irregularities in . . . the Thursday books."

"Which ones?" I asked, suddenly worried that Thursday5 might have taken her failure to heart.

"The first four. Since you know them quite well and no one else wants to touch them or her with a barge pole, I thought you might want to check it out."

"What sorts of irregularities?"

"Small ones," said Bradshaw, handing me a sheet of paper. "Nothing you'd notice from the Outland unless you were a committed fan. I'm thinking it might be the early stage of a breakdown."

He didn't mean a breakdown in the Outlander sense. In the BookWorld a breakdown meant an internal collapse of the character's pattern of reason—the rules that made one predictable and understandable. Some, like Lucy Deane, collapsed spontaneously and with an annoying regularity; others just crumbled slowly from within, usually as a result of irreconcilable conflicts within their character. In either case, replacement by a fully trained-up generic was the only option. Of course, it might be nothing and very possible that Thursday1–4 was just angry about being fired and venting her spleen on the co-characters in the series.

"I'll check her out."

"Good," said Bradshaw, turning to Zhark and Tiggy-Winkle. "And you two—I want you all geared up and ready to try to get into 'The Speckled Band' by way of 'The Disintegrator Ray' by fourteen hundred hours."

Bradshaw looked at his clipboard and then vanished. We all stood up.

"Do you want us to come with you?" asked Zhark. "Strictly speaking, your checking up on Thursday1–4 is a conflict-of-interest transgression."

"I'll be fine," I said, and the pair of them wished me well and vanished, like Bradshaw, into thin air.

26.

Thursday Next

I was only vaguely consulted when the first four of the Thursday Next books were constructed. I was asked about my car, my house, and I even lent them a photo album (which I never got back). I was also introduced to the bland and faceless generic who would eventually become Thursday1–4. The rest was created from newspaper reports and just plucked from the air. If I'd cared more about how it all was going to turn out, perhaps I would have given them more time.

After another fruitless argument with the dispatcher at Trans-Genre Taxis, who told me they had two drivers off sick and it wasn't their fault but they would "see what could be done," I took the elevator down to the sixth floor of the Great Library and walked to the section of shelving that carried all five of the Thursday books, from *The Eyre Affair* all the way through to *The Great Samuel Pepys Fiasco.* There was every edition, too—from publisher's proof to hardback, large print and mass-market paperback. I picked up a copy of *The Eyre Affair* and looked carefully for a way in. I knew that the book was first-person narrative, and having a second me clearly visible to readers would be wildly confusing—if the book wasn't confusing enough already. I soon found what I was looking for: a time lapse of six weeks after Landen's death near the beginning of the book. I scanned the page for the correct place, and, using an oblique, nonappearing-entry method taught to me by Miss Havisham, I slipped unseen into the end of chapter one.

I arrived in the written Swindon just as the sun was dipping below the horizon, and I was standing opposite our house in the Old Town. Or at least it was the *remains* of our house. The fire had just been put out, and the building was now a blackened ruin, the still-hot timbers steaming as they were doused with water. Through the twinkling of blue and red emergency lights, I could see a small figure sitting in the back of an ambulance, a blanket draped across her shoulders. The legal necessity of removing Landen from the series was actually a blessing in disguise for the publishers. It freed up their Thursday romantically and also gave a reason for her psychotic personality. Boy, was this book ever *crap*.

I waited in the crowd for a moment until I could sense that the chapter was over, then approached Thursday1–4, who had her back to me and was talking to a badly realized version of Bowden, who in this book was known by the legally unactionable "Crowden Babel."

"Good evening," I said, and Thursday jumped as though stuck with a cattle prod.

"What are you doing here?" she asked without turning around.

"Text Grand Central saw a few wrinkles in the narrative, and you're too unpleasant for anyone other than me to come and have a look."

"It's okay," she said, "everything's fine. It's probably a Storycode Engine on the fritz. A buildup of irony on the dialogue injectors or something."

She seemed jittery but still didn't want to turn and look at me straight on.

"You sure?"

"Of course I'm sure—do you think I don't know my own book? I'm afraid I must go. I've got to run through some lines with the replacement Hades."

"Wait," I said, and grabbed her arm. I pulled her around to face . . . *someone else entirely*. It wasn't Thursday1–4. It was a woman with the same coloring and build, clothes and general appearance, but it wasn't her.

"Who the hell are you?" I demanded.

She sighed heavily and shrugged. "I'm . . . I'm . . . a character understudy."

"I can see that. Do you have a name?"

"Alice-PON-24330," she replied resignedly.

"This series isn't up for maintenance for years. What are you doing here?"

She bit her lip, looked away and shifted her weight uneasily. "If she finds I've talked . . . well, she has a *temper*."

"And I don't?"

She said nothing. I turned to Crowden Babel. "Where is she?"

He rubbed his face but said nothing. It seemed I was the only person *not* frightened by Thursday1–4.

"Listen," I said to Babel, pointing at Alice-PON-24330, "she's just an understudy and is like a phone number—replaceable. You're in every book and have a lot more to lose. Now, either you talk to me right this minute and it goes no further or we turn you over to Jurisfiction and thirty tons of prime-quality shit is going to descend on you from a very great height."

Babel scratched the back of his head. "She does this every now and then. She thinks the series is too small for her."

Babel and the ersatz Thursday glanced nervously at each other. There was something else going on. This wasn't just a simple substitution so Thursday1–4 could have a break.

"Somebody better start talking, or you'll discover where she gets her temper from. Now, *where has she gone?*"

Babel looked nervously around. "She came back *furious*. Said you'd fired her on false pretenses and she wanted to get some . . . serious payback."

"What sort of payback?"

"I don't know."

"If you're lying to me!"

"I swear on the life of the Great Panjan—"

"I know where she is," said the ersatz Thursday in a quiet voice. "What the hell. When she discovers I've talked to you, I'll be dead anyway. She's out . . . in the *real world*!"

This was serious. Substitution and illegal pagerunning were one thing, but crossing over to the real world was quite another. I could legally erase her on sight, and the way I felt right now, I—

My thoughts were interrupted because both Crowden and the understudy had looked anxiously toward the burned-out shell of the house. I suddenly had a very nasty thought, and my insides changed to lead. I could barely say the word, but I did:

"Landen?"

"Yes," said the understudy in a soft voice. "She wanted to know what it was . . . to *love.*"

I felt anger well up inside me. I pulled out my TravelBook and read as I walked toward the house. As I did so, the evening light brightened, the emergency vehicles faded back into fiction, and the house, which burned to a husk in *The Eyre Affair,* was suddenly perfect again as I moved back into the real world. My mouth felt dry after the jump, and I could feel a headache coming on. I broke into a panicky sweat and dumped my jacket and bag in the front garden but kept my pistol and slipped a spare eraserhead into my back pocket. I very quietly stepped up to the front door and silently slipped the key into the lock.

The house was silent aside from the thumping of my heart, which in my heightened state of anxiety was almost deafening. I had planned to lie in wait for her, but a glance down at the hall table made me reappraise the situation. My house keys and distinctive grammasite key ring were already lying where I left them—*but I still had mine in my hand.* I felt powerfully thirsty, too, and was badly dehydrated—the most annoying side effect of my return to the Outland. I looked through to the kitchen and could see a pitcher of half-finished juice on the kitchen drainer. If I didn't drink something soon, I'd pass out. On the other hand, Thursday1–4 was somewhere in the house, waiting for Landen or rummaging in our sock drawer or something. I silently crept along the downstairs hallway, checked the front room, then went through to the dining room beyond and from there to the kitchen. The only thing I noticed out of place was a book of family holiday snapshots open on the coffee table. I moved into the kitchen and was about to take a swig of juice straight from the pitcher when I heard a noise that turned my blood to ice. I dropped the pitcher, which shattered on the kitchen floor with a concussion that echoed around the house.

Pickwick woke up in her basket and started plocking at everything in sight until she saw who it was and went back to sleep. I heard voices upstairs and the sound of footsteps padding across the bedroom floor. I held my pistol at arm's length and walked slowly down the hall to the stairs. The sound that had made me drop the pitcher was *Landen*, but it was the sort of sound that only *I* ever heard him make—something that was for me and me alone.

I rounded the newel post and looked up. Almost immediately Thursday1–4 stepped onto the landing, completely naked and holding her automatic. Fictional she might have been, but out here she was as deadly as any real person. We stared at each other for a moment, and she fired. I felt her shot whine past me and embed itself in the doorframe. At almost exactly the same time, I fired my pistol. There was a low thud, and the air wobbled as though momentarily seen through a milk bottle. She jumped back into the bedroom as the wide spread of the eraserhead hit harmlessly on the walls and stairs—the charge only affected anything *textual*. She'd know my weapon was a single shot, so I turned on my heels and ran back through the front room, breaking the pistol open to reload. The cartridge ejected with a soft *thwup*, and I yanked the spare out of my back pocket and pushed it into the breech. There was a detonation and another whine of a near miss as I jumped across the breakfast table and snapped the pistol shut with a flick of my wrist. I pulled the heavy oak kitchen table to shield me, and three shots smashed into the wood. I heard the sound of footsteps running away and rose to fire at her retreating form. The dull thud of the eraserhead echoed around the room, and there was a mild hiss as it struck its mark. I heard the front door open, I got up—slightly too quickly—and the room went squiffy. I staggered to the sink and drank from the running tap and then, still feeling light-headed but tolerably alert, stumbled up the hall to the open front door. There was a small scattering of fine text on the doorstep and more leading out into the front garden, where I saw her automatic lying on the garden path. I turned and yelled upstairs, "Stay where you are, Land!" and then followed the trail of text to the front gate, where there was a random sprinkling of letters. I cursed. There wasn't enough here to be fatal—I'd probably just clipped her and caused a small part of her to unravel. It was no big deal. She could have another body part written exclusively for her down in the Well.

My shoulder bag was still where I'd left it in the front garden, and I rummaged inside for a spare eraserhead. I slipped the shiny cartridge into the barrel, then stopped. Something was *wrong.* I searched the bag more frantically, then all around the area nearby, but found only a light smattering of text. The wounded Thursday1–4 had been here—*and taken my TravelBook.* I looked around, closed the pistol and followed the small trail of letters to the garden gate, where they ended abruptly. I gazed out into the empty street. Nothing. She had jumped out, back to where she belonged—and with my TravelBook. My *TravelBook.*

I wiped the sweat from my brow and muttered, "Shit-shit-shit-*SHIT.*"

I turned and ran back to the house but then stopped as I suddenly had a series of terrible thoughts. Thursday1–4's adventures ranged across several years, so she wasn't particularly age-specific. Landen couldn't know that it was not me but my fictional counterpart he'd just made love to. I didn't bear him any malice—I mean, it wasn't as if he'd slept with another woman or anything. But because he knew nothing about Jurisfiction and it was better for our relationship that he *never* knew, there was only one course of action I could take.

"Hang on, Land!" I yelled upstairs. "I'm okay. Just stay where you are."

"Why?" he yelled back.

"Just do as I ask, sweetheart."

I grabbed the dustpan and brush and hurriedly swept up the text that littered the front step and the path, and when I heard the distant wail of the police sirens, I went back indoors, took off all my clothes, stashed them behind the sofa and ran upstairs.

"What's going on?" asked Land, who had just gotten his leg and trousers on. I wrapped myself in a robe but couldn't look at him and just sat at the dressing table, clenching and unclenching my fists to try to control the violent thoughts. Then I realized: After what she'd done, I could think about wringing her badly written neck as much as I wanted. I was a woman wronged. Dangerously violent thoughts were *allowed.* I'd get her for this, but I was in no hurry. She had nowhere to go. I knew *exactly* where I could find her.

"Nothing's going on," I said in a quiet voice. "Everything's fine."

27.

Bound to the Outland

Although we never really saw eye to eye with the local police force when we were SpecOps, we always used to help them out if they got into a jam, and the young ones never forgot it. Hard not to, really, when some lunatic plucks you from the jaws of a werewolf or something. Because of this I was still granted favors in return. Not parking tickets, unfortunately—just the big stuff.

By the time the police arrived, I had regained control of myself. I picked up Thursday1–4's clothes with a disdainful finger and thumb and deposited them in the laundry basket, in which I would take them out to burn them later that evening. I went through the pockets of her jacket but found only an empty wallet and a few coins. I knew I was going to have to admit to owning her automatic, so I had to hope they would take my previous exemplary conduct into account before citing me on any illegal-firearms charges. While I explained it all to the cops, Landen called Joffy's partner, Miles, to get him to pick up the girls from school, and we eventually tracked Friday down at Mum's, where he'd been discussing with his aunt the merits of the guitar riff on the second track of *Hosing the Dolly*.

"So let me get this straight," said Detective Inspector Jamison an hour later, thumbing through his notes. "You were both upstairs . . . er, *naked* when you heard a noise. You, Mrs. Parke-Laine-Next, went downstairs to investigate with an illegally held

Glock nine-millimeter. You saw this man whom you identified as 'Felix8,' an associate of the deceased Acheron Hades, whom you last met sixteen years ago. He was armed, and you fired at him once when he was standing at the door, once when he was running to the kitchen, then three times as he hid behind the kitchen table. He then made his escape from the house without firing a single shot. Is that correct?"

"Quite correct, Officer."

"Hmm," he said, and his sergeant whispered something in his ear and handed him a fax. Jamison looked at it, then at me. "You're *sure* it was Felix8?"

"Yes—why?"

He placed the fax on the table and slid it across.

"The body of missing father of two Danny Chance was discovered in a shallow grave in the Savernake Forest three years ago. It was skeletal by then and only identifiable by his dental records."

"That's not possible," I murmured, with good reason. Even if he hadn't been in the house this afternoon, I'd certainly seen him yesterday.

"I know that Hades and Felix are tied up in all manner of weird shit, so I'm not going to insist you *didn't* see him, but I thought you should know this."

"Thank you, Officer," I muttered, reading through the report, which was unequivocal; it even said the bones had been in the ground a good ten years. Aornis had been right—Cocytus *had* killed him like a stray dog.

Inspector Jamison turned to Landen. "Mr. Parke-Laine? May we speak to you now?"

They finally left at nine in the evening and we called Miles to bring the kids back. We'd been given the all-clear to tidy up, and to be honest it didn't sound as though they were gong to make a big deal of it. It didn't look as if they would even bother to prosecute; they knew about Felix8—everyone did. He, Hades and Aornis were as much a part of popular culture as Robin Hood. And that was it. They took the Glock nine-millimeter, privately told me that it was an honor to meet me and that I could expect their report to be lost before being passed to the prosecutor, and then they were gone.

"Darling?" said Landen as soon as the kids had been safely returned home.

"Yes?"

"Something's bothering you."

"You mean aside from having an amoral lunatic who died fifteen years ago try to kill us?"

"Yes. There's something else on your mind."

Damn. Found out. Lucky I had *several* things on my mind I could call upon.

"I went to visit Aornis."

"You did? Why?"

"It was about Felix8. I should have told you: He was hanging around the house yesterday. Millon spotted him, and Spike nabbed him—but he escaped. I thought Aornis might have an idea why he's suddenly emerged after all these years."

"Did Aornis . . . say anything about us?" asked Landen. "Friday, Me, Tuesday, Jenny?"

"She asked how everyone was, but only in an ironic way. I don't think she was concerned in the least—quite the opposite."

"Did she say anything else?"

I turned to look at him, and he was gazing at me with such concern that I rested a hand on his cheek.

"Sweetheart—what's the matter? She can't harm us any longer."

"No," said Landen with a sigh, "she can't. I just wondered if she said anything—anything at all. Even if you remembered it later."

I frowned. Landen knew about Aornis's powers because I'd told him, but his specific interest seemed somehow unwarranted.

"Yeah. She said that she was going to bust out with the help of someone 'on the outside.'"

He took my hands in his and stared into my eyes. "Thursday—sweetheart—promise me something?"

I laughed at his dramatic earnestness but stopped when I saw he was serious.

"Two minds with but a single thought," I told him, "two hearts that beat as one."

"That was good. Who said that?"

"Mycroft."

"Ah! Well, here it is: Don't let Aornis out."

"Why should I want to do that?"

"Trust me, darling. Even if you forget your own name, remember this: *Don't let Aornis out.*"

"Babes—"

But he rested his finger on my lips, and I was quiet. Aornis was the least of my worries. Without my TravelBook I was marooned in the Outland.

We had dinner late. Even Friday was vaguely impressed by the three bullet holes in the table. They were so close they almost looked like one.

When he saw them, he said, "Nice grouping, Mum."

"Firearms are no joking matter, young man."

"That's our Thursday," said Landen with a smile. "When she shoots up our furniture, she does as little damage as possible."

I looked at them all and laughed. It was an emotional release, and tears sprang to my eyes. I helped myself to more salad and regarded Friday. There was still the possibility of his replacement by the-Friday-that-could-have-been hanging over him. The thing was, I couldn't do anything about it. There's never anywhere to hide from the ChronoGuard. But the other Friday had told me I had forty-eight hours until they might attempt such a thing, and that wasn't up until midmorning the day after tomorrow.

"Fri," I said, "have you thought any more about the time industry?"

"Lots," he said, "and the answer's still no."

Landen and I exchanged looks.

"Have you ever wondered," remarked Friday in a languid monotone from behind a curtain of oily hair, "how nostalgia isn't what it used to be?"

I smiled. Dopey witticisms at least showed he was *trying* to be clever, even if for the greater part of the day he was asleep.

"Yes," I replied, "and imagine a world where there were no hypothetical situations."

"I'm *serious*," he said, mildly annoyed.

"Sorry!" I replied. "It's just difficult to know what you're thinking when I can't see your face. I might as well converse to the side of a yak."

He parted his hair so I could see his eyes. He looked a lot like his father did at that age. Not that I knew him then, of course, but from photographs.

"Nostalgia used to have a minimum twenty years before it kicked in," he said in all seriousness, "but now it's getting shorter and shorter. By the late eighties, people were doing seventies stuff, but by the mid-nineties the eighties-revival thing was in full swing. It's now 2002, and already people are talking about the nineties—soon nostalgia will catch up with the present and we won't have any need for it."

"Good thing, too, if you ask me," I said. "I got rid of all my seventies rubbish as soon as I could and never regretted it for a second."

There was an indignant plock from Pickwick.

"Present company excepted."

"I think the seventies are underrated," said Landen. "Admittedly, fashion wasn't terrific, but there's been no better decade for sitcoms."

"Where's Jenny?"

"I took her dinner up to her," said Friday. "She said she needed to do her homework."

I frowned as I thought of something, but Landen clapped his hands together and said, "Oh, yes! Did you hear that the British bobsled team has been disqualified for using the banned force 'gravity' to enhance performance?"

"No."

"Apparently so. And it transpires that the illegal use of gravity to boost speed is endemic within most downhill winter sports."

"I wondered why they managed to go so fast," I replied thoughtfully.

Much later that night, when the lights were out, I was staring at the glow of the streetlamps on the ceiling and thinking about Thursday1–4 and what I'd do to her when I caught her. It wasn't terribly pleasant.

"Land?" I whispered in the darkness.

"Yes?"

"That time we . . . made love today."

"What about it?"

"I was just thinking—how did you rate it? Y'know, on a one-to-ten?"

"Truthfully?"

"Truthfully."

"You won't be pissed off at me?"

"Promise."

There was a pause. I held my breath.

"We've had better. *Much* better. In fact, I thought you were pretty terrible."

I hugged him. At least there was one piece of good news today.

28.

The Discreet Charm of the Outland

The real charm of the Outland was the richness of detail and the *texture*. In the BookWorld a pig is generally just pink and goes oink. Because of this, most fictional pigs are simply a uniform flesh color without any of the tough bristles and innumerable scabs and skin abrasions, shit and dirt that makes a pig a pig. And it's not just pigs. A carrot is simply a rod of orange. Sometimes living in the BookWorld is like living in Legoland.

The stupidity surplus had been beaten into second place by the news that the militant wing of the no-choice movement had been causing trouble in Manchester. Windows were broken, cars overturned, and there were at least a dozen arrests. With a nation driven by the concept of choice, a growing faction of citizens who thought life was simpler when options were limited had banded themselves together into what they called the "no-choicers" and demanded the choice to have no choice. Prime Minister Redmond van de Poste condemned the violence but explained that the choice of choice over "just better services" was something the *previous* administration had chosen and was thus itself a no-choice principle for the current administration. Alfredo Traficcone, MP, leader of the opposition Prevailing Wind Party, was quick to jump on the bandwagon, proclaiming that it was the inalienable right of all citizens to have the choice over whether they have choice or not. The no-choicers had suggested that there should be a referendum to settle the matter once and for all, something that the opposition "choice" faction had no option but to agree with. More sinisterly, the militant wing known only as NOPTION was keen to go further and demanded that there should be only one option on the ballot paper—the no-choice one.

It was eight-thirty, and the girls had already gone to school.

"Jenny didn't eat her toast again," I said, setting the plate with its uneaten contents next to the sink. "That girl hardly eats a thing."

"Leave it outside Friday's door," said Landen. "He can have it for lunch when he gets up—*if* he gets up."

The front doorbell had rung, and I checked on who it might be through the front-room windows before opening the door to reveal . . . Friday. The *other* Friday.

"Hello!" I said cheerily. "Would you like to come in?"

"I'm in a bit of a hurry," he replied. "I just wondered whether you'd thought about my offer of replacement yesterday. Hi, Dad!"

Landen had joined us at the door. "Hello, son."

"This," I said by way of introduction, "is the Friday I was telling you about—the one we were supposed to have."

"At your service," said Friday politely. "And your answer? I'm sorry to push you on this, but time travel has still to be invented and we have to look very carefully at our options."

Landen and I glanced at each other. We'd already made up our mind.

"The answer's no, Sweetpea. We're going to keep *our* Friday."

Friday's face fell, and he glared at us. "This is so typical of you. Here I am a respected member of the ChronoGuard, and you're still treating me like I'm a kid!"

"Friday!"

"How stupid can you both be? The history of the world hangs in the balance, and all you can do is worry about your lazy shitbag of a son."

"You talk like that to your mother and you can go to your room."

"He *is* in his room, Land."

"Right. Well . . . you know what I mean."

Friday snorted, glared at us both, told me that I really shouldn't call him "Sweetpea" anymore and walked off, slamming the garden gate behind him.

I turned to Landen. "Are we doing the right thing?"

"Friday told us to dissuade him from joining the ChronoGuard, and that's what we're doing."

I narrowed my eyes, trying to remember.

"He did? When?"

"At our wedding bash? When Lavoisier turned up looking for your father?"

"Shit," I said, suddenly remembering. Lavoisier was my least favorite ChronoGuard operative, and on that occasion he had a partner with him—a lad of about twenty-five who'd looked vaguely familiar. We figured it out several years later. It was Friday *himself*, and his advice to us was unequivocal: "If you ever have a son who wants to be in the ChronoGuard, try to dissuade him." Perhaps it wasn't just a complaint—perhaps it had been . . . a *warning*.

Landen placed a hand on my waist and said, "I think we should follow his best advice and see where it leaves us."

"And the End of Time?"

"Didn't your father say that the world was *always* five minutes from total annihilation? Besides, it's not until Friday evening. It'll work itself out."

I took the tram into work and was so deep in thought I missed my stop and had to walk back from MycroTech. Without my TravelBook I was effectively stuck in the real world, but instead of feeling a sense of profound loss as I had expected, I felt something more akin to *relief*. In my final day as the LBOCS, I had scotched any chance of book interactivity or the preemptive strike on Speedy Muffler and the ramshackle Racy Novel, and the only worrying loose end was dealing with slutty bitchface Thursday1–4. That was if she hadn't been erased on sight for making an unauthorized trip to the Outland. Well, I could always hope. Jurisfiction had gotten on without me for centuries and would doubtless continue to do so. There was another big plus point, too: I wasn't lying to Landen quite as much. Okay, I still did a bit of SpecOps work, but at least this way I could downgrade my fibs from "outrageous" to a more manageable "whopping." All of a sudden, I felt really quite happy—and I didn't often feel that way. If there hadn't been a major problem with Acme's overdraft and the potential for a devastating chronoclasm in two and a half days, everything might be just perfect.

"You look happy," said Bowden as I walked into the office at Acme.

"Aren't I always?"

"No," he said, "hardly at all."

"Well, this is the new me. Have you noticed how much the birds are singing this morning?"

"They always sing like that."

"Then . . . the sky is always that blue, yes?"

"Yes. May I ask what's brought on this sudden change?"

"The BookWorld. I've stopped going there. It's over."

"Well," said Bowden, "that's *excellent* news!"

"It is, isn't it? More time for Landen and the kids."

"No," said Bowden, choosing his words carefully, "I mean excellent news for Acme—we might finally get rid of the backlog."

"Of undercover SpecOps work?"

"Of *carpets*."

"You mean you can make a profit selling carpets?" I asked, having never really given it a great deal of thought.

"Have you seen the order books? They're full. More work than we can handle. Everyone needs floor coverings, Thurs—and if you can give some of your time to get these orders filled, then we won't need the extra cash from your illegal-cheese activities."

He handed me a clipboard.

"All these customers need to be contacted and given the best deal we can."

"Which is?"

"Just smile, chat, take the measurements, and I'll do the rest."

"Then *you* go."

"No, the big selling point for Acme is that Thursday Next—the Z-4 *celebrity* Thursday Next—comes and talks to you about your floor-covering needs. That's how we keep our heads above water. That's how we can support all these ex-SpecOps employees."

"C'mon," I said doubtfully, "ex-celebrities don't do retail."

"After the disaster of the *Eyre Affair* movie, Lola Vavoom started a chain of builders' merchants."

"She did, didn't she?"

I took the clipboard and stared at the list. It was long. Business *was* good. But Bowden's attention was suddenly elsewhere.

"Is that who I think it is?" he asked, looking toward the front of the store. I followed his gaze. Standing next to the cushioned-linoleum display was a man in a long dark coat. When he saw us watching him, he reached into his pocket and flashed a badge of some sort.

"Shit," I murmured under my breath. "Flanker."

"He probably wants to buy a carpet," said Bowden with a heavy helping of misplaced optimism.

Commander Flanker was our old nemesis from SO-1, the SpecOps department that policed other SpecOps departments. Flanker had adapted well to the disbanding of the service. Before, he made life miserable for SpecOps agents he thought were corrupt, and now he made life miserable for *ex*-SpecOps agents he thought were corrupt. We had crossed swords many times in the past, but not since the disbandment. We regarded it as a good test of our discretion and secrecy that we had never seen him at Acme Carpets. Then again, perhaps we were kidding ourselves. He might know all about us but thought flushing out renegade operatives just wasn't worth his effort—especially when we were actually doing a service that no one else wanted to do.

I walked quickly to the front of the shop.

"Good morning, Ms. Next," he said, glancing with ill-disguised mirth at my name embroidered above the company logo on my jacket. "Literary Detective at SO-27 to carpet layer? Quite a fall, don't you think?"

"It depends on your point of view," I said cheerfully. "Everyone needs carpets—but not everyone needs SpecOps. Is this a social call?"

"My wife has read all your books."

"They're not *my* books," I told him in an exasperated tone. "I had absolutely no say in their content—for the first four anyway."

"Those were the ones she liked. The violent ones full of sex and death."

"Did you come all this way to give me your wife's analysis of my books?"

"No," he said, "that was just the friendly breaking-the-ice part."

"It isn't working. Is there a floor covering I could interest you in?"

"Axminster."

"We can certainly help you with *that*," I replied professionally. "Living room or bedroom? We have some very hard-wearing wool/acrylic at extremely competitive prices—and we've a special this week on underlayment and free installation."

"It was Axminster *Purple* I was referring to," he said slowly, staring at me intently. My heart jumped but I masked it well. Axminster Purple wasn't a carpet at all, of course, although to be honest there probably *was* an Axminster in purple, if I looked. No, he was referring to the semi-exotic cheese, one that I'd been trading in only a couple of days ago. Flanker showed me his badge. He was CEA—the Cheese Enforcement Agency.

"You're not here for the carpets, are you?"

"I know you have form for cheese smuggling, Next. There was a lump of Rhayder Speckled found beneath a Hispano-Suiza in '86, and you've been busted twice for possession since then. The second time you were caught with six kilos of Streaky Durham. You were lucky to be fined only for possession and not trading without a license."

"Did you come here to talk about my past misdemeanors?"

"No. I've come to you for information. While cheese smuggling is illegal, it's considered a low priority. The CEA has always been a small department more interested in collecting duty than banging up harmless cheeseheads. That's all changed."

"It has?"

"I'm afraid so," replied Flanker grimly. "There's a new cheese on the block. Something powerful enough to make a user's head vanish in a ball of fire."

"That's a figure of speech for 'really powerful,' right?"

"No," said Flanker with deadly seriousness. "The victim's head really *does* vanish in a ball of fire. It's a killer, Next—and addictive. It's apparently the finest and most powerful cheese ever designed."

This was worrying. I never regarded my cheese smuggling as anything more than harmless fun, cash for Acme and to supply something that should be legal anyway. If a cheese that I'd furnished had killed someone, I would face the music. Mind you, I'd tried most of what I'd flogged, and it was, after all, only cheese. Okay, so the taste of a particularly powerful cheese might render you unconscious or make your tongue numb for a week, but it never killed anyone—until now.

"Does this cheese have a name?" I asked, wondering if there'd been a bad batch of Machynlleth Wedi Marw.

"It only has a code name: X-14. Rumor says it's so powerful that it has to be kept chained to the floor. We managed to procure a half ounce. A technician dropped it by mistake, and this was the result."

He showed me a photograph of a smoking ruin.

"The remains of our central cheese-testing facility."

He put the photograph away and stared at me. Of course, I *had* seen some X-14. It'd been chained up in the back of Pryce's truck the night of the cheese buy. Owen had declined to even show it to me. I'd traded with him every month for over eight years, and I never thought he was the sort of person to knowingly peddle anything dangerous. He was like me: someone who just loved cheese. I wouldn't snitch on him, not yet—not before I had more information.

"I don't know anything," I said at length, "but I can make inquiries."

Flanker seemed to be satisfied with this, handed me his card and said in a stony voice, "I'll expect your call."

He turned and walked out of the store to a waiting Range Rover and drove off.

"Trouble for us?" asked Bowden as soon as I returned.

"No," I replied thoughtfully, "trouble for me."

He sighed. "That's a relief."

I took a deep breath and thought for a moment. Communications into the Socialist Republic of Wales were nonexistent—when I wanted to contact Pryce, I had to use a shortwave wireless transmitter at prearranged times. There was nothing I could do for at least forty-eight hours.

"So," continued Bowden, handing me the clipboard with the list of people wanting quotes on it, "how about some Acme Carpets stuff?"

"What about SpecOps work?" I asked. "How's that looking?"

"Stig's still on the case of the *Diatrymas* and has at least a half dozen outstanding chimeras to track down. Spike has a few biters on the books, and there's talk of another SEB over in Reading."

It was getting desperate. I loved Acme, but only insofar as it was excellent cover and I never actually had to do anything carpet-related.

"And us? The ex–Literary Detectives?"

"Still nothing, Thursday."

"What about Mrs. Mattock over in the Old Town? She still wants us to find her first editions, surely?"

"No," said Bowden. "She called yesterday and said she was selling her books and replacing them with cable TV—she wanted to watch *England's Funniest Chain-Saw Mishaps*."

"And I felt so good just now."

"Face it," said Bowden sadly, "books are finished. No one wants to invest the time in them anymore."

"I don't believe you," I replied, an optimist to the end. "I reckon if we went over to the Booktastic! megastore, they'd tell us that books are still being sold hand over fist to hard-core story aficionados. In fact, I'll bet you that jar of cookies you've got hidden under your desk that you think no one knows about."

"And if they're not?"

"I'll spend a day installing carpets and pressing flesh as the Acme Carpets celebrity saleswoman."

It was a deal. Acme was on a trading estate with about twenty or so outlets, but, unusually, it was the only carpet showroom—we always suspected that Spike might have a hand in scaring off the competition, but we never saw him do it. Between us and Booktastic! there were three sporting-goods outlets all selling exactly the same goods at exactly the same price and, since they were three branches of the same store, with the same sales staff, too. The two discount electrical shops actually *were* competitors but still spookily managed to sell the same goods at the same price, although "sell" in this context actually meant "serve as brief custodian between outlet and landfill."

"Hmm," I said as we stood inside the entrance of Booktastic! and stared at the floor display units liberally stacked with CDs, DVDs, computer games, peripherals and special-interest magazines. "I'm sure there was a book in here last time I came in. Excuse me?"

A shop assistant stopped and stared at us in a vacant sort of way.

"I was wondering if you had any books."

"Any *what*?"

"Books. Y'know—about so big and full of words arranged in a specific order to give the effect of reality?"

"You mean DVDs?"

"No, I mean *books*. They're kind of old-fashioned."

"Ah!" she said. "What you mean are *videotapes*."

"No, what I mean are *books*."

We'd exhausted the sum total of her knowledge, so she went into default mode. "You'll have to see the manager. She's in the coffee shop."

"Which one?" I asked, looking around. There appeared to be three—and this wasn't Booktastic!'s biggest outlet either.

"That one."

We thanked her and walked past boxed sets of obscure sixties TV series that were better—and safer—within the rose-tinted glow of memory.

"This is all so wrong," I said, beginning to think I might lose the bet. "Less than five years ago, this place was all books and nothing else. What the hell's going on?"

We arrived at the coffee shop and couldn't see the manager, until we noticed that they had opened a smaller branch of the coffee shop actually *inside* the existing one, and named it "X-press" or "On-the-Go" or "More Profit" or something.

"Thursday Next," I said to the manager, whose name we discovered was Dawn.

"A great pleasure," she replied. "I did *so* love your books—especially the ones with all the killing and gratuitous sex."

"I'm not really like that in real life," I replied. "My friend Bowden and I wondered if you'd sold many books recently or, failing that, if you have any or know what one is?"

"I'm sure there are a few somewhere," she said, and with a "woman on a mission" stride led us around most of the outlet. We walked past computer peripherals, stationery, chocolate, illuminated world globes and pretty gift boxes to put things in until we found a single rack of long-forgotten paperbacks on a shelf below the boxed set of *Hale & Pace Outtakes Volumes 1–8* and *The Very Best of Little and Large*, which Bowden said was an oxymoron.

"Here we are!" she said, wiping away the cobwebs and dust.

"I suppose we must have the full collection of every book ever written!"

"Very nearly," I replied. "Thanks for your help."

And that was how I found myself in an Acme van with Spike, who had been coerced by Bowden to do an honest day's carpeting in exchange for a week's washing for him and Betty. I hadn't been out on the road with Spike for a number of years, either for the weird shit we used to do from time to time or for any carpet-related work, so he was particularly talkative. As we drove to our first installation, he told me about a recent assignment.

". . . so I says to him, 'Yo, Dracula! Have you come to watch the eclipse with us?' You should have seen his face. He was back in his coffin quicker than shit from a goose, and then when he heard us laughing, he came back out and said with his arms folded, 'I suppose you think that's funny?' and I said that I thought it *was* perhaps the funniest thing I'd seen for years, especially since he'd tripped and fallen headfirst into his coffin, and then he got all shitty and tried to bite me, so I rammed a sharpened stake through his heart and struck his head from his body."

He laughed and shook his head. "Oh, man, did *that* crease us up."

"My amusement might have ended with the sharpened-stake thing," I confessed, "but I like the idea of Dracula falling flat on his face."

"He did that a lot. Clumsy as hell. That biting-the-neck thing? He was going for the *breast* and missed. Now he pretends that's what he was aiming for all along. Jerk. Is this number eight?"

It was. We parked, got out and knocked at the door.

"Major Pickles?" said Spike as a very elderly man with a pleasant expression answered the door. He was small and slender and in good health. His snow white hair was immaculately combed, a pencil mustache graced his upper lip, and he was wearing a blazer with a regimental badge sewn on the breast.

"Yes?"

"Good morning. We're from Acme Carpets."

"Jolly good!" said Major Pickles, who hobbled into the house and ushered us to a room that was devoid of any sort of floor covering. "It's to go down there," he said, pointing at the floor.

"Right," said Spike, who I could tell was in a mischievous mood. "My associate here will begin carpeting operations while I view the selection of tea and cookies on offer. Thursday—the carpet."

I sighed and surveyed the room, which was decorated with stripy green wallpaper and framed pictures of Major Pickles's notable wartime achievements—it looked as if he'd been quite a formidable soldier. It seemed a shame that he was in a rather miserable house in one of the more run-down areas of Swindon. On the plus side, at least he was getting a new carpet. I went to the van and brought in the toolbox, vacuum cleaner, grippers and a nail gun. I was just putting on my knee pads when Spike and Pickles came back into the room.

"Jaffa cakes!" exclaimed Major Pickles, placing a tray on the windowsill. "Mr. Stoker here said that you were allergic to anything without chocolate on it."

"You're very kind to indulge my partner's bizarre and somewhat disrespectful sense of humor," I said. "Thank you."

"Well," he said in a kindly manner, "I'll leave you to get along, then."

And he tottered out the door. As soon as he had gone, Spike leaned close to me and said, "Did you see that!?!"

"See what?"

He opened the door a crack and pointed at Pickles, who was limping down the corridor to the kitchen. "His *feet*."

I looked, and the hair on the back of my neck rose. There was a reason Major Pickles was hobbling—just visible beneath the hems of his trouser legs were *hooves*.

"Right," said Spike as I looked up at him. "The cloven one."

"Major Pickles is the *devil*?"

"Nah!" said Spike, sniggering as if I were a simpleton. "If that

was Mephistopheles, you'd *really* know about it. Firstly, the air would be thick with the choking stench of brimstone and decay, and we'd be knee-deep in the departed souls of the damned, writhing in perpetual agony as their bodies were repeatedly pierced with the barbed spears of the tormentors. And secondly, we'd never have got Jaffa cakes. Probably rich tea or graham crackers."

"Yeah, I hate them, too. But listen, if not Satan, then who?"

Spike closed the door carefully. "A demi-devil or junior demon or something, sent to precipitate mankind's fall into the eternal river of effluent that is the bowels of hell. Let's see if we can't get a make on this guy. Have a look in the backyard and tell me if you see anything unusual."

I peered out the window as Spike looked around the room.

"I can see the old carpet piled up in the carport," I said, "and an almost-brand-new washing machine."

"How does the carpet look?"

"It seems perfect."

"Figures. Look here."

He pointed to an old cookie jar that was sitting on the mantelpiece. The lid was half off, and clearly visible inside was a wad of banknotes.

"Bingo!" said Spike, drawing out the hefty wad. They were all fifty-pound notes—easily a grand. "This is demi-demon Raum, if I'm not mistaken. He tempts men to eternal damnation by the sin of theft."

"Come on!" I said, mildly skeptical. "If Lucifer has everyone that had stolen something, he'd have more souls than he'd know what to deal with."

"You're right," agreed Spike. "The parameters of sin have become blurred over the years. A theft worthy of damnation has to be deceitful, cowardly and *loathsome*—like from a charming and defenseless pensioner war veteran. So what Raum does is stash the real Major Pickles in a closet somewhere, assume his form, leaves the cash in plain sight, and some poor boob chances his luck. He counts his blessings, has a good few evenings out and forgets all about it until Judgment Day. And then—*shazam!* He's having his eyeballs gouged out with a spoon. And then again. And again . . . and *again*."

"I . . . get the picture. So this Raum guy's a big deal, right?"

"Nah—pretty much a small-timer," said Spike, replacing the money. "First sphere, tenth throne—any lower and he'd be in the second hierarchy and confined to hell rather than doing the cushy number up here, harvesting souls for Lucifer and attempting to engineer the fall of man."

"Is there a lot of this about?" I asked. "Demons, I mean—hanging around ready to tempt us?"

Spike shrugged. "In Swindon? No. And there'll be one less if I can do anything about it."

He flipped open his cell phone and dialed a number, then pointed at the floor. "You better get those grippers down if we're to finish by lunchtime. I'm kidding. He doesn't want a carpet; we're only here to be tempted—remember all that stuff in the backyard? Hi, Betty? It's Dad. I've got a five-five in progress with a tenth-throner name of Raum. Will you have a look in Wheatley's and see how to cast him out? Thanks." He paused for a moment, looked at me and added, "Perhaps it wasn't Felix8 at all. Perhaps he was . . . *Felix9.* After all, the linking factor between the Felixes was only ever his face, yes?"

"Good point," I said, wondering quite how Spike might be so relaxed about the whole demon thing that he could be thinking about the Felix problem at the same time.

"Betty?" said Spike into his phone. "I'm still here. . . . Cold steel? No problem. Have you done your homework? . . . Well, you'd better get started. One more thing: Bowden said he'd do the washing for us, so get all the curtains down. . . . Love you, too. Bye."

He snapped his phone shut and looked around the room for something made of steel. He picked up the nail gun, muttered, "Damn, galvanized" then rummaged in the toolbox. The best he could find was a long screwdriver, but he rejected this because it was chrome-plated.

"Can't we just go away and deal with Raum later?"

"Doesn't work like that," he said, peering out the window to see if there was anything steel within reach, which there wasn't. "We deal with this clown right now or not at all."

He opened the door a crack and peeked out.

"Okay, he's in the front room. Here's the plan: You gain his attention while I go into the kitchen and find something made of steel. Then I send him back to the second sphere."

"What if you're mistaken?" I asked. "He might be suffering from some—I don't know—rare genetic disorder that makes him grow hooves."

Spike fixed me with a piercing stare. "Have you even *heard* of such a thing?"

"No."

"Then let's do it. I hope there's a Sabatier or a tire iron or something—it'll be a pretty messy job with an eggbeater."

So while Spike slipped into the kitchen, I went to the door of the front room where Major Pickles was watching TV. He was seated on a floral-patterned settee with a cup of tea and a slice of fruitcake on a table nearby.

"Hello, young lady," he said amiably. "Done already?"

"No," I said, trying to appear unflustered, "but we're going to use the nail gun, and it might make some noise."

"Oh, that's quite all right," he said. "I was at Tobruk, you know."

"Really? What was it like?"

"My dear girl, the *noise*—and you couldn't get a decent drink anywhere."

"So a nail gun is no problem?"

"Nostalgic, my dear—fire away."

Spike hadn't yet reappeared, so I carried on. "Good. Right, well— Hey, is that *Bedazzled* you're watching?"

"Yes," he replied, "the Brendan Fraser version—*such* a broad head, but very funny."

"I met him once," I said, stalling for time, "at the launch party for the *Eyre Affair* movie. He played the part of—"

"Thursday?"

It was Spike, calling from the kitchen. I smiled and said to Major Pickles, "Would you excuse me for just one moment?"

Pickles nodded politely, and I walked to the kitchen, which was, strangely enough, empty. Not a sign of Spike anywhere. It had two doors, and the only other entrance, the back door, had a broom leaned up against it. I was about to open the fridge to look for him when I heard a voice.

"I'm up here."

I glanced up. Spike was pinned to the ceiling with thirty or so knives, scissors and other sharp objects, all stuck through the periphery of his clothing and making him look like the victim of an overenthusiastic circus knife thrower.

"What are you doing?" I hissed. "We're supposed to be dealing with the Raum guy."

"What am I *doing*? Oh, just admiring the view—why, what do you *think* I'm doing?"

I shrugged.

"Thursday," added Spike in a quiet voice, "I think he's onto us."

I turned to the door and jumped in fright because Major Pickles had crept up without my realizing. But it wasn't the little old gent I'd a seen a few moments ago; this Pickles had two large horns sticking out of his head, yellow eyes like a cat's, and he was dressed in a loincloth. He was lean and muscular and had shiny, bright red skin—a bit like those ducks that hang in Chinese-restaurant windows. He also smelled strongly of sewage.

"Well," said Raum in a guttural, rasping voice that sounded like a box of rusty nails, "Thursday Next. What a surprise!" He looked up. "And Mr. Stoker, I presume—believe me, you are *very* unpopular from where I come from!"

I made a move to thump him, but he was too quick, and a moment later I was thrown to the ceiling with a force so hard it cracked the plaster. I didn't drop; I was held, face pointing down, not by any knives or scissors but the action of an unearthly force that felt as if I were being sat upon by a small walrus.

"Thursday," added Spike in a quiet voice, "I think he's onto us."

"Two unsullied souls," growled Raum sadly. "To His Infernal Majesty, *worthless*."

"I'm warning you," said Spike in a masterful display of misplaced optimism, "give yourself up and I'll not be too hard on you."

"SILENCE!" roared Raum, so loudly that two of the kitchen windows shattered. He laughed a deep, demonic cackle, then carried on. "Just so this morning hasn't been a complete waste, I am prepared to offer a deal: Either you both die in an exceptionally painful manner and I relinquish all rights to your souls, or one of you gives yourself to me—and I free the other!"

"How about a game of chess?" suggested Spike.

"Oh, no!" said Raum, wagging a reproachful finger. "We don't fall for *that* one anymore. Now, who's it going to be?"

"You can take me," said Spike.

"No!" I cried, but Raum merely laughed. He laughed long and loud. He laughed again. Then some more. He laughed so long, in fact, that Spike and I looked at each other. But still Raum laughed. The plates and cups smashed on the dresser, and glasses that were upside down on the drainer broke into smithereens. More laughter. Louder, longer, harder, until suddenly and quite without warning he exploded into a million tiny fragments that filled the small kitchen like a red mist. Released from the ceiling, I fell to the floor via the kitchen table, which was luckily a bit frail and had nothing on it. I was slightly dazed but got up to see . . . the *real* Major Pickles, standing where Raum had been, still holding the steel bayonet that had dispatched the demon back to hell.

"Hah!" said the elderly little gent with an aggressive twinkle in his eye. "They don't like the taste of cold steel up 'em!"

He had several days of stubble and was dressed in torn pajamas and covered in soil.

"Are you okay?" I asked him.

"He thought he could keep me prisoner in the garden shed," replied the pensioner resolutely, "but it was only fifteen yards nor-noreast under the patio to the geranium bed."

"You dug your way out?"

"Yes, and would have been quicker, too, if I'd had a soup spoon instead of this."

He showed me a very worn and bent teaspoon.

"Or a spade?" I ventured.

"Hah!" he snorted contemptuously. "Spades are for losers." He looked up and noticed Spike. "I say, you there, sir—get off my ceiling this minute."

"Nothing I'd like better."

So we got Spike down and explained as best we could to the sprightly nonagenarian just who Raum was, something that he seemed to have very little trouble understanding.

"Good Lord, man!" he said at last. "You mean I killed a demon? There's a notch for the cricket bat, and no mistake."

"Sadly, no," replied Spike. "You just relegated him to the second sphere—he'll not reappear on earth for a decade or two and will get a serious lashing from the Dark One into the bargain."

"Better than he deserves," replied Major Pickles, checking the cookie jar. "The rotten blighter has pigged all my Jaffa cakes."

"Spike," I said, pointing at a desk diary I'd found on the counter, "we're not the only people who have had an appointment this morning."

He and Major Pickles bent over to have a look, and there it was. This morning was the first of three days of soul entrapment that Raum had planned for the house-call professionals of Swindon, and we had been the third potential damnees. The first, an electrician, Raum had crossed out and made a note: "sickeningly pleasant." The next, however, was for a new washing machine, and Raum had made three checks next to the name of the company: Wessex Kitchens. I rummaged through the papers on the countertop and found a job sheet—the workman had been someone called Hans Towwel.

"Blast!" said Spike. "I *hate* it when Satan obtains a soul. Don't get me wrong, some people deserve to be tortured for all eternity, but damnation without the possibility of salvation—it's like a three-strike life sentence without the possibility of parole."

I nodded in agreement. Obscene though the crime was, eternal damnation was several punishments too far.

"All this defeatist claptrap is making me sick to the craw," growled Major Pickles. "No one is going to hell on my account—what happens if we get the money back?"

Spike snapped his fingers.

"Pickles, you're a genius! Mr. Towwel doesn't join the legion of the damned until he actually makes use of his ill-gotten gains. Thursday, call Wessex Kitchens and find out where he is—we need to get to him before he spends any of the cash."

Ten minutes later we were heading at high speed toward the Greasy Monk, a popular medieval-themed eatery not far from the rebuilt cathedral of St. Zvlkx. I had tried to call Towwel's cell phone, but it was switched off, and when I explained that there was a substantial sum of money missing from Major Pickles's house, the boss of Wessex Kitchens said he was horrified—and promised to meet us there.

The restaurant was filled to capacity, as the cathedral of St. Zvlkx had just been nominated as the first GSD drop-around-if-you-want-but-hey-no-one's-forcing-you place of worship/contemplation/meditation, and the many followers/adherents/vaguely interested parties of the single unified faith were having lunch and discussing ways in which they could best use the new multifaith for overwhelming good.

As soon as we pushed open the doors Spike yelled, "Hans Towwel?" in his most commanding voice, and in the silence that followed, a man in a navy blue coverall signaled to us from behind a wooden plate of bread and dripping.

"Problems?" he said as we walked up.

"Could be," said Spike. "Did you pay for that meal with the money you pinched from Major Pickles?"

"Did I what?"

"You heard him," I said. "Did you pay for that meal with the money you stole from Major Pickles?"

"Ballocks to you!" he said, getting up. Spike, who was pretty strong, pushed the man hard back down into his seat.

"Listen," said Spike in a quiet voice, "we're not cops, and we don't give a shit about the money, and we don't give a shit about you—but we do give a shit about your *soul*. Now, just tell us: Have you spent any of the cash or not?"

"That's well sweet, isn't it?" growled Towwel. "Some cash is missing so you blame the workingman."

"Towwel?" said a crumpled and untidy-looking man in a crumpled and untidy-looking suit, who had just arrived. "Is what they say true?"

"Who are you?" asked Spike.

"Mr. Hedge Moulting of Wessex Kitchens," said the untidy man, offering us a business card. "I must say I am shocked and appalled by our employee's behavior—how much was taken?"

"Now, look here!" said Towwel, growing angrier by the second, which caused Mr. Moulting of Wessex Kitchens to flinch and hide behind Spike. "I don't steal from people. Not from customers, not from pensioners, not from you, not from *anyone*!"

"You should be ashamed of yourself!" said Moulting, still half hidden behind Spike. "You're *fired*—and don't expect a reference."

"How do we know *you* didn't take it?" demanded Towwel.

"Me?" exclaimed Moulting. "How dare you!"

"*You* made a random inspection of my work this morning, and you're a sleazy piece of crap—I say *you* took it."

"An outrageous accusation!" yelled Moulting, waving a threatening finger in Towwel's direction. "You'll never install a washing machine in this town again, and what's more I will make it my duty—nay, pleasure—to see you convicted of this heinous crime. A thousand pounds? From a *war veteran*? You deserve all you're going to get!"

There was silence for a moment.

"Mr. Moulting," said Spike, "we never said how much was stolen. As I said to Mr. Towwel here, we don't give a shit about the money. We're here to save a soul from the torment of eternal damnation. It was a diabolical entrapment from one of Old Scratch's accomplices. If you've got the money and haven't spent any of it, then just drop it in the nearest poor box, and your soul is clear. If you *have* spent some of the cash, then there's nothing anyone can do for you."

I turned to Mr. Towwel. "Sorry to have accused you unjustly, sir. If you need a job, call me anytime at Acme Carpets."

And we walked out, bumping aside Moulting as we went. His shaking hand reached for a chair back to steady himself. He had turned pale and was sweating, trembling with the fear of the man who is condemned to eternal hellfire and knows it.

We recarpeted Major Pickles's entire house with the finest carpet we had. We also did his shopping, his washing and bought him two dozen packets of Jaffa cakes. After that, the three of us sat down and nattered all afternoon, drinking tea and telling stories. We parted the best of friends and left our phone numbers on his fridge so he could call us if he needed anything. I even suggested he give Polly a call if he wanted some company.

"I never realized carpet laying could be so much fun," I said as we finally drove away.

"Me neither," replied Spike. "Do you think Bowden will be pissed off that we've done this one for free and it took us all day?"

"Nah," I replied with a smile, "I'm sure he'll be just fine about it."

29.

Time Out of Joint

I never did get my head around time's carefree propensity to paradox. My father didn't exist, yet I was still born, and time travel had never been invented, but they still hoped that it might. There were currently two versions of Friday, and I had met him several times in the past—or was it the future? It gave me a dull ache in the head when I thought about it.

How was work?" asked Landen when I walked in the door.

"Quite good fun," I replied. "The floor-covering business is definitely looking up. How are things with you?"

"Good, too—lots of work done."

"On *The Mews of Doom*?" I asked, still hopeful about Scampton-Tappett and remembering that I had sent a note down to *Bananas for Edward* for him to swap books. He'd cost me a thousand book-guineas, and I was sure as hell going to get my money's worth.

"No. I've been working on Spike's weird-shit self-help book: *Collecting the Undead*."

Damn and blast again.

I recalled a news item I had overheard on the tram home.

"Hey, do you know what Redmond van de Poste's Address to the Nation is all about?"

"Rumor says it's going to be about the stupidity surplus. Apparently his top advisers have come up with a plan that will deal with the excess in a manner that won't damage economic interests and might actually generate new business opportunities."

"He'll top the ratings with that one—I only hope he doesn't generate more stupidity. You know how stupidity tends to breed off itself. How are the girls?"

"They're fine. I'm just playing Scrabble with Tuesday. Is it cheating for her to use Nextian Geometry to bridge *two* triple-word scores with a word of only six letters?"

"I suppose. Where's Jenny?"

"She's made a camp in the attic."

"Again?"

Something niggled in my head once more. Something I was meant to do. "Land?"

"Yuh?"

"Nothing. I'll get it."

There was someone at the door, and whoever it was had knocked, rather than rung, which is always mildly ominous. I opened the door, and it was Friday, or at least it was the clean-cut, nongrunty version. He wasn't alone either—he had two of his ChronoGuard friends with him, and they all looked a bit serious. Despite the dapper light blue ChronoGuard uniforms, they all looked too young to get drunk or vote, let alone do something as awesomely responsible as surf the timestream. It was like letting a twelve-year-old do your epidural.

"Hello, Sweetpea!" I said. "Are these your friends?"

"They're *colleagues*," said Friday in a pointed fashion. "We're here on official business."

"Goodness!" I said, attempting not to patronize him with motherly pride and failing spectacularly. "Would you all like a glass of milk and a cookie or something?"

But Friday, it seemed, wasn't in much of a mood for milk—or a cookie.

"Not now, Mum. There's only forty-eight hours of time left, and we *still* haven't invented time travel."

"Maybe you can't," I replied. "Maybe it's impossible."

"We used the technology to get here," said Friday with impeccable logic, "so the possibility still exists, no matter how slight. We've got every available agent strung out across the timestream doing a fingertip search of all potential areas of discovery. Now, where is he?"

"Your father?"

"No, *him.* Friday—the other me."

"Don't you know? Isn't this all ancient history?"

"Time is not as it should be. If it were, we'd have solved it all by now. So where is he?"

"Are you here to replace him?"

"No, we just want to talk."

"He's out practicing with his band."

"He is *not.* Would it surprise you to learn that there was no band called the Gobshites?"

"Oh, no!" I said with a shudder. "He didn't call it the Wankers after all, did he?"

"No, no, Mum—*there is no band.*"

"He's definitely doing his band thing," I assured him, inviting them in and picking the telephone off the hall table. "I'll call Toby's dad. They use their garage for practice. It's the perfect venue—both Toby's parents are partially deaf."

"Then there's not much point in phoning them, now, is there?" said the cockier of Friday's friends.

"What's your name?"

"Nigel," said the one who had spoken, a bit sheepishly.

"No one likes a smart-ass, Nigel."

I stared at him, and he looked away, pretending to find some fluff on his uniform.

"Hi, is that Toby's dad?" I said as the phone connected. "It's Friday's mum here. . . . No, I'm not like that—it only happens in the book. My question is: Are the boys jamming in your garage?"

I looked at Friday and his friends.

"Not for at least three months? I didn't know that. Thank you. Good night."

I put the phone down.

"So where is he?" I asked.

"We don't know," replied the other Friday, "and since he's a free radical whose movements are entirely independent of the SHE, we have no way of knowing where or when he is. The feckless, dopey, teenage act was a good one and had us all fooled—you especially."

I narrowed my eyes. This was a surprising development. "What are you saying?"

"We've had some new information, and we think Friday might be actually *causing* the nondiscovery of the technology—conspiring with his future self to overthrow the ChronoGuard!"

"Sounds like a trumped-up bullshit charge for you to replace him," I said, beginning to get annoyed.

"I'm serious, Mum. Friday is a dangerous historical fundamentalist who will do whatever it takes to achieve his own narrow agenda—to keep time as it was originally meant to run. If we don't stop him, then the whole of history will roll up and there'll be nothing left of any of us!"

"If he's so dangerous," I said slowly, "then why haven't you eradicated him?"

Friday took a deep breath. "Mum? Like . . . *duh*. He's a younger version of me and the future director-general. If we get rid of him, we get rid of ourselves. He's clever, I'll grant him that. But if he can stop time travel from being discovered, then he knows how it was invented in the first place. We need to speak to him. Now—where is he?"

"I don't rat out my son, son," I said in a mildly confusing way.

"*I'm* your son, Mum."

"And I wouldn't rat you out either, Sweetpea."

Friday took a step forward and raised his voice a notch. "Mum, this is important. If you have any idea where he is, then you're going to have to tell us—and don't call me Sweetpea in front of my friends."

"I don't know where he is—Sweetpea—and if you want to talk to me in that tone of voice, you'll go to your room."

"This is beyond room, Mother."

"Mum. It's *Mum*. Friday always calls me Mum."

"I'm Friday, Mum—*your* Friday."

"No," I said, "you're *another* Friday—someone he *might* become. And do you know, I think I prefer the one who can barely talk and thinks soap is a type of TV show?"

Friday glared at me angrily. "You've got ten hours to hand him over. Harboring a time terrorist is a serious offense, and the punishment unspeakably unpleasant."

I wasn't fazed by his threats.

"Are you sure you know what you're doing?" I asked.

"Of course!"

"Then, by definition, *so does he*. Why don't you take your SO-12 buddies and go play in the timestream until dinner?"

Friday made a harrumph noise, turned on his heels and departed, with his friends following quickly behind.

I closed the door and walked through to the hall where Landen was leaning on the newel post staring at me. He'd been listening to every word.

"Pumpkin, just what the hell's going on?"

"I'm not sure myself, darling, but I'm beginning to think that Friday's been making monkeys out of the pair of us."

"Which Friday?"

"The hairy one that grunts a lot. He's not a dozy slacker after all—he's working undercover as some sort of historical fundamentalist. We need some answers, and I think I know where to find them. Friday may have tricked his parents, the SHE and half the ChronoGuard, but there's one person no teenage boy ever managed to fool."

"And that is?"

"His younger sister."

"I can't believe it took you so long to figure out," said Tuesday, who agreed to spill the beans on her brother for the bargain price of a new bicycle, a thirty-pound gift card to MathWorld and lasagna three nights in a row. "He didn't stomp on Barney Plotz either—he forged the letters and the phone call. He needed the time to conduct what he called his . . . investigations. I don't know what they were, but he was at the public library a lot—and over at Gran's."

"Gran's? Why Gran's? He *likes* his food."

"I don't know," said Tuesday, thinking long and hard about it. "He said it was something to do with Mycroft and a chronuption of staggering proportions."

"That boy," I muttered grimly, "has got some serious explaining to do."

30.
Now Is the Winter

One of the biggest wastes of money in recent years was the Anti-Smite shield, designed to protect mankind (or Britain, at the very least) from an overzealous deity eager to cleanse the population of sin. Funded initially by Chancellor Yorrick Kaine, the project was halted after his ignominious fall from grace. Canceled but not forgotten, the network of transmission towers still lies dotted about the country, a silent testament to Kaine's erratic and somewhat costly administration.

My mother answered the door when we knocked, and she seemed vaguely surprised to see us all. Landen and I were there as concerned parents, of course, and Tuesday was there as she was the only one who might be able to understand Mycroft's work, if that was what was required.

"Is it Sunday lunchtime already?" asked my mother.

"No, Mother. Is Friday here?"

"Friday? Goodness me, no! I haven't seen him for over—"

"It's all right, Gran," came a familiar voice from the living-room door. "There's no more call for subterfuge."

It was Friday—*our* Friday, the grunty, smelly one, who up until an hour ago was someone we thought wouldn't know what "subterfuge" meant, let alone be able to pronounce it. He had changed. There seemed to be a much more upright bearing about him. Perhaps it was because he wasn't dragging his feet when he walked, and he actually looked at us when he spoke. Despite this, he still *seemed* like a sad-teenager cliché: spots, long unkempt hair, and with clothes so baggy you could dress three people out of the material and still have enough to make some curtains.

"Why don't you tell us what's going on?" I asked.

"You wouldn't understand."

I fixed him with my best "Son, you are in *so* much trouble" look. "You'd be amazed what I can understand."

"Okay," he said, drawing a deep breath. "You've heard that the ChronoGuard is using time-travel technology now in the almost certain knowledge that it's invented in the future?"

"I get the *principle,*" I replied somewhat guardedly, as I still had no idea how you could use something that had yet to be invented.

"As weird as it might seem," explained Friday, "the principle is sound. Many things happen solely because of the curious human foible of a preconceived notion's altering the outcome. More simply put: If we convince ourselves that something is possible, it becomes so. It's called the *Schrödinger Night Fever* principle."

"I don't understand."

"It's simple. If you go to see *Saturday Night Fever* expecting it to be good, it's a corker. However, if you go *expecting* it to be a crock of shit, it's that, too. Thus *Saturday Night Fever* can exist in two mutually opposing states *at the very same time,* yet only by the weight of our expectations. From this principle we can deduce that *any* opposing states can be governed by human expectation—even, as in the case of retro-deficit-engineering, the present use of a future technology."

"I *think* I understand that," said Landen. "Does it work with *any* John Travolta movie?"

"Only the artistically ambiguous ones," replied Friday, "such as *Pulp Fiction* and *Face/Off*. *Battlefield Earth* doesn't work, because it's a stinker no matter how much you think you're going to like it, and *Get Shorty* doesn't work either, because you'd be hard-pressed not to enjoy it, irrespective of any preconceived notions."

"It's a beautiful principle," I said admiringly. "Yours?"

"Sadly not," replied Friday with a smile. "Much as I'd like to claim it, the credit belongs to an intellect far superior to mine—Tuesday. Way to go, sis."

Tuesday squirmed with joy at getting a compliment from her big brother, but still none of it made any real sense.

"So how does this relate to Mycroft and time travel?"

"Simple," said Friday. "The obscenely complex technologies that the ChronoGuard uses to power up the time engines contravene one essential premise that is at the very core of science: that disorder will always stay the same or increase. More simply stated, you can put a pig in a machine to make a sausage, but you can't put a sausage in a machine to make a pig. It's the Second Law of Thermodynamics. One of the most rigid tenets of our understanding of the physical world. You can't reverse the arrow of time to make something *un*happen—whether it be unscrambling eggs or unmaking a historical event."

"The recipe for unscrambled eggs," I murmured, suddenly remembering a family dinner we had about the time of the *Jane Eyre* episode. "He was scribbling it on a napkin, and Polly made him stop. They had an argument—that's how I remember it."

"Right," said Friday. "The recipe was actually an equation that showed how the Second Law of Thermodynamics could be modified to allow a reversibility of time's arrow. That you *could* unbake a cake with almost breathless simplicity. The recipe for unscrambled eggs is at the heart of reversing the flow of time—without it, *there is no time travel*!"

"So," I said slowly, "the whole of the ChronoGuard's ability to move around in time rests on their getting hold of this recipe?"

"That's about the tune of it, Mum."

"So where is it?" asked Landen. "Logically, it *must* still exist, or the likelihood of time travel drops to zero. Since your future self just popped up twenty minutes ago to make veiled threats, the possibility remains that it will be discovered sometime before the End of Time—sometime in the next forty-eight hours."

"Right," said Friday, "and that's what I've been doing with Polly for the past two weeks—trying to find where Mycroft put it. Once

I've got the recipe, I can destroy it: The possibility of time travel drops to zero, and it's good night, Vienna, for the ChronoGuard."

"Why would you want that?"

"The less you know, Mum, the better."

"They say you're a dangerous historical fundamentalist," I added cautiously. "A terrorist of time."

"But they would say that, wouldn't they? The Friday you met—he's okay. He's following orders, but he doesn't know what I know. If he did, he'd be trying to destroy the recipe, the same as me. The Standard History Eventline is bullshit, and all they're doing is trying to protect their temporal-phony-baloney jobs."

"How do you know this?"

"I become director-general of the ChronoGuard when I'm thirty-six. In the final year before retirement, at seventy-eight, I'm inducted into the ChronoGuard Star Chamber—the ruling elite. It was there that I discovered something so devastating that if it became public knowledge would shut down the industry in an instant. And the time business is worth six hundred billion a year—*minimum*."

"Tell them what it is," said Polly, who'd been standing at his side. "If anything happens to you, then at least one of us might be able to carry on."

Friday nodded and took a deep breath. "Has anyone noticed how short attention spans seem to have cast a certain lassitude across the nation?"

"Do I ever," I replied, rolling my eyes and thinking of the endlessly downward clicking of the Read-O-Meter. "No one's reading books anymore. They seem to prefer the mind-numbing spectacle of easily digested trash TV and celebrity tittle-tattle."

"Exactly," said Friday. "The long view has been eroded. We can't see beyond six months, if that, and short-termism will spell our end. But the thing is, it needn't be that way—there's a *reason* for it. The time engines don't just need vast quantities of power—they need to run on time. Not punctuality, but time *itself*. Even a temporal leap of a few minutes will use up an infinitesimally small amount of the abstract concept. Not the hard *clock* time but the soft stuff that keeps events firmly embedded in a small cocoon of prolonged event—the *Now*."

"Oooh!" murmured Tuesday, who twigged it first. "*They've been mining the Now!*"

"Exactly, sis," said Friday, sweeping the hair from his eyes. "The Short Now is the direct result of the time industry's unthinking depredations. If the ChronoGuard continues as it is, within a few years there won't be any Now at all, and the world will move into a Dark Age of eternal indifference."

"You mean TV could get *worse*?" asked Landen.

"*Much* worse," replied Friday grimly. "At the rate the Now is being eroded, by this time next year *Samaritan Kidney Swap* will be considered the height of scholarly erudition. But easily digestible TV is not the cause—it's the effect. A Short Now will also spell the gradual collapse of forward planning, and mankind will slowly strangulate itself in a downward spiral of uncaring self-interest and short-term instant gratification."

There was a bleak silence as we took this on board. We could see it all now. Short attention spans, a general malaise, no tolerance, no respect, no rules. Short-termism. No wonder we were seeing Outlander ReadRates go into free fall. The Short Now would hate books; too much thought required for not enough gratification. It brought home the urgency to find the recipe, wherever it was: Without unscrambled eggs, there was no time travel, no more depredation of the Now, and we could look to a brighter future of long-term thought—and more reading. Simple.

"Shouldn't this be a matter for public debate?" asked Landen.

"What would that achieve, Dad? The ChronoGuard doesn't have to *disprove* that the reduction of the Now is caused by humans—they only have to create doubt. They'll always be Short Now deniers, and the debate will become so long and drawn out that as soon as we realize there *is* a problem, we won't care enough to want to do anything about it. This issue is not for debate—the ChronoGuard *cannot* get hold of that recipe. I'm staking my career on it. And believe me, I would have had an excellent career to stake."

There was silence after Friday's speech. We all realized that he was right, of course, but I was also thinking about how proud I was of him and how refreshing it was to hear such eloquence and moral lucidity from such a grubby and disheveled individual who was wearing a WAYNE SKUNK IS THE BALLOCKS T-shirt.

Polly sighed, breaking the silence. "If only Mycroft were alive. we could ask him where he put it."

And then I *understood.*

"Aunt," I said, "come with me. Friday—you, too."

It was dusk by now, and the last rays of evening light were shining through the dusty windows of Mycroft's workshop. It seemed somehow shabbier in the twilight.

"All those memories!" breathed Polly, hobbling across the concrete floor with Friday holding her arm. "What a life. Yes indeed, what a life. I've not been in here since before he . . . you know."

"Don't be startled," I told her, "but I've seen Mycroft twice in here over the past two days. He came back to tell us something, and until now I had no idea what it was. Polly?"

Her eyes had filled with tears as she stared into the dim emptiness of the workshop. I followed her gaze, and as my eyes became accustomed to the light, I could see him, too. Mycroft's opacity was low, and the color seemed to have drained from his body. He was barely there at all.

"Hello, Poll," he said with a smile, his voice a low rumble. "You're looking positively *radiant*!"

"Oh, Crofty!" she murmured. "You're such a fibber—I'm a doddering wreck ready for the scrap heap. But one that has missed you *so* much!"

"Mycroft," I said in a respectful whisper, "I don't want to keep you from your wife, but time is short. I know why you came back."

"You mean it wasn't Farquitt or the chairs?"

"No. It was about the recipe for unscrambled eggs."

"We need to know," added Polly, "where you left it."

"Is that all?" laughed Mycroft. "Why, goodness—I put in my jacket pocket!"

He was beginning to fade, and his voice sounded hollow and empty. His post-life time was almost up.

"And *after* that?"

He faded some more. I was worried that if I blinked, he'd go completely.

"Which jacket, my darling?" asked Polly.

"The one you gave me for Christmas," came an ethereal whisper, "the blue one . . . with the large checks."

"Crofty?"

But he had vanished. Friday and I rushed to support Polly, who had gone a bit wobbly at the knees.

"Damn!" said Friday. "When does he next come back?"

"He doesn't," I said. "That was it."

"Then we're no closer to knowing where it is," said Friday. "I've been through all his clothes—there isn't one with blue checks in his closet."

"There's a reason for that," said Polly, her eyes glistening with tears. "He left it on the *Hesperus*. I scolded him at the time, but now I see why he did it."

"Mum? Does this make any sense to you?"

"Yes," I said with a smile. "It's somewhere the ChronoGuard can't get to it. Back in 1985, before he used the Prose Portal to send Polly into 'I Wandered Lonely as a Cloud,' he tested it on himself. The jacket is right where he left it—in the teeth of an Atlantic gale inside Henry Longfellow's poem 'The Wreck of the Hesperus.'"

"Inside the *BookWorld*?"

"Right," I replied, "and nothing—repeat, *nothing*—would compel me to return there. In two days the ChronoGuard will be gone, and the slow repair of the Now can begin. You did good, Sweetpea."

"Thanks, Mum," he said, "but please—don't call me Sweetpea."

31.

Spending the Surplus

The Commonsense Party's first major policy reversal of perceived current wisdom was with the scrapping of performance targets, league standings and the attempt to make subtle human problems into figures on a graph that could be solved quickly and easily through "initiatives." Arguing that important bodies such as the Health Service should have the emphasis on care and not on administration, the Commonsense Party forced through legislation that essentially argued, "If it takes us ten years to get into the shit, it will take us twenty years to get out—and that journey starts *now.*"

We stayed at Mum's for dinner, although "dinner" in this context might best be described as a loose collection of foodstuffs tossed randomly into a large saucepan and then boiled for as long as it took for all taste to vanish, never to return. Because of this we missed Redmond van de Poste's Address to the Nation, something that didn't really trouble us, as the last address had been, as they always were, unbelievably dreary but astute and of vital importance. It was just so good to talk to Friday again one-to-one. I'd forgotten how pleasant he actually was. He lost no time in telling me that he was going to have to stay undercover as a lazy good-for-nothing until the ChronoGuard had ceased operations—and this meant that I shouldn't even *attempt* to wake him until at least midday, or two on weekends.

"How convenient," I observed.

Tuesday had been thoughtful for some time and finally asked, "But can't the ChronoGuard go back to the time between when Great-Uncle Mycroft wrote the recipe and when he left it on the *Hesperus*?"

"Don't worry," said Friday with a wink. "It was only twenty-eight minutes, and the older me has it covered at the other end. The only thing we have to do is make sure the recipe stays in 'The Wreck of the Hesperus.' We can win this fight with nothing more than inaction, which as a teenager suits me just fine."

It was only as we were driving home that I suddenly thought of Jenny.

"Oh, my God!" I said in a panic. "We left Jenny at home on her own!"

Landen took hold of my arm and squeezed it, and I felt Friday rest his hand on my shoulder.

"It's all right, darling, calm down," Landen soothed. "We left her with Mrs. Berko-Boyler."

I frowned. "No, we *didn't*. You said she was making a camp in the attic. We came straight out. How could we have forgotten?"

"Sweetheart," said Landen with a deep breath, "there is no Jenny."

"What do you you mean?" I demanded, chuckling at the stupidity of his comment. "Of course there's a Jenny!"

"Dad's right," said Friday soothingly. "There has never been a Jenny."

"But I can *remember* her!"

"It's *Aornis*, Mum," added Tuesday. "She gave you this mindworm seven years ago, and we can't get rid of it."

"I don't understand," I said beginning to panic. "I can remember everything about her! Her laugh, the holidays, the time she fell off her bicycle and broke her arm, her birth—*everything*!"

"Aornis did this to you for *revenge*," said Landen. "After she couldn't wipe me from your memory, she left you with this—that's what she's doing her forty-year stretch for."

"The bitch!" I yelled. "I'll kill her for this!"

"Language, Mum," said Tuesday. "I'm only twelve. Besides, even if you did kill her, we think Jenny would still be with you."

"Oh, *shit*," I said as reason started to replace confusion and anger. "That's why she never turns up at mealtimes."

"We pretend there *is* a Jenny to minimize the onset of an attack," said Landen. "It's why we keep her bedroom as it is and why you'll find her stuff all around the house—so when you're alone, you don't go into a missing-daughter panic."

"The evil little cow!" I muttered, rubbing my face. "But now that I know, we can do something about it, right?"

"It's not as easy as that, sweetheart," said Landen with a note of sadness in his voice. "Aornis is truly vindictive—in a few minutes you won't remember any of this and you'll again believe that you have a daughter named Jenny."

"You mean," I said slowly, "I've done this before?"

We pulled up outside the house, and Landen turned off the engine. There was silence in the car.

"Sometimes you can go weeks without an attack," said Landen quietly. "At other times you can have two or three an hour."

"Is that why you work from home?"

"Yeah. We can't have you going to school every day expecting to pick up a daughter who isn't there."

"So . . . you've explained all this to me before?"

"Many times, darling."

I sighed deeply. "I feel like a complete twit," I said in a soft voice. "Is this my first attack today?"

"It's the third," said Landen. "It's been a bad week."

I looked at them all in turn, and they were all staring back at me with such a sense of loving concern for my well-being that I burst into tears.

"It's all right, Mum," said Tuesday, holding my hand. "We'll look after you."

"You are the best, most loving, supportive family anyone

could ever have," I said through my sobs. "I'm so sorry if I'm a burden."

They all told me not to be so bloody silly, I told them not to swear, and Landen gave me his handkerchief for my tears.

"So," I said, wiping my eyes, "how does it work? How do I stop remembering the fact that there's no Jenny?"

"We have our ways. Jenny's at a sleepover with Ingrid. Okay?"

"Okay."

He leaned across and kissed me, smiled and said to the kids, "Right, team, do your stuff."

Friday poked Tuesday hard in the ribs, and she squealed, "What was *that* for!?"

"For being a geek!"

"I'd rather be a geek than a duh-brain. And what's more, Strontium Goat is rubbish and Wayne Skunk couldn't play a guitar if his life depended on it!"

"Say that again!"

"Will you two cut it out!" I said crossly. "Honestly, I think Friday's proved he's no duh-brain over the Short Now thing, so just pack it in. Right. I know your gran gave us some food, but does anybody want anything proper to eat?"

"There's some pizza in the freezer," said Landen. "We can have that."

We all got out of the car and walked up to the house with Friday and Tuesday bickering.

"Geek."

"Duh-brain."

"Geek."

"Duh-brain."

"I said *cut it out*." I suddenly thought of something. "Land, where's Jenny?"

"At a sleepover with Ingrid."

"Oh, yeah. Again?"

"Thick as thieves, those two."

"Yeah," I said with a frown, "thick as thieves, those two."

Bowden called during dinner. This was unusual for him, but not totally unexpected. Spike and I had crept away from Acme like naughty schoolkids, as we didn't want to get into trouble over the cost of Major Pickles's carpet, not to mention that it had taken us both all day and we'd done nothing else.

"It's not great, is it?" said Bowden in the overserious tone he used when he was annoyed, upset or angry. To be honest, I had the most shares in Acme, but he *was* the managing director, so day-to-day operations were up to him.

"I don't think it's all *that* bad," I said, going on the defensive.

"Are you insane?" replied Bowden. "It's a disaster!"

"We've had bigger problems," I said, beginning to get annoyed. "I think it's best to keep a sense of proportion, don't you?"

"Well, yes," he replied, "but if we let this sort of thing take a hold, you never know where it might end up."

I was pissed off now.

"Bowden," I said, "just cool it. Spike got stuck to the ceiling by Raum, and if Pickles hadn't given the demi-devil the cold steel, we'd both be pushing up daisies."

There was silence on the line for a moment, until Bowden said in a quiet voice, "I'm talking about van de Poste's Address to the Nation—what are *you* talking about?"

"Oh—nothing. What did he say?"

"Switch on the telly and you'll see."

I asked Tuesday to switch channels. OWL-TV was airing the popular current-affairs show *Fresh Air with Tudor Webastow,* and Tudor, who was perhaps not the best but certainly the tallest reporter on TV, was interviewing the Commonsense minister of culture, Cherie Yogert, MP.

". . . and the first classic to be turned into a reality book show?"

"*Pride and Prejudice,*" announced Yogert proudly. "It will be renamed *The Bennets* and will be serialized live in your household copy the day after tomorrow. Set in starchy early-nineteenth-century England, the series will feature Mr. and Mrs. Bennet and their five daughters being given tasks and then voted out of the house one by one, with the winner going on to feature in *Northanger Abbey,* which itself will be the subject of more 'readeractive' changes."

"So what van de Poste is sanctioning," remarked Webastow slowly, "is the wholesale plunder of everything the literary world holds dear."

"Not *everything,*" corrected Ms. Yogert. "Only books penned by English authors. We don't have the right to do dumb things with other nations' books—they can do that for themselves. But," she went on, "I think 'plunder' would be too strong a word. We would prefer to obfuscate the issue by using nonsensical jargon such as 'market-led changes' or 'user-choice enhancements.' For centuries now, the classics have been dreary, overlong and incomprehensible to anyone without a university education. Reality book shows are the way forward, and the Interactive Book Council are the people to do it for us!"

"Am I hearing this right?"

"Unfortunately," murmured Landen, who was standing next to me.

"We have been suffering under the yoke of the Stalinist principle of one-author books," continued Ms. Yogert, "and in the modern world we must strive to bring democracy to the writing process."

"I don't think any authors would regard their writing process as creative totalitarianism," said Webastow uneasily. "But we'll move on. As I understand it, the technology that will enable you to alter the story line of a book will change it permanently, and in every known copy. Do you not think it would be prudent to leave the originals as they are and write *alternative* versions?"

Yogert smiled at him patronizingly. "If we did that," she replied, "it would barely be stupid at all, and the Commonsense

Party takes the stupidity surplus problem *extremely* seriously. Prime Minister van de Poste has pledged to not only reduce the current surplus to zero within a year but to also cut all idiocy emissions by seventy percent in 2020. This requires unpopular decisions, and he had to compare the interests of a few die-hard, elitist, dweeby, bespectacled book fans with those of the general voting public. Better still, because this idea is *so* idiotic that the loss of a single classic—say, *Jane Eyre*—will offset the entire nation's stupidity for an entire year. Since we have the potential to overwrite *all* the English classics to reader choice, we can do *really* stupid things with impunity. Who knows? We may even run a stupidity *deficit*—and can then afford to take on other nations' idiocy at huge national profit. We see the UK as leading the stupidity-offset-trading industry—and the idiocy of *that* idea will simply be offset against the annihilation of *Vanity Fair*. Simple, isn't it?"

I realized I was still holding the phone. "Bowden, are you there?"

"I'm here."

"This stinks to high heaven. Can you find out something about this so-called Interactive Book Council? I've never heard of such a thing. Call me back."

I returned my attention to the TV.

"And when we've lost all the classics and the stupidity surplus has once again ballooned?" asked Webastow. "What happens then?"

"Well," said Ms. Yogert with a shrug, "we'll cross that bridge when we come to it, eh?"

"You'll forgive me for saying this," said Webastow, looking over his glasses, "but this is the most harebrained piece of unadulterated stupidity that any government has ever undertaken *anywhere*."

"Thank you very much," replied Ms. Yogert courteously. "I'll make sure your compliments are forwarded to Prime Minister van de Poste."

The program changed to a report on how the "interactive book" might work. Something about "new technologies" and "user-defined narrative." It was all baloney. I knew what was going on. It was

Senator Jobsworth. He'd pushed through that interactive book project of Baxter's. Worse, he'd planned this all along—witness the large throughput conduits in *Pride and Prejudice* and the recent upgrading of all of Austen's work. I wasn't that concerned with how they'd managed to overturn my veto or even open an office in the real world—what worried me was that I needed to be in the BookWorld to stop the nation's entire literary heritage from being sacrificed on the altar of popularism.

The phone rang. It was Bowden again. I made a trifling and wholly unbelievable excuse about looking for a hammer, then vanished into the garage so Landen couldn't hear the conversation.

"The Interactive Book Council is run out of an office in West London," Bowden reported when I was safely perched on the lawn mower. "It was incorporated a month ago and has the capacity to take a thousand simultaneous calls—yet the office itself is barely larger than the one at Acme."

"They must have figured a way to transfer the calls en masse to the BookWorld," I replied. "I'm sure a thousand Mrs. Danvers would be overjoyed to be working in a call center rather than bullying characters or dealing with rampant mispellings."

I told Bowden I'd try to think of something and hung up. I stepped out of the garage and went back into the living room, my heart thumping. This was why I had the veto—to protect the BookWorld from the stupefyingly shortsighted decisions of the Council of Genres. But first things first. I had to contact Bradshaw and see what kind of reaction Jurisfiction was having to the wholesale slaughter of literary treasures—but how? JurisTech had never devised a two-way communication link between the BookWorld and the Outland, as I was the only one ever likely to use it.

"Are you all right, Mum?" asked Tuesday.

"Yes, poppet, I'm fine," I said, tousling her hair. "I've just got to muse on this awhile."

I went upstairs to my office, which had been converted from the old box room, and sat down to think. The more I thought, the worse things looked. If the CofG had discounted my veto and forced the interactivity issue, it was entirely possible that they would also be attacking Speedy Muffler and Racy Novel. The only agency able to police these matters was Jurisfiction—but it worked to Text Grand Central's orders, which was *itself* under the control of the Council of Genres, so Jobsworth was ultimately in command of Jurisfiction—and he could do with it what he wanted.

I sighed, leaned forward and absently pulled out my hair tie, then rubbed at my scalp with my fingertips. Commander Bradshaw would never have agreed to this interactivity garbage and would resign out of principle—as he had hundreds of times before. And if I were there, I could reaffirm my veto. It was a right given me by the Great Panjandrum, and not even Jobsworth would go against *her* will. This was all well and good but for one thing: I'd never even *considered* the possibility of losing my TravelBook, so I'd never worked out an emergency strategy for getting into the BookWorld without it.

The only person I knew who could bookjump without a book was Mrs. Nakajima, and she was in retirement at Thornfield Hall. Ex–Jurisfiction agent Harris Tweed had been banished permanently to the Outland, and without his TravelBook he was as marooned as I was. Ex-chancellor Yorrick Kaine, real these days and currently licking his wounds from a cell at Parkhurst, was no help at all, and neither was the only other fictionaut I knew still living, Cliff Hangar. I thought again about Commander Bradshaw. He'd certainly want to contact me and was a man of formidable resources—if *I* were him, how would I go about contacting someone in the real world? I checked my e-mails but found nothing and looked to see if I had any messages on my cell phone, which I hadn't. My mobilefootnoterphone, naturally, was devoid of a signal.

I leaned back in my chair to think more clearly and let my eyes wander around the room. I had a good collection of books, amassed during my long career as a Literary Detective. Major and minor classics, but little of any great value. I stopped and thought for a moment, then started to rummage through my bookshelf until I found what I was looking for—one of Commander Bradshaw's novels. Not one he wrote, of course, but one of the ones that *featured* him. There were twenty-three in the series, written between 1888 and 1922, and all featured Bradshaw either shooting large animals, finding lost civilizations or stopping "Johnny Foreigner" from causing mischief in British East Africa. He had been out of print for over sixty years and hadn't been read at all for more than ten. Since no one was reading him, he could say what he wanted in his own books, and I would be able to read what he said. But there were a few problems: one, that twenty-three books would take a lot of reading; two, that Text Grand Central would know if his books were being read; and three, that it was simply a one-way conduit, and if he *did* leave a message, he would never know if it was me who'd read it.

I opened *Two Years Amongst the Umpopo* and flicked through the pages to see if anything caught my eye, such as a double line space or something. It didn't, so I picked up *Tilapia, the Devil-Fish of Lake Rudolph* and, after that, *The Man-Eaters of Nakuru*. It was only while I was idly thumbing through *Bradshaw Defies the Kaiser* that I hit pay dirt. The text of the book remained unaltered, but the *dedication* had changed. Bradshaw was smart; only a variance in the *story* would be noticed at Text Grand Central—they wouldn't know I was reading it at all. I took the book back to my desk and read:

> Thursday, D'girl.
>
> If you can read this, you have realized that something is seriously squiffy in the BookWorld. Plans had been afoot for weeks, and none of us had seen them. Thursday1–4 (yes, it's true) has taken your place as the CofG's LBOCS and is rubber-stamping all of Jobsworth's idiotic schemes. The interactivity idea is going ahead full speed, and even now Danverclones are

massing on the borders of Racy Novel, ready to invade. Evil Thursday has loaded Text Grand Central with her toadies in order to keep a careful watch for any textual anomalies that might give them—and her—a clue as to whether you have returned. For it is this that Evil Thursday fears more than anything: *that you will return, unmask her as an impostor and retake your place.* She has suspended Jurisfiction and had all agents confined to their books, and she now commands a legion of Danverclones, who are waiting to capture you should you appear in the BookWorld. We stole back your TravelBook and have left it for you with Captain Carver inside *It Was a Dark and Stormy Night* if you can somehow find a way in. This dedication will self-erase in two readings. Good luck, old girl—and Melanie sends her love.

Bradshaw.

I read the dedication again and watched as the words slowly dissolved from the page. Good old Bradshaw. I had been to *It Was a Dark and Stormy Night* a couple of times, mostly for training. It was a maritime adventure set aboard a tramp steamer on the Tasman Sea in 1924. It was a good choice, because it came under the deregulated area of the library known as Vanity Publishing. Text Grand Central wouldn't even know I was there. I replaced *Bradshaw Defies the Kaiser* on the shelf, then unlocked the bottom drawer and took out my pistol and eraserhead cartridges. I stuffed them in my bag, noted that it was almost ten and knocked on Friday's door.

"Darling?"

He looked up from the copy of *Strontmania* he was reading.

"Yuh?"

"I'm sorry, Sweetpea, but I have to go back to the BookWorld. It may put the unscrambled-eggs recipe in jeopardy."

He sighed and stared at me. "I knew you would."

"How?"

He beckoned me to the window and pointed to three figures

sitting on a wall opposite the house. "The one in the middle is the other me. It shows there is still a *chance* they'll get hold of the recipe. If we'd won, they'd be long gone."

"Don't worry," I said, laying a hand on his. "I know how important the length of the Now is to all of us. I won't go anywhere near 'The Wreck of the Hesperus.' "

"Mum," he said in a quiet voice, "if you get back home and I'm polite, well-mannered and with short hair, don't be too hard on me, eh?"

He was worried about being replaced.

"It won't come to that, Sweetpea. I'll defend your right to be smelly and uncommunicative . . . with my *life*."

We hugged and I said good-bye, then did the same to Tuesday, who was reading in bed, giggling over the risible imperfections of the Special Theory of Relativity. She knew I was going somewhere serious, so she got out of bed to give me an extra hug just in case. I hugged her back, tucked her in, told her not to make Einstein look *too* much of a clot in case it made her look cocky. I then went to say good-bye to Jenny and can remember doing so, although for some reason Friday and Tuesday picked that moment to argue about the brightness of the hall light. After sorting them out, I went downstairs to Landen.

"Land," I said, unsure of what to say, since I rarely got emergency call-outs for carpet laying, and to pretend I did now would be such an obvious lie, "you do know I love you?"

"More than you realize, sweetheart."

"And you trust me?"

"Of course."

"Good. I've got to go and—"

"Do some emergency carpet laying?"

I smiled. "Yeah. Wish me luck."

We hugged, I put on my jacket and left the house, hailing a cab to take me to the Clary-LaMarr Travelport. When I was safely on the bullet train to Saknussemm, I took out my cell phone and keyed in a number. I stared out at the dark Wessex countryside that zipped past so fast the few streetlamps I could see were almost orange streaks. The cell was picked up, and I paused, heart thumping, before speaking.

"My name's Thursday Next. I'd like to speak to John Henry Goliath. You're going to have to wake him. It's a matter of some importance."

32.

The *Austen Rover* Roving

The basis for the *Austen Rover,* I learned much later, was a bus that the Goliath Corporation had bought in 1952 to transport its employees to the coast on "works days out," a lamentable lapse in Goliath's otherwise fine record of rampant worker exploitation. The error was discovered after eight years and the day trips discontinued. True to form, Goliath docked the wages of all who attended and charged them for the trip—with back-dated interest.

"The *Austen Rover* has two separate systems," explained Dr. Anne Wirthlass, "the transfictional propulsion unit and the book-navigation protocol. The former we have worked out—the latter is something you need to update us on."

It was almost noon of the following day, and I was being brought up to speed on the *Rover*'s complexities by the brilliant Dr. Wirthlass, who had thanked me profusely for changing my mind so close to the time before they were to fire themselves off into the unknown.

"It was the least I could do," I replied, keeping the real reason to myself.

There had been an excited buzz among the technicians in the lab that morning, and I had been introduced to more specialists in an hour than I'd met in a lifetime. John Henry Goliath himself was on hand to smooth over any problems we might have, and there had already been a propulsion test. The *Austen Rover* had been chained to the floor, and the engines had been spooled up. With a deafening roar, the *Rover* had flexed at the chains while an inky black void had opened up in front of it. The engines had been throttled back, and the void had closed. It didn't have the quiet subtleness of Mycroft's Prose Portal, but it had certainly been impressive.

That had been three hours earlier. Right now we were in the control room, and I'd been trying to explain to them just what form the BookWorld takes, which was a bit odd, as it was really only *my* interpretation of it, and I had a feeling that if they accepted *my* way, it would become *the* way, so I was careful not to describe anything that might be problematical later. I spread a sheet of paper on the table and drew a rough schematic of the various genres that made up the BookWorld, but without too many precise locations—just enough for them to get us inside and then to *It Was a Dark and Stormy Night* without any problems.

"The Nothing is a big place," I said without fear of understatement, "and mostly empty. Theoretical storyologists have calculated that the readable BookWorld makes up only twenty-two percent of visible reading matter—the remainder is the unobservable remnants of long-lost books, forgotten oral tradition and ideas still locked in writers' heads. We call it 'dark reading matter.'"

"Why is so much of it unread and untold?"

I shrugged. "We're not altogether sure, but we think ninety-eight percent of the world's fiction was wiped out by the accidental death of an Iron Age storyteller about three thousand years ago. It was what we call a 'mass erasure'—we wouldn't see anything of that size until human perfidy, fire and mold wiped out seventy-five percent of Greek drama at the CE boundary. The reason I mention it is that navigating through the Nothing could be more treacherous than you imagine—colliding with a lost work of Aeschylus or being pulled apart by the Hemingway 'lost suitcase of manuscripts' could bring your trip to a painfully verbose. And incorrectly punctuated. End."

Dr. Wirthlass nodded sagely.

I drew a rough circle near the Maritime Adventure (Civilian) genre. "We think that this area is heavy with detritus from an unknown genre—possibly Squid Action/Adventure—that failed to fully form a century ago. Twice a year Maritime is pelted with small fragments of ideas and snatches of inner monologue regarding important invertebrate issues that don't do much harm, but bookjumping through this zone has always been a bit bumpy. If we wanted to go from Maritime to Frontier quickly and easily, we wouldn't jump direct but go through Western."

We talked along these lines for a good four hours; it surprised me that I knew so much about the BookWorld without really having had to sit down and learn it, and it also surprised me to what an advanced stage the Goliath Book Project had progressed. By agreement they would drop me on page 68 of *It Was a Dark and Stormy Night* before slingshotting back to Goliath, then await my return and a debrief before attempting any further travel. I had made my demands clearly when I'd spoken to John Henry the previous evening. They would do this my way or not at all, something that he was happy to agree with. He also proposed some sort of business partnership where I could oversee the whole *Austen Rover* project and determine in what direction book tourism would go. I still didn't like the idea of it, but if the alternative was the wholesale loss of all the classics through reality book shows, then I'd pretend to go along. I told John Henry we could discuss the precise details upon my return. Throughout the day I'd been having nagging doubts about cozying up to Goliath despite their entreaties, and in an afternoon rest break I wandered into the employees' canteen area, where there was a TV showing a program all about the upcoming *Pride and Prejudice* reality show.

"Welcome to *Bennetmania*," said a lively young man with painfully fashionable facial hair. He was presenting one of several reality book TV shows that had been rushed onto the schedules to cater to the latest fad. ". . . And our studio panel will be here to give an up-to-date analysis of the book's unfolding drama as soon as it begins. Dr. Nessecitar, our resident pseudopyschologist, will point out the bleeding obvious about the Bennet housemates' progress, and our resident experts will give their opinions and advice on whom should be voted out. But first let's have a rundown on who our housemates actually are."

I stood and stared with a kind of numb fascination as a jaunty tune started up under an annoyingly buoyant voice-over that accompanied "artists' impressions" of the family.

"Mr. Bennet is the father of the clan, and when he's not chastizing his younger daughters for their silliness or teasing his wife, he likes nothing better than to sit in his study and conduct his affairs. His wife is Mrs. Bennet, who has a brother in trade and is convinced that her daughters should marry up. This old bunny is highly unstable, prone to panic attacks and socially awkward, so keep your eyes fixed on her for some seriously good fireworks."

The illustration changed to that of the sisters, with each being highlighted in turn as the voice-over described them.

"None of the daughters will inherit Longbourn due to the lack of an heir, and the apparent absence of any suitable males in Meryton makes the issue of potential husbands a major concern. Curvaceous, doe-eyed Jane, twenty-two, is the beauty of the family, with a kindly temperament to match. And if Bingley looks at another woman, hold on for the waterworks! Next in line is the thinker of the house and Mr. Bennet's favorite: Lizzie, who is twenty. Willful, skillful and adept with words, she is certainly one to watch—never mind the looks, check out the subtext! Third eldest is Mary, who just likes to read and criticize the rest of them. Dreary and unappealing, and we don't think she'll last long. Kitty and Lydia are the two youngest of the Bennets and the silliest and most excitable of them all, especially when there's a uniform around, or even the sniff of a party. Impetuous and uncontrollable—these are the two that all eyes will be riveted upon!"

The music ended, and the annoying presenter came back onscreen.

"There you have it. Seven Bennets, one house, three chapters, one task, one eviction. Bookies are already taking bets as to who's for the bullet. Tune in tomorrow at eleven P.M. with your book in hand to read the housemates' first task as it is set, and join us for the reading of *The Bennets—live!*"

I switched off the set and walked back to the Book Project lab, all doubts over the wisdom of my actions dispelled from my mind.

By six that evening, the *Austen Rover* was primed and ready to go. Although there was seating for twelve, the crew was to be only the four of us—myself, Dr. Wirthlass and two technicians, whose sole function was to monitor the systems and collect data. I called Landen before we left and told him I'd be home before bedtime. I didn't see any problems. After all, I'd been prancing around the inside of the BookWorld for near on twenty years and had faced almost all the terrors that could be thrown in my direction. I felt as safe and confident inside fiction as I did walking down the street in Swindon. I'd turn up at the CofG, reveal Thursday1–4 as an impostor, put everything to rights and be back in time to take Jenny to her piano lesson. Simple. But if it *was* that simple, why did my insides feel so leaden?

John Henry Goliath came to see us off, and we all shook hands before the door closed and sealed itself with a hermetic hiss. The doctor and the two technicians were too busy to be worried over the risks, something that I felt myself but tried not to show. After a half-hour countdown, Wirthlass fired up the main reactors, released the handbrake, rang the bell twice and engaged the gravity engines.

And with a mild tingling sensation, we were somewhere else entirely.

33.

Somewhere Else Entirely

The BookWorld was generally agreed to be only part of a much larger Bookverse, but quite how big it was and what percentage was unobservable was a matter of hot debate among booklogians. The fundamental rules of the Bookverse were also contentious. Some factions argued that the Bookverse was constantly expanding as new books were written, but others argued convincingly of a steady-state Bookverse, where ideas were endlessly recycled. A third faction who called themselves "simplists" argued that there was a single fundamental rule that governed all story: If it works, it works.

The darkness drifted away like morning mist, leaving us hovering above a slate gray sea with empty horizons in all directions. The sky was the same color as the sea and stretched across the heavens like a blanket, heavy and oppressive. A light breeze blew flecks of foam from the tops of the waves, and positioned not thirty feet below us was an old steamer of riveted construction. The vessel was making a leisurely pace through the waves, a trail of black smoke issuing languidly from her funnel and the stern trailing a creamy wake as the ship rose and fell in the seas.

"That'll be the *Auberon*," I said, craning my neck to see if I could spot Captain Carver in the wheelhouse. I couldn't, so I asked Wirthlass to move closer and try to land the *Rover* on the aft hold cover so I could step aboard. She expertly moved the bus in behind the bridge and gently lowered it onto the boards, which creaked ominously under the weight. The door of the coach hissed opened, and a strong whiff of salty air mixed with coal smoke drifted in. I could feel the rhythmic thump of the engine and the swell of the ocean through the decking. I took my bag and stepped from the *Rover,* but I hadn't gone three paces when all of a sudden I realized there was something badly wrong. This ship wasn't the *Auberon,* and if that was the case, this book certainly wasn't *Dark and Stormy Night.*

"Okay, we've got a problem," I said, turning back to the *Rover* only to find Dr. Wirthlass standing in the doorway—holding a pistol and *smiling.*

"*Ballocks,*" I muttered, which was about as succinct as I could be, given the sudden change of circumstance.

"Ballocks indeed," replied Dr. Wirthlass. "We've waited over fifteen years for this moment."

"Before now I'd always thought patience was a virtue," I murmured, "not the secret weapon of the vengeful."

She shook her head and smiled again. "You're *exactly* how he described you. An ardent moralist, a Goody Two-shoes, pathologically eager to do what's best and what's right." She looked around at the ship, which heeled in the swell. "So this place is particularly apt—and the perfect place for you to spend the rest of your pitifully short life."

"What do you want?"

"Nothing. Nothing at all. With you trapped here, we have everything I want. We'll be off to the *Hesperus* now, Ms. Next—to find that recipe."

"You know about the unscrambled eggs?" I asked, shocked at the sudden turn of events.

"We're Goliath," she said simply, "and information is power. With the End of Time due tomorrow evening, it will be something of a challenge, but listen: I like a challenge, and I have the knowledge of your defeat to freshen my mind and make the task that much more enjoyable."

"You'll never find it," I said. "Longfellow is at the other end of the BookWorld, and Poetry is the place you'll discover—"

I checked myself. I wasn't helping these people, no matter how acute the perils.

"Discover what?" asked Wirthlass with a frown.

"Never mind."

"We'll be fine," she replied. "We just needed your expertise to make the initial jump. We're not *quite* so stupid as you think."

I couldn't believe that I'd been hoodwinked by Goliath again. I had to hand it to them—this plan had been hatched and executed *beautifully*.

"How long have you known about the recipe?"

"That's just the weirdest thing of it." Dr. Wirthlass smiled. "On the one hand, only a day, but on the other . . . over fifteen years."

"Retrospective investment," I whispered, suddenly understanding. In their desperation, the ChronoGuard was breaking every single rule they'd ever made.

"Right! The Star Chamber lost confidence in your son's ability to secure the future, so they called Lavoisier out of retirement to see if there weren't *other* avenues to explore. He approached John Henry yesterday at breakfast time to ask him if the long-abandoned Book Project could be brought up to speed. Since it couldn't, Lavoisier suggested that they restart the project fifteen years ago so it could be ready for the End of Time tomorrow evening. John Henry agreed with certain *conditions*, and I must say we only just made it."

"This is something of a mindf**k," I replied, with no possibility of understatement. "What does Goliath get out of it?"

"How do you think we survived being taken over by the Toast Marketing Board? Two days ago Goliath was just a bad memory, with John Henry in debtors' prison and me working for International Pencils. When you have friends in the time industry, anything is possible. The ChronoGuard will be willing to offer us almost untold patronage for the recipe to unscramble eggs and, with it, the secret to travel in time. And in return? A corporation allowed to speculate freely in *time*. Finally we will be able to bring our 'big plan' to fruition."

"And that plan is . . . ?"

"To own . . . everything."

"In a world with a Short Now?"

"Of course! With a compliant population only interested in the self and instant gratification, we can flog all manner of worthless crap as the 'latest thing to have.' There'll be big profits, Next—and by subtly choosing from whom the Now is mined, the Long Now Überclass can sit back and enjoy the benefits that will be theirs and theirs alone."

I stared at Wirthlass, wondering if I could rush her. It seemed doubtful, since I was at least ten feet away, and the two technicians still on board the *Rover* also looked as if they had weapons.

"Okay," said the doctor, "we're all about done here. Enjoy your imprisonment. You'll know what it was like for my husband. Two years in "The Raven," Next—*two years*. He still has nightmares, even today."

"You're Jack Schitt's *wife*?"

She smiled again. "Now you're getting it. My full name is Dr. Anne Wirthlass-Schitt, but if you'd known, it might have been a bit of a giveaway, hmm? Bye-bye now."

The door swung shut, the bell rang twice, there was a low hiss and the *Austen Rover* lifted off. They hovered for a moment and then slowly rotated, expertly missed the crane derrick, rose above the height of the funnel and then became long and drawn out like a piece of elastic before vanishing with a faint pop. I was left standing on the deck, biting my lip in frustration and anger. I took a deep breath and calmed myself. The reality book show of *The Bennets* wasn't due to start until tomorrow morning, so there was always hope. I looked around. The steamer rolled gently in the swell, the smoke drifted across the stern past the fluttering red ensign, and the beat of the engine echoed up through the steel deck. I knew I wasn't in *Dark and Stormy Night*, because the ship wasn't a rusty old tub held together by paint, but I was certainly *somewhere*, and somewhere was better than nowhere. It was only when I arrived there and was out of ideas, time and essential metabolic functions that I was going to give up.

I trotted up the companionway, ducked into the galley and made my way up the ladder to the bridge, where a boy not much older than Friday was holding the ship's wheel.

"Who's in command?" I asked, a bit breathless.

"Why, *you,* of course," replied the lad.

"I'm not."

"Then why are you a-wearin' the cap?"

I put up my hands to check, and strangely enough, I *was* wearing the captain's cap. I took it off and stared at it stupidly.

"What book is this?"

"No book I knows of, Cap'n. What be your orders?"

I looked out of the wheelhouse ahead but could see nothing except a gray sea meeting a gray sky. The light was soft and directionless, and for the first time I felt a shiver of dread. Something about this place was undeniably *creepy,* but I couldn't put my finger on it. I went to the navigation desk and looked at the chart. There was nothing on it but the pale blueness of open ocean, and a cursory look in the drawers of the desk told me that every chart was the same. Whatever this place was, this was all there was of it. I had to assume I was somewhere in the Maritime genre, but a quick glance at my mobilefootnoterphone and the absence of any signal told me that I was several thousand volumes beyond our repeater station in the Hornblower series, and if that was the case, I was right on the periphery of the genre—as good as lost. I tapped my finger on the desk and thought hard. Panic was the mind killer, and I still had several hours to figure this out. If I was no further on in ten hours' time—*then* I could panic.

"What are your orders, Cap'n?" asked the lad at the wheel again.

"What's your name?"

"Baldwin."

"I'm Thursday. Thursday Next."

"Good to know you, Cap'n Next."

"Have you heard my name? Or of Jurisfiction?"

He shook his head.

"Right. Tell me, Baldwin, do you know this ship well?"

"As well as I know meself," he replied proudly.

"Is there a core-containment room?"

"Not that I knows of."

So we weren't in a published work.

"How about a Storycode Engine anywhere on board?"

He frowned and looked confused. "There's an *ordinary* engine room. I don't know nuffin' 'bout no *Storycode*."

I scratched my head. Without a Storycode Engine, we were either nonfiction or something in the oral tradition. Those were the upbeat possibilities: I might also be in a forgotten story, a dead writer's unrealized idea or even a handwritten short story stuck in a desk drawer somewhere—the dark reading matter.

"What year is this?"

"Spring of 1932, Cap'n."

"And the purpose of this voyage?"

"Not for the likes of me to know, Cap'n."

"But *something* must happen!"

"Oh, aye," he said more confidently, "things most *definite* happen!"

"What sort of things?"

"*Difficult* things, Cap'n."

As if in answer to his enigmatic comment, someone shouted my name. I walked out onto the port wing, where a man in a first officer's uniform was on the deck below. He was in his mid-fifties and looked vaguely cultured, but somehow out of place, as though his service in the merchant navy had been to remove him from problems at home.

"Captain Next?" he said.

"Yes, sort of."

"First Officer William Fitzwilliam at your service, ma'am. We've got a problem with the passengers!"

"Can't you deal with it?"

"No, ma'am—*you're* the captain."

I descended and met Fitzwilliam at the foot of the ladder. He led me into the paneled wardroom, where there were three people waiting for us. The first man was standing stiffly with his arms folded and looked aggrieved. He was well dressed in a black morning coat and wore a small pince-nez perched on the end of his nose. The other two were obviously man and wife. The woman was of an unhealthy pallor, had recently been crying and was being comforted by her husband, who every now and then shot an angry glance at the first man.

"I'm very busy," I told them. "What's the problem here?"

"My name is Mr. Langdon," said the married man, wringing his hands. "My wife, Louise, here suffers from Zachary's syndrome, and without the necessary medicine she will die."

"I'm very sorry to hear that," I said, "but what can I do?"

"That man has the medicine!" cried Langdon, pointing an accusatory finger at the man in the pince-nez. "Yet he refuses to sell it to me!"

"Is this true?"

"My name is Dr. Glister," said the man, nodding politely. "I have the medicine, it is true, but the price is two thousand guineas, and Mr. and Mrs. Langdon have only a thousand guineas and not the capacity to borrow more!"

"Well," I said to the doctor, "I think it would be a kindly gesture to lower the price, don't you?"

"I wish that I could," replied Dr. Glister, "but this medicine cost me everything I possessed to develop. It destroyed my health and damaged my reputation. If I do not recoup my losses, I will be forced into ruin, my property will be repossessed, and my six children will become destitute. I am sympathetic to Mrs. Langdon's trouble, but this is a fiscal issue."

"Listen," I said to the Langdons, "it's not up to me. The medicine is Dr. Glister's property for him to dispose of as he wishes."

"But she needs the medicine *now*," pleaded Mr. Langdon. "If she doesn't get it, she will die. You are the captain on this ship and so have the ultimate authority. You *must* make the decision."

I sighed. I had a lot more important things to deal with right now.

"Dr. Glister, give him the medicine for a thousand guineas. Mr. Langdon, you will work to repay Dr. Glister *no matter what*. Understand?"

"But my livelihood!" wailed Glister.

"I place Mrs. Langdon's *definite* death above the *possibility* of your penury, Dr. Glister."

"But this is nothing short of theft!" he replied, outraged at my words. "And I have done nothing wrong—only discovered a cure for a fatal illness. I deserve better treatment than this!"

"You do, you're right. But I know nothing of you, nor the Langdons. My decision is based only on the saving of a life. Will you excuse me?"

Baldwin had called from the wheelhouse, and I quickly scooted up the stairs.

"What is it?"

He pointed to something about a mile off the starboard bow. I picked up a pair of binoculars and trained it on the distant object. Finally some good luck. It looked like a "turmoil," the name we gave to a small, localized disruption in the fabric of the written word. This was how heavy weather in the BookWorld got started: A turmoil would soon progress into a powerful WordStorm able to uproot words, ideas and even people, then carry them with it across the empty darkness of the Nothing, eventually dumping them on distant books several genres distant. It was my way out. I'd never hitched a ride on a WordStorm before, but it didn't look too difficult. Dorothy, after all, had no real problems with the tornado.

"Alter course to starboard thirty degrees," I said. "We're going to intercept the WordStorm. How long do you think it will take for us to get there, Baldwin?"

"Twenty minutes, Cap'n."

It would be a close thing. Turmoils increase their pace until a rotating tube rises up into the heavens, filled with small sections of plot and anything else it can suck up. Then, with a flurry of distorted sense, it lifts off and vanishes. I wouldn't get this chance again.

"Is that wise, Captain?" asked First Officer Fitzwilliam, who had joined us on the bridge. "I've seen storms like that. They can do serious damage—and we have forty passengers, many of them women and children."

"Then you can lower me in a lifeboat ahead of the storm."

"And leave us without a lifeboat?"

"Yes . . . *no* . . . I don't know. Fitzwilliam?"

"Yes, Captain?"

"What is this place?"

"I don't know what you mean, Captain."

"I mean—"

"Cap'n," said Baldwin, pointing off of the port side of the ship, "isn't that a lifeboat?"

I turned my attention to the area in which he pointed. It *was* a lifeboat, with what looked like several people, all slumped and apparently unconscious. *Damn.* I looked again, hoping for confirmation that they might already be dead, but saw nothing to tell me either way. I frowned to myself. Had I just hoped for them to be dead?

"You can pick them up after you've dropped me off," I said. "It'll only mean an extra forty minutes for them, and I really need to get out of here."

I saw Fitzwilliam and Baldwin exchange glances. But as we watched, the lifeboat was caught by a wave and capsized, casting the occupants into the sea. We could see now that they *were* alive, and as they scrabbled weakly to cling to the upturned boat, I gave the order.

"Turn about. Reduce power and stand by to pick up survivors."

"Aye-aye, Cap'n," said Baldwin, spinning the wheel as Fitzwilliam rung up "slow ahead" on the engine-room telegraph. I walked out onto the starboard wing and watched despondently as the turmoil developed into a WordStorm. Within the twenty minutes it took to intercept the lifeboat, the whirling mass of narrative distortion lifted off, taking part of the description of the ocean with it. There was a ragged dark hole for an instant, and then the sea washed in to fill the anomaly, and in a few moments everything was back to normal. Perhaps I should have left the lifeboat. After all, the Long Now and the classics were more important than several fictional castaways. Mind you, if I'd been on that lifeboat, I know what I would have wanted.

"Captain!"

It was Dr. Glister.

"I don't want to know about your arguments with the Langdons," I told him.

"No, no," he replied in something of a panic, "you *cannot* pick up these castaways!"

"Why not?"

"They have Squurd's disease."

"They have *what*?"

We walked into the wheelhouse and out again onto the port wing, where Fitzwilliam was directing the rescue operation. The lifeboat was still ahead of us at least a hundred yards. The ship was moving forward slowly, a cling net had been thrown over the side, and several burly sailors were making ready to pick up the castaways.

"Look carefully at the survivors," urged Dr. Glister, and I trained my binoculars on the small group. Now that they were closer, I could see that their faces were covered with unsightly green pustules.

I lowered the binoculars and looked at Dr. Glister. "What's the prognosis?"

"A hundred percent fatal, and highly contagious. Bring them on board and we'll be looking at a minimum of twenty percent casualties. We don't reach port for six months, and these poor wretches will already have died in agony long before we could get any help to them."

I rubbed my temples. "You're completely sure of this?"

He nodded. I took a deep breath.

"Fitzwilliam?"

"Yes, Captain?"

"Break off the rescue."

"What?"

"You heard me. These people have a contagious fatal illness, and I won't risk my passengers' lives saving castaways who will die no matter what we do."

"But, Captain!" he protested. "We *never* leave a man in the water!"

"We're doing it today, Fitzwilliam. Do you understand?"

He glared at me menacingly, then leaned over the rail and repeated my order, making sure the men knew who had made it. After that, he went into the wheelhouse, rang up "full ahead," and the vessel shuddered as we made extra speed and steamed on.

"Come inside," said Dr. Glister.

"No," I said. "I'm staying here. I won't hide from the men I've condemned to death."

And I stood there and watched as the lifeboat and the men drifted astern of the ship and were soon lost to view in the seas.

It was with a heavy heart that I walked back into the wheelhouse and sat in the captain's chair. Baldwin was silent, gazing straight ahead.

"It was the right thing to do," I muttered, to no one in particular. "And what's more, I could have used the WordStorm to escape after all."

"Things happen here," muttered Baldwin. "*Difficult* things."

I suddenly had a thought, but hoped upon hope I was wrong. "What's the name of this ship?"

"The ship?" replied Baldwin cheerily. "It's the steamship *Moral Dilemma,* Cap'n."

I covered my face with my hands and groaned. Anne Wirthlass-Schitt and her obnoxious husband had not been kidding when they said they'd chosen this place especially for me. My nerves were already badly frayed, and I felt the heavy hand of guilt pressing upon me. I'd only been here an hour—what would I be like in a week, or a month? Truly, I was trapped in an unenviable place: adrift on the Hypothetical Ocean, in command of the *Moral Dilemma*.

"Captain?"

It was the cook this time. He was unshaven and wearing a white uniform that had so many food stains on it that it was hard to say where stain ended and uniform began.

"Yes?" I said, somewhat wearily.

"Begging your pardon, but there's been a gross underestimation on the provisions."

"And?"

"We don't get into port for another six months," the cook continued, referring to a grubby sheet of calculations he had on him, "and we only have enough to feed the crew and passengers on strict rations for two-thirds of that time."

"What are you saying?"

"That all forty of us will starve long before we reach port."

I beckoned Fitzwilliam over. "There wouldn't be another port closer than that, would there?"

"No, Captain," he answered. "Port Conjecture is the only port there is."

"I thought so. And no fish either?"

"Not in these waters."

"Other ships?"

"None."

I got it now. These were the "difficult things" Baldwin had spoken of, and they were mine and mine alone to deal with. The ship, the sea and the people on it might be hypothetical—but they could suffer and die the same as anyone.

"Thank you, Cook," I said. "I'll let you know of my decision."

He gave a lazy salute and was gone.

"Well, Fitzwilliam," I said, doing some simple math on a piece of paper, "there's enough food for twenty-six people to survive until we reach port. Do you think we could find fourteen volunteers to throw themselves over the side to ensure the survival of the rest?"

"I doubt it."

"Then I have something of a problem. Is my primary sense of duty as captain to see to it that as many people as possible survive on my ship, or is it my moral obligation not to conduct or condone murder?"

"The men in the lifeboat just now wouldn't see you as anything but a murderer."

"Perhaps so, but this one's harder; it's not a case of *inaction* to bring about a circumstance, but *action*. This is what I'm going to do. Anyone under eighteen is excluded, as are six essential crew to keep the ship going. All the rest will choose straws—thirteen will go over the side."

"If they don't want to go?"

"Then I will throw them over."

"You'll hang for it."

"I won't. I'll be the fourteenth."

"Very . . . *selfless*," murmured Fitzwilliam, "but even after your crew and age exclusions, thirty-one passengers are still under eighteen. You will still have to select seven of them. Will you be able to throw *them* overboard, the children, the innocents?"

"But I save the rest, right?"

"It's not for me to say," said Fitzwilliam quietly. "I am not the captain."

I closed my eyes and took a deep breath, my heart thumping and a cold panic roiling inside me. I had to do terrible things in order to save others, and I'm not sure I could even do it—and thus imperil everyone's life. I stopped for a moment and thought. The dilemmas had been getting progressively worse since I arrived. Perhaps this place—wherever it was—was quirkily responsive to my decisions. I decided to try something.

"No," I said. "I'm not going to kill anyone simply because an abstract ethical situation demands it. We're going to sail on as we are and trust to providence that we meet another ship. If we don't, then we may die, but we will have at least done the right thing by one another."

There was a distant rumble of thunder in the distance, and the boat heeled over. I wondered what would be next.

"Begging your pardon, Captain, but I bring bad news." It was a steward whom I hadn't seen before.

"And . . . ?"

"We have a gentleman in the wardroom who claims there is a bomb on board the ship—and it's set to go off in ten minutes."

I allowed myself a wry smile. The rapidly changing scenarios seemed to have a clumsy intelligence to them. It was possible this was something in the oral tradition, but I couldn't be sure. If this small world were somehow sentient, though, it could be beaten. To vanquish it, I needed to find its weakness, and it had just supplied one: *impatience.* It didn't want a long, drawn-out starvation for the passengers; it wanted me to commit a hands-on murder for the greater good—and soon.

"Show me."

I followed the steward down into the wardroom, where a man was sitting in a chair in the middle of the room. He looked sallow and had fine, wispy blond hair and small eyes that stared intently at me as I walked in. A burly sailor named McTavish, who was tattoo and Scotsman in a three-to-four ratio, was standing guard over him. There was no one else in the room—there didn't need to be. It was a hypothetical situation.

"Your name, sir?"

"Jebediah Salford. And I have hidden a bomb—"

"I heard. And naturally you won't tell me where it is?"

"Naturally."

"This bomb," I went on, "will sink the ship, potentially leading to many deaths?"

"Indeed, I hope so," replied Jebediah cheerily.

"Your own included?"

"I fear no death."

I paused for thought. It was a classic and overused ethical dilemma. Would I, as an essentially good person, reduce myself to torturing someone for the greater good? It was a puzzle that had been discussed for many years, generally by those to whom it has no chance of becoming real. But the way in which the scenarios came on thick and fast suggested that whoever was running this show had a prurient interest in seeing just how far a decent person could be pushed before doing bad things. I could almost feel the architect of the dilemma gloating over me from afar. I would have to stall him if I could.

"Fitzwilliam? Have all passengers go on deck, close all watertight doors, and have every crew member and able-bodied passenger look for the bomb."

"Captain," he said, "that's a waste of time. There *is* a bomb, but you can't find it. The decision has to be made here and now, in this wardroom."

Damn. Outmaneuvered.

"How many lifeboats do we have?" I asked, getting increasingly desperate.

"Only one left, ma'am—with room for ten."

"Shit. How long do we have left before this bomb goes off?"

"Seven minutes."

If this were the real world and in a situation as black and white as this, there wasn't a decision to make. I would use all force necessary to get the information. But, most important, submit myself to scrutiny afterward. If you permit or conduct torture, you must be personally responsible for your actions—it's the kind of decision where it's best to have the threat of prison looming behind you. But the thing was, on board this ship here and now, it didn't look as though torturing him would actually achieve anything at all. He would eventually tell me, the bomb would be found—and the next dilemma would begin. And they would carry on, again and again, worse and worse, until I had done everything I would never have done and the passengers of this vessel were drowned, eaten or murdered. It was hell for me, but it would be hell for them, too. I sat down heavily on a nearby chair, put my head in hands and stared at the floor.

"Captain," said Fitzwilliam, "we only have five minutes. You *must* torture this person."

"Yeah, yeah," I mumbled incoherently, "I know."

"We will all die," he continued. "*Again.*"

I looked up into his eyes. I'd never noticed how incredibly blue they were.

"You all die in the end, don't you?" I said miserably. "No matter what I do. It's just one increasingly bad dilemma after another until everyone's dead, right?"

"Four minutes, Captain."

"Am I right?"

Fitzwilliam looked away.

"I asked you a question, Number One."

He looked up at me, and he seemed to have tears in his eyes. "We have all been drowned," he said in a quiet voice, "over a thousand times each. We have been eaten, blown up and suffered fatal illnesses. The drownings are the worst. Each time I can feel the smothering effect of water, the blind panic as I suffocate—"

"Fitzwilliam," I demanded, "where is this damnable place?"

He took a deep breath and lowered his voice. "We're oral tradition, but we're not in a story—we're an *ethics seminar.*"

"You mean you're all hypothetical characters during a lecture?"

Fitzwilliam nodded miserably. The steward somewhat chillingly handed me a pair of pliers, while reminding me in an urgent whisper that there were only three minutes left.

I looked down at the pliers in an absent sort of way, at Jebediah, then back to Fitzwilliam, who was staring at the floor. So much suffering on board this ship, and for so long. Perhaps there *was* another way out. The thing was, to take such radical action in the oral tradition risked the life of the lecturer giving the talk. But what was more important? The well-being of one real-life ethics professor or the relentless torture of his subjects, who had to undergo his sadistic and relentless hypothetical dilemmas for two-hour sessions three times a week? When you tell a tragic story, someone dies for real in the BookWorld. I was in the oral tradition. Potentially the best storytelling there was—and the most destructive.

"McTavish, prepare the lifeboat for launching. I'm leaving."

McTavish looked at Fitzwilliam, who shrugged, and the large Scotsman and his tattoos departed.

"That isn't one of the options," said Fitzwilliam. "You can't do it."

"I have experience of the oral tradition," I told him. "All these scenarios are taking place only because I am here to preside in judgment upon them. This whole thing goes just one way: in a downward spiral of increasingly impossible moral dilemmas that will leave everyone dead except myself and one other, whom I will be forced to kill and eat or something. If I take myself out of the equation, you are free to sail across the sea unhampered, unimpeded—and safe."

"But that might . . . that might—"

"Harm the lecturer, even kill him? Possibly. If the bomb goes off, you'll know I've failed and he's okay. If it doesn't, you'll all be safe."

"And you?" he asked. "What about you?"

I patted him on the shoulder. "Don't worry about me. I think you've all suffered enough on account of the Outland."

"But surely . . . we can pick you up again if all goes well?"

"No," I said, "that's not how it works. It can't be a trick. I have to cast myself adrift."

I trotted out of the wardroom and to the side of the ship, where McTavish had already lowered the lifeboat. It was being held against the scramble net by lines fore and aft clutched by deckhands, and it thumped against the hull as the waves caught it. As I put my leg over the rail to climb down, Fitzwilliam grasped my arm. He wasn't trying to stop me—he wanted to shake me by the hand.

"Good-bye, Captain—and thank you."

I smiled. "Think you'll make Port Conjecture?"

He smiled back. "We'll give it our best shot."

I climbed down the scramble net and into the lifeboat. They let go fore and aft, and the boat rocked violently as the bow wave caught it. For a moment I thought it would go over, but it stayed upright, and I rapidly fell behind as the ship steamed on.

I counted off the seconds until the bomb was meant to explode, but, thankfully, it didn't, and across the sea I heard the cheer of forty people celebrating their release. I couldn't share in their elation, because in a university somewhere back home the ethics lecturer had suddenly keeled over with an aneurysm. They'd call a doctor, and with a bit of luck he'd pull through. He might even lecture again, but not with this crew.

The *Moral Dilemma* was at least a quarter mile away by now, and within ten minutes the steamer was just a smudge of smoke on the horizon. In another half hour, it had vanished completely, and I was on my own in a gray sea that lasted forever in all directions. I looked through my shoulder bag and found a bar of chocolate, which I ate in a despondent manner and then just sat in the bow of the lifeboat and stared up at the gray sky, feeling hopelessly lost. I leaned back and closed my eyes.

Had I done the right thing? I had no idea. The lecturer couldn't have known the suffering he was putting his hypothetical characters through, but even if he had, perhaps he'd justify it by reasoning that the suffering was worth the benefits to his students. If he survived, I'd be able to ask him his opinion. But that wasn't likely. Rescue seemed a very remote possibility, and that was at the nub of the whole ethical-dilemma argument. You never come out on top, no matter what. The only way to win the game is not to play.

34.

Rescue/Capture

There was only one Jurisfiction agent who worked exclusively in the oral tradition. He was named Ski, rarely spoke and wore a tall hat in the manner of Lincoln—but that was the sum total of his recognizable features. When appearing at the Jurisfiction offices, he was always insubstantial, flickering in and out like a badly tuned TV. Despite this he did some of the best work in the OralTrad I'd seen. Rumor had it that he was a discarded Childhood Imaginary Friend, which accounted for his inconsolable melancholy.

When I awoke, nothing had changed. The sea was still gray, the sky a dull overcast. The water was choppy but not dangerously so and had a sort of twenty-second pattern of movement to it. With nothing better to do, I sat up and watched the waves as they rose and fell. By fixing my eyes on a random part of the ocean, I could see that the same wave would come around again like a loop in a film. Most of the BookWorld was like that. Fictional forests had only eight different trees, a beach five different pebbles, a sky twelve different clouds. It was what made the real world so rich by comparison. I looked at my watch. The reality book show of *The Bennets* would be replacing *Pride and Prejudice* in three hours, and the first task of the household would be unveiled in two. Equally bad, that worthless shit Wirthlass-Schitt might well have the recipe by now and would be hoofing it back to Goliath. But then again, she might not. I'd visited enough Poetry to know that it's an emotionally draining place and on a completely different level. Whereas story is processed in the mind in a straightforward manner, poetry bypasses rational thought and goes straight to the limbic system and lights it up like a brushfire. It's the crack cocaine of the literary world.

My mind, I knew, was wandering. It was intentional. If I didn't let it, it returned like an annoying default setting to Landen and the kids. Whenever I thought of them, my eyes welled up, and that was no good for anything. Perhaps, I mused, instead of lying to Landen after the Minotaur had shot me in 1988, I should have just stayed at home and led a blameless life of unabashed domestication. Washing, cleaning and making meals. Okay, with *some* part-time work down at Acme in case I went nuts. But no SpecOps stuff. None. *Except* maybe dispatching a teensy-weensy chimera. Or two. And if Spike needed a hand? Well, I couldn't say no, now could—[1]

My thoughts were interrupted by my mobilefootnoterphone. Until now it had been resolutely silent. I dug it out of my bag and stared at it hopefully. There was still no signal, which meant that *someone else* was within a radius of about 10 million words. Not far in a shelf of Russian novels, perhaps, but out here in the oral tradition it could mean over a thousand stories or more. It was entirely possible that whoever it was wasn't a friend at all, but anything was better than slow starvation, so I keyed the mike and pretended I was a communications expert from OFF-FNOP, the watchdog responsible for overseeing the network.

"OFF-FNOP tech number . . . um, 76542: Request user ident."

I looked carefully all around me, but the horizon was clear. There was nothing at all, just endless gray. It was like—[2]

I paused. Footnoterphones weren't like normal phones—they were textual. It was impossible to tell who was talking. It was a bit

[1] ffffffgghuhfdffffffggggoooonpicUp . . . passslcccccwwww.

[2] kkkkkcar45kAR45%%%%bloody hellfire!>>>>>>sodding jjjjjjjjj Bureaucrats even out here+eeee.

like text messages back home, but without the dopey CUL8R shorthand nonsense.

"I say again: Request user ident."

I looked around desperately, but still nothing. I hoped it wasn't another poor twit like me, compelled to take over the reins as ethical arbiter.[3]

My heart suddenly leaped. Whoever it was, was somewhere close—and didn't read like anyone who would do me harm. I needed to tell the person how to find me, but the only directions I could think of were "I'm near a wave," which was marginally less useful than "I'm in a boat." Then I had an idea.

"If you can hear me," I said into my phone, "head for the rainstorm of text."

I tucked the phone in my pocket and took out my pistol. I released the safety, pointed it into the air and fired. There was a low thud, and the air seemed to wobble as the eraserhead arced high into the sky. It was a risky move, as it would almost certainly be picked up by the weather stations dotted around the genres and from there to Text Grand Central. If they were looking for me, they'd know instantly where I was.

It took a few seconds for the charge to reach the thick stratus of cloud, but when it hit, the effect can be described only as spectacular. There was a yellow-and-green starburst, and the textual clouds changed rapidly from gray to black as the words dissolved, taking the meaning with them. A dark cloud of letters was soon fluttering down toward the sea like chaff, a pillar of text that could be seen for miles. They landed on me and the boat, but mostly the sea, where they settled like autumn leaves on a lake.

I looked up and saw that the hole in the clouds was already healing itself, and within a few minutes the text would start to sink. I opened the pistol and reloaded, but I didn't need to fire a

[3] jjjjjjjahagssffffffssss-Is anyone out there? All I dddddd can see is endless BLEEDING ocean-///////.

second time. On the horizon and heading toward me was a small dot that gradually grew bigger and bigger until it was overhead, then circled twice before it slowed to a stop, hovering in the air right next to the lifeboat. The driver rolled down his window and consulted a clipboard.

"Are you Ms. Next?" he asked, which was mildly surprising, to say the least.

"Yes, I am."

"And you ordered me?"

"Yes, yes I did."

"Well, you better get in, then."

I was still in mild shock at the turn of events but quickly gathered my thoughts and my belongings and climbed into the yellow vehicle. It was dented and dirty and had the familiar TransGenre Taxis logo on the door. I'd never been so glad to see a cab in my entire life.

I settled myself into the backseat as the driver switched on the meter, turned to me with a grin and said, "Had the devil's job finding you, darling—where to?"

It was a good point. I thought for a moment. *Pride and Prejudice* was definitely in dire peril, but if the Now got any shorter, then *all* books were in danger—and a lot more besides.

"Longfellow," I said, "and make it snappy. I think we're going to have some unwanted company."

The cabbie raised his eyebrows, pressed on the accelerator, and we were soon scooting across the sea at a good rate of knots.

He caught my eye in the rearview mirror. "Are you in some kind of trouble?"

"The worst kind," I replied, thinking that I was going to have to trust this cabbie to do the right thing. "I'm subject to a shoot-to-kill order from the CofG, but it's bullshit. I'm a Jurisfiction agent, and I could seriously do with some help right now."

"Bureaucrats!" he snorted disparagingly, then thought hard for a moment and added, "Next, Next—you wouldn't be *Thursday* Next, would you?"

"That's me."

"I like your books a lot. Especially the early ones with all the killing and gratuitous sex."

"I'm not like that. I'm—"

"Whoa!"

The cabbie swerved abruptly, and I was thrown violently to the other side of the taxi. I looked out the rear window and could see a figure in a long black dress hit the sea in a cascade of foam. They were onto me already.

"That was strange," said the cabbie, "but I could have sworn that was a fifty-something, creepy-looking housekeeper dressed entirely in black."

"It was a Danverclone," I said. "There'll be more."

He clicked down the central locking and turned to stare at me. "You've really pissed someone off good and proper, haven't you?"

"Not without good reason— Look out!"

He swerved again as another Danverclone bounced off the hood and stared at me in a very unnerving way as she flew past the window. I watched her cartwheel across the the waves behind us. That was the thing about Danverclones. They were wholly expendable.

A moment later a heavy thump on the roof shook the cab. I looked behind, but no one had fallen off, and then I heard a noise like an angle grinder from above. It was another Danverclone on the roof, and she was planning on getting in.

"This is too heavy for me," said the cabbie, whose sense of fair play was rapidly departing. "I've got a livelihood and a very expensive backstory to support."

"I'll buy you a fleet of new cabs," I told him somewhat urgently. "And MasterBackstoryist Grnksghty is a personal friend of mine; he'll spin you a backstory of your choice."

Before the cabbie could answer, another Mrs. Danvers landed heavily on the hood near the radiator. She stared at us for a moment and then, by pushing her fingers into the steel bodywork, began to crawl up the hood toward us, lips pursed tightly, the slipstream flapping her clothes and tugging at her tightly combed black hair. She wore the same small dark glasses as the rest of them, but you didn't need to see her eyes to guess her murderous intent.

"I'm going to have to turn you in," said the cabbie as yet another Danverclone landed on the taxi with a crash that shattered the side window. She hung on to the roof trim and flapped around for a bit before finally getting a hold, and then, reaching in through the broken window, she fumbled for the door handle. I reached across, flicked off the lock and kicked the door open, dislodging the Danverclone, who seemed to hang in the air for a moment before a large wave caught her and she was left behind the rapidly moving taxi.

"I'm not sure I can help you any further," continued the cabbie. "This is some seriously bad shit you're gotten yourself into."

"I'm from the Outland," I told him as another two Danvers fell past, vainly flailing their arms as they attempted to catch hold of the taxi. "Ever wanted something Outlandish? I can get it for you."

"Anything?" asked the cabbie. There was a screech of metal from the roof as the Danverclone up there began to cut her way in. Sparks fell from the roof as the angle grinder bit into the metal.

"*Anything!*"

"Well, now," said the cabbie, ignoring still another Danvers, who landed on the one crawling up the hood. There was the sort of sound a squeaky toy makes when you sit on it heavily, and then they both bounced off and were gone. "What I'd really like," he continued, completely unfazed, "is an original Hoppity Hop."

It seemed an unusual request until you realized just how

valuable Outlander memorabilia was. I'd once seen two generics almost kill each other over a traffic cone.

"Orange and with a face on the front?"

"Is there any other? You'll find a seat belt in the back," he said. "I suggest you use it."

I didn't even have time to search for it before he suddenly pointed the cab straight up and went into a vertical climb toward the clouds. He turned to look at me, raised his eyebrows and smiled. He thought it was something of a lark. I was . . . well, *concerned.* I looked behind me as the Mrs. Danvers fell from the roof along with the gasoline-driven grinder and tumbled in a spiraling manner toward the sea, which was now far below. A few moments later, we were enveloped by the soft grayness of the clouds, and almost immediately, but without any sensation of having righted ourselves, we left the cloud on an even keel and were moving slowly between a squadron of French sailing ships and a lone British one. That might have been nothing to worry about, except that they were both armed naval vessels and were firing salvos at one another, and every now and again a hot ball of iron would sail spectacularly close to the cab with a whizzing noise.

"I had that Admiral Hornblower in the back of my cab once," said the taxidriver, chatting amiably to me in that curious way cabbies do when they talk over their shoulder and look at the road at the same time. "What a gent. Tipped me a sovereign and then tried to press me into service."

"Where are we?" I asked.

"C. S. Forester's *Ship of the Line,*" replied the cabbie. "We'll hang a left after the HMS *Sutherland* and move through *The African Queen* to join the cross-Maritime thoroughfare at *The Old Man and the Sea.* Once there we'll double back through *The Sea Wolf* and come out at *Moby-Dick,* which neatly sidesteps *Treasure Island,* as it's usually jammed at this hour."

"Wouldn't it be better to go via *20,000 Leagues Under the Sea* and hang a left at *Robinson Crusoe*?"

I could see him staring at me in the rearview mirror. "You

want to try it that way?" he asked, annoyed that I might question his judgment."

"No," I replied hastily. "We'll do what you think best."

He seemed happier at this. "Okeydokey. Whereabouts in Longfellow were you wanting to go?"

" 'The Wreck of the Hesperus.' "

He turned around to stare at me. "*Hesperus?* You're one whole heap of trouble, lady. I'll drop you off at 'A Psalm of Life,' and you can walk from there."

I glared at him. "An original Hoppity Hop was it? *Boxed?*"

He sighed. It was a good deal, and he knew it.

"Okay," he said at last. "*Hesperus* it is."

We moved slowly past a small steam launch that was shooting some rapids on the Ulanga, and the cabbie spoke again. "So what's your story?"

"I was replaced by my written other self, who is rubber-stamping the CofG's most harebrained schemes with the woeful compliance of our prime minister back home. You've heard about *Pride and Prejudice* being serialized as a reality book show called *The Bennets*? That's what I'm trying to stop. You got a name?"

"Colin."

We fell silent for a moment as we followed the Ulanga downriver to where it joined the Bora and then into the lake, where the gunboat *Königin Luise* lay at anchor. I busied myself reloading my pistol and checking the last two eraserheads. I even took the pistol's holster and clipped it to my belt. I didn't like these things, but I was going to be prepared. Mind you, if they decided to send in the clones, I'd be in serious shit. There were seven thousand Danvers and only one of me. I'd have to erase over three thousand per cartridge, and I didn't think they'd all gather themselves in a convenient heap for me. I pulled out my cell phone and stared at it. We were in full signal, but they'd have a trace on me for sure.

"Use mine," said Colin, who'd been watching me. He passed his footnoterphone back to me, and I called Bradshaw.

"Commander? It's Thursday."[4]

"I'm in a taxi heading toward *Moby-Dick* via *The Old Man and the Sea*."[5]

"Apparently not. How are things?"[6]

"No; I've got to destroy something in *Hesperus* that will hopefully raise the Outlander ReadRates. As soon as I'm done there, I'll go straight to Jobsworth."[7]

I looked out of the window. We were over the sea once again, but this time the weather was brighter. Two small whaling boats, each with five men at the oars, were pulling toward a disturbance in the water, and as I watched, a mighty, gray-white bulk erupted from beneath the green water and shattered one of the small boats, pitching the hapless occupants into the sea.

"I'm just coming out the far end of *Moby-Dick*. Do you have anything for me at all?"[8]

I closed the phone and handed it back. If Bradshaw was short on ideas, the situation was more hopeless than I had imagined. We crossed from Maritime to Poetry by way of *The Rime of the Ancient Mariner*, and after hiding momentarily in the waste of wild dunes, marram and sand of "False Dawn" while a foot patrol of Danvers moved past, we were off again and turned into Longfellow by way of "The Lighthouse."

"Hold up a moment," I said to Colin, and we pulled up beneath a rocky ledge on a limestone spur that led out in the deep purple of the twilight to a lighthouse, its beam a sudden radiance of light that swept around the bay.

"This isn't a wait-and-return job, is it?" he asked nervously.

[4] "Thursday! Great Scott, girl! Where are you?"

[5] "Wouldn't it be better to go via *20,000 Leagues Under the Sea* and hang a left at *Robinson Crusoe*?"

[6] "Not good. Can you get up to the CofG straightaway?"

[7] "Good luck, old girl. You'll need it. Where are you now?"

[8] "Not a thing. I'm under house arrest. You're all alone on this one, Thursday. Best of British and all that."

"I'm afraid it is. How close can you get me to the actual wrecking of the *Hesperus*?"

He sucked in air through his teeth and scratched his nose. "During the gale itself, not close at all. The reef of Norman's Woe during the storm is not somewhere you'd like to be. Forget the wind and the rain—it's the cold."

I knew what he meant. Poetry was an emotional roller coaster of a form that could heighten the senses almost beyond straining. The sun was always brighter, the skies bluer, and forests steamed six times as much after a summer shower and felt twelve times earthier. Love was ten times stronger, and happiness, hope and charity rose to a level that made your head spin with giddy well-being. On the other side of the coin, it also made the darker side of existence twenty times worse—tragedy and despair were bleaker, more malevolent. As the saying goes, "They don't do nuffing by half measures down at Poetry."

"So how close?" I asked.

"Daybreak, three verses from the end."

"Okay," I said, "let's do it."

He released the handbrake and motored slowly forward. The light moved from twilight to dawn as we entered "The Wreck of the Hesperus." The sky was still leaden, and a stiff wind scoured the foreshore, even though the worst of the storm had passed. The taxi drew to a halt on the sea beach, and I opened the door and stepped out. I suddenly felt a feeling of strong loss and despair, but knowing full well that these were simply emotions seeping out of the overcharged fabric of the poem, I attempted to give it no heed. Colin got out as well, and we exchanged nervous looks. The sea beach was littered with the wreckage of the *Hesperus*, reduced to little more than matchwood by the gale. I pulled my jacket collar close against the wind and trudged up the shoreline.

"What are we looking for?" asked Colin, who had joined me.

"Remains of a yellow tour bus," I said, "or a tasteless blue jacket with large checks."

"Nothing too specific, then?"

* * *

Most of the flotsam was wood, barrels, ropes and the odd personal artifact. We came across a drowned sailor, but he wasn't someone from the *Rover.* Colin became emotional over the loss of life and lamented how the sailor had been "sorely taken from the bosom of his family" and "given his soul to the storm" before I told him to pull himself together. We reached some rocks and chanced across a fisherman, staring with a numbed expression at a section of mast that gently rose and fell in the sheltered water of an inlet. Lashed to the mast was a body. Her long brown hair was floating like seaweed, and the intense cold had frozen her features in the expression she'd last worn in life—of abject terror. She was wearing a heavy seaman's coat, which hadn't done much good, and I waded into the icy water to look closer. Ordinarily I wouldn't have, but something was *wrong.* This should have been the body of a young girl—the skipper's daughter. But it wasn't. It was a middle-aged woman. It was Wirthlass-Schitt. Her eyelashes were encrusted with frozen salt, and she stared blankly out at the world, her face suffused with fear.

"She saved me."

It was a little girl's voice, and I turned. She was aged no more than nine and was wrapped in a Goliath-issue down jacket. She looked confused, as well she might; she hadn't survived the storm for over 163 years. Wirthlass-Schitt had underestimated the power not only of the BookWorld, the raw energy of Poetry . . . but also *herself.* Despite her primary goal of corporate duty, she couldn't leave a child to drown. She'd done what she thought was right and suffered the consequences. It was what I was trying to warn her about. The thing you discover in Poetry . . . is your *true* personality. The annoying thing was, she'd done it all for nothing. A cleanup gang from Jurisfiction would be down later, putting everything chillingly to rights. It was why I didn't like to do "the rhyming stuff."

Colin, overcome by the heavy emotions that pervaded the air like fog, had begun to cry. "O wearisome world!" he sobbed.

I checked Anne's collar and found a small necklace on her cold flesh. I pulled it off and then stopped. If she'd been on the *Hesperus*, perhaps she had picked up his jacket?

The seaman's coat was like cardboard, and I eased it open at the collar to look beneath. My heart fell. She wasn't wearing the jacket, and after checking her pockets I found that she wasn't carrying the recipe either. I took a deep breath, and my emotions, enhanced by the poem, suddenly fell to rock bottom. Wirthlass-Schitt must have given the jacket to her crewmates—and if it was back at Goliath, I'd have a snowball's chance in hell of getting to it. Friday had entrusted me with the protection of the Long Now, and I had failed him. I waded back to shore and started sniffing as large, salty tears ran down my face.

"Oh, *please* dry up," I said to Colin, who was sobbing into his hankie next to me. "You've got me started now."

"But the sadness drapes heavily on my countenance!" he whimpered.

We sat on the foreshore next to the fisherman, who was still looking aghast, and sobbed quietly as though our hearts would break. The young girl came and sat down next to me. She patted my hand reassuringly.

"I didn't *want* to be rescued anyway," she announced. "If I survive, the whole point of the poem is lost—Henry will be *furious*."

"Don't worry," I said. "It'll all be repaired."

"And everyone keeps on giving me their jackets," she continued in a huffy tone. "Honestly, it gets harder and harder to freeze to death these days. There's this one that Anne gave me," she added, thumbing the thick pile on the blue Goliath jacket, "and the one the old man gave me seventeen years ago."

"Really, I'm not interested in—"

I stopped sobbing as a bright shaft of sunlight cut through the storm clouds of my melancholia.

"Do . . . you still have it?"

"Of course!"

And she unzipped the Goliath jacket to reveal—a man's blue

jacket in large checks. Never had I been happier to see a more tasteless garment. I quickly rummaged through the pockets and found a yo-yo string, a very old bag of jelly beans, a domino, a screwdriver, an invention for cooking the perfect hard-boiled egg and . . . wrapped in a plastic freezer bag, a paper napkin with a simple equation written upon it. I gave the young girl a hug, my feeling of elation quadrupled by the magnifying effect of Poetry. I breathed a sigh of relief. *Found!* Without wasting a moment, I tore the recipe into small pieces and ate them.

"Riublf," I said to Colin with my mouth full, "leb's get goinf."

"I don't think we're going anywhere, Ms. Next."

I looked up and saw what he meant. Occupying every square inch of space—on the sea beach, the foreshore, the dunes and even standing in the sea—were hundreds upon hundreds of identical black-clad Mrs. Danvers, staring at me malevolently. We'd killed five of their number recently, so I guessed they wouldn't be that pleased. Mind you, they were always pretty miserable, so it might have had nothing to do with it. I instinctively grasped the butt of my pistol, but it was pointless—like using a peashooter against a T-54 battle tank.

"Well," I said, swallowing the last piece of the recipe and addressing the nearest Danverclone, "you'd better take me to your leader."

35.

The Bees, the Bees

The Danverclones had advanced a good deal since their accidental creation from the original Mrs. Danvers in *Rebecca*. At first, they had simply been creepy, fifty-something housekeepers with bad attitude, but now they had weapons training as well. A standard Danverclone was a fearless yet generally vapid drone who would willingly die to follow orders. But just recently an elite force of Danverclones had arisen, with not only weaponry but a sound working knowledge of the BookWorld. Even I would think twice before tackling this bunch. We called them the SWOT team.

The Danverclones moved in silently. With bewildering speed and a tentacle-like movement of their bony limbs, four of them grasped my arms while another took my shoulder bag and a sixth removed my pistol. A seventh, who appeared to be the platoon commander, spoke briefly into a mobilefootnoterphone:

"Target Number One located and in custody."

She then snapped the phone shut and used a brief series of hand signals to the other Mrs. Danvers, who began to jump out of the poem, beginning with the ones right at the back. I looked across at Colin, who was also being held tightly. A Danverclone had pulled his taxi license from his wallet and held it up in front of him before tearing it in two and tossing the halves in the air. He glanced at me and looked severely annoyed, but not with me—more with the Danverclones and the circumstances. I was just wondering where they would take me when there was a faint crackle in the air and my recently appointed least-favorite person was standing right in front of me. She was dressed in all her black leather finery, twin automatics on her hips and a long black greatcoat that fell to the ground. She leered at me as she appeared, and I thought about spitting in her eye but decided against it—she was too far away, and if I'd missed, I would just have looked even more enfeebled.

"Well, well," said Thursday1–4, "the great Thursday Next finally brought to book."

"Wow!" I replied. "Black is surely the color of choice today."

She ignored me and continued, "Do you know, it's going to be fun being you. Senator Jobsworth has extended me all the rights that are usually yours—you in the BookWorld, you at the CofG, you in the much-awaited and now greenlighted *Thursday Next Returns—This Time It's Personal* and you in the Outland. That's the bit I like best. As much Landen as I want." She leaned closer and lowered her voice. "And believe me, I want a *lot*."

I gave an almighty howl of anger and struggled to break loose from the Danvers, but without any luck. The clones all sniggered, and Thursday1–4 smiled unpleasantly.

"It's time for you to vanish, Thursday," she growled.

She tossed a pair of handcuffs to the Danvers, who pulled my arms behind my back and secured them. Thursday1–4 held on to me, took my shoulder bag from a nearby clone and began to walk away when the commander of the Mrs. Danvers contingent said, "I have orders to take her direct to the Île Saint-Joseph within *Papillon* as per your original plan, Ms. Next1–4."

The other me turned to the Mrs. Danvers, looked her up and down and sneered, "You've done your job, Danny—you'll be rewarded. This is *my* prisoner."

But Mrs. Danvers had an order, and Danvers only do one thing: They do as they're told—and, until countermanded by a written order, they do it rather well.

"I have my *written* instructions," the clone said more firmly, and the other Danvers took a menacing step toward us, three of them producing weapons from within the folds of their black dresses.

"I'm countermanding your order."

"No," said Mrs. Danvers. "I have my orders, and I *will* carry them out."

"Listen here shitface," said Thursday1–4 with a snarl, "I'm the new Mrs. de Winter now—*geddit*?"

Mrs. Danvers took a step back in shocked amazement, and in that short moment Thursday1–4 held tightly to my arm and jumped us both out.

I was expecting a ready dug grave—or worse, a shovel and a place for *me* to dig one, but there wasn't. Instead the place where we'd arrived looked more like the sitting room of a Georgian country house of moderate means somewhere, and, thankfully, there wasn't a shovel in sight—but there was a Bradshaw, five Bennet sisters and Mr. Bennet, who were all staring at me expectantly, which was somewhat confusing.

"Ah!" said Bradshaw. "Thank goodness for that. Sorry to keep you in the dark, old girl, but I knew my footnoterphone was bugged. We've got to get you across to the CofG, but right now we have a serious and very pressing problem."

"O-kay," I said slowly and in great puzzlement. I looked across at Thursday who was rapidly divesting herself of the weapons and leather apparel.

"I actually *swore*," she muttered unhappily, holding one of the automatics with a disdainful finger and thumb. "And these clothes! Made from *animal skins* . . ."

My mouth may have dropped open at this. "Thursday5?" I mumbled. "That's *you*?"

She nodded shyly and shrugged. Underneath the leathers, I noticed, was her usual attire of naturally dyed cotton, crocheted sweater and Birkenstocks. She had taken her failure over the Minotaur to heart and made good. Perhaps I'd been too hasty over her assessment.

"We knew you were in the BookWorld, but then you disappeared off the radar," said Bradshaw. "Where have you been the past ten hours?"

"I was trapped in a moral dilemma. Any news from the Outland? I mean, are people buying into this whole reality book thing?"

"And how!" exclaimed Bradshaw. "The news from the CofG is that a half million people are waiting to see how *The Bennets* will turn out, as the idea of being able to change a major classic has huge appeal—it's the latest fad in the Outland, and you know how the Outlanders like fads."

"Sometimes I think they like little else."

Bradshaw looked at his watch. "There's only six minutes before *Pride and Prejudice* as we know it is going to be rewritten and lost forever, and we don't have a seriously good plan of action. In fact," he added, "we don't have *any* plan of action."

Everyone stared at me. Twenty seconds ago I thought I was almost certainly dead; now I was expected at short notice to fashion a plan of infinite subtlety to save one of our greatest novels from being reduced to a mind-numbing morass of transient popular entertainment.

"Right," I said as I attempted to gather my thoughts. "Lizzie?"

"Here, ma'am," said the second-eldest Bennet sister, bobbing respectfully.

"Fill me in. How does this reality-book thing work? Have you been given any instructions?"

"We've not been told much, ma'am. We are expected to collect ourselves in the house, but instead of looking for husbands and happiness, we are to undertake a preset task of an altogether *curious* nature. And as we do so," she added sorrowfully, "our new actions and words are indelibly burned into the new edition of our book."

I looked around the room. They were *still* all staring at me expectantly.

"Let me see the task."

She handed me a sheet of paper. It was on Interactive Book Council letterhead and read:

TASK ONE

Chapters 1 to 3 (one hour's reading time)

All Housemates Must Participate

The housemates will gather in the parlor of Longbourn and make bee costumes. After that, the housemates will be expected to act like bees. One of the housemates, dressed as a bee, will ask Mr. Bingley to organize a fancy-dress costume ball where everyone is required to dress as a bee. The housemate who is judged to have made the best bee costume and to have done the most satisfactory bee impersonation will win the first round and be allowed to put up two housemates for eviction. The voting Outlander public will decide who is to go. Housemates will be expected to go to the diary room and talk about whatever comes into their heads, no matter how dreary.

I put down the sheet of paper. This was a good deal worse than I'd expected, and my expectations hadn't been high.

"I'm *not* dressing up as a bee," announced Mr. Bennet indignantly. "The very idea. You girls may indulge in such silliness, but *I* shall withdraw to my study."

"Father," said Lizzie, "remember we are doing this to ensure that the Outland ReadRates do not continue to fall in the precipitous manner that has marked their progress in recent years. It is a sacrifice, to be sure, but one that we should shoulder with determination and dignity—for the good of the BookWorld."

"I'll dress as a bee!" cried Lydia excitedly, jumping up and down.

"Me, too!" added Kitty. "I will be the finest bee in Meryton!"

"You shall not, for I shall!" returned Lydia, and they joined hands and danced around the room. I looked at Mary, who turned her eyes heavenward and returned to her book.

"Well," said Jane good-naturedly, "I shall dress as a bee if it is for the greater good—do you suppose Mr. Bingley will *also* be required to dress as a bee? And whether," she added somewhat daringly, "we might get to see each other again, as bees?"

"It doesn't state as such," replied Mr. Bennet, looking at the task again, "but I expect Mr. Bingley will be requested to make an idiot of himself in the fullness of time—and Darcy, too, I should wager."

"Where's Mrs. Bennet?" I asked, having not seen her since I'd arrived.

"We had to put poor Mama in the cupboard again," explained Lizzie, pointing at a large wardrobe, which Thursday5 opened to reveal that yes, Mrs. Bennet was indeed inside, stock-still and staring with blank eyes into the middle distance.

"It calms her," explained Jane as Thursday5 closed the wardrobe door again. "We have to commit dear Mama to the wardrobe quite often during the book."

"Yes," added Lizzie thoughtfully, "I fear she will not take to the bee task. While there are daughters unmarried, Mama has only one thing on her mind, and she is liable to get . . . agitated and cause a dreadful scene. Do you think that will spoil the task?"

"No," I said wearily. "The worse it gets, the better reality it is, if you see what I mean."

"I'm afraid I don't."

"Thursday, old girl," interrupted Bradshaw, who'd been staring at his watch, "how's this for a suggestion? Everyone hides so there's no book at all."

"Out of the question!" intoned Mr. Bennet. "I will not hide my family from view and skulk in my own home. No indeed. No matter how silly we may look, we shall be here in the front room when the new book begins."

"Wait a moment," I said. "This first section lasts an hour's reading time, yes?"

Lizzie nodded.

I took the piece of paper with the task written upon it and

pulled a pen from my top pocket, put three broad lines through the task and started to write my own. When I had finished, I handed it to Lizzie, who looked at it thoughtfully and then passed it to her father.

"Oh, boo!" said Lydia, crossing her arms and jutting out a lip. "And I did *so* want to become a bee!"

"I'm going to read this out loud," announced Mr. Bennet, "since we must all, as a family, agree to undertake this new task—or not. He looked around at everyone, who all nodded their agreement, except Lydia and Kitty, who were poking each other, and Mrs. Bennet, who couldn't, as she was still "relaxing" in the closet.

" 'First Task. Chapters One to Three,' " he began. " 'Mr. Bennet, of Longbourn House in Meryton, should be encouraged by his wife to visit Mr. Bingley, who has taken up residence at nearby Netherfield Park. Mr. Bingley shall return the visit without meeting the daughters, and a ball must take place. In this ball Mr. Bingley and Jane Bennet are to dance together. Mr. Darcy is also to attend, and he shall be considered rude, proud and aloof by Lizzie and the rest of the family. At the same time, we are to learn much of the Bennet marriage, and their daughters, and their prospects. The reading public can vote on whether Jane and Bingley are to dance a second time. Mrs. Bennet is free to do "her own thing" throughout.' "

Mr. Bennet stopped reading, gave a smile and looked around the room. "Well, my children?"

"It sounds like an *excellent* task," said Jane, clapping her hands together. "Lizzie?"

"I confess I cannot fault it."

"Then it is agreed," opined Mr. Bennet with a twinkle in his eye. "Truly an audacious plan—and it *might just work*. How long before we begin?"

"Forty-seven seconds," answered Bradshaw, consulting his pocketwatch.

"I don't understand," said Lydia. "This new task—isn't that what usually happens?"

"Duh," replied Kitty, making a face.

"Places, everyone," said Mr. Bennet, and they all obediently sat in their allotted chairs. "Lizzie, are you ready to narrate?"

"Yes, Father."

"Good. Mary, would you let Mrs. Bennet out of the cupboard? Then we can begin."

Myself, Thursday5 and Bradshaw scurried out into the corridor as Lizzie began the reality book show with words that rang like chimes, loud and clear in the canon of English literature:

"'It is a truth universally acknowledged,'" we heard her say through the closed door, "'that a single man in possession of a good fortune, must be in want of a wife.'"

"Thursday," said Bradshaw as he, Thursday5 and I walked to the entrance hall, "we've kept the book exactly as it is—but only until the Council of Genres and the Interactive Book people find out what we've done. And then they'll be down here in a flash!"

"I know," I replied, "so I haven't got much time to change the CofG's mind over this interactivity nonsense. Stay here and try to stall them as long as possible. It's my guess they'll let this first task run its course and do the stupid bee thing for task two. Wish me luck."

"I do," said Bradshaw grimly, "and you're going to need it."

"Here," said Thursday5, handing me an emergency TravelBook and my bag. "You'll need these as much as luck."

I didn't waste a moment. I opened the TravelBook, read the required text and was soon back in the Great Library.

36.

Senator Jobsworth

Senatorial positions in the Council of Genres are generally pulled from the ranks of the individual book council members, who officiate on all internal book matters. They are usually minor characters with a lot of time on their hands, so aside from a few notable exceptions, the Council of Genres is populated entirely by unimaginative D-4s. They meddle, but they don't do it very well. It is one of the CofG's strengths.

I impatiently drummed my fingers on the wall of the elevator as I rose to the twenty-sixth floor of the Great Library and the Council of Genres. I checked in my bag and found I still had two eraserheads but wasn't sure if a show of force was the correct way to go about this. If what Bradshaw had said was true and Evil Thursday was commanding a legion of Danvers, I might not even have a chance to plead my own case, let alone *Pride and Prejudice*'s.

I decided that the best course of action was simply to wing it and was just wondering how I should approach even this strategy when the elevator doors opened and I was confronted by *myself*, staring back at me from the corridor. The same jacket, the same hair, trousers, boots—everything except a black glove on her left hand, which covered the eraserhead wound, I imagined. Bradshaw was right—Thursday1–4 had divested herself of her own identity and taken mine—along with my standing, integrity and reputation—an awesome weapon for her to wield. Not only as the CofG's LBOCS and as a trusted member of Jurisfiction, but *everything.* Jobsworth, in all his dreary ignorance, probably thought that this *was* me, having undergone a bizarre and—to him—entirely fortuitous change of mind about policy directives.

We stared at each other for a moment, she with a sort of numbed look of disbelief, and I—I hoped—with the expression that a wife rightly reserves for someone who has slept with her husband.

"Meddling fool!" she said at last, waving a copy of *Pride and Prejudice* that she'd been reading. "I can only think this is your doing. You may have won the first round, but it's merely a postponement—we'll have the reality book show back on track after the first three chapters have run their course!"

"I'm going to erase you," I said in a quiet voice, "and, what's more, *enjoy it.*"

She stared at me with a vague look of triumph. "Then I was wrong," she replied. "We *are* alike."

I didn't have time to answer. She took to her heels and ran off down the corridor toward the debating chamber. I followed; if we were externally identical, then the first to plead her case to the CofG had a clear advantage.

Thinking about it later, the pair of us running hell for leather down the corridors must have been quite a sight, but probably not *that* unusual, given the somewhat curious nature of fiction. Annoyingly, we were evenly matched in speed and stamina, and her ten-foot head start was still there when we arrived at the main debating chamber's door two minutes and many startled CofG employees later. She had to slow down at the door, and as she did so, I made a flying tackle and grabbed her around the waist. Toppled by the momentum, the pair of us went sprawling headlong on the carpet, much to the astonishment of three heavily armed Danverclones who were just inside the door.

The strange thing about fighting with yourself is that not only are you of equal weight, strength and skill, but you both know all the same moves. After we had grappled and rolled around on the carpet for about five minutes and achieved nothing but a lot of grunting and strained muscles, my mind started to shift and think about other ways in which to win—something my opponent did at *exactly* the same moment—and we both switched tactics and went for each other's throats. The most this achieved was that Landen's birthday locket was torn off, something that drove me to a rage I never knew I had.

I knocked her hand away, rolled on top of her and punched her hard in the face. She went limp, and I climbed off, breathing hard, picked up my bag and locket and turned to Jobsworth and the rest of the security council, who had come into the corridor to watch.

"Arrest her," I panted, wiping a small amount of blood from my lip, "and bind her well."

Jobsworth looked at me and the other Thursday, then beckoned to the Danverclones to do as I asked.

She was still groggy but seemed to regain enough consciousness to yell, "Wait, wait! She's not the real Thursday—I am!"

Jobsworth, Barksdale and Baxter all swiveled their heads to me, and even the Danverclones took notice. In the CofG, my veto counted for everything, and if there was any doubt at all over which was the correct Thursday, I had to quash it here and now.

"Want me to prove it?" I said. "Here it is: The interactive book project stops *now*."

Jobsworth's face fell. "Stop it? But you were all for it not less than an hour ago!"

"That wasn't me," I said, pointing an accusing finger at the disheveled and now-defeated Thursday, who was at that moment being cuffed by the Danverclones. "It was the *other* Thursday, the one from the crappy-as-hell TN series, who has been trying, for reasons of her own personal vindictiveness, to screw up everything I've worked so hard to achieve."

"She's lying!" said the other Thursday, who now had her arms secured behind her back and still seemed unsteady from when I'd hit her. "*She's* the ersatz Thursday—*I'm* the real one!"

"You want more proof?" I said. "Okay. I'm also reinforcing my veto on the insane decision to invade the Racy Novel genre. Diplomacy is the key. And I want all Jurisfiction agents released from their books and returned to work."

"But that was *your* idea!" muttered Jobsworth, who, poor fellow, was still confused. "You said there was a bad apple at Jurisfiction and you needed to flush it out!"

"Not me," I said. "Her. To keep me from returning. And if you need any more proof, here's the clincher: We're *not* going to have her reduced to text. She's going to spend the next two years contemplating her navel within the pages of *The Great Samuel Pepys Fiasco.* She's smart and resourceful, so we'll keep her in isolation in case she wants to try to be me again, and if she even *attempts* to escape, she'll be reduced to text."

Jobsworth needed no further convincing.

"It shall be so," he said in a faintly pompous way, and the other Thursday was dragged off, still uselessly proclaiming her unbogusness.

I took a deep breath and sat down at my desk. I could feel a bruise coming up on the side of my neck and my knee hurt. I stretched my hand and rubbed it where I'd struck her.

"Well," said Baxter, "I can't say I'm glad you've decided against either invading Racy Novel or canceling the reality book shows, but I am a lot happier that you are the one making the wrong decisions, and not some poorly written wannabe. What the hell was she up to?"

"As you say. Just a jumped-up generic who wanted to be real. Better put a Textual Sieve Lockdown on *The Great Samuel Pepys Fiasco* both in and out—I don't want to even *entertain* the possibility of someone rescuing her."

Jobsworth nodded to one of his aides to do as I'd asked and

also—very reluctantly—to put a halt to the interactivity project and the Racy Novel invasion plans.

"But look here," said Colonel Barksdale, who seemed to be somewhat miffed that he wasn't going to spearhead an invasion of Racy Novel, "we can't just ignore Speedy Muffler and those heathens."

"And we shan't," I replied. "After we have followed all possible diplomatic channels, *then* we'll have a look at other means of keeping them in check—and I rule out nothing."

Barksdale stared at me, unconvinced.

"Trust me," I said. "I'm Thursday Next. I know what I'm doing."

He seemed to find some solace in this—my name counted for a lot.

"Right," I said, "I'm bushed. I'm going to go home. We'll discuss things tomorrow, right?"

"Very well," replied Jobsworth stonily. "We can talk at length then about the falling ReadRates and what you intend to do about them."

I didn't reply and left his office. But instead of going back to Swindon, I took a walk in the corridors of power at the CofG. Everything was busy as usual, the debating chamber in full swing, and there was little—if any—evidence that we were no longer at war or rewriting the classics. I stopped by the large picture window that faced out onto the other towers. I'd never really looked out of here for any length of time before, but now, with time and the BookWorld as my servant, I stared out, musing upon the new responsibilities that I had and how I would exercise them first.

I was still undecided twenty minutes later when Bradshaw tapped me lightly on the shoulder. "Old girl?"

He startled me, and I looked around, took one glance at who was with him and drew my automatic.

"Whoa, whoa!" said Bradshaw hurriedly. "This is *Thursday5*."

"How do you know?" I barked, pointing my gun directly at her, my sensibilities keenly alert to any sort of look-alike subterfuge.

"How do we know it isn't the evil bad Thursday back here in disguise or something?"

Bradshaw looked mildly shocked at my suggestion. "Because she's not left my side since we last saw you, old girl."

"Are you sure?"

"Absolutely! Here, I'll prove it." He turned to Thursday5. "What were the names of the von Trapp children in *The Sound of Music*?"

Thursday5 didn't pause for an instant and recited in one breath: "Kurt, Friedrich, Louisa, Brigitta, Marta, Gretl and Liesl."

"You see?"

"You're right," I said. "Only a total drip like Thursday5 would know *that*—or at least," I added hurriedly, "that's what Evil Thursday would think."

I clicked on the safety and lowered the gun.

"I'm sorry," I said. "It's been a tough day, and my nerves are in shreds. I need to get home and have a long, hot bath and then a martini."

Thursday5 thought for a moment. "After you've drunk the long, hot bath," she observed, "you'll never have room for the martini."

"Say what?"

"Never mind."

"We just came to congratulate you," said Bradshaw, "on rere-versing the vetoes. *Pride and Prejudice* is running precisely as it should, and without the Interactive Book Council idiots to set any new tasks, we're in the clear. The Bennets wanted me to send you their very best and to tell you to drop around for tea sometime."

"How very proper of them," I said absently, feeling a bit hot and bothered and wanting them to go away. "If there's nothing else . . . ?"

"Not really," replied Bradshaw, "but we wondered: Why did you lock her up in *The Great Samuel Pepys Fiasco*?"

I shrugged. "Punishment to fit the crime, I guess. Are you questioning my judgment?"

"Of course not, old girl," replied Bradshaw genially, exchanging a glance with Thursday5.

"*That* explains why I can't get back in," murmured Thursday5 in dismay. "Is this permanent? I know my book's unreadable—but it's home."

"Listen," I said, rubbing my scalp, "that's your problem. Since when were you part of the decision-making process?"

Bradshaw's mobilefootnoterphone rang.

"Excuse me," he said, and wandered off to answer it.

"It's been a long day," murmured Thursday5, staring out the window at the view. "You must be tired. Do you want me to fetch you a chai?"

"No, I don't drink any of that rubbish. What were you saying about the hot bath and the martini again?"

She didn't have time to answer.

"That was Text Grand Central," said Bradshaw as he returned. "We've been getting some Major Narrative Flexations inside *The Great Samuel Pepys Fiasco.* It seems the entire first chapter has broken away from the rest of the book."

"What?"

"As I said. It's a good thing no one reads it these days. We've tracked Thursday to page two hundred and eight."

I took a deep breath and looked at Bradshaw and Thursday5 in turn. "This is unfinished business," I said quietly. "I'm going to put an end to her once and for all."

They didn't try to argue with me. I should have killed her there and then in the corridor. What *was* I thinking of?

"The book's been two-way-sieved," said Bradshaw. "Call me when you're about to jump, and I'll get Text Grand Central to open you a portal. As soon as you're in, we'll close it down and you'll both be trapped. Do you have your mobilefootnoterphone?"

I nodded.

"Then call me when you're done. Use Mrs. Bradshaw's middle name so I know it's you and *really* you. Good luck."

I thanked them, and they walked off down the corridor before evaporating from view. I tried to calm my nerves and told myself that facing Thursday couldn't be *that* bad, but the consequences if I failed were high indeed. I took another deep breath, wiped my sweaty palms on my trousers, made the call to Bradshaw and jumped all the way to page 208 of *The Great Samuel Pepys Fiasco.*

37.

The Great Samuel Pepys Fiasco

The *real* adventure that came to be known as *The Great Samuel Pepys Fiasco* was my first proper sojourn into nonfiction, which was, as the title suggests, one of my more embarrassing failures. I don't really know why, but nothing ever went right. I tried to convey a sense of well-meaning optimism in the book where I was caught between two impossible situations, but it came across as mostly inept fumbling, with a lot of hugging and essential oils.

I came to earth in Swindon. Or at least, the *Fiasco* touchy-feely version of Swindon, which was sunny and blue-skied and every garden an annoying splash of bright primary colors that gave me a headache. The houses were perfect, the cars clean, and everything was insanely neat and orderly. I pulled out my automatic, removed the clip to check it, replaced it and released the safety. There would be no escape for her this time. I knew she was unarmed, but somehow that didn't fill me with such confidence; after all, she was almost infinitely resourceful. The thing was, *so was I.* After I'd killed her, I would just jump out and everything would be right—forever. I could reinstate the interactive book project before the readers had finished the first three chapters—then go to the Outland and savor the joys of Landen once more. Following that and after paying a small amount of lip service to diplomacy, I could also deploy two legions of Mrs. Danvers into Racy Novel. Who knows? I might even lead the attack myself.

That, I had discovered, was the best thing about being Thursday Next—you could do anything you damn well pleased and no one would, could or dared oppose you. I had only two problems to deal with right now: disposing of the *real* Thursday Next and trying to figure out Mrs. Bradshaw's middle name, the code word to get out. I hadn't a clue—I'd never even met her.

I pulled the glove off my hand and looked at where the mottled flesh still showed signs of the eraserhead. I rubbed the itchy skin, then moved to the side of the street and walked toward where this version of Thursday's house was located. It was the same as the one that was burned down in the first chapter of my book, so I knew the way. But the strange thing was, the street was completely deserted. Nothing moved. Not a person, not a cat, squirrel—*nothing.* I stopped at a car that was abandoned in the street and looked in the open passenger door. The key was still in the ignition. Whoever had once populated this book had left—and in a hurry.

I carried on walking slowly down the road. That pompous fool Bradshaw had mentioned something about a chapter breaking away from the main book—perhaps that was where all the background characters were. But it didn't matter. Thursday was here now, and she was the one I was after. I reached the garden gate of Landen5's house and padded cautiously up the path, past the perfectly planted flowers and windows so clean and sparkly they almost weren't there. Holding my gun outstretched, I stepped quietly inside the house.

Thursday5's idea of home furnishing was different from mine and the real Thursday's. For a start, the floor covering was seagrass, and the curtains were an odiously old-fashioned tie-dye. I also noticed to my disgust that there were Tibetan mandalas in frames upon the wall and dream catchers hanging from the ceiling. I stepped closer to the pictures on the mantelpiece and found one of Thursday5 and Landen5 at Glastonbury. They had their faces painted as flowers and were grinning stupidly and hugging each other, with Pickwick5 sitting between them. It was quite sickeningly twee, to be honest.

"I would have done the same."

I turned. Thursday was leaning on the doorway that led through to the kitchen. It was an easy shot, but I didn't take it. I wanted to relish the moment.

"What would you have done the same?" I asked.

"I would have spared you, too. I'll admit it, your impersonation of me was about the most plausible I'll ever see. I'm not sure there's anyone out there who would have spotted it. But I didn't think you could keep it up. The *real* you would soon bubble to the surface. Because, like it or not, you're not enough of me to carry it off. To be me you need the seventeen years of Jurisfiction experience—the sort of experience that means I can take on people like you and come out victorious."

I laughed at her presumption. "I think you overestimate your own abilities, Outlander. I'm the one holding the gun. Perhaps you're a little bit right, but I *can* and *will* be you, given time. Everything you have, everything you are. Your job, your family, your *husband*. I can go back to the Outland and take over from where you left off—and probably have a lot more fun doing it, too."

I pointed my gun at her and began to squeeze the trigger, then stopped. She didn't seem particularly troubled, and that worried me.

"Can you hear that?" she asked.

"Hear what?"

She cupped a hand to her ear. "That."

And now that she mentioned it, I *could* hear something. A soft thrumming noise that seemed to reverberate through the ground.

"What is it?" I asked, and was shocked to discover that my voice came out cracked and . . . afraid.

"Take a look for yourself," she said, pointing outside.

I wiped the sweat from my brow and backed out the door, still keeping my gun firmly trained on her. I ran down to the garden gate and looked up the street. The houses at the end of the road seemed to have lost definition and were being eaten away by a billowing cloud of sand.

"What the hell's that?" I snapped.

"You'd know," she replied quietly, "if only you'd gone to Jurisfiction classes instead of wasting your time on the shooting range."

I looked at the mailbox on the corner of the street, and it seemed to crumble to fragments in front of my eyes and then was taken up into the cloud of dust and debris that was being sucked into a vortex high above us. I pulled out my footnoterphone and frantically dialed Bradshaw's number.

"But you don't know Melanie Bradshaw's middle name," observed Thursday, "do you?"

I lowered the phone and stared at her uselessly. It was a setup. Thursday must have spoken to Bradshaw, and together they'd tricked me into coming here.

"It's *Jenny*," she added. "I named my second daughter after her. But it won't help you. I told Bradshaw not to lift the Textual Sieve on any account, password or not. As soon as you were inside and the generics were safely evacuated, he was instructed to begin . . . the *erasure* of the entire book."

"How did you contact him?" I asked.

"He contacted *me*," she replied. "Thursday5 suggested to Bradshaw that you might have pulled the same trick as she did. I couldn't get out, but we could trick you *in*."

She looked at her watch.

"And in another eight minutes, this book and everything in it—you included, will be gone."

I looked around and saw to my horror that the erasure had crept up without my noticing and was less than ten feet away—we were standing on the only piece of remaining land, a rough circle a hundred feet across containing only Landen's house and its neighbors. But they wouldn't stay for long, and even as I watched, the roofs were turning to dust and being whirled away, consumed by the erasure. The dull roar was increasing, and I had to raise my voice to be heard.

"But this will erase you, too!" I shouted.

"Maybe not—it depends on you."

She beckoned me back into the house as the garden gate turned to smoke and was carried away into the dust cloud. As soon as we were in the kitchen, she turned to me.

"You won't need that," she said, pointing at my gun. I fumbled the reholstering clumsily, and it fell to the floor with a clatter. I didn't stoop to pick it up. I looked out the window into the back garden. The shed and the apple tree had both gone, and the erasure was slowly eating its way across the lawn. The ceiling was starting to look blotchy, and as I watched, the front door turned to dust and was blown away in the wind.

"Ballocks!" I said, as realization suddenly dawned. Not that I was going to be erased, no. It was the cold and sobering revelation that I wasn't nearly as smart as I thought I was. I'd met a foe immeasurably superior to me, and I would suffer the consequences of my own arrogance. The question was, would I give her the pleasure of knowing it? But on reflection she didn't want or need that sort of pleasure, and everything suddenly seemed that much more peaceful.

I said instead, "I'm truly flattered."

"Flattered?" she inquired. "About what?"

The ceiling departed in a cloud of swirling dust, and the walls started to erode downward with the pictures, mantel and furniture rapidly crumbling away to a fine debris that was sucked up into the whirlwind directly above us.

"I'm flattered," I repeated, "because you'd erase a whole book and give your own life just to be rid of me. I must have been a worthy adversary, right?"

She sensed my change of heart and gave me a faint smile.

"You almost defeated me," said Thursday, "and you still might. But if I *do* survive this," she added, "it is my gift to you."

The walls had almost gone, and the seagrass flooring was crumbling under my feet. Thursday opened a door in the kitchen, beyond which a concrete flight of steps led downward. She beckoned me to follow, and we trotted down into a spacious subterranean vault shaped like the inside of a barrel. Upon a large plinth, there were two prongs across which a weak spark occasionally fired. The noise of the wind had subdued, but I knew it was only a matter of time before the erasure reached us.

"This is the core-containment room," explained Thursday. "You'd know about that if you'd listened in class."

"How," I asked, "is your survival a gift to me?"

"That's easily explained," replied Thursday, removing some pieces of packing case from the wall to reveal a riveted iron hatch. "Behind there is the only method of escape—across the emptiness of the Nothing."

The inference wasn't lost on me. The Nothing didn't support textual life—I'd be stripped away to letters in an instant if I tried to escape across it. But Thursday wasn't text: She was flesh and blood and *could* survive.

"I can't get out of here on my own," she added, "so I need your help."

I didn't understand to begin with. I frowned, and then it hit me. She wasn't offering me forgiveness, a second chance or rescue—I was far too bitter and twisted for that. No, she was offering me the one thing that I *would* never, *could* never have. She was offering me redemption. After all I'd done to her, all the things I'd *planned* to do, she was willing to risk her life to give me one small chance to atone. And what's more, *she knew I would take it*. She was right. We were more alike than I thought.

The roof fell away in patches as the erasure started to pull the containment room apart.

"What do I do?"

She indicated the twin latching mechanisms that were positioned eight feet apart. I held the handle and pulled it down on the count of three. The hatch sprung open, revealing an empty, black void.

"Thank you," she said as the erasure crept inexorably across the room. The sum total of the book was now a disk less than eight feet across, and we were in the middle of what looked like a swirling cloud of dirt and detritus, while all about us the wind nibbled away at the remaining fabric of the book, reducing it to undescriptive textdust.

"What will it be like?" I asked as Thursday peered out into the inky blackness.

"I can't tell you," she replied. "No one knows what happens after erasure."

I offered her my hand to shake. "If you ever turn this into one of your adventures," I asked, "will you make me at least vaguely sympathetic? I'd like to think there was a small amount of your humanity in me."

She took my hand and shook it. It was warmer than I'd imagined.

"I'm sorry about sleeping with your husband," I added as I felt the floor grow soft beneath my feet. "And I think this is yours."

And I gave her the locket that had come off when we fought.

As soon as Thursday1–4 returned my locket, I knew that she had finally learned something about me and, by reflection, *her*. She was lost and she knew it, so helping me open the hatch and handing over the locket could only be altruism—the first time she had acted thus and the last time she acted at all. I climbed partially out of the hatch into the Nothing. There was barely anything left of the book at all, just the vaguest crackle of its spark growing weaker and weaker. I was still holding Thursday1–4's hand as I saw her body start to break up, like sandstone eroded by wind. Her hair was being whipped by the currents of air, but she looked peaceful.

She smiled and said, "I just got it."

"Got what?"

"Something Thursday5 said about hot baths and a martini."

Her face started to break down, and I felt her hand crumble within mine like crusty, sun-baked sand. There was almost nothing left of *Fiasco* at all, and it was time to go.

She smiled again, and her face fell away into dust, her hand turned to sand in mine, and the spark crackled and went out. I let go and was—

gone
Evil
Thursday
leg
is
deed
dead
book
gone

Cold Comfort
FARM
ISBN
0140188691

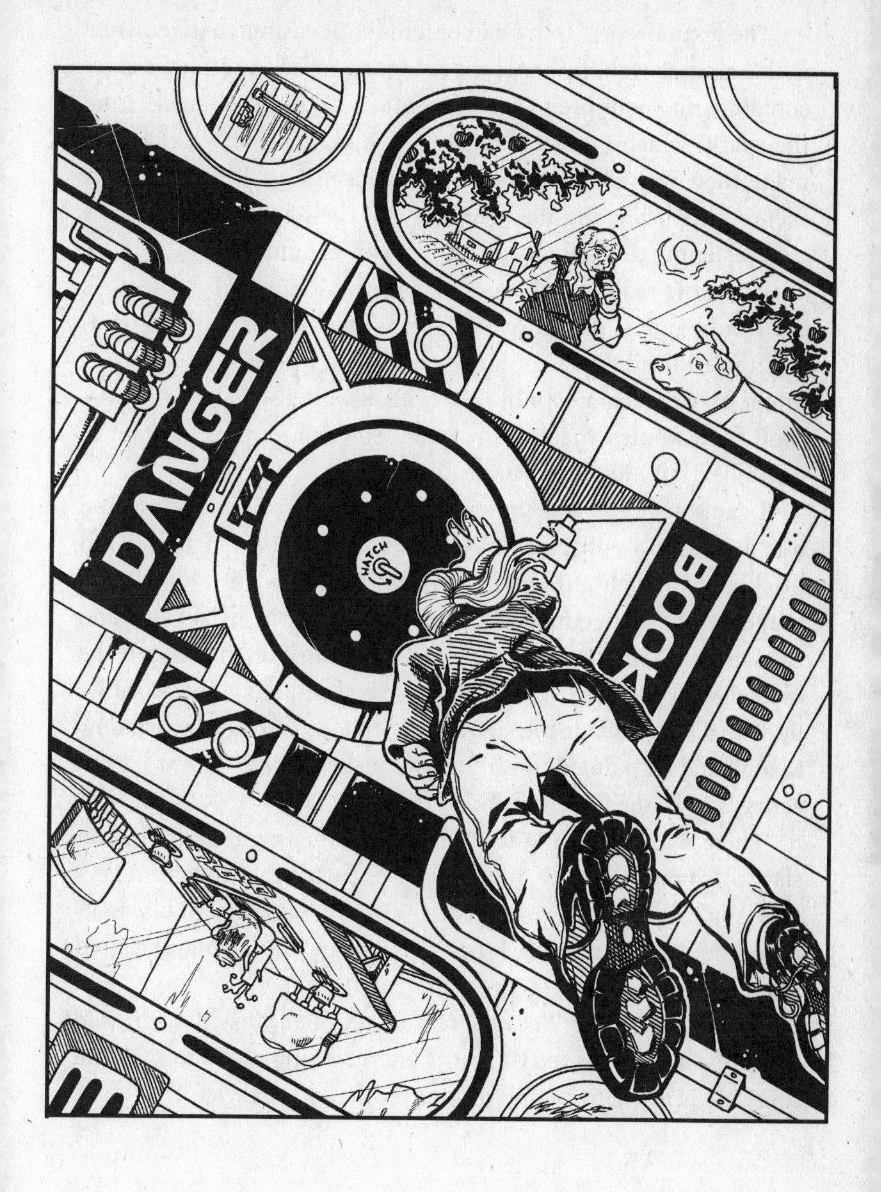
DANGER
HATCH
BOOK

The textual world that I had become so accustomed to returned with a strange wobbling sensation. I found myself in another core-containment room pretty much identical to the first—aside from the spark, which crackled twenty times more brightly as readers made their way through the book. I picked myself up, shut and secured the hatch and made my way up the steps and toward the exit, fastening the locket around my neck as I did so.

I couldn't really say I was saddened by Thursday1–4's loss, as she would almost certainly have killed me and done untold damage if she'd lived. But I couldn't help feeling a sense of guilt that I might have done more for her. After all, it wasn't strictly her fault—she'd been written that way. I sighed. She had found a little bit of me in her, but I knew there was some of her in me, too.

I cautiously opened the containment room door and peered out. I was in a collection of farm buildings constructed of red brick and in such a dilapidated state of disrepair it looked as if they were held together only by the moss in the brickwork and the lichen on the roof. I spotted Adam Lambsbreath through the kitchen window, where he was scraping ineffectually at the washing-up with a twig. I made the sign for a telephone through the window at him, and he pointed toward the woodshed across the yard. I ran across and pushed open the door.

There was something nasty sitting in the corner making odd slavering noises to itself, but I paid it no heed other than to reflect that Ada Doom had been right after all, and found the public footnoterphone that I needed. I dialed Bradshaw's number and waited impatiently for him to answer.

"It's me," I said. "Your plan worked: She's dust. I'm in *Cold Comfort Farm*, page sixty-eight. Can you bring a cab to pick me up? This is going to be one serious mother of a debrief."

38.
The End of Time

No one ever did find out who the members of the ChronoGuard Star Chamber were, nor what their relationship with the Goliath Corporation actually was. But it was noted that some investment opportunities taken by the multinational were *so* fortuitous and *so* prudent and *so* longsighted that they seemed statistically impossible. There were never any whistle-blowers, so the extent of any chronuption was never known, nor ever would be.

By the time I arrived back home, it was dark. Landen heard my key in the latch and met me in the hallway to give me a long hug, which I gratefully received—and returned.

"What's the news on the reality book show?"

"Canceled. Van de Poste has been on the TV and radio explaining that due to a technical error, the project has been shelved—and that the stupidity surplus would be discharged instead by reinvigorating the astronomically expensive and questionably useful Anti-Smite shield."

"And *Pride and Prejudice*?"

"Running exactly as it ever did. But here's the good bit: All the readers who bought copies of the book to see the Bennets dress up as bees continued reading to see if Lizzie and Jane would get their men and if Lydia would come to a sticky end. Naturally, all the new readers were delighted at what happened—so much so that people with the name of Wickham have had to go into hiding."

"Just like the old days," I said with a smile.

The passion for books was returning. I thought for a moment and walked over to the bookcase, pulled out my copy of *The Great Samuel Pepys Fiasco* and riffled through the pages. They were blank, every single one.

"How are Friday and the girls?" I asked, dropping the book into the wastepaper basket.

"Friday is out. The girls are in bed."

"And Pickwick?"

"Still bald and a bit dopey. So . . . you managed to do what you set out to do?"

"Yes," I said quietly, "and Land, I can't lie to you anymore. The Acme Carpets stuff is just a front."

"I know," he said softly. "You still do all that SpecOps work, don't you?"

"Yes. But, Land, that's a front, too."

He placed a hand on my cheek and stared into my eyes. "I know about Jurisfiction as well, Thurs."

I frowned. I hadn't expected this. "You knew? Since when?"

"Since about three days after you'd said you'd given it up."

I stared at him. "You *knew* I was lying to you all those years?"

"Pumpkin," he said as he gently ushered me into the house and closed the door behind us, "you do love me, don't you?"

"Yes, but—"

He put his finger to my lips. "Hang on a minute. I know you do, and I love it that you do. But if you care *too* much about upsetting me, then you won't do the things you have to do, and those things are important—not just to me but to *everyone*."

"Then . . . you're not cross I've been lying to you for fourteen years?"

"Thursday, you mean *everything* to me. Not just because you're cute, smart, funny and have a devastatingly good figure and boobs to die for, *but that you do right for right's sake*—it's what you are and what you do. Even if I never get my magnum opus published, I will still die secure in the knowledge that my time on this planet was well spent—giving support, love and security to someone who actually *makes a difference.*"

"Oh, *Land,*" I said, burying my head in his shoulder, "you're making me go all misty!"

And I hugged him again, while he rubbed my back and said that everything was all right. We stood like this for some time until I suddenly had a thought.

"Land," I said slowly, "*how* much do you know?"

"Mr. and Mrs. Bradshaw tell me quite a lot, and Spike and Bowden often call to keep me updated."

"The rotten swines!" I said with a smile. "They're always telling me to spill the beans to you!"

"We *all* care about you, Thursday."

This was abundantly true, but I couldn't get Thursday1–4 and her brief sojourn to the real world out of my mind. "What about . . . *other* stuff?"

Landen knew exactly what I was talking about. "I only figured out she was the *written* Thursday when you came back upstairs."

"How?"

"Because it was only then I realized she hadn't been wearing the necklace I gave you for your birthday."

"Oh," I said, fingering the locket around my neck. There was silence for a moment as we both considered what had happened. Eventually I said, "But she was a terrible lay, right?"

"*Hopeless.*"

And we both laughed. We would never mention it again.

"Listen," said Landen, "there's someone to see you in the front room."

"Who?"

"Just go in. I'll make some tea."

I walked into the living room, where a tall man was standing at the mantel with his back to me, looking at the framed pictures of the family.

"That's us holidaying on the Isle of Skye," I said in a soft voice, "at the Old Man of Storr. Jenny's not there because she was in a huff and sat in the car, and you can just see Pickwick's head at the edge of the frame."

"I remember it well," he said, and turned to face me. It was Friday, of course. Not *my* Friday but his older self. He was about sixty, and handsome to boot. His hair was graying at the temples, and the smile wrinkles around his eyes made me think of Landen. He was wearing the pale blue uniform of the ChronoGuard, the shoulder emblazoned with the five gold pips of director-general. But it wasn't the day-to-day uniform, it was ceremonial dress. This was a special occasion.

"Hi, Mum."

"Hi, Sweetpea. So you *did* make it to director-general after all!"

He shrugged and smiled. "I did and I didn't. I'm here, but I can't be. It's like everything else that we've done in the past to change the present—we were definitely there, but we couldn't have been. The one thing you learn about the time business is that mutually opposing states can comfortably coexist."

"Like *Saturday Night Fever* being excellent and crap at the same time?"

"Kind of. When it comes to traveling about in the timestream, paradox is always a cozy bedfellow—you get used to living with it." He looked at his watch. "You destroyed the recipe, didn't you?"

"I ate it."

"Good. I've just come to tell you that with only twenty-three minutes to go until the End of Time and without the equation for unscrambling eggs, the Star Chamber has conceded that the continued existence of time travel is retrospectively insupportable. We're closing down the time engines right now. All operatives are being demobilized. Enloopment facilities are being emptied and places found for the inmates in conventional prisons."

"She was right after all," I said quietly.

"I'm sorry?"

"Aornis. I *did* get her out of the loop."

"We're making quite sure that all prisoners with 'special requirements' are being looked after properly, Mum."

"I hope so. What about the other inventions built using retro-deficit-engineering?"

"They'll stay. The microchip and Gravitube *will* be invented, so it's not a problem—but there won't be any new retro-deficit technologies. More important, the Standard History Eventline will stay as it was when we switch off the engines."

"None of the history-rolling-up-like-a-carpet, then?"

"Possibly—but not very likely."

"And Goliath gets to stay as it is?"

"I'm afraid so." He paused briefly, then sighed. "So many things I could have done, might have done, have done and haven't done. I'm going to miss it all."

He looked at me intently. This was my son, but it wasn't. It was him as he *might* have turned out but never would. I still loved him, but it was the only time in my life where I was glad to say good-bye.

"What about the Now?"

"It'll recover, given time. Keep people reading books, Mum; it helps to reinforce and strengthen the indefinable moment that anchors us in the here-and-now. Strive for the Long Now. It's the only thing that will save us. Well," he added with finality, giving me a kiss on the cheek, "I'll be going. I've got to do some paperwork before I switch off the last engine."

"What will happen to you?"

He smiled again. "The Friday *Last*? I wink out of existence. And do you know, I'm not bothered. I've no idea what the future will bring to the Friday *Present*, and that's a concept I'll gladly die for."

I felt tears come to my eyes, which was silly, really. This was only the possibility of Friday, not the actual one.

"Don't cry, Mum. I'll see you when I get up tomorrow—and you know I'm going to sleep in, right?"

He hugged me again, and in an instant he was gone. I wandered through to the kitchen and rested my hand on Landen's back as he poured some milk in my tea. We sat at the kitchen table until, untold trillions years in the future, time came to a halt. There was no erasure of history, no distant thunder, no "we interrupt this broadcast" on the wireless—nothing. The technology had gone for good and the ChronoGuard with it. Strictly speaking, neither of them had ever been. But as *our* Friday pointed out the following day, they *were* still there, echoes from the past that would make themselves known as anachronisms in ancient texts and artifacts that were out of place and out of time. The most celebrated of these would be the discovery of a fossilized 1956 Volkswagen Beetle preserved in Precambrian rock strata. In the glove box, they would find the remains of the following day's paper featuring the car's discovery—and a very worthwhile tip for the winner of the three-thirty at Kempton Park.

"Well, that's it," I said after we had waited for another five minutes and found ourselves still in a state of pleasantly welcome existence. "The ChronoGuard has shut itself down, and time travel is as it should be: technically, logically and theoretically . . . *impossible.*"

"Good thing, too," replied Landen. "It always made my head ache. In fact, I was thinking of doing a self-help book for SF novelists eager to write about time travel. It would consist of a single word: *Don't.*"

I laughed, and we heard a key turn in the front door. It turned out to be Friday, and I recoiled in shock when he walked into the kitchen. He had short hair and was wearing a suit and tie.

As I stood there with my mouth open, he said, "Good evening, Mother. Good evening, Father. I trust I am not too late for some sustenance?"

"Oh, my God!" I cried in horror. "They *replaced* you!"

Neither Landen nor Friday could hold it in for long, and they both collapsed into a sea of giggles. He hadn't been replaced at all—he'd just had a haircut.

"Oh, very funny," I said, arms folded and severely unamused. "Next you'll be telling me Jenny is a mindworm or something."

"She is," said Landen, and it was my turn to burst out laughing at the ridiculousness of the suggestion. They didn't find it at all funny. Honestly, some people have no sense of humor.

39.

A Woman Named Thursday Next

The Special Operations Network was instigated to handle policing duties considered either too unusual or too specialized to be tackled by the regular force. There were thirty departments in all, starting at the more mundane Neighborly Disputes (SO-30) and going on to Literary Detectives (SO-27) and Art Crime (SO-24). Anything below SO-20 was restricted information, so what they got up to was anyone's guess. What *is* known is that the individual operatives themselves are slightly unbalanced. "If you want to be a SpecOp," the saying goes, "act kinda weird."

My father had a face that could stop a clock. I don't mean that he was ugly or anything; it was a phrase the ChronoGuard used to describe someone who had the power to reduce time to an ultra-slow trickle. Dad had been a colonel in the ChronoGuard and kept his work very quiet. So quiet, in fact, that we didn't know he'd gone rogue at all until his timekeeping buddies raided our house one morning clutching a Seize & Eradication Order open-dated at both ends and demanded to know where and when he was. Dad has remained at liberty ever since; we learned from his subsequent visits that he regarded the whole service as "morally and historically corrupt" and was fighting a one-man war against the bureaucrats within the Office for Special Stemporal Temp . . . Tability. *Temporal* . . . Stemp . . . Special—

"Why don't we just hold it right there?" I said before Thursday5 tied her tongue in knots.

"I'm sorry," she said with a sigh. "I think my biorhythms must be out of whack."

"Remember what we talked about?" I asked her, raising an eyebrow.

"Or perhaps it's just a tricky line to say. Here goes: Special . . . Temporal . . . *Stability*. Got it!" She smiled proudly at her accomplishment. Then a stab of self-doubt crossed her face. "But aside from that, I'm doing okay, right?"

"You're doing fine."

We were standing in the opening chapter of *The Eyre Affair*, or at least the refurbished first chapter. Evil Thursday's erasure caused a few ruffled feathers at Text Grand Central, especially when Alice-PON-24330 said that while happy to keep the series running for the time being, she was not that keen about taking on the role permanently—what with all the sex, guns, swearing and stuff. There were talks of scrapping the series until I had a brain wave. With the erasure of *The Great Samuel Pepys Fiasco*, Thursday5 was now bookless and needed a place to live; *she* could take over. Clearly, there had to be a few changes—quite a lot actually—but I didn't mind; in fact, I welcomed it. I applied for a whole raft of internal plot adjustments, and Senator Jobsworth, still eager to make amends and keep his job after the reality book farrago, was only too happy to accede to my wishes—as long as I at least *tried* to make the series commercial.

"Can we get a move on?" asked Gerry, the first assistant imaginator. "If we don't get to the end of this chapter by lunchtime, we're going to get behind schedule for the scene at Gad's Hill tomorrow."

I left them to it and walked to the back of Stanford Brookes's café in London, faithfully re-created from my memory and the place where the new *Eyre Affair* starts, rather than at a burned-out house belonging to Landen, where, in point of fact, I didn't live for another two years. I watched as the imaginators, characters and technicians translated the story into storycode text to be uploaded to the engines at TGC—and eventually to replace the existing TN series. Perhaps, I mused to myself, life might be getting back to normal after all.

It had been a month since we'd erased *Pepys Fiasco,* and Racy Novel, despite all manner of threats, had to admit that dirty-bomb technology was still very much in the early stages, so Feminist and Ecclesiastical breathed a combined sigh of relief and returned to arguing with each other about the malecentricity of religion.

At the same time, the gentle elongation of the Now was beginning to take effect: The Read-O-Meter had been steadily clicking upward as ReadRates once again began to rise. In the Outland the reality TV craze was now fortunately on the wane—*Samaritan Kidney Swap* had so few viewers that by the second week they became desperate and threatened to shoot a puppy on live TV unless a million people phoned in. They had 2 million complaints and were closed down. Bowden and I visited Booktastic! a week ago to find they now had two entire sections of books because, as the manager explained, "there had been a sudden demand."

As part of the whole ChronoGuard decommissioning process, Dad had been reactualized from his state of quasi nonexistence and turned up at Mum's carrying a small suitcase and a bunch of flowers. We had a terrific reunion for him, and I invited Major Pickles along, who seemed to hit it off rather well with Aunt Polly.

On other matters, I traveled to Goliathopolis to meet with Jack Schitt and return his wife's necklace, with an explanation of what had happened to her on board the *Hesperus.* He took the jewelry and the details of her death in stony silence, thanked me and was gone. John Henry Goliath made no appearance, and I didn't tell anyone at Goliath that the *Austen Rover* was, as far as we knew, still adrift without power in intragenre space somewhere between Poetry and Maritime. I didn't know whether this was the end of the Book Project or not, but TGC was taking no chances and had erected a battery of Textual Sieves in the direction of the Outland and marked any potential transfictional incursions as "high priority."

I walked out of the café to where Isambard Kingdom Buñuel was waiting for me. We were standing in Hangar Three among the fabric of *Affair,* ready to be bolted in. Buñuel had already built a reasonable facsimile of Swindon that included my mum's house and the Literary Detectives' office, and he was just getting started on Thornfield Hall, Rochester's house.

"We've pensketched the real Thornfield," he explained, showing me some drawings for approval, "but we were kind of thinkworthing how your Porsche was painted?"

"Do you know Escher's *Reptiles*?"

"Yes."

"It's like that—only in red, blue and green."

"How about the Prose Portal?"

I thought for a moment. "A sort of large leatherbound book covered in knobs, dials and knife switches."

He made a note. "And the unextincted Pickwick?"

"About so high and not very bright."

"Did you bring some snapimagery?"

I rummaged in my shoulder bag, brought out a wad of snaps and went through them.

"That's Pickers when she still had feathers. It's blurred because she blinked and fell over, but it's probably the best. And this is Landen, and that's Joffy, and that's Landen again just before his trousers caught fire—that was *hilarious*—and this is Mycroft and Polly. You don't need pictures of Friday, Tuesday or Jenny do you?"

"Only Friday birth-plus-two for *Something Rotten*."

"Here," I said, selecting one from the stack. "This was taken on his second birthday."

Buñuel recoiled in shock. "What's that strangeturbing stickbrownymass on his face? Some species of alien facehugger or somewhat?"

"No, no," I said hurriedly, "that's chocolate cake. He didn't master the fine art of cutlery until . . . well, he's yet to figure it out, actually."

"Can I temporown these?" asked Buñuel. "I'll have them snoodled up to St. Tabularasa's to see what they can do."

"Be my guest."

The book preproduction had been going on for about two weeks now, and as soon as Buñuel had constructed everything for *The Eyre Affair,* he could move on to the more complex build for *Lost in a Good Book*.

"Is there anything you'll be able to salvage from the old series?" I asked, always thinking economically.

"Indeedly-so," he answered. "Acheron Hades and all his heavisters can be brought across pretty much unaltered. Delamare, Hobbes, Felix7 and 8, Müller—a few different lines here and there and you'll never know the difference."

"You're right," I said slowly as an odd thought started to germinate in my mind.

"A few of the other iddybiddyparts we can scavenge," added Buñuel, "but most of it will be a newbuild. The warmspect the Council of Genres holds for you is reflected in the high costcash."

"What was that?" I asked. "I was miles away."

"I was mouthsounding that the budget for the new TN series—"

"I'm sorry," I replied in a distracted manner, "would you excuse me for a moment?"

I walked to where Colin was waiting for me in his brand-new taxi. Under the TransGenre Taxis logo, they had added "*By Appointment to Thursday Next*" in an elegant cursive font. I didn't ordinarily endorse anything, but they had told me I would always be 'priority one', so I figured it was worth it.

"Where to, Ms. Next?" he asked as I climbed in.

"Great Library, floor six."

"Righto."

He pulled off, braked abruptly as he nearly hit a shiny black

Ford motorcar, yelled at the other driver, then accelerated rapidly toward the wall of the hangar that opened like a dark void in front of us.

"Thanks for the Hoppity Hop," he said as the hole closed behind us and we motored slowly past the almost limitless quantity of books in the Great Library. "I'll be dining out on that for months. Any chance you can get me a Lava Lite?"

"Not unless you save my life again."

I noted the alphabetically listed books on the shelves of the library and saw that we were getting close. "Just drop me past the next reading desk."

"Visiting Tom Jones?"

"No."

"*Bridget* Jones?"

"No. Just drop me about . . . *here*."

He stopped next to the bookcase, and I got out, told him he didn't need to wait and to put the fare on my account, and he vanished.

I was in the Great Library standing opposite the original Thursday Next series, the one kept going by Alice-PON-24330, and I was here because of something Buñuel had said. Spike and I had never figured out how Felix8 had managed to escape, and since his skeletal remains were found up on the Savernake, Spike had suggested quite rightly that he had been not Felix8 but *Felix9*. But Spike could have been wrong. What if the Felix I had met was the *written* Felix8? It would explain how he had gotten out of the Weirdshitorium—he'd just melted back into his book.

I took a deep breath. I didn't want to go anywhere near the old TN series, but this begged further investigation. I picked up the first in the series and read myself inside.

Within a few moments, the Great Library was no more and I was instead aboard an airship floating high over the home counties. But this wasn't one of the small fifty-seaters that plied the skies these days; it was a "Hotel Class" leviathan, designed to roam the globe in style and opulence during the halcyon days of the airship. I was in what had once been the observation deck, but many of the Plexiglas windows had been lost, and the shabby craft rattled and creaked as its lumbering bulk pushed through the air. The icy slipstream blew into the belly of the craft where I stood and made me shiver, while the rush of air and incessant flap of loose fabric were a constant percussive accompaniment to the rhythmic growl of the eight engines. The aluminum latticework construction was apparent wherever I looked, and to my left a door gave access to a precipitous veranda where first-class passengers would once have had a unique bird's-eye view of the docking and landing procedure. In the real world, these monsters had been melted down into scrap long ago, the job of repeater stations for TV and wireless signals now taken over by pilotless drones in the upper atmosphere. But it was kind of nostalgic to see one again, even in this illusory form.

I wasn't in the main action, the "better dead than read" adage as important to me as to anyone else. The narrative was actually next door in the main dining room, where Thursday, a.k.a. Alice-PON-24330, was attempting to outwit Acheron Hades. This wasn't how it *really* happened, of course—Acheron's hideout had actually been in Merthyr Tydfil's abandoned Penderyn Hotel in the Socialist Republic of Wales. It was dramatic license—and fairly bold dramatic license at that.

There was a burst of gunfire from next door, some shouting and then more shots. I positioned myself behind the door as Felix8 came running through the way he usually did, escaping from Bowden and myself once Acheron leaped into the pages of *Jane Eyre*. As soon as he was inside, he relaxed, since he was officially "out of the story." I saw him grin to himself and click on the safety of his machine pistol.

"Hello, Felix8."

He turned and stared at me. "Well, well," he said after a pause. "Will the real Thursday Next please stand up?"

"Just drop the gun."

"I'm not really violent," he said. "It's just the part I play. The real Felix8—now, that's someone you should keep an eye on."

"Drop the gun, Felix. I won't ask you again."

His eyes darted around the room, and I saw his hand tighten on the grip of his gun.

"Don't even *think* about it," I told him, pointing my pistol in his general direction. "This is loaded with eraserhead. Put the gun on the floor—but *really* slowly."

Felix8, fully aware of the destructive power of an eraserhead, gently laid his weapon on the ground, and I told him to kick it to one side.

"How did you get into the real world?"

"I don't know what you mean."

"You were in the *real* Swindon five weeks ago. Do you know the penalty for pagerunning?"

He said nothing.

"I'll remind you. It's erasure. And if you read the papers, you know that I'll erase a whole book if required."

"I've never been out of *The Eyre Affair*," he replied. "I'm just a C-3 generic trying to do my best in a lousy book."

"You're lying."

"That it's a lousy book?"

"You know what I mean. Keep your hands in the air."

I walked behind him and, jamming my pistol firmly against his back, searched his pockets. Given the obsession that members of the BookWorld held for the Outland, I reckoned it was impossible that he'd been all the way to Swindon and not returned with a few Outlandish mementos to sell or barter. And so it proved. In one pocket I found a joke rubber chicken and a digital watch, in the other a packet of Cup-a-Soup and a Mars bar. I chucked them on the floor in front of him.

"Where did you get these, then?"

He was silent, and I backed off a few yards before telling him to turn slowly around and face me.

"Now," I said, "let's have some answers: You're too mediocre to have hatched this yourself, so you're working for someone. Who is it?"

Felix8 gave no answer, and the airship banked slightly as it made a trifling correction to its course. The aluminum-framed door to the exterior promenade walkway swung open and then clattered shut again. It was dusk, and two miles below, the small orange jewels that were the streetlights had begun to wink on.

"Okay," I said, "here's the deal: You tell me what you know and I'll let you go. Play the hard man and it's a one-way trip to the Text Sea. Understand?"

"I've only *eighteen* words and one scene," he said at last. "One lousy scene! Do you have any idea what that's like?"

"It's the hand you were dealt," I told him, "the job you do. You can't change that. Again: *Who sent you into the Outland to kill me?*"

He stared at me without emotion. "And I would have done it, too, if it wasn't for that idiot stalker. Mind you, Johnson blew it as well, so I'm in good company."

This was more worrying. "Mr. Johnson" was the pseudonym used by the Minotaur—and he'd referred to my murder as "a job," so this looked to be better organized than I'd thought.

"Who ordered my death? And why me?"

Felix8 smiled. "You *do* flatter yourself, Ms. Next. You're not the only one they want, you're not the only one they'll get. And now I shall take my leave of you."

He moved toward the exterior door that clattered in the breeze, opened it and stepped out onto the exterior promenade. I ran forward and yelled "Hold it!"—but it was too late. With a swing of his leg, Felix8 slipped neatly over the rail and went tumbling off into space. I ran to the rail and looked down. Already he was a small figure spiraling slowly downward as the airship droned on. I felt a curious sickly feeling as he became nothing more than a small dot and then disappeared from view.

"Damn!" I shouted, and slapped the parapet with my palm. I took a deep breath, went inside out of the chill wind, pulled out my mobilefootnoterphone and pressed the speed-dial connection to the Cheshire Cat, who had assumed command of Text Grand Central.[1]

"Chesh, it's Thursday."[2]

"I've lost a C-3 generic Felix8 from page two hundred and seventy-eight of *The Eyre Affair,* ISBN 0-14-200180-5. I'm going to need an emergency replacement ASAP."[3]

"No."[4]

"Blast," I muttered. "Can you find out who's been dicking around with the Textual Sieves and get it lifted? I've no urge to hang around a cold airship for any longer than I have to."[5]

I told him that I'd be fine if he'd just call me back when the sieve was lifted, then snapped the phone shut. I pulled my jacket up around my neck and stamped my feet to keep warm. I leaned against an aluminum girder and stared out at the mauve twilight, where even now I could see stars begin to appear. Felix8 would have hit the ground so hard his text would have fused with the surrounding description; when we found him, we'd have to cut him from the earth. Either way he'd not be doing any talking.

I started thinking of people who might want me to kill me but stopped counting when I reached sixty-seven. This would be harder than I thought. But . . . what did Felix8 say: that I shouldn't flatter myself . . . *it wasn't just me*? The more I thought about it, the stranger it seemed, until suddenly, with a flash of realization, I knew what was going on. Sherlock Holmes, Temperance Brennan, the Good Soldier Svejk and myself—kill us and you kill not

[1] "*Prego! Il Gatto del Cheshire.*"

[2] "Sorry—just practicing for my holidays in Brindisi this year. What can I do for you?"

[3] "Sure. Say, did you order a Textual Sieve Lockdown on *The Eyre Affair*?"

[4] "Well, you've got one. Mesh is set to ultrafine and timelocked—not even a period is going to get out of that book for at least twenty minutes."

[5] "*No problems,* Outlander *amiga*. Do you want me to keep you company?"

just the individual, but the *series*. It seemed too bizarre to comprehend, but it had to be the truth—*there was a serial killer loose in the BookWorld.*

I looked around the airship, and my heart fell. They'd tried to kill me twice already, and who was to say they wouldn't try again? And here I was, trapped ten thousand feet in the air by a Textual Sieve that no one had ordered, hanging beneath 20 million cubic feet of highly flammable hydrogen. I pulled out my cell phone and hurriedly redialed the cat.[6]

"No questions, Chesh—I need a parachute and I need it *now.*"

As if in answer, there was a bright flare from the rear of the airship as a small charge exploded in one of the gas cells. Within a second this had ignited the cell next to it, and I could see the bright flare arc out into the dusk; the airship quivered gently and started to drop at the stern as it lost lift.

"I need that parachute!" I yelled into my phone as a third gas cell erupted, vaporizing the fabric covering and sending a shower of sparks out either side of the craft. The tail-down attitude increased as the fourth gas cell erupted, followed quickly by the fifth and sixth, and I grabbed a handrail to steady myself.

"Goddamn it!" I yelled to no one in particular. "How hard can it be to get a parachute around here?!" The airship trembled again as another explosion ripped through the envelope, and with an unpleasant feeling of lightness I felt the craft very slowly begin to fall. As I looked down to see where we were heading and how fast, twelve parachutes of varying styles, colors and vintage appeared in front of me. I grabbed the most modern-looking, stepped into the leg straps and quickly pulled it onto my back as the ship was again rocked by a series of explosions. I clicked the catch on the front of the webbing and without even pausing for breath, leaped over the rail and out into the cold evening air. There was a sudden sense of rapid acceleration, and I tumbled for a while, eventually coming to

[6] *"Prego! Il Gatto del Cheshire."*

rest on my back, the air rushing past me, flapping my clothes and tugging at my hair. Far above me the airship was now a chrysanthemum of fire that looked destructively elegant, and from even this distance I could feel the heat on my face. As the airship grew smaller, I snapped out of my reverie and looked for a toggle or something to deploy the chute. I found it across my chest and pulled as hard as I could. Nothing happened for a moment, and I was just thinking that the chute had failed when there was a *whap* and a jerk as it opened. But before I had even *begun* to sigh with relief, there was a thump as I landed on the ground, bounced twice and ended up inside the lines and the canopy, which billowed around me. I scrambled clear, released the harness, pulled out my phone and pressed the speed dial for Bradshaw, running as fast as I could across the empty and undescribed land as the flaming hulk of the airship fell slowly and gracefully in the evening sky, the blackened skeleton of the stricken ship silhouetted dark against the orange fireball above it, an angry flaming mass that even now was beginning to spread to the fabric of the book, as the clouds and sky started to glow with the green iridescence of text before it spontaneously combusts.

"It's Thursday," I panted, running to get clear of the airship before it hit the ground, "and I think we've got a situation. . . ."

My Thanks to:

My very dear Lipali **Mari Roberts**, for countless hours of research, assistance and for looking after her writer and partner in the throes of creation. I hope that in the fullness of time I might do the same for her.

Molly Stern and **Carolyn Mays**, the finest editors in the galaxy, to whom I am always grateful for support and guidance. And by extension, to the hordes of unsung heroes and heroines at Hodder and Penguin who diligently support and promote me and my work.

My grateful thanks goes to **Kathy Reichs** for allowing Dr. Temperance Brennan to make a guest appearance in this book.

Jordan Fforde, my own teenage son, who is a fine, upstanding young man and displays nothing like the worst excesses of Friday's idleness, and who served only vaguely as any sort of reference material.

Bill Mudron and **Dylan Meconis** of Portland, Oregon, for their outstanding artwork completed in record time and with an understanding of the author's brief that left me breathless. Further examples of their work and contact details for commissions can be found at www.thequirkybird.com (Dylan) and www.excelsiorstudios.net (Bill).

Professor **John Sutherland** for his Puzzles in Fiction series of books, which continue to fascinate and inspire.

The Paragon tearooms exist in the same or greater splendor in which they are referred to in the pages of this novel. They can be found on the main street of Katoomba, in the Blue Mountain region of New South Wales, Australia, and no visit to the area would be complete without your attendance. Who knows—you may even see a giant hedgehog and a tyrannical leader of the known universe sharing a booth and discussing Irritable Vowel Syndrome in hushed tones.

This novel was written in BOOK V8.3 and was sequenced using a Mark XXIV ImaginoTransferenceRecording Device. Harley Farley was the imaginator. Generics supplied and trained by St. Tabularasa's. Holes were filled by apprentices at the HoleSmiths' Guild, and echolocation and postcreative grammatization was undertaken by Outland contractors at Hodder and Penguin.

The "Galactic Cleansing" policy carried out by Emperor Zhark is a personal vision of the emperor's, and its inclusion in this work does not constitute tacit approval by the author or the publisher for any such projects, howsoever conducted.

Get into the Classics

...aboard the *Austen Rover!*

Brontë * Trollope * Austen * Thackeray * Dickens

Goliath proudly presents the very latest in advanced tourist technology. Visit all your favorite books from the comfort and safety of our transfictional tour bus and see the classics as you've never seen them before. Tours begin March 2003 and bookings are now being taken at Goliath Holidays, Inc.

Goliath Transfictional Holidays is a division of the Goliath Corporation. Goliath death waivers will apply. Goats, salt and elderly relatives' body parts now accepted as payment. Goliath. A name in market saturation and corporate greed for over six decades. Goliath. For all you'll ever need—ever. www.goliathcorp.com.

BRITONS!

TO DO DUMB THINGS

The Nation's Stupidity Surplus is higher now than at any time in recorded history. The citizenry must work together to destroy this menace, and YOU can do your part. Drop into your local Stupidity Offset Centre and ask to speak to the Duty Clot.

THINK SMART–THINK DUMB

Issued by the Commonsense Party on behalf of the Nation

Thursday Next will return in:

The War of the Words

or

Last Among Prequels

or

Apocalypse Next

or

Dark Reading Matter

or

Paragraph Lost

or

Herrings Red

or

The Palimpsest of Dr. Caligari

or

The Legion of the Danvers

or

Some Other Title Entirely